something like stories

volume two

Jay Bell Books

www.jaybellbooks.com

Did you buy this book? If so, thank you for putting food on our table! Making money as an independent artist isn't easy, so your support is greatly appreciated. Come give me a hug!

Did you pirate this book? If so, there are a couple of ways you can still help out. If you enjoy the story, please take the time to leave a nice review somewhere, such as an online retail store (my preference), or on any blog or forum. Word of mouth is an unbeatable form of advertising, so if you can recommend this book to friends with more cash to spare, that would be awesome too!

Something Like Stories: Volume 2

ISBN: 978-1-7338597-7-6

Cover art by Andreas Bell: www.andreasbell.com

-=Books by Jay Bell=-

The Something Like... series

#1 Something Like Summer
#2 Something Like Autumn
#3 Something Like Winter
#4 Something Like Spring
#5 Something Like Lightning
#6 Something Like Thunder
#7 Something Like Stories - Volume One
#8 Something Like Hail
#9 Something Like Rain
#10 Something Like Stories - Volume Two
#11 Something Like Forever
#12 Something Like Stories - Volume Three

The Loka Legends series

#1 The Cat in the Cradle
#2 From Darkness to Darkness

Other Novels

Kamikaze Boys
Hell's Pawn
Straight Boy

Other Short Stories

Language Lessons
Like & Subscribe
The Boy at the Bottom of the Fountain

Foreword

Welcome to another collection of short stories! Many of these were written for a wonderful little site called Patreon, which enables people to support the creative endeavors of their favorite artists. Starting in November 2015, I challenged myself to produce weekly content for my supporters. This included monthly holiday-themed stories, all twelve of which you'll find included in this book. Those start with Thanksgiving, since that's the order they were written and published in. Considering that this series didn't begin with the first season of the year, not beginning with New Year's somehow seems appropriate. But first we kick off with *Something Like Infinity*, a story I began writing on the set of the *Something Like Summer* movie.

The joy of writing shorter pieces is that it allows readers to explore characters who are unlikely to ever get their own books. I hope you enjoy the journey. The *Something Like...* series is winding down, so this may be the last chance to revisit many of these characters, although I hope that most of them have already taken up permanent residence in your heart.

Happy reading!

-Jay Bell
April 2017

Table of Contents

Something Like Infinity

by Jay Bell

The Woodlands, 1997

Words are like names. They define us. Take for instance someone named Will. He might be called William at his workplace, hoping to sound more adult. He might be Billy to his family, since he'll always remain a little boy in their eyes. The guys down at the bar might call him Bill, and his lover might use a special pet name. Sometimes we choose our titles. Usually they are assigned to us. Either way, we often utilize a variety of names to distinguish the different roles we play. Words are much the same. Like names, they help define our concept of the world. This is best demonstrated with examples outside our language that offer more nuance than English. Does an emotional state exist between like and love? Spanish suggests so. Te quiro. *Or how about a small shared meal between breakfast and lunch, or between lunch and dinner?* Merendar *is the word for that. Have you ever sought a term for the period of casual conversation that follows eating with family and friends?* Sobremesa *is the word you seek. The true lesson here is that, rather than limiting us, language can help us better understand ourselves and our surroundings. All it takes is a previously undiscovered word to change our perspective, or a new name to give us a fresh start.*

Señor Langdon blinked, then looked up from his pad of notebook paper. The students in his class were still hunched over their desks as they struggled with the practice test. Aside from Daniel Wigmore, who prided himself on being the first to complete any assignment, and Julie Snyder, who had wanted to take French instead and expressed her disdain of Spanish by stubbornly ignoring assignments. No concern of his, because at the end of the day, Señor Langdon would resume the boring life of Ross Langdon.

He returned his attention to the lesson he was preparing, hoping to instill in his students that learning a language was more than memorizing a new vocabulary with a different grammatical system. Once the Spanish language had sunk into their thick skulls, they would never again see things in quite the same way.

He decided to ditch the line about pet names. Any mention of a lover might be considered inappropriate. Plus it was a painful reminder that he didn't have one of his own.

Ross worked on revising his lesson until the bell rang. The students groaned. He felt like joining them. Only his two star pupils had completed the assignment. With less than a month left in the school year, they really should have this material down already. "Just leave your tests where they are," Ross said. "I'll take a look, and we can go over them tomorrow."

The only responses he received were rolled eyes or apathetic shrugs. Except for Daniel Wigmore, whose freckled face smiled proudly. Ross would check his paper first, just in case speed had tripped him up. Daniel normally pulled in A's regardless of haste. The kid had an annoying personality, but he would probably be the next Bill Gates.

Ross watched the classroom empty faster than it ever filled. Stomach grumbling with hunger, he walked down the rows of desks, collecting each test until he had a neat stack. He decided to look them over while treating himself to one of the cafeteria's burgers. When doused with enough ketchup, they tasted bearable. The burgers, not the tests, but he was nearly hungry enough to try the latter. Ross was heading for the door, attention on Daniel's paper, when he saw in his peripheral vision that the doorway was closed. Odd. He reached up while still searching for errors, intending to push the door open, but instead of chilly metal, his palm pressed against warm cotton.

Ross glanced up in confusion, finding a man rather than a door, although the toned chest was nearly as firm. Then he noticed the police uniform and jerked away. His glasses slipped, cheeks already burning as he pushed them back up his nose. The police officer had barely moved. His dark eyes scanned Ross critically before one of the finely arched eyebrows rose.

"Mr. Langdon?" the officer inquired.

"Señor Langdon," he repeated out of habit, which was silly, because his entire family was hopelessly white and from nowhere more exotic than Oklahoma. He only called himself "Señor" for this class.

"Senior Langdon," the officer amended, his pronunciation off. "I'd like to ask you a few questions."

Ross searched his memory for any criminal acts he might

have committed, no matter how trivial. Parking tickets? Littering? Sampling a cherry tomato from the grocery store before buying them, just to be sure they were sweet enough? He hadn't done any of those things lately, but it didn't take long to leap to another possibility: One of the students, or someone's parents, had discovered the truth. His big dark secret. He was certain it would end his teaching career. "I was just about to have lunch," he replied, hoping to avoid the inevitable. "Maybe later?"

The officer didn't move, which was unfortunate, because he was still blocking the only path to freedom. "This won't take long."

Ross nodded, accepting his fate. "Okay." He gestured to his desk, realizing too late that the officer would have nowhere to sit. He moved behind it anyway to feel more secure and remained standing. The officer stood on the opposite side as they sized each other up. His dark hair was bleached on top, platinum blonde except where the roots had grown out, a stark contrast to the dark eyes. He could be of Hispanic heritage. Perhaps that might help establish comradery. But would that translate to leniency? Ross glanced down at the badge, seeking a last name. This didn't go unnoticed.

"My name is Officer Adler."

"Adler," Ross repeated, even though it didn't tell him much. The name sounded German. Didn't it mean eagle? Or perhaps hawk, which would be appropriate considering the sensation of being watched by one. "What can I do for you, sir?"

"I'm investigating a series of arsons."

Fire starting? He was in the clear! "Oh thank god!"

Now the officer really appeared suspicious, probably because Ross had practically swiped the back of his arm across his sweaty forehead and said, *"Phew! That was a close one!"*

"Are you feeling all right?" Adler inquired.

"Low blood sugar, that's all. You were saying?"

"The fires began last year, toward the end of summer. We now believe a student at this school could be responsible."

Ross shook his head. "If so, none of them have confided in me. I would have reported it."

"The reason I'm here," Adler continued, "is because I had an encounter with the perpetrator recently. He shouted at me as he fled the scene. In Spanish."

"Oh! So you saw what he looked like? You should have come sooner when the students were still here."

"The night in question was dark," Adler said. "I was unable to determine much except his age and—" He closed his eyes briefly, as if getting sidetracked. "That's beside the point. I'm here because I need your help. I wrote down what the suspect shouted. Or at least I tried to." He unbuttoned the chest pocket of his shirt and pulled out a folded piece of paper, which he handed over.

Ross took it with interest. The handwriting was messy and angular, the Spanish just a phonic representation of what the officer had heard, but enough had been captured to interpret. All nervousness forgotten, he sat down, grabbed his red pen, and started making corrections. He became so absorbed in his work that he was unsure how much time passed. When he looked up again, Adler was still standing there, watching him patiently.

"What does it say?"

Ross leaned back. "*¡Eres muy lento, así nunca me vas a alcanzar gordinflón!*"

"Translation?"

Ross cleared his throat. "You're too slow, you'll never catch me. Erm."

"Is that all?"

"*Gordinflón*. Fat ass."

Adler glared.

"His words, not mine," Ross said hurriedly. "From what I can see, you're all muscle!"

The officer's expression became difficult to read. He didn't seem offended, but still, it probably wasn't a good idea to praise the body of any visiting law enforcement agent, no matter how tight it might appear.

"Blood sugar," Ross repeated. "I get lightheaded when hungry. Sorry."

Adler leaned over the desk, tapping the translated paper. "This sounds advanced."

"It's not exactly complicated, but it *is* flawless. Then again, I could be inadvertently fixing mistakes that were spoken, instead of correcting what you managed to write down."

"Uh-huh. How many of your students are capable of saying something like that, even incorrectly? The guys in particular."

Ross shrugged. "A few. I don't know. They're not really my students."

"Meaning?"

"Didn't the office tell you? I'm just a substitute for Señora Vega. She's been having health problems all year, so I've been here for most of her absence."

"Long enough to narrow down the list?"

"Maybe," Ross said. Now that the focus wasn't on him, he didn't feel so intimidated. Despite his claim that he would have reported any student who spoke to him about illegal activity, he wasn't likely to. Not automatically or without knowing the circumstances. He didn't want to see any of these kids get into trouble. After all, he'd been in high school himself only six short years ago. Ross remembered how difficult the world could be at that age, and how dealing with bullying, divorcing parents, academic pressure, or just angst over the future in general had driven him and his friends to do all sorts of irresponsible things. But they hadn't burnt down any buildings. "These fires, how bad are they?"

Adler pushed away from the desk to stand upright again. "They're getting worse. It began with small fires in open fields and empty lots. Lately the arsonist has focused on park benches and playground equipment. Mailboxes too, the large public ones on street corners."

"But no private property," Ross said dismissively.

Adler noticed this indifference. "Actually, private property has been involved too, and I'll remind you that destroying mail is a federal offense."

"Of course. Right. Have you considered that the accused might not be one of my students? This is Texas, after all. The arsonist could be a native Spanish-speaker."

Adler placed his hands on his belt. "I have reason to believe otherwise. Now if you could please draw up a list of names, I'll take it from there."

"Sure. It's just… They're all so young."

Officer Adler exhaled, his face handsome even when tense with impatience. "I understand that it's your job to care for these kids and keep them safe. We share that duty and conviction. If one of these fires gets out of control, people could be hurt, including your students or even the arsonist himself. And you're right, these kids are still young. The judge will take that into consideration."

Ross stared into dark unwavering eyes, finding only sincerity there. "Okay. What else can you tell me about the suspect?"

Adler considered him a moment, then spun around and marched to the classroom door to close it, shutting out the ambient hallway noise. When he returned to the desk, he rested one set of knuckles on the surface. "What I'm about to say doesn't leave this room. Understand?"

Ross nodded.

"The suspect was caught in a compromising situation."

Ross tried to decipher this. "He was taking a dump?"

Officer Adler's jaw clenched, either out of annoyance or an attempt to hold back laughter. "He wasn't alone, so there might be two perpetrators involved. Both are male and were in a partial state of undress. One of them was on his knees."

This time Ross made damn sure to maintain his poker face because the conversation had ventured into dangerous territory again. "I see."

"Good." The officer's nod was curt. "Does this narrow the field?"

Ross felt his temper rising. "You're asking me to *out* my students? I wouldn't even if I could! But no, it doesn't narrow the field because none of them have confided in me about such things. Considering the social backlash that comes with being openly gay, I can't say I blame them. And frankly, now that I know what you're really after, I no longer feel like helping you with your investigation."

Adler's nostrils flared, but his tone was even when he spoke. "I'm just as interested in preserving their anonymity as you are. In fact..." He clenched his jaw and shook his head again. "Never mind. All I want to do is prevent more fires. The rest can remain off record."

"Simple as that?" Ross challenged. "It won't be in your report?"

Adler glowered. "I wasn't the only one there. My partner feels it might be important. I'm hoping to prove otherwise. For now, I've convinced her to keep it under wraps."

"Wow. Really?"

"Really!"

Ross stared, trying to see past the handsome face to the substance beyond. He didn't know this man, but Adler seemed noble enough. Or maybe that's what Ross wanted to believe. Regardless, such issues were sensitive. Potentially life-changing and even life-threatening, so he held his tongue.

"Help me," Adler pleaded. "If we stop the arsonist now, the rest can be ignored."

Was that coercion? Name a suspect or we'll make this about sexual orientation instead? Then again, if he refused to comply, other teachers would be interviewed, and they might not be as discrete with their knowledge. "Fine."

"You'll help me?"

"I'll need a little time, but yes."

"Thank you." Adler visibly relaxed. "Think it over. I realize none of your students would be out to you, but you might be able to eliminate anyone with a girlfriend. That, combined with the necessary skill in Spanish..."

Ross nodded again. "I'll see what I can do."

"Good." Officer Adler pulled out a business card and was about to hand it over. Then he thought twice, flipped it over, and grabbed Ross's red pen to scribble on the back. "This is my home number. I can't stress how important this case is to me, so please, don't hesitate to call as soon as you have a list."

"Will do."

"Thanks."

They stood facing each other. Then Officer Adler nodded cordially, pivoted, and marched toward the door. Ross watched him go. His feelings for the man were conflicted, but one thing was certain: Adler wasn't a *Gordinflón*, because that ass was firm and fine!

Ross decided to eat his lunch in the teachers' lounge, needing time alone to organize his thoughts. He didn't want to start viewing each student with unfair suspicion. The breakroom was mostly empty, just three other souls present, but two of them were venomous. Coach Reynolds had thinning red hair and a pug nose. His face often flushed when he complained about foreigners, liberals, or any other demographic he found offensive. Then there was Mrs. Jones, the journalism teacher. She was a waspish woman who chose her words more carefully, all of them cutting. Ross wavered in the doorway, experiencing a flashback to the eighth grade when his family first moved to Texas and lunch became a daily struggle to find an empty seat near a friendly face.

Then he saw Ms. Hughes, the science teacher with a heavy build and acne scars across her cheeks. She was good company, so he sat down across from her. Mrs. Jones raised her eyebrows at this, probably because she often talked bad about Ms. Hughes behind her back. Or maybe she disapproved of him, a lowly substitute, using the teachers' lounge. Ross ignored her and pulled out the sandwich he had packed in the morning—the one that made a cafeteria burger look scrumptious by comparison. He might have a gift for foreign languages, but he was no chef!

"Care for some chips?" Ms. Hughes said, offering the bag she was snacking from.

"Thank you, no," Ross replied, wishing the others would stop staring at him.

Coach Reynolds was the first to look away. "As I was saying," he grumbled, "there should be a screening process. Proof of nationality. Most of these schools cram as many Mexicans on their soccer teams as possible, just because they're good at the game, but if they weren't born in this country—"

Mrs. Jones held up her hand, cutting off this rant, attention still on Ross. "Was that a police officer I saw entering your classroom?"

Jesus, did she have spies everywhere? Few things seemed to escape her notice. He nodded, taking a handful of chips after all and intending to stuff them into his mouth so he couldn't speak.

"What did he want?" Mrs. Jones pressed.

"He just needed something translated," Ross said, a cluster of Doritos about to plug his maw.

"Anything of interest?"

He sighed and set the chips on the same flattened paper bag where his sandwich rested. "Not really. A suspect yelled a few words at him that the officer didn't understand."

"Lucky you," Ms. Hughes said cheerfully. "Sounds like something out of a TV show, the police needing to consult with us. I've always wanted that to happen. Surely it's just a matter of time before a global emergency strikes that only a science teacher can solve."

Ross chuckled in appreciation. "Don't give up hope yet. What would you do if they asked you about the melting ice caps?"

"Dry ice," Ms. Hughes responded. "Lots of it, dropped by helicopters at both global poles. I don't think it would help, but all that fog sure would look cool."

Ross grinned. "Throw in some lasers and Pink Floyd's *Dark Side of the Moon* and you've got yourself a party!"

Mrs. Jones wasn't amused by this exchange. "You would think the police department would have their own resources," she said, "rather than needing to consult with a substitute."

Ross shrugged. "I'm cheap labor." And an amateur detective, because he had his own case to solve. An idea occurred to him: Maybe the journalism teacher's nosiness could be used to his advantage. He didn't know of any gay students, but if rumors were floating around, she would have heard them. He couldn't reveal what Officer Adler had divulged, but if he was clever… "Actually, I've been meaning to discuss something with you. A friend of mine sent me a newspaper from a different school. They have a large number of Mexican students, much like we do, and so they run additional articles in Spanish. Not only does that give them a sense of community, but it's good practice for the students learning the language."

Mrs. Jones crossed her arms over her chest. "How am I supposed to edit a newspaper I can't even read?"

"Well, you could always learn, or ask for my—"

"Where exactly is this school located?"

"New Mexico," Ross answered, knowing the paper and not the idea would become the topic. "Santa Fe to be precise."

"Sounds awfully liberal to me," Coach Reynolds interjected.

Ross nodded. "I suppose so. They certainly have more resources for students then we do, such as a gay-straight alliance that—"

Coach Reynolds turned a darker shade of pink. "A what?"

"It's for—"

"I know what it's for!" Coach Reynolds snarled.

"Then there was no need to interrupt him," Ms. Hughes pointed out. "I, for one, think it's a wonderful idea."

Mrs. Jones sneered. "You would. We have no need for such things in this school."

"There aren't any gay students enrolled here?" Ross asked innocently.

"That's beside the point," Mrs. Jones said. She exchanged a look with Coach Reynolds.

The older man smirked. "Bendly."

"Who?" Ross asked with a dry mouth.

"Ben Bentley," Mrs. Jones said, not bothering to address him directly. "I showed you the poem, didn't I?"

"Yes." Coach Reynolds laughed without warmth. "I could have told you sooner from the limp-wristed way he throws a ball."

Ms. Hughes slammed her palm against the table. "This conversation strikes me as highly inappropriate! And tasteless!"

Mrs. Jones refused to be chastised. "It's hardly a secret."

"Right," Coach Reynolds said. "The kid—what's it called? Fell out? Everyone knows."

"Came out," Ms. Hughes corrected. "That must have taken tremendous courage."

"It certainly didn't take smarts," the coach cackled. "He should have asked the Wizard of Oz for brains instead."

"He deserves our respect," Ms. Hughes insisted, but no one backed her up. Not even Ross, because he was too worried to take sides on this matter, lest he draw attention to himself.

"So," Mrs. Jones said. She nodded in his direction, making him think he was busted. "You feel the school paper should be written in Spanish, and that we need a gay support group for one solitary student."

"I think," Ross said, standing and abandoning his lunch, "that this conversation has ventured into a direction I never intended."

"Funny how that always seems to happen among certain company," Ms. Hughes said.

Ross couldn't bring himself to respond. He felt too guilty for not supporting her position, and too disgusted by the bigoted attitudes of the other teachers, so he turned and left the room. He was angry at himself, but what could he do? He loved teaching—*loved* it!—and saying too much could cost him his job. Maybe he was being foolish. This was just a substitute position. Losing it wouldn't change much. But if he stayed quiet and finished the assignment without controversy, he could take the good reference and move to a different city. Somewhere far away from The Woodlands. Santa Fe held appeal because the paper he had mentioned was real. Not all schools were as backward as this one.

Ross was putting as much distance as possible between himself and the teachers' lounge when he heard someone call his name. Ms. Hughes. She was struggling to keep up, her expression concerned. "A moment," she puffed. "Please."

"Sure," Ross said, feeling it was the least he could do. An apology was on his lips, but she spoke first.

"Is he in trouble?"

"Sorry?"

"Ben Bentley. With the visit from the police, I thought maybe…" Whatever her fears were, they remained unspoken.

"I don't know," Ross admitted. He hadn't had time to consider the implications. Ben was gay, the right age, and a student in his Spanish class. That certainly raised suspicion, although Ben's language skills weren't that great, from what he could remember. "What can you tell me about him?"

"Don't bother checking with the office," she replied. "You won't find anything."

"But you know something."

"Only that he has a good heart. And yes, it has led him into trouble before, but nothing too serious. I'm not like some of the other teachers here. I don't judge and I don't gossip, but I am invested in the lives of my students. What exactly was the officer asking about?"

"Arson."

Ms. Hughes shook her head instantly. "No. It isn't Ben."

"You're probably right. Don't worry about it. Please."

"If only that were a choice."

Ross offered his hand before they parted. The decision was spontaneous, and in retrospect, a little odd, but he didn't often meet another teacher who cared so much. More than that, she seemed like a decent human being. She shook his hand, clearly still concerned, but he couldn't offer any further comfort. Then he continued down the hall, eyes on the scuffed floor as he silently cursed Officer Adler for dragging him into this mess.

Señor Langdon was on edge, overseeing the same practice quiz he had given before lunch and the two periods that had followed. He didn't divide his attention between the class and a future lesson. Instead he focused on each student, and as much as he hated it, made each a suspect in his mind. Ronnie Adams had a decent understanding of the Spanish language, taking the new words he learned and twisting them to make jokes. The guy sitting one chair over, Craig Thompson, was his guaranteed laugh-track. They were friends, that much was clear, but were they more? He started to picture them in a compromising situation before he felt uncomfortable and banished the image from his mind. Besides, he was fairly certain that Ronnie had a girlfriend, since he had made her the topic of a presentation once.

He crossed them both off his mental list and continued to scan the room. At least he didn't need to consider the girls. His eyes settled briefly on Mike Simmons, who was seriously overweight and unlikely to outrun anyone. He looked at and dismissed George Rohrer, who could write Spanish, but was too bashful to speak it. Then there was Tim Wyman, who wasn't struggling with the quiz so much as working methodically. Deliberately slow, like someone who knew all the answers but didn't want to let on. His grades in this class were nearly perfect, if Ross recalled correctly, and Tim was certainly athletic enough to outrun someone like Adler despite the officer's toned muscles, broad chest, and narrow hips.

Ross started to imagine a different sort of compromising situation, one that involved handcuffs and the teachers' lounge. He snapped out of it when he saw Tim glance at the clock. Class was almost over, and Tim must have realized this, because he breezed through the rest of the test. He moved from question to question, answering each like it was basic arithmetic. No doubt about it, he had been holding back! Ross casually flipped open the grade book and noticed the consistently high scores next to Tim's name. Funny, since he rarely raised his hand to volunteer an answer or ask a question. As understanding as Ross tried to be, he couldn't let such things slide.

The bell rang. He stood along with his students. "Leave the tests where they are," he shouted over the rising noise. The last period of the day was always followed by a desperate exodus. "Mr. Wyman, if I could speak with you, please."

Ross didn't know what he would say. Or do. Should he frisk the guy for lighters and matches? What if he found them? Citizen's arrest?

"How's it going, Señor Langdon?"

Tim was standing before his desk, his silver eyes a striking contrast to the deeply tanned skin. One of his parents could be a native speaker, and if so, Tim might have been raised bilingual. Ross decided to slip into Spanish to test him.

«You've been doing well. I'm impressed by your grades.»

Tim's brow crinkled. He made a face like someone concentrating. "*Muchas gracias.*"

So much thought needed for a phrase that everyone in this country knew? One thing was for sure, Tim's Spanish was better than his acting. «I feel you could be in a more advanced class.»

«Really? No. This one is challenging enough.»

«This charade is ludicrous.» Ross watched his face closely for a reaction, knowing the words were too advanced for any of his students. Sure enough, Tim's cheeks grew a little red and his jaw clenched.

"Sorry," Tim said, reverting to English. "You lost me there."

«Then I'll discuss the matter with your parents instead.»

«Please don't!» Tim's shoulders slumped. «Damn it!»

Ross shook his head disapprovingly. "You're already fluent."

"My Spanish isn't perfect." Now those striking eyes were pleading with him. Tim was a handsome guy. He probably knew that and used it to his advantage, but Ross wasn't persuaded by such things.

"Your Spanish is good enough that you don't need my help. Do you know how that makes me feel? Normally when one of my students does well, like yourself, I'm proud. Teaching is my passion and what I've dedicated my life to. So when I find out someone in my class already knows what I have to offer, I feel foolish instead."

"I *have* learned from you," Tim said. "I swear. My mom is Mexican, but we speak English at home, so I don't get much practice. That's what I'm here for. It's been helpful."

"You're here for an easy A."

"It's been helpful," Tim repeated. His jaw clenched again. "And yeah, I'm under a lot of pressure from my parents. I can barely keep up with my other classes, so having one that's a little easier…"

Ross hadn't been a teacher for long, but he had already seen how some parents pushed their children. Often these students were like Tim, who appeared perfect from the outside and were expected to be that way on the inside as well. "You need to pull your weight," Ross said. "There isn't much left to the school year, but you can still help other students. I have a few in my class who won't pass without tutoring."

Tim groaned. "Seriously?"

"It's either that or I really can contact your parents."

Tim raised his hands, palms outward. "Okay, okay! No problem. Just tell me who."

Ross said the first name that came to mind. The one that kept popping up in his thoughts ever since lunch break. "Ben Bentley."

Tim grew still, his expression disturbingly neutral. He was still handsome, but more like a store mannequin now. Cold. As was his response. "No."

"No?" Ross repeated incredulously.

Tim gave a barely perceptible shake of the head. "Sorry, but no."

Ross struggled to understand why Tim's tone had grown so hard. Was it Ben's sexuality? Or had he stumbled upon the truth? Officer Adler had found two young men in a compromising situation, and at least one of them had been fast and fluent enough to race away while shouting insults in Spanish. With a chill, he realized he had found the culprit. Tim Wyman was the arsonist! But how to proceed?

"Okay," he said quickly. "Someone else then. Julie Snyder. She doesn't think Spanish is romantic like French is. Maybe you can convince her otherwise."

Tim returned to life and flashed a disarming smile. "Of course!" he said in upbeat tones. "Just tell me when and where, and I'll do my best. Thanks for being so understanding, Señor Langdon."

"I'm pleased we reached an agreement." He gestured to the door, eager for Tim to leave. "I'll let you know the details tomorrow."

"Okay." Tim kept smiling. "Thanks again."

"No problem."

Ross remained rigid until Tim disappeared into the hall. Then he scrambled for his wallet and pulled out a business card with red inked numbers on the back. Time to call in the cavalry!

Ross lived alone in a one-bedroom apartment. Having a roommate would be nice. Not only would sharing the apartment have split the cost of rent and utilities in half, he also would have had someone to talk to or watch TV with. His best friend had moved way after graduating from college, his other friends already had living arrangements, and advertising for a roommate—a stranger—would make his secret harder to maintain. Ross was out to family and friends, but they knew to be discrete because of his occupation.

Not that he was completely alone. He had pets! His landlord didn't allow much when it came to animals. Nothing with fur. Just feathers or fins. Ross had opted for fish.

He stood in front of their tank. Marie and Pierre were black skirt tetras and feeding them always took top priority. When in a silly mood, Ross would give a Mr. Rogers-inspired speech while doing so. "Welcome, neighbor! So nice to have you. Doesn't it feel nice to do good things for others?"

Tonight he skipped the speech and hurried to feed his fish so he could stand in his narrow kitchen next to the phone. Then he took out Officer Adler's card again to stare at the number on the flip side. All he needed to do was call. He had the perfect excuse. Something held him back regardless. He laughed when he realized what. His appearance! As ridiculous as it sounded, he wanted to make sure his hair looked okay.

Ross set down the card and went into the bathroom. First he polished his black-framed glasses. Once they were back on his nose, he made sure his thick chestnut-brown hair was swept back, just how he liked it. Ross patted his stomach, pleased that he had given up eating instant pasta a few months back. No need to diet at the moment. After brushing his teeth, he smiled at himself, pretending he was facing a hunky police officer instead. Before his nerves could get the best of him again, he hurried back to the kitchen. He punched each numbered key carefully. Then he held the phone to his ear and the breath in his lungs.

"Richard," a voice grunted.

"Huh?" Ross replied. "Sorry, I must have the wrong…" He remembered the full name on the other side of the card. "Officer Adler?"

"Speaking," the voice replied.

"Hi, this is Señor Langdon. Um, from school. The high one. School, that is. High school." Going great so far!

The voice on the other ended sounded receptive enough. "I

didn't expect you to call so soon. Do you have the list ready?"

"Not exactly. I might have something better."

"You know who the arsonist is."

Ross hesitated, twirling a finger around the phone's cord. "I had an interesting conversation, let's put it that way."

The unmistakable sound of a pen clicking preceded the response. "Go ahead. What's his name?"

"It's just a theory," Ross said. "I'm not sure I'm comfortable naming anyone."

"The details of the conversation then," Adler replied, sounding less patient.

"What will you do? Arrest him?"

"Arrest who? You haven't told me anything."

"I'm just trying to understand how the process works." He heard a sigh but pressed on. "Listen, can we meet somewhere? I'd feel better if we did this face to face."

"Uh huh," Adler replied. "I can come over there or we can meet at McDonald's. Up to you."

"I'm not a big fan of the golden arches."

"I only suggested it as a public place. We can do Jack in the Box, Whataburger, or whatever you like."

"Chinese?" Ross suggested.

The line was quiet a moment. "You want to eat together? I thought you only wanted to meet."

"Might as well do so over dinner. Or do you have plans?"

"No," Adler said, still sounding uncertain. The pen could be heard clicking over and over again. "All right. Name the spot."

Ross did so, heart pounding as he gave directions.

"I think I know the area."

"Good!" Ross said. "See you in about an hour?"

"Sure. See you then."

The line went dead. Was it sad to be excited about a dinner that clearly wasn't a date? In the end Ross decided he didn't care. He couldn't remember the last time a handsome man had sat across from him during a meal. At this point, he'd take whatever he could get!

Ross arrived at the Chinese restaurant wearing a comfortable T-shirt and a worn pair of jeans. The place offered an affordable buffet and attracted mostly college students, so no need to dress up. Besides, he didn't want to appear as desperate as he felt. He regretted this decision when Officer Adler showed up wearing a dress shirt, tight jeans, and freshly styled hair. Or maybe he always looked that way when off duty. Some guys were more attractive when in uniform, but Richard did just fine without it too.

Ross stood up from the table and offered his hand. "Thank you for meeting me like this, Officer Alder."

"Richard," Adler responded, shaking his hand. "I'm off duty, and it's going to seem weird if people overhear you say 'officer' to someone in plain clothes. They'll think I'm undercover."

Ross imagined him under *his* covers and tittered nervously. "That makes sense. I already told the waitress we both want the buffet. Is that okay?"

Richard shrugged. "Sure."

They walked to the buffet together and stood side-by-side as they loaded up their plates. Ross snuck a few glances at him. Officer Adler was gone. For now, at least. Just like the lesson he had been working on earlier, a new name revealed a new aspect to a person, and this one felt more real. Never had he considered that police officers had private lives or engaged in the mundane activities that everyone else did. Paying bills, taking out the trash, and so on. Had they met this way instead, he would have assumed Richard was a young professional, someone in the finance industry or maybe a law firm intern. Richard's presence in this everyday environment made Ross feel even more frustrated that they could never be together. Gay people were less likely to join the police force, and even if by some miracle Richard was one of the few, well, he was probably already taken.

As they sat at the table, Ross casually checked for a wedding ring. He didn't see one, but rather than torturing himself with fantasies, he focused on relaying what he had learned.

"So it's got to be him," Ross said at the end of his story. "I found the arsonist!"

Richard didn't seem to share this conviction. "Maybe."

"Maybe? Are you kidding? This student can speak Spanish, he's athletic enough to outrun you—"

"—the perpetrator had a head start," Richard made sure to point out.

"Okay, but those things combined with Tom's uneasy

relationship with Bob—" AKA Tim and Ben. Ross had changed the names to protect the innocent, even though he was sure they were actually guilty. "I really believe this is the perpetrator in question. Or however you guys say it."

Richard fought down amusement. "This other person, the one the arsonist might be involved with, you said his name was Bob Biggins?"

"Mm-hm."

"And the kid who called me a fat ass, he's Tom Wilcox?"

Ross squirmed. "Yep!"

"Two fires were set that night," Richard said, spearing a batter-fried piece of chicken with his fork and dragging it through orange sauce. "A real estate sign and a welcome mat, both at the home of another student."

"Okay." Ross shrugged. "What's your point?"

"That I don't understand why our two lovers set the fires and then reconvened at the playground so they could... entertain each other."

"Maybe that's how they get their kicks. They obviously like doing it in public. Maybe they're thrill-seekers."

Richard tried holding back a smile and failed. He had the prettiest teeth. "I think it's a good lead," he said. "But I need more to go on. Parents tend to get defensive when you accuse their children of arson, not to mention the other situation."

Ross scowled. "You promised to leave that part out!"

"I don't know if I can," Richard replied. "As I said, my partner feels it's important and—"

"This is exactly why I didn't trust you. I knew you wouldn't understand. You're going to ruin the lives of these—"

"Hey, I'm trying to be careful and—"

"You have no idea! Seriously. You're clueless!"

"And you aren't?"

Ross raised his chin defiantly. "No, I'm not. I know exactly what it's like to fear being who I really am, and even though I'm not ashamed, sometimes there's too much at stake."

"You're not listening. I *do* understand. I feel that way every single day."

Ross stared. "What?"

Richard glared at the empty table next to theirs. "Nothing."

It didn't sound like nothing to him! "Hold on, are you saying that you're—"

"Drop it," Richard said, tossing his napkin next to his plate. "Thank you for your help."

"You can't leave yet!" Ross stood, feeling panicked. Pressing the topic of sexuality would only scare Richard off so he switched back to one that would interest him more. "Tom and Bob aren't their real names."

"I figured." Richard pulled out his wallet. "I'm sure I have enough to go on."

"Please," Ross tried. "I'm sorry. I just get defensive because they're my students. Most of them yawn through my classes, and I get treated like a second-class citizen by other teachers, but I don't care. All I want is to broaden minds and give these kids a better future. That's why I put up with the abuse. Someday I want to be a permanent employee with my own class, but until then, I'll do my time in the trenches."

Richard hesitated. "I'm hoping to make detective."

"So we both have reasons for overreacting." Ross tried a smile. "I'm sorry if I offended you."

"You're fine," Richard said, pocketing his wallet. "This has been a difficult case for me. I wish it was just about the fires. I really do."

They sat again, Ross wanting to learn about the person across from him. "So becoming a detective, what does that entail exactly?"

"Experience," Richard said. "I've only been a street cop for a few years, and without trying to sound arrogant, I'm good. I bring in the numbers without harassing people who don't deserve it. I'd like to think I have an above-average understanding of how the human mind works, and I've taught myself to notice the world around me. That might sound simple, but most people aren't aware of what surrounds them. Speaking of which, where did that come from?"

He pointed across the table. Ross followed his gaze, then laughed while rubbing his wrist. "My tattoo?"

"Yes. You either got it before meeting me for dinner, or you have some way of hiding it while at work."

"Make up."

"Seriously?"

"Yup!" Ross looked down at the line of black ink that looped back on itself like a bow. "I've had more than one job interview go wrong because of it, and the superintendent of my current school has a strict policy about tattoos and piercings."

"What does it signify?" Richard asked. "I know it's the symbol for infinity, but what made you choose that?"

"It's personal."

Richard laughed. "Oh I see! You can ask me questions, but when I try to do the same…"

"Exactly. Back to you becoming a detective. What needs to happen? A certain amount of solved cases? Catching someone on the most wanted list?"

"That would help. Broadening my own mind wouldn't hurt either. I shouldn't have needed to come to you for help."

Ross scrunched up his nose. "You can't blame yourself for not speaking Spanish."

"I can, because it's a useful skill in my line of work."

"I could teach you."

Richard cocked his head. "Wouldn't that be difficult?"

"I don't mean to sound arrogant," Ross said with a smile, "but I'm pretty good at my job too. So besides work, what keeps you occupied? A busy personal life?"

Richard snorted. "No."

"Oh!"

"You sound happy."

"Only because it sometimes feels like I'm the only single guy my age."

"If that's the kind of personal life you mean, then yeah, I'm single, but it's by choice. I do perfectly fine with the ladies. Right now I'm focusing on my career."

"Oh."

"Now you sound disappointed."

Ross frowned. "There's such a thing as being *too* observant, you know."

He was right though. Ross did feel disappointed. He didn't want to hear about Richard's luck with women. Just this once he wished that he could meet someone who was intelligent, handsome, kind, *and* gay. Okay, maybe that was a tall order, but he had tried to keep himself in check this time. It was only because had Richard hinted earlier— Actually, Ross was no longer sure what that was about, and he intended to keep digging until he found out. "So when you're not chasing bad guys, what do you do for fun?"

"I like movies."

"About?"

"Chasing bad guys."

"I should have known."

Richard smiled. "And others too. Comedies. Thrillers. Musicals."

Ross raised an eyebrow. "Musicals? Really?"

Richard's face turned red. "What's wrong with that?"

"Nothing! Really." Ross was tired of beating around the bush. "It's just that you're going out of your way to keep sexual orientation out of your investigation. That level of sympathy is unusual."

"Is it?"

"Yes. But only for a straight man. You said earlier that you understand what it's like to be closeted, so I'm guessing you have a gay brother or sister. Unless you yourself are gay."

Richard stared at him evenly. "You're very observant."

Ross grinned. "Maybe I'll make detective someday."

"You also leap to conclusions." Richard lowered his voice. "I'm not gay. But I did have an experience once."

"An experience?"

He nodded. "When I was younger. No one found out, but I can imagine what might have happened if they did. That's why I'm able to sympathize."

Richard had been open with him, so it only seemed fair to do the same.

"Just so you know—"

Richard spoke before he could finish. "I wouldn't be a good detective if I hadn't figured you out already."

"Am I that obvious?"

Richard shook his head. "No."

Ross sighed. "Even if I was, I wish it didn't matter."

"Same here. Like I said before, I'll try to keep my partner focused on the arson."

"So what's next?" Ross asked, keeping the question intentionally vague. Gay or not, he liked spending time with this man. Now that they were done eating, he wouldn't mind watching a movie together. Even one about chasing bad guys. Richard's mind was still on business though.

"You need to find out what you can about both boys. Talk to… What was his name?"

"Ben," Ross said, deciding to trust him at last. "Ben Bentley."

Richard nodded. "Talk to him and see what sort of impression you get. Maybe get both guys in the same room together and see if there's a reaction. It could be that Tom—"

"Tim."

"—that Tim doesn't like Ben because he's gay."

Ross shook his head. "I don't think so. If he had made a face or said something homophobic, that would have been more natural. The way he went so still felt like a practiced response."

"You speak from experience?"

"Yes," Ross admitted. "I do."

Richard studied him and nodded. "Definitely get them together, but make it look like an accident."

"What am I looking for exactly?"

"Facts," Richard replied. "That might sound simple, but believe me, people will do anything in their power to hide the truth. Our job is to find it again."

As he stood and returned to the buffet for another serving, Ross tried to decide which interested him most: the amorous arsonists, or the open-minded officer.

Ross was in full detective mode, starting first thing in the morning. Ms. Hughes had said something the other day that struck him as odd. She had insisted he shouldn't contact the front office about Ben, and despite having had no intention of doing so, now he felt he should. Carefully. Most teachers didn't stroll into the office and demand to know dirt on a specific student. If a record of disciplinary action existed, normally he would have to go through the principal to get it. Lucky for him, the secretary was a hopeless gossip, and few things made her happier than someone asking a juicy question.

"So," Ross said after making the prerequisite small talk with her, "I've got this kid in third period, Ben Bentley."

"Oh *him,*" Jessica leaned across the desk, her voice already a conspiring whisper. "You know he's light in the loafers, right?"

"I don't think I've seen him ever wear loafers," Ross said, smiling to show he was only kidding. "Is he trouble? Anything I should be concerned about? You know how we substitutes get the worst side of students."

"Just don't leave your classroom unlocked," Jessica said, widening her eyes meaningfully.

"I don't follow. Did he steal something?"

"No." She looked behind her to make sure the hallway to the principal's office was still empty. When she spoke again, her voice was so quiet he could barely hear her. "Bentley trashed the journalism room. He knocked over furniture, tore up photos in the dark room, and then took a fire extinguisher to it all."

A fire extinguisher? An ironic tool for an arsonist to use, but it did match the theme. Sort of. "Why? What was his reason?"

"No idea, but old Mrs. Jones nearly died of a heart attack."

Jessica covered her mouth to hold back laughter. Ross felt like joining her. The idea of trashing Mrs. Jones's classroom had never occurred to him, but if anyone had it coming, she did. Still, this was serious. Thinking dark thoughts and acting on them were two different things. Ben had a history of vandalism. That, when combined with everything else, made him even more of a suspect. Ross was tempted to call Richard and declare the case closed. Rather than be accused of jumping to conclusions again, he decided to wait until third period. Ross would talk with Ben in person and see what sort of impression he got. And he would set a small trap.

"Could you do me a favor?" he said to Jessica. "I need to get a message to one of my students, Tim Wyman. Could you ask him to meet me in my classroom during lunch break? He promised to help tutor another student of mine."

Tim would be passing on information all right, but Ross would be the one taking notes, watching as Ben and Tim came face to face, partners in crime, exposed at last.

Ross was enjoying himself a little too much. He taught his third period class with dramatic flair, often cocking an eyebrow as if the secrets of his students were laid bare for him to see. He even toyed with them, introducing vocabulary words like vandalism and crime, looking to Ben each time for a reaction. All this revealed was just how little he paid attention. Anytime that Ross checked on him, Ben was either staring down at his book, or at one of the wall posters. In particular the one that used a painter's palette to teach the Spanish words for colors, which for whatever reason, caused him to sigh despondently, and in at least one instance, to glare. Strange kid.

When the bell rang, Ross was prepared. "Okay class, don't forget your assignment for tomorrow. Act out a scene with your partner, five lines of dialog *each*. Be creative and have fun! Ben, if I could see you for a moment?"

The irritated expression remained. "Fine."

Fine? Substitute teachers were used to a lack of respect, but so far, he hadn't had trouble with Ben. Ross closed the classroom door, giving them privacy, and then turned. Ben stood in front of the desk, arms crossed over his chest.

Rather than place himself behind it, Ross sat on the desk, angling himself to face Ben in what he hoped was a more personable approach. "I'm concerned about your grades."

Ben shrugged. "I find it difficult to concentrate in this class."

"Any particular reason?"

"Yes."

Ross waited for a more in-depth explanation, but it didn't come. Ben stood his ground, brow knotted in open aggression. Where was the good heart Ms. Hughes had praised?

"Is there anything I can do to help?" he tried.

"Is Señora Vega ever coming back?" The spiteful tone left no room for interpretation.

"I see. You feel my teaching is the issue."

"*You're* the problem," Ben said, clenching his jaw. Then he shook his head and kept his gaze down. "Never mind. Sorry. I'll try to get my grades up."

"You'll have to work hard. The school year is almost over." Ross decided grades didn't matter right now. "If you don't mind me asking, what exactly did I do wrong?"

Ben raised his head. He was a nice-looking kid with soft dark-blond hair and brown eyes that normally didn't appear so furious. "You really want to know?"

"Of course!"

"One of the first times you subbed, someone asked you how to say 'faggot' in Spanish. You probably don't even remember. I do. Wanna guess why? Because every day in this stupid school feels like a war, and I'm the only one on my side. Just try to picture that, then imagine how crappy it feels when the enemy is given a new word—a new weapon—to use against you."

"*Mariposa,*" Ross said, understanding at last. "It doesn't mean what you—"

"It means 'butterfly.' I know." Ben clenched his jaw and turned his head away. He seemed to be holding back tears.

"I'm sorry," Ross said. "I always get asked questions like that. Cuss words are the first thing anyone wants to learn in a new language. I decided a long time ago to always give an answer, but a harmless one. When people ask me how to say 'shit,' I teach them how to say 'manure.' If it's 'bitch' they want to know, I teach them *perra,* a female dog. I choose harmless words so these students at least learn something. Just not what they wanted. I didn't expect those words to be used to hurt anyone. Including you."

"Well they did," Ben said, looking defiant again, "and right now it's the last word I *ever* want to hear."

"I'm terribly sorry," Ross said, feeling guilty, "and I understand where you're coming from."

"Do you?" Ben challenged.

In a different world, a liberal East or West Coast school perhaps, Ross would have confided in him. *Don't worry, you're not alone! I'm gay too, and I know how bad slurs can hurt.* But he was deep in the heart of conservative Texas, dealing with an angry teenager who already resented him. Giving him ammo could be disastrous. Or maybe it would help ease his anger. Ross hated feeling shackled, just because of who he loved. Other teachers could mention their relationships, the families waiting for them at home, without fear of persecution. They would never have to choose between their job and the urge to comfort a student who was hurting emotionally. Then again, maybe helping one person was worth throwing away his dreams. Ross wasn't sure he could live with himself otherwise. "Listen—"

—knock knock knock—

He took a deep breath and sighed at the interruption. "That'll be Tim Wyman."

"What?" Ben's eyes went wide, proving they knew each other.

In fact, he looked downright panicked, which was more of a reaction than Ross had expected. "Is that a problem?"

"Yes," Ben whispered, all aggression gone from his voice. "I can't explain, but please, just get rid of him."

Ross studied him a moment. Ben's reaction wasn't the fear of being caught. Something else was going on, and when he realized what, he felt guilt right down to his core. "Okay. Just a sec."

He went to the door, opening it just a crack. Tim was standing there, concerned expression shifting effortlessly to one more charming. That smile was like a deadly weapon. Even Ross found himself struggling to form a coherent sentence. He could imagine how a guy like Ben might fall for him, and how devastating the end of that relationship would be.

"Spanish tutor reporting for duty," Tim said easily.

"Great, uh, I'm not actually ready for you today so um... Goodbye."

He shut the door and pressed his back to it. No need because few students, when told they didn't need to work, stuck around to argue. He noticed Ben's vulnerable expression. "I take it you two know each other?"

Ben nodded once. "We used to."

"But not anymore?"

The jaw clenched, followed by steely resolve. "No. Not anymore."

"I see." Ross gathered his thoughts, then walked back to the desk. "I really am sorry about my carelessness. For what it's worth, butterflies are magnificent creatures. As you know, they begin life as caterpillars, which if you think about it, do a much better job of blending into their surroundings. They're green, with just enough stripes to mimic a pattern of shadow, and despite this natural ability to hide, they still listen to the urge to climb high and put themselves in a vulnerable state. When a caterpillar emerges from its cocoon, it's more colorful and delicate than before. They only end up drawing more attention to themselves, but butterflies are the lucky ones. They're destined for more than just crawling around and chewing on leaves. They're meant to fly."

Ben swallowed and took a deep breath. His eyes were watery, and he looked as though he had much to explain, but in the end he merely shook his head and said, "I'll try to improve my grades."

Ross shoved aside his disappointment and tried to find some way to help. "I can give you an extra credit assignment. That should be enough to earn a passing grade."

Ben nodded, his fingers clutching the straps of his backpack. "Can I go?"

"Of course."

Ben went to the door and hesitated, perhaps worrying that Tim hadn't gotten far enough away yet.

"It won't always be like this," Ross said.

Ben spun around. "What do you mean?"

"That most of us are smart enough to outgrow the high school mentality. College is a different place, and if history is anything to go by, someday attitudes will change in the adult world as well. You'll soon leave these struggles behind. Name-calling and foolish teachers who are careless with the knowledge they impart, you'll rise above it all. Just you wait and see. In the meantime, I admire your bravery. You're an inspiration."

Ben considered him. Then he nodded. "Thanks."

If he was still worried about running into Tim, Ben didn't show it as he opened the door and slipped into the hallway to continue fighting his war.

The teachers' lounge was mercifully empty. Ross only returned there to fetch the sandwich he had prepared, intending to eat it in his car to avoid bigoted teachers. Instead he found Ms. Hughes sitting alone at the long table, quietly turning the pages of a tattered paperback. He nodded in greeting when she looked up and decided to join her. She set aside the book, waiting until he had swallowed his first bite before asking a question.

"Solve any more crimes lately?"

"Not really," he replied.

"How did the last case go? I never heard the conclusion."

"I'd rather not talk about it," he said, taking another bite so he couldn't speak. As he chewed and swallowed, he realized there were other issues that troubled him. "Do you think it's important to be a good role model?"

"To our students?" Ms. Hughes chuckled. "While I'd like to believe they look up to us and base their behavior on our own, the truth is we barely register. We're just tiresome old people who get in the way of their social lives."

"I didn't expect you to be so cynical."

"I'm not! That's exactly how it should be. I want my students to form their own opinions. If the current generation always followed the lead of the previous, progress wouldn't be made. Oh sure, I wish they admired all my accumulated wisdom and came to me for advice, but that's not how it works. Instead I try to enjoy those rare occasions when I can actually make a difference, and yes, that's when I try to be a good role model."

"Madam," Ross wagged a finger at her, "you should be

principal. Or superintendent. Maybe even president!"

Ms. Hughes laughed. "That'll be the day. No, I'm happy here on the frontline where I feel like I can accomplish more."

"How?" Ross asked, setting down his sandwich. "Aside from trying to cram their heads full of knowledge, what other options do we have?"

Ms. Hughes took a deep breath. "We can do what's best for them, even though it's not always what's right."

"I don't follow."

"We're expected to enforce rules, and generally there are very good reasons for those rules, but not in every situation. And not for every student."

"You make exceptions?"

Ms. Hughes shook her head. "I make judgment calls. Even when they put me at risk. Like I said, it's so rare that we can actually make a difference. When the opportunity presents itself, I grab hold."

Ross mulled over her words, picking up his sandwich for another bite of turkey and mustard. After taking a swig of cola, he reached a decision. "The previous case you asked about? The one involving Ben? Everyone is going to be okay. I'll make sure of it."

Ms. Hughes smiled. "I'm very glad to hear that."

Carpet vacuumed, toilet scrubbed, and kitchen counters wiped. Even *hors d'oeuvres* had been prepared, if Ritz crackers topped by slices of cheese and ham could even be called that. Still, it was safer than attempting to cook a real meal. A full belly also meant it was harder to get a buzz, and he needed Richard Adler to be a little drunk tonight. That would—in theory—make him more agreeable to suggestion. Ross tried to ignore the nervousness building in his stomach as he walked the apartment, performing one final inspection.

He was considering pouring himself a drink to get a head start when he heard a knock on the door. He hurried to the living room and opened it, finding a police officer there in full uniform.

Richard looked him up and down. Then his eyes moved to the scented candle burning on the coffee table and the small plate of crackers next to it. "You wanted to see me?"

"Are you on duty?" Ross asked, failing to hide his concern.

"I just finished my shift. You said you had important

information for me that, apparently, couldn't be shared over the phone. Again."

"I do have a flair for the dramatic!" Ross stepped aside. "Come in."

He waited until Richard had passed him before checking out the slope of his shoulders and the curve of his butt. Ross loved the uniform a little too much. "Please, sit down. Would you like a drink?" He moved to the kitchen instead of waiting for an answer, hurriedly pouring two glasses of white wine.

When he returned, Richard was standing next to the fish tank and tapping on the glass.

"Don't do that, please," Ross said, moving to join him. "I don't think they like it."

"Normally I wouldn't. When's the last time you checked on them?"

"When I got home!" Ross answered defensively. He had made sure the tank was clean when preparing for the evening. He looked at the aquarium to see what he had missed and his heart sank. There, on the water's surface, a sideways fish no longer moved.

"Are you kidding me?" Ross moaned.

"Oh." Richard cleared his throat. "I'm sorry. You must have been very attached to it."

"Not really," Ross said, but his heart still felt heavy. "I don't even know if that's Marie or Pierre."

"They're French?"

"They're scientists," Ross said with a sigh. "At least their real-life counterparts were. The Curies were pioneers, especially her, in the field of radiology."

Richard bent over to peer through the aquarium. "I think you've got a widow on your hands, because this one is Marie."

"How can you tell?"

"Something about the eyelashes."

Ross managed a laugh. Then he set aside the wine glasses and took out the small net he used to scoop out the aquarium. "Do you mind if I take care of this? I don't want to leave her in there with a dead body."

"No problem," Richard said. "Do you want to bury him or—"

"Burial at sea," Ross said without humor. He scooped up Pierre, then walked to the bathroom toilet to dispose of the body, feeling terrible. He was reaching for the lever to flush when Richard placed a hand over his to stop him.

"Say something first," he said.

"What?" Ross replied, distracted by the minimal physical contact, which already felt electric.

"Say something." Richard withdrew his hand. "He was your pet, right?"

Ross nodded. "Okay. Uh. Let's see… Pierre, you were a good little fish. I tried to make you happy, even though you probably would have liked a bigger tank. Or your freedom. I'll make sure Marie isn't lonely. She's still got me, I promise. Just two old spinsters with no one but each other for company." He looked up sharply, wishing he hadn't spoken so openly, but Richard wasn't laughing. Instead he nodded in approval.

"Is it easier if I do it?"

"No," Ross said. "I'd better. Like you said, he was my pet."

The toilet flushed, the little black fish disappearing in a swirl of water.

Richard patted him on the back. "Let's see about that drink."

They returned to the living room and picked up their glasses.

"To Pierre," Richard said.

"To Pierre," Ross repeated, his heart filling with both sorrow and affection. He didn't know which feeling he wanted to focus on, so he settled on filling his stomach with wine instead.

Richard did too, taking in the details of the room. "You live alone?"

"Yup," Ross said, trying to sound upbeat. He didn't want to ruin the evening. He could sort out his feelings later. "Make yourself at home." He led by example, sitting on the couch and curling up his legs. When Richard sat on the opposite end of the couch, Ross angled his body toward him. "Is that a real gun?"

"It's definitely not a theater prop! Does that make you uncomfortable?"

"I don't know," Ross admitted, raising his glass again, mostly to keep his guest drinking. He hadn't been this desperate to get another guy drunk since sophomore year of high school when a cute new guy had joined the debate team. Nothing happened then except them both getting sick, but he had tried. His motivation tonight was nobler. "So tell me about your day."

"There's not much to report. Wrote some tickets for the usual things. Had a domestic violence call from a man who locked himself in his car because his wife caught him cheating. She was taking a golf club to the windshield when we got there."

"Serves him right," Ross said. "What else?"

"An emergency call that turned out to be a prank from two kids skipping school. Not the smartest move. Speaking of misbehaving students…"

"Have a cracker," Ross said, reaching for the plate and holding it out.

"Thanks." Richard took one but didn't eat. "Listen, is this a social call or—"

"—just a prank? Ha ha. I thought it would be nice to talk. That's all."

"And I thought you had information."

"I do, but it can wait. What do you think of the wine?"

Richard took another gulp, nodding appreciatively. "It's nice."

Ross did the same, the first hint of warmth spreading through him. "Can I ask you a question? What did you mean the other night when you said you 'had an experience.'"

"That's very personal," Richard replied.

Ross shrugged. "I don't mind getting personal."

"Fine. A story for a story. Tell me about your tattoo."

Ross took another sip and set the glass on the table. Then he moved closer so a cushion no longer separated them. He held out his arm, wrist up. "Look closely."

Richard set aside both drink and cracker, then bent over to peer at the tattoo. "What am I supposed to be seeing?"

"Notice the scar?"

Richard gently took his wrist and held it closer to his face. "I think so. Wait. Is this—"

"I was fifteen years old," Ross explained. "I had figured out that I'm gay, which honestly, felt like one more problem added to the pile. I didn't have the best relationship with my dad, I was getting picked on at school, and I was pretty sure God hated me. Teenage Ross was a mess. Solving my problems seemed impossible, so I decided to escape them."

Richard's head shot up, expression sympathetic. "I'm sorry."

"It's fine. After I made the first cut and blood poured out, I quickly realized that I didn't want to die. First of all, the cut hurt like hell, so I wasn't about to do the same thing to the other wrist. Secondly, if all those jerks in my life hated me, the last thing I wanted was to let them win. I went from sad to angry in the blink of an eye. Or the cut of a blade, I suppose. I put a shirt over the cut and had my mom drive me to the emergency room. She was so upset that we nearly ended up dying in a car wreck instead. That would have been ironic, huh?"

Richard's brow furrowed, the hand holding his wrist tightening. "How can you joke about this?"

"Because, as crazy as it sounds, my suicide attempt was empowering. For me it was a turning point. Yeah, it was one of the darkest moments of my life, but it was also when I finally decided to fight back. That's what the tattoo is about. Infinity. I'll never give up. I'll never turn my back on life again. I'll always keep trying, keep feeling, keep loving… All of it. While I'm still alive, I'm going to give it everything I've got."

"That's very brave," Richard said, tracing his thumb across the scar.

"I don't always live up to the promise," Ross said. He reached out and moved Richard's thumb along the line of black ink instead. "I try my best though. That's all any of us can do."

He was enjoying the physical contact and didn't want it to end. Richard felt differently. He let go of Ross's wrist, reached for his drink, and drained the glass.

"Refill?" Ross offered.

"Yeah. Please."

Ross stood and went to the kitchen, bringing the bottle back with him. He topped off his own glass and refilled Richard's before taking a seat on the far end of the couch again, not wanting to crowd his guest and make him uncomfortable. "That's my story. Let's hear yours."

Richard groaned. "It's embarrassing. Ask me anything else."

Ross shook his head. "Embarrassing stories are my favorite kind. Come on. I poured my heart out to you. Tell me about this experience you had."

Richard's eyes were shining as he took another swig for courage. "Fine. I was in college and working toward my associate's degree. While at a Halloween party, I meet this guy. Let's call him Tarzan since that's how he was dressed that night. All he wore was a—what are they called? A loincloth! Keep in mind that his muscles were in plain view. I couldn't stop staring."

"You're attracted to guys?"

Richard shrugged. "At the time I was just envious. I wanted my body to look like his, so I struck up a conversation, trying to learn his routine or whatever. Soon the guy suggests we work out together. Awesome. The next week I meet him at the gym and it turned into a regular thing. We never really talked much, which bothered me because I like to talk, but Tarzan never gave me anything to work with. So one day, I'm standing there spotting him. He's doing bench presses wearing nothing but a tiny pair of shorts. I'm bored out of my mind, and when that happens..."

"What? Did you get a boner?"

Richard nodded. "It just happened. I'm staring at all this pumped-up muscle, and before I know it, one of my own is getting pumped as well. His head isn't far from my crotch, and the athletic shorts I'm wearing are totally tenting at this point."

Ross laughed. "What happened?"

"Forget spotting! I ran for the bathroom. The humiliation was enough to get things under control. Even worse was having to face him again. I had to though. He was my ride. I hit the showers first to get that awkwardness out of the way. Then I went and waited by the car. Tarzan finally shows up in the parking lot and he's glaring at me, so I start apologizing. Then he grunts something about us going back to his place to watch a movie."

"No!"

"Yes! Keep in mind we had never done anything social. Besides that initial conversation at the party and a bunch of work-out sessions, we were as good as strangers. I accepted his offer, thinking he was trying to prove he's cool about the situation."

"Were you hoping for more?"

Richard grinned. "Maybe. We make it halfway through an Arnold Schwarzenegger movie—the sci-fi one where he gets a tracking device pulled out of his nose—when Tarzan whips out a surprise of his own. Simple as that. He doesn't say a damn thing. He just waves it like someone offering a dog a bone."

"And what did you do?"

Richard winked. "Ruff ruff!"

"You went down on him?"

"Hell yeah! I might have been confused about what it all meant, but I knew what I wanted."

Ross let his eyes dart over the police uniform again. "So you're gay?"

"No. I like women. Correction, I *love* women. I'm bisexual, with an emphasis on the sexual part when it comes to guys. I find them attractive, and I like the idea of messing around, but it's never been emotional."

"Not even with Tarzan?"

"Nope. He was the only one, in fact. The same events played out a few times before our workout sessions stopped as suddenly as they began."

"Closet case," Ross said dismissively.

"Honestly? I think he was straight and too socially inept to get any. Maybe he finally found a girl who disliked talking as much as he did."

"Tarzan never reciprocated?"

"No."

"And you've never loved a guy before."

"I haven't, but that doesn't mean I can't relate to your situation." Richard was a lot more relaxed than when he first arrived, spreading himself out and sinking into the cushions. "The station where I work is full of testosterone. Nobody knows about me, but I still take a lot of flak because I don't have the same good ol' boy mentality. So I get why you don't want to attract attention to yourself, and why you're so concerned about your students. Speaking of which, what did you learn?"

Ross eyed the wine glasses on the coffee table, wishing they were emptier. This was it! "I talked to Ben today. We were wrong. Kind of. Ben and Tim are a couple, or were, but they're not the arsonists."

"Why do you say that?"

Because he didn't want it to be true. "Instinct? Ben is a good kid. Trust me, he's not the one you're looking for."

"And Tim?"

"Uh… If he was a bad person, Ben wouldn't have dated him."

"Except it sounds like they've broken up. Maybe that's the reason why; Ben got tired of Tim wanting to burn down everything. I looked him up, by the way."

"Who?"

"Tim."

Ross sat upright. "How?"

"We have yearbooks at the station. You'd be surprised how often they come in handy. It might have been dark that night, but I shined my light right into his eyes. They're distinct. I remember them. Tim is the guy I chased. I'm certain."

"Okay," Ross said, "but that doesn't mean he's the arsonist. He's only guilty of having sex in public. Considering the circumstances, you can't really blame them. Right?"

Richard didn't respond right away. He reached for his glass and took another swig. "I'm sorry. He's the most likely suspect. I can't ignore that."

"Yes, you can! Just let this one go. Who besides us will know?"

"My partner." Richard sighed. "Listen, the first week I was on the job, I responded to a call about a shoplifter. I showed up at the store expecting to see a punky teenager. Instead it's someone ten years older than me. Some people steal for the thrill, or because they feel entitled, but this woman obviously didn't have much. Even worse, she was stealing baby formula. Had it been alcohol instead, or cigarettes…" He shook his head. "I didn't want to arrest her, but the store owner insisted on pressing charges. I offered to pay for the baby formula, but he was adamant. Even though I hated myself for it, I had to bring her in. Now I know that I did the right thing."

"How can you say that?"

"Because I'm not a judge. My job is to know the law and to enforce it. This woman needed help, but that's what welfare programs are for. Or what about the baby? Doesn't it deserve to be fed? I had no idea what condition the baby was in because it wasn't with her. Maybe this person had a drug problem. If so, what sort of environment is that for a child? If I had been asked to investigate further, I would have, but you have to trust the system. I'm sure Child Protective Services got involved, and that the judge she went before was more concerned with finding a solution than a sentence."

"You can't know that."

"Right, because I can't know everything. Your job is no different. Normally you focus on teaching, and when there are disciplinary problems, what then?"

"I send them to the principal."

"And I send them to the court system. It doesn't matter how

much we like or relate to a person. If they're breaking the rules, they face the consequences."

"More so than normal in this circumstance," Ross argued. "What if their parents kick them out of the house? Or they get beat up at school because they can't help who they love? They could be killed!"

Richard sighed. "I know. But what if I look away, like you're asking me to, and they end up burning down the school? What if people die because I chose to turn a blind eye?"

Ross couldn't argue with that. "I'll talk to them. Tomorrow. I'll tell Tim especially that I know about the fires, and that if I hear about one more being set, I'll have no choice but to alert the authorities."

Richard shook his head. "You could be putting yourself in danger."

"That's my choice to make. Besides, I've got a big strong police officer looking out for me."

Richard managed a smile, but not much of one. "I don't like this."

"Just give me one more day. Let me talk to them. We'll see how they react and take it from there. Okay? Great!" He picked up the bottle. "More wine?"

Richard laughed. "It's a good thing my judgment is impaired. Otherwise I would never agree to such a stupid scheme."

"That was the plan," Ross said, filling their glasses.

"I want to hear from you right after you talk to them. Call me. I won't wait for another dinner or whatever."

"I thought you liked spending time with me?"

"I do," Richard said. "A little too much. It's not the wine that made me agree."

"No?"

"Not at all. I've got a strong tolerance."

"Oh." Ross couldn't say the same. He didn't indulge often. There were too many alcoholics in his family, so he tried to drink sparingly. Right now his head was buzzing, enough that he didn't think twice about what he asked next. "Can I see your gun?"

"Absolutely not!" Richard noticed the shameless grin that accompanied this question. "Wait, you mean…"

"Yup!"

"Still concerned it's fake?"

"Only one way to prove otherwise."

Richard set down his glass and leaned back, hand on his belt. "You sure about this?"

Ross abandoned his glass too, crawling forward with a smile. "Ruff ruff," he said.

On some mornings, Ross wished for a doctor who made house calls, not that he needed help guessing the diagnosis: headache with a slight case of heartache. He was suffering both and didn't regret either. Sure he had drunk too much wine last night, and stayed up late into the night talking to Richard. And yes, his jaw was still sore from other activities, because Richard was more challenging than he had expected. All of it had been blissful and anything but superficial. This attraction went beyond the uniform or Richard's impressive sidearm. Ross admired his integrity and passion for justice, even though he didn't share his faith in the system. When it came to rules, Ross sided with Ms. Hughes. Doing what was best wasn't always the same as doing what was right. Not for the first time, he wished he and Richard had met without the complication of an unsolved crime. At least not one that involved his students. Speaking of which, Ross returned his attention to the ongoing presentation, remembering that he had his own job to do.

«Good morning for you,» Ben said in seriously broken Spanish. «How much is the meat expensive?»

«Cheap, my friend,» replied his partner, grinning at the class instead of looking at his conversation partner. «The meal is so fresh!»

«Here is a wallet,» Ben said carefully. «For meat.»

«Thank you, nice customer! Good night!»

Ross resisted a groan. «Very good. Please take a seat.» When this failed to provoke a response, he switched to English. "You can sit down now." Just once he would like to have a student who surpassed his expectations. He checked his list for the next pair of partners. "Daniel Wigmore," he said, feeling more hopeful. "And Julie Snyder." Ugh. What a combination! One was an over-achiever and the other refused to participate. Still, he was interested to see how the conversation would go. They each had five lines to recite. Once they were both standing in front of the class, Daniel began.

«Hello, park ranger. Could you please tell me the name of this forest?»

«No.»

«It's very beautiful here!»

«Yes.»

«I think I'll go for a hike. Can you recommend a good destination?»

«No.»

«I see. Is that smoke I smell?»

«Yes.»

«We had better run before the entire forest burns down!»

«Maybe.»

"Thank you," Ross said with an exasperated sigh. "Julie, I expected more from you. Daniel, that was... unique." As skilled as his Spanish was, Daniel got a little too creative when implementing it. He was unlikely to have such a conversation with a real park ranger. Ben's attempt to buy some sort of meat or meal was a more practical application, even though he'd managed to bungle it. At least Daniel had been inspired to think outside the box, and not for the first time. Previously he had responded to essay questions by writing about a dramatic plane crash, or once an orphanage that had burnt down, except he had accidentally chosen the wrong word and— Ross blinked, seeing a pattern that he should have noticed sooner. Explosions and fires. If he didn't have a class staring at him, he would have torn through old assignments, seeking more evidence.

Instead he called another pair of names, only halfway paying attention as he sized Daniel up. He wasn't athletic, although the gangly arms and legs probably helped put distance between him and anyone in pursuit. His light frame could give him an edge on someone like Officer Adler, whose heavy muscles might slow him down. And hadn't Richard mentioned that the arsonist had gotten a head start?

And yet, Tim had already been identified, thanks to his yearbook photo, so it was a moot point. He and Daniel didn't have similar eyes. It was unlikely to be a case of mistaken identity. Unless... What if Ben and Tim being in the park that night was a complete coincidence?

For the rest of the period, Ross tried to decide on a course of action. He had planned on talking to Ben after class, but when the bell rang, he asked Daniel to stay behind instead. «You have a gift for this language,» he said.

«Thank you very much,» Daniel replied, smiling eagerly in return. He was awkward. The red hair probably drew enough insults. Ross's brother had suffered the same treatment. But the way Daniel didn't know when to hold back, when to play it cool instead of boasting about his achievements, probably didn't help him make friends. It wasn't difficult to imagine him needing to exorcise some of his frustration.

«There seems to be a theme. Do you understand?»

Daniel nodded.

"*Incendio*," Ross said, mouth dry. "Do you know that word?"

"*Incendio*?" Daniel replied. "No, sir. What's it mean?"

"Arson." Ross watched carefully for a reaction, but he couldn't have missed it. Daniel's face lit up. Then he grinned, as if he were delighted. "*Incendio!*"

"Right," Ross said, trying to keep his own expression neutral. "You've chosen fire as a theme before. Try to broaden your scope. You're a smart young man. Choose something different next time."

"I will, sir." Daniel replied. "Thank you."

"Enjoy your lunch."

As soon as Daniel was gone, Ross decided he would hurry to the teachers' lounge and, assuming he found privacy, call Richard to tell him what he had learned. Officer Adler would show up in full uniform, probably with his partner in tow, to arrest Daniel. Then he and Ross could finally put this entire mess to bed, leaving them free to pursue whatever potential they had. A relationship? A lifetime spent together? Who knew!

Ross frowned. He liked the idea of being with Richard. What sat uneasy with him was the idea of ratting out *any* of his students. Not just Ben and Tim. Sure, he felt slightly more protective of them, due to his own sexuality, but Ross also knew how difficult being young could be, and how easy it was to make mistakes at their age without realizing the seriousness of the ramifications.

"Just a moment, please!"

Daniel was on his way out the door, but he stopped and turned around. "Sir?"

Ross walked over to meet him. "It's a funny coincidence, your chosen theme, because there have been a series of fires lately. Intentional fires. Arson."

Daniel appeared genuinely concerned. "Really?"

"Yes. I know the investigating police officer, and he says he's close to catching the perpetrator. In fact, the arsonist is someone at this school."

Daniel swallowed. "Oh. That's terrible."

"I agree. It'll all be over because the police have a trap in place. One more fire and they're convinced they'll catch who's setting them. Don't ask me how. Maybe they're following that person around, I don't know. My point is that you shouldn't joke about fires right now. That could have serious consequences."

Daniel went pale. "I'm sorry."

"It's fine," Ross said, giving him a friendly pat on the arm. "You didn't mean any harm. I just don't want anyone getting the wrong idea about you. How are you doing in general? I remember how difficult high school was. Not the classes or grades. I did fine there. So do you! You're very gifted, Daniel. Other students don't always appreciate that, do they? Sometimes they hold it against you, am I right?"

Daniel nodded numbly.

"I've been there myself. Don't let it get you down. Your intelligence will make you successful. Everything life has to offer will be within your grasp, as long as you make the right decisions. But for now, maybe let other people share the spotlight with you. School doesn't have to be a competition. Let your grades speak for themselves, and if anyone gives you a hard time, come talk to me. Okay?"

"Okay," Daniel said. "Thank you, sir."

"No problem."

Ross watched him leave, feeling pleased with how the conversation had gone. The sensation was fleeting because he still had a very determined police officer to deal with. One who had given him until the end of the day to find his arsonist.

Ross threw open the door before Richard could knock. He had been pacing back and forth, peering through the peephole at regular intervals, anxious about this encounter. Judging from the other man's expression, he was right to be.

"I'm here on business," Richard said. Or perhaps Officer Adler was more appropriate, because not only was he in uniform, he was using his slightly deeper professional voice. Only one thing seemed out of place: a plastic bag he held that was filled with water and two black fish.

"Awwww!" Ross said, reaching for it instinctively.

"Oh." Richard cleared his throat. "Right. First this, then business."

"Sounds like a plan," Ross said with a smile. "Come in!"

"I hope you don't mind. I know you're probably still missing Pierre, but I did some research on Marie Curie. She had two daughters. Did you know that?"

"No," Ross admitted. "Or if I did, I must have forgotten."

"She did," Richard said, walking with him toward the fish tank. "I didn't want Marie to be alone, so this is Irene and Eve."

"Yay!" Ross enthused, taking the bag from him. "You even got the right kind. These are black skirt tetras!"

Richard puffed up his chest in pride. "Like I said, I try to be observant. The guy at the pet store said you're supposed to let the water temperature adjust gradually."

Ross nodded, already lowering the bag into the aquarium. "You're so sweet! What a great idea too. I really think Marie has been depressed lately."

"You were supposed to call me during the day."

Ross turned to face him, surprised by the sudden change of topic. "I got sidetracked, but I have good news. Do you want another drink? Or more of my famous Ritz crackers?"

Richard shook his head. "I told you yesterday that I didn't want another dinner date. I want the truth!"

"Do you regret what happened?"

Richard exhaled. "No. I don't." He put his hands on his hips. "Tell me what's going on. No small talk, no drinks. None of the other stuff either. Please."

Ross nodded. "Okay. I found the arsonist and it's not Ben or Tim. I happened to notice that one of my students is preoccupied with fire. I had a talk with him after class and—well, there's little room for doubt. It's him."

"That's great!" Richard unbuttoned a shirt pocket and took out a small pad of paper. "What's his name?"

"About that..."

"Not this again! Are you serious?"

"He's a—"

"Let me guess, a good kid?"

Ross nodded enthusiastically. "Yes. He's very intelligent. Maybe a little socially awkward, but he's got potential."

Richard glowered. "That doesn't matter."

"Sorry?"

"I have a job to do. You're obstructing justice."

Ross laughed, thinking it was a joke. "Are you going to arrest me?"

"I'm damn near tempted!" Richard roared. He walked deeper into the living room, pinching the bridge of his nose. "This needs to stop. I like you, I really do. What I said the other day about my attraction to guys being only sexual? I'm not so sure anymore. Do you know what my favorite part of last night was?"

Ross grinned, remembering what they had called it. "Friendly fire?"

"Nope. It was talking to you before we got down to business. Afterwards too. Don't get me wrong, I enjoyed all the stuff in between, but it's you I like. Your personality, your thoughts… All of you."

"Wow," Ross said, at a loss for words. "Thanks."

"This case," Richard said, holding up a finger and continuing to pace, "is in our way. We need to put it behind us so we can freely explore our potential. Assuming you even want that."

"I like you too!" Ross said, taking a step closer. "Mind if I show you how much?"

Richard's expression remained grim. "Not now. Just tell me the name of the arsonist. Please."

Ross sighed. "I already talked to him about it. I told him the police were closing in, and that all it would take is one more fire to catch the culprit. He's done. You have my word."

"That's not enough."

"Why not?" Ross said indignantly.

"Because you can't control what this person will and won't do! That's not a promise you can keep. Only he can."

"Okay, then how about this? If there's another fire—just one—then I'll tell you his name."

Richard stopped moving, head hung low as he shook it. "This is like Tommy Wilson all over again."

"Tommy who?"

"When my sister was fourteen, she started dating this guy from another school. Tommy lived in the next county over, far enough away that it was too long to walk or bike, so she started taking our parents' car."

"She knew how to drive already?"

"Not officially, but she still managed to get to Tommy's place and back. I was scared for her. My sister kept reassuring me that everything would be fine. This went on for weeks. I wanted to tell my parents, but she begged me not to." Richard paused, eyes unfocused as he stared into the past. "I remained silent. Just like she wanted. One night she and Tommy were out for a joyride. They thought it would be fun, the idiots! That's when she ran a red light and the car was sideswiped."

"Oh my god! Was she—"

"My sister was fine, but Tommy suffered brain trauma. I had met him a few times before. He was always nice and even brought me a bunch of his old comics when he found out I liked them. The accident left him unable to speak. He recovered eventually, but he still doesn't sound normal, and frankly, I don't think it's just his words that are jumbled. So basically, because I held my tongue like my sister asked me to, someone ended up with brain damage. A good kid too. Tommy also had potential."

"You can't blame yourself for that."

Richard scowled. "I can, and I do! Yes, it was my sister's fault, and his, but I also had a choice. I had the power to prevent what happened. I didn't, and that's exactly the sort of situation you're putting me in now."

"Okay." Ross nodded. "I can understand where you're coming from, but I need to tell you a story too. Or at least continue one. Remember my suicide attempt? I talked about all the abuse I had gone through, but do you know what pushed me over the edge? I failed physical education. I had a coach who was really mean, and he told me if I didn't do enough pushups… The details don't matter. Failing PE doesn't matter! What a joke, but back then, it felt like the end of the world to me. I knew I would get teased even more, and my parents would be angry, so I decided to call it quits. Small things seem like a really big deal when you're that age, especially if you're already dealing with being bullied. So it's not just that I like these students. I'm trying to prevent them from getting hurt or wanting to hurt themselves."

Richard crossed his arms over his chest. "So you never give them failing grades, even if they deserve it?"

"I give them another chance. Extra credit or makeup tests. And yeah, I do have students like Julie Snyder who still don't give a crap and fail. But not before I try my hardest to help them help themselves." Ross rolled his eyes. "That sounds cheesy. Forget I said anything."

"It's not cheesy," Richard murmured. "I like that about you. But in this one circumstance, I need you to let me do my job. I told my superiors I had a strong lead. They're expecting results!"

Ross steeled himself. "I won't give you his name. If you really do like me, then I'm asking you for this one favor. I realize we don't know each other very well yet, but I think we could go far. It's not hard to imagine us falling in love and being together for years, if not decades. I truly believe that could happen. Do you?"

Richard's reply was hoarse. "Yeah."

"Then do this for that guy, the Ross in the future who you love more than anything, and I promise when we finally reach that day, I won't have asked you for anything else. Hell, I'll never ask you for another favor again! I just need one from you. In advance."

"That's very romantic," Richard said, "but it's also manipulative. If I do this for you, then that's it between us. We're finished. I won't date someone who uses my own feelings against me."

"That's not what I'm trying to do!"

"Decide," Richard said. "It's either me or him."

Ross was surprised to find it wasn't an easy choice. He had only known this man for a few days, but he really did believe in their potential together. He could see their future as if it were already written: a little two-bedroom apartment that they would share, maybe even a dog. Richard would be gallant and insist they adopt it from a shelter. Wouldn't that be cute? Then again, Ross had his own sense of nobility. He wouldn't betray one of his students. Not when he was convinced that the threat was over. "I need to think of my students' needs before my own. I'm sorry."

"So am I," Richard said, heading for the door. He turned around after opening it. "I wish we'd had more time together."

"So do I," Ross said softly.

Richard clenched his jaw, then strode toward him, closing the distance. He took Ross's head in his hands and kissed him like they would never have another chance. Only when Richard broke away and left the apartment, not turning around on his way out, did Ross realize that's exactly what it had been. Their last kiss, their final goodbye.

Love sucks. If that's even what it had been. Ross spent the next week feeling deflated. Life had been so exciting, if only briefly. A crime to solve and a passionate affair with a police officer. What could be better, and what did he have to look forward to now? Summer school, where the students were even less enthusiastic? He considered his current class, most of them with their heads lowered in concentration as they took a test. This wasn't a practice run. Only Julie Snyder—still protesting until the very end—wasn't trying. And Ben Bentley, who was in a daze, his expression despondent. Ross was pretty sure it matched his own. Lovesick. Their eyes met briefly before Ben panicked and resumed working on his test. However long he and Tim had been together, Ross hoped it had been more than a few lousy days.

He found himself wishing Daniel would start another fire, freeing Ross from any obligation. So far—for better or worse—Daniel seemed to be taking their talk to heart. He even seemed more confident, not just when it came to school work, but also when interacting with other students. That was good. At least Ross's sacrifice hadn't been in vain.

He whiled away the rest of the period by staring at the calendar and calculating how long it would take for Richard to forgive him. Would three months suffice? Six? A year? Richard would probably be in a relationship by then. Ross felt confident about his own status. Hopelessly alone, as usual. When the bell rang and the classroom emptied, he collected the tests, put them in a drawer, and turned to face the door, hoping to find it occupied by a gruff police officer. It wasn't. Then he went to the teachers' lounge. Ross was eager for anyone to be there, even Coach Reynolds, because listening to him spew hate was better than facing the silence of his apartment.

The lounge wasn't empty, but Ross didn't recognize the teachers there. Only the principal, Mrs. Newman, who was pouring herself a cup of coffee. She smiled when noticing Ross.

"Señor Langdon!" she declared. "I've got good news for you!"

"I could use it," Ross replied.

"Señora Vega is back on her feet again. She'll be returning to teach the summer courses we talked about."

In other words, Ross would soon be out of work again.

"That's great," he managed.

"Isn't it?" Mrs. Newman continued to smile. "You should take a nice trip somewhere. Do some traveling. Maybe to Mexico! I imagine that would help keep your language skills sharp."

His finances were in such poor condition that a trip anywhere was out of the question. No, he could look forward to another summer of waiting tables, unless he could find a new assignment. "This is a nice school," he said, already feeling pathetic. "I'll miss it. Keep me in mind if a full-time position opens up."

"Will do," Mrs. Newman said, already turning away to speak with one of the full-fledged teachers.

The sun might be shining outside, but the rest of Ross's day was gloomy and gray. What he wanted, more than anything, was a sympathetic shoulder to rest his head on. He would do just about anything for another cozy night at home with a certain someone. Instead the apartment would be empty like his future now seemed.

When all you have is nothing, at least you've got nothing to lose.

Ross's uncle had told him that. At the time he'd been too young to grasp the double meaning, or how it related to his uncle's gambling problem. Now it made perfect sense. Ross had nothing to lose at this point, which was oddly liberating. He could do absolutely anything, and matters couldn't get much worse. Even if they did, at least his life would be more interesting. He thought of a number of plans, some too crazy for him, but one wasn't so bad. At the very least, it gave him an excuse to see Richard again.

Ross spent his free period writing a letter. After school he went directly to the police station. "I'd like to speak with Officer Adler," he told the receptionist.

"Just a moment," the man said, consulting his computer. Then he lifted his phone and had a clipped conversation before hanging up. "Officer Adler is still out on patrol, but a different officer would be happy to assist you. What's this about exactly?"

Ross shook his head. "Adler is the only one I'll talk to. Will he be back soon?"

"Is an hour soon?"

"Sure. I'll wait."

The receptionist made a face, but Ross ignored this and sat in the waiting area. The chairs were painfully uncomfortable, and many of the people he saw gave him the creeps, but he was determined not to give up. More than an hour passed, Ross fighting against boredom and despair, when a familiar voice finally pulled him free.

"Mr. Langdon. How may I help you?" Richard's expression was all business. Only the barely withheld emotion in his eyes suggested that feelings remained between them.

Ross shot to his feet. "Is there somewhere private we can talk?"

A subtle shake of the head. Then a repeated question. "How may I help you?"

Ross swallowed and held out the letter he'd written. "This is a signed confession," he whispered. "I'm the arsonist."

Richard clenched his jaw. "No, you're not."

"This says I am."

"Why?"

Ross looked around to make sure they weren't overheard. "So the case can be closed and your superiors won't be angry. I want you to make detective."

Richard stared hard at him. Then he snatched away the letter. "Fine," he said, gesturing to a glass door where officers were coming and going. "Right this way."

Ross walked to the door with unwavering resolve and waited there. Richard followed, using a special pass to gain entry. He held the door open, eyebrows raised expectantly. Goodbye freedom! Ross walked forward on stiff legs, questioning his own actions. A long hallway led past more doors, voices and typical office noises drifting out from each.

"Hold on a second," Richard said.

"What?" Ross responded, the hope in his voice transparent.

"Turn around. I need to cuff you."

"Oh." He had thought of this happening before, but in a warm bedroom instead of a cold concrete hallway. The handcuffs closed painfully tight around his wrists.

Richard placed a hand on his shoulder to guide him. "This way."

He was led to a room as bleak as the hallway. Just four white walls, a small table, and two chairs. Richard shut the door behind them, the click echoing with finality. This was it. He was under arrest.

"You have the right to remain silent," Richard said, standing in front of him. "You also have the right to explain why you thought a stupid ruse like this would work." He stepped forward menacingly. "Anything you say may be used against you in a court of law."

Ross stumbled backward, hands bumping against the wall. "I'm doing this for you!"

"You have the right to an attorney," Richard continued, "although a psychologist might be more appropriate. I'm thinking of starting therapy too. Maybe then I could finally get you out of my head."

"Wait, what?"

Richard grabbed him by the shoulders and brought their mouths together. A hand on the back of his head stopped it from hitting the hard wall as lips pressed against his hungrily. Ross eagerly reciprocated, almost crying out in protest when Richard pulled back enough to speak.

"Knowing and understanding your rights as I have explained them, are you willing to answer my questions without an attorney present?"

"Yes," Ross breathed.

"Good. What's the name of the arsonist?"

Not this again! "But you promised—"

"And I need you to start trusting me. Otherwise it's never going to work. Now then, what's the name of the arsonist?"

"Daniel Wigmore," Ross answered.

"Good." Richard nodded. "One more fire and he's mine. That was the deal, right?"

His heart skipped a beat. "Yes! Um… It's the rest of the deal I'm starting to have second thoughts about."

"I figured. Turn around."

Ross did as he was told, relieved when the handcuffs were unlocked and removed. As soon as his arms were free, he used them to hug Richard. "I could use an extra chance too," he murmured.

"I'll need to examine the evidence first." Richard unfolded the letter, laughing after reading a few lines. "Could your plan be any more dramatic?"

"Yes, actually. I was considering one where I would set a big fire and wait at the scene of the crime for you to arrest me."

"That would have been stupid."

"And another where I frame Julie Snyder for the crime, because if one of my students was going to take the fall, I'd rather it be her."

"You've moved on from obstructing justice to fraud. I'm so proud of you."

"I also toyed with the idea of figuring out where you patrol and speeding through the area every day, getting speeding ticket after speeding ticket, just so I could see you."

"I'm flattered. And a little frightened. You should probably stop while you're ahead."

"Okay." Ross looked into those dark shining eyes and resisted a sigh. "That future we talked about. Do you think we can still get there?"

Richard nodded slowly. "I think it's in the public's best interest if I keep an eye on you."

"You'll take me into custody? House arrest? That sort of thing?"

"Yes. Although this time, no more mixing business with pleasure. Then again…"

"What?"

"I talked to my head of department about learning Spanish. He thinks it would be a good idea. Not just for me, but for the other officers as well. It would mean extra hours for you, which might not be easy to juggle with a day job, but—"

"I'm your man," Ross blurted out. Then he chuckled. "In more than one way. I hope."

Richard grabbed him around the waist for a kiss. "My man? I like the sound of that."

Ross sighed wistfully. He took it all back. Love didn't suck. In fact, it was pretty damn excellent.

The final day of school had arrived. Ross was reminded of how eager his younger self had been for the semester to end and summer to begin, if only to escape the bullies. How ironic that he had signed up for a lifetime of this. Although maybe not. Thanks to a certain police officer, his career path now had a few forks, and he was still uncertain how far down this one he would wander. He was already working on a lesson plan, repurposing the one he had begun writing on that fateful day when Officer Adler had barged into his life. Ross looked up, almost expecting to see him there. All he saw were students who were talking freely. In English, sadly. Even though Ross had given them a free period to do whatever they liked, he still couldn't help wishing that some of them would take the initiative and speak the new language they had learned.

He tuned in on the various conversations, happy when he heard some snippets of Spanish after all. Daniel Wigmore, of course, but he was interacting with students with whom he usually didn't. Sure he was translating obscene sentences into Spanish for the others' amusement, but if it helped him fit in and made next year easier, then so be it. Ross pretended not to notice and resumed working on his lesson until the bell rang.

"Have a nice summer!" he called, but he was already forgotten as his students fled the room, craving their freedom.

All but one, that is.

"Señor Langdon," Ben said, approaching his desk. "Do you have a minute?"

Ross closed his lesson book. "Sure!"

"I just wanted to say thank you. Or apologize. Both, really." Ben shook his head and started over. "I know I haven't been a very good student. Especially lately. It's not your fault. I guess I have negative associations with Spanish now, and that's made it hard to stay motivated."

He thought of Tim Wyman's fluency in the language. It wasn't difficult to imagine how that could be used romantically. And how much those memories would hurt when their relationship came to an end.

"You did fine," Ross said generously. "Foreign languages aren't for everyone, although sometimes it's just a matter of finding one that resonates with you. French maybe, or perhaps Italian?"

Ben shrugged. "I think I'll stick to English. I still can't believe I passed!"

Technically he hadn't, but Ross had snuck a few extra points on Ben's final test, just to make sure he would. "You earned that D minus!" he said in upbeat tones, trying to be encouraging.

When he realized how ridiculous this sounded, he laughed.

Ben did too. "I'll take what I can get. I also wanted to say that I'm sorry if I was rude to you or anything. It's been a rough year. Actually, it was really great up until the end."

The year still had many months left, but he didn't think that was the end Ben was referring to. "I'm sorry to hear that. Are you looking forward to the summer break at least?"

Ben took a deep breath and exhaled. "This is going to sound really dramatic, but have you ever felt like you had nothing to look forward to?"

"Yes," Ross said instantly. "Very recently, in fact. I kept trudging along, and eventually, I discovered that life had some welcome surprises in store for me. I didn't sit around feeling sorry for myself though. That's important. If you're not happy with your life, do whatever it takes to change it. As long as you aren't hurting yourself or others, don't hold back. We create our own happy endings."

Ben considered this. Then he grinned. "You're pretty cool, you know that? Not many teachers care like you do. About our grades, sure, but not the rest of it. They don't care how we feel or what we're going through."

"Some do," Ross said. "Don't give up hope there either."

"I'm tempted to take your class again, but I guess that wouldn't be doing either of us a favor."

"No," Ross said with a chuckle, "probably not, but I wouldn't mind. Although I don't think I'll be here next year. Señora Vega will have returned by then."

"Oh." Ben frowned. "That sucks."

"Between you and me, I think so too."

"Well, wherever you end up," Ben said, "just know that I think you're awesome, and I bet a bunch of other people do too."

Ross could only think of one he was sure about, because the morning had begun with Richard telling him—and showing him—just how appreciated he was. "Wherever *you* end up, I wish only the best for you too. Just keep being true to yourself. Some people don't learn that lesson until late in their lives, if ever at all. You're ahead of the game, Ben. Keep it that way."

Ben nodded. "I'll try. See you around!"

Ross wasn't sure they would ever cross paths again, but he

wouldn't forget the brave boy with a sad heart. In a way he felt a certain kinship with him, although Ross hoped he had already found his own happily-ever-after in the form of a police officer with an unshakable sense of justice and a body that wouldn't quit. The thought made him laugh, and he kept on smiling as he imagined a relationship that would outlast the decades, surviving every obstacle and hardship to prove that love could be infinite.

Something Like Turkey

by Jay Bell

Austin, 2013

Won't your family feel loved when they see how much care and consideration you put into preparing this cherished staple of American cuisine! Simply truss the turkey, tent with aluminum foil, and slow-roast at two-hundred and twenty-five degrees for twelve hours, basting every two to three hours, increasing heat by one hundred degrees for the final hour before resting the bird thirty minutes prior to carving. Just don't let your family see how easy it is! Instead, bask in their smiling faces and words of praise, knowing that you've provided them with a truly special day.

Ben peered at the cookbook, the words blurring together. He tried to make sense of them until the sting of sweat forced him to close his eyes. After wiping them with his forearm, he squatted to gaze through the window of the oven door. Twelve hours of work. The stupid bird better be worth it! Ben had set his alarm for three in the morning, rushing downstairs to preheat the oven. Once the turkey had been placed inside, he returned to bed, trying to get a few more hours of sleep but unable to, instead suffering through visions of the house burning down thanks to an untended oven. Eventually he gave up, returning to the kitchen to baste the turkey while a stupid foil tent stood in the way. Then he started work on the other dishes, and before he knew it, noon had come and gone.

Ben looked around the kitchen and nearly wept. The counters were cluttered with dirty pots, greasy pans, smudged cutting boards, and crusted plates. Farther away, the kitchen table was filled with covered dishes and pies, some that he had prepared, some that had been brought by his guests. And speaking of guests.... Ben spun around, making sure that nobody had attempted to invade this most sacred of spaces. Anyone who tried was shooed out, no matter how good their intentions. Allison kept offering to help, and as kind as that was, her presence made him doubly nervous. That also went for her husband Brian, who really knew how to roast and grill. Or Davis, their son, who had crawled into the kitchen after Chinchilla and almost caused Ben to trip and drop a baking dish full of scalloped potatoes. And then there was Tim.

Ben sighed. Most of the effort was for him. During this time of year his boyfriend would always talk about Eric with shining eyes, reminiscing about the epic parties he had thrown and the vast feasts he conjured up. Eric's cooking skills were legendary. Ben's? Not even close, but he wanted to overcome this for Tim. How often had Ben gotten nostalgic and rambled on and on about the memories he and Jace had made together? Tim was always cool about that, usually responding with phrases like, "I'm glad someone was there to make you happy. You deserved that." Well, lately Ben thought Tim had earned a special treat for being patient, and for having come so far. While Ben knew he couldn't take Eric's place any more than Tim could take Jace's, he at least wanted to honor Eric's memory by providing a memorable meal, and in the process, hopefully give Tim a happy reminder of the past.

Ben opened the oven, forgetting once again to avoid the initial wave of heat. He blinked against this, certain he had singed his eyebrows. Then he grabbed an oven mitt—already having learned that lesson the hard way—and pulled the pan free, setting it on the stovetop. He was supposed to let it sit for thirty minutes, but he couldn't resist peeking. Lifting the foil tent, he expected steam to fill the air with the mouth-watering aroma of roasted turkey. No steam, but there was definitely a smell, and it wasn't good. The scent matched the appearance of the bird, which seemed be mummified. No big deal. He just needed to baste it again. There weren't any juices left at the bottom of the pan, so Ben decided a little white wine would do the trick. He grabbed an open bottle from the fridge, pouring a few glugs over the bird. Past an initial sizzle, the wine just rolled off.

Ben stifled a groan, fearing it would attract attention. Instead he grabbed a fork, poked at a meatier section of the turkey, and was rewarded with a crunching noise. He knew that a crispy skin was desirable, but crispy meat? That wasn't right. Ben set down the fork, clutching both hands into fists and resisting the urge to start punching the loathsome bird. Instead he forced himself to take a deep breath. Maybe he could salvage enough to serve at least *some* turkey. He resumed poking at it, either finding dry meat or softer parts that were flavorless aside from a hint of the wine he had poured. Then, feeling obscene, he stuck his finger into the cavity filled with stuffing and winced at the soggy coldness. How had he managed that?

Ben consulted the recipe once more. He had chosen one of Eric's old cookbooks from the seventies. The photographs were various shades of brown and orange with highlights of mustard yellow and olive green. He had found that amusing, but now he treated the tome as if it were treacherous. Evil. The Necronomicon! He noticed the part about increasing the heat and checked the oven, which was now at four hundred and—Wait. Ben eyed the recipe yet again. He knew he had increased the heat toward the end, but it was currently set way too high, meaning that…

Now he did groan out loud. For the last twelve hours, the oven had been one hundred degrees above the recommended temperature. He had overcooked the turkey while somehow managing to create heat-resistant stuffing. Could it get any worse?

"Need any help in there?" Brian called from the living room.

"No!" Ben shouted in response. Damn it! What was he going to do now? He considered his options. Grocery stores sold pre-roasted turkeys, right up front and ready to go, catering to incompetent chefs like himself. He would make an excuse to go there, grab one, and swap it out for his own, like an infant switched at birth. Ben imagined a turkey with his smile and Tim's eyes. Then he shook the unfortunate mental image from his mind and headed for the living room.

He was greeted by eager faces. Not just Allison and her family, or Tim, who already appeared proud, but also Jason and William, who had their share of issues recently. A crappy Thanksgiving meal certainly wouldn't help.

"Everything okay?" Allison asked, always able to read him.

"I forgot something?" Ben said, not meaning for it to sound like a question. He cleared his throat and tried again. "I need to run to the store."

"I can—" Tim began.

"No! You'll get the wrong thing."

"What exactly do you need?" Allison asked, clearly enjoying herself. "We could ask Marcello to pick it up on his way over. Actually, his giant house probably has its own grocery store."

"I need cranberry sauce," Ben said, glaring at her. "A very particular kind. Besides, I don't want to trouble him."

"Okay, okay!" she responded, raising her hands in surrender. "Just trying to prevent us all from starving to death."

"We can wait," William declared, "but it won't be easy because it sure smells good!"

Nice guy. Maybe too nice, because seated next to him, Jason shook his head with a hint of irritation.

"I'll be right back," Ben said. "Nobody goes in the kitchen! You hear me? I mean it. Stay out!"

His guests exchanged glances and resumed watching television, or in Jason and William's case, having a heated but hushed discussion. Ben hurried to the front room to collect his keys and a light jacket, then sprinted outside to the separate garage. He was opening the driver-side door when Allison came skipping into the garage, grinning at him as she went to the passenger side.

"What are you doing?" Ben asked her.

"Making sure you drive safely," she replied.

Before he could protest, she slipped inside the car. Ben climbed in too, started the engine, and backed out.

"What happened?" Allison asked when they were on the road. "I smelled something burning. One of the pies?"

"The turkey," he said with a sigh.

"Ouch!"

"Yeah. You don't want to know how many hours I sank into that stupid thing. I hate this holiday. Why couldn't the pilgrims have ordered pizza instead?"

"I read they didn't even have turkey," Allison said. "Just wild fowl and venison, if I remember right, both of which are easier to cook."

"You aren't making me feel better," Ben grumbled.

"Sorry. This is exactly why I don't do Thanksgiving. I tried the year Davis was born. My dad and I never bothered once we were on our own, but I wanted to give my son what I didn't have, so I tried."

"And?"

"It ended in tears."

"For you or for him?"

Allison thought about it. "For everyone involved."

Ben grimaced. "There might be a few tears tonight if we can't find another turkey."

"The grocery store banks on these sorts of disasters," Allison said reassuringly. "They'll make you pay out the nose, but they'll have what you need."

This lifted his spirits. They plummeted again when he and Allison walked into the supermarket's deli section. A large broiler sat next to a sign advertising roasted turkeys, but it was empty. One look at the haggard employee working there filled him with despair.

"Sold out," she said, anticipating their question. "Must be a lot of first-timers this year!"

"There must be one left somewhere," Ben said, not hiding his desperation. "Maybe you were saving one for yourself. If so, name your price and I'll make you rich!"

The woman laughed. "I'm a vegetarian, so no hidden stash. You've given me an idea for next year though! Don't worry, you'll find more turkeys in the meat section."

Why didn't she say so sooner? Ben started running toward that department, returning only to grab Allison's hand so he could drag her along. He went straight to the butcher counter and asked for a whole turkey. The man pointed silently. Ben spun around to look in the indicated direction and saw a freezer stuffed full of large misshapen balls covered in frost. Frozen turkeys.

"Okay," Allison said. "No big deal. We can thaw one out using warm water in the sink."

"Try a bathtub instead," Ben said, approaching the freezer and eyeing the massive lumps. "And then another twelve hours cooking time." He shook his head. "No way."

"You can cook them faster than that."

He looked to her, feeling hopeful. "Really? How fast?"

Allison cocked her head, and after a quick mental calculation said, "Two or three hours."

"We'll all be dead by then!"

"You're being dramatic."

"I'm not." Ben bit his bottom lip. "Another store?"

Allison sighed. "Fine."

The results were the same. The deli at the next location was also sold out, but they did have two roasted Cornish hens left, which definitely wouldn't stretch to feed seven guests plus himself. Besides, as he said to Allison, "It has to be turkey! You can't have a perfect Thanksgiving without turkey!"

"We can try more stores," Allison said, "but I think you should make your peace with what we find here."

"Fine," Ben said, tromping to the meat section. That's where inspiration stuck. He grabbed from a nearby peg and held up a package of lunch meat. "It's turkey!" he said, grinning like a madman. "*And* it's conveniently sliced. No need to carve it. Ha ha! I'll just heat it up a little and it'll be just as good."

"I'm going along with this plan," Allison said, "but only because I'm worried about your mental health."

"It'll be fine," Ben said, feeling manic. "You'll see!"

After buying the lunch meat—and the Cornish hens, just to be safe—Ben felt better. Only on the drive home did he begin to lose confidence. If processed lunch meat was good enough for Thanksgiving, nobody would bother slaving over a hot stove. And why the hell did that cookbook of Eric's insist he needed to cook the turkey for twelve hours when Allison said it could be done in only two? If he was destined to ruin dinner, he could have at least slept in.

"You realize there's no reason to stress about this," Allison said when he kept grunting in frustration. "We're all adults, and there's plenty of food. Some of which I know is edible because I brought it."

"You're right," Ben said. "As usual. The Cornish hens will be good. We'll all have to share, but I'm sure I can do something creative with the turkey slices. Who wants a traditional Thanksgiving anyway? How boring would that be?"

He heard a dull pop and the wheel jerked to one side before he regained control. Ben checked his mirrors, then looked around for an explanation, the steering still sluggish.

"Sounds like a flat," Allison said. "Better pull over."

Ben did so, his mood nosediving again. "I take it back," he said once they were parked on the shoulder and standing in front of a tire just as deflated as he felt. "Boring is good. I should have driven us all to my mom's house. She puts out the same spread every year—roasted turkey, cranberry sauce, oven-hot buns, and *the* most amazing green beans."

"You're not helping," Allison said, clutching at her grumbling stomach.

"I'm hungry too. For stuffing. That sounds the best right now. Oh, and for all her faults, you haven't lived until you've tried Karen's pie."

"Unfortunate word choice," Allison said, making a face. "Let's get this thing changed so we can go home and eat."

"No problem." Ben took out his wallet and slid out a card. His roadside assistance plan. Tim was adamant about such things, insisting on adding Ben to his membership in case of emergencies. He patted himself, searching for his phone before he remembered that he had left it at home. Then he turned a hopeful expression on Allison.

"Nada," she said. "I had to sprint to catch up before you left. I don't have anything with me."

"Great!" Ben declared, frowning at the card and hoping for a magic button that would summon help. Or at least instructions that would tell him what to do. "Um…"

Allison sighed. "You don't know how to change a tire, do you?"

"No. Do you?"

"Yes, but I'm a woman! This is your job."

"Oh no!" Ben said, shaking his head. "That's not how gender equality works! You don't get the benefits without having to take on the bad stuff too. I think you changing my tire would really prove how strongly you feel about women being equal to men."

"I'm about to prove my equality by giving you a serious beat down!"

"We both know who would win that fight," Ben said.

"Me?"

"Exactly. So there's no point. I concede."

Allison laughed. "Okay, let's change it together. Deal?"

"Deal."

They went around to the back of his car and opened the trunk. This puzzled him until the flooring was moved away, revealing a spare tire, a jack, and some sort of crowbar thing. "You learn something new every day," he murmured. "I didn't know this was in here."

Allison glanced over in surprise. "You're kidding!"

"Yes?" he said. Then he feigned a scowl. "Don't shove me into your predefined gender categories! Not all men are familiar with cars."

"I'm willing to do most of the work," Allison said, "if you spare me the misguided lectures."

"I love you!" Ben declared. "So what do we do now?"

"First we get the bolts off and then we jack it up." Allison paused. "I think that's the right order."

"We're doomed," Ben said.

"Probably. Ready?"

Ben didn't feel the need to prove his masculinity, but he also didn't want his friend to feel taken advantage of, so he took the initiative. How difficult could it be to twist a few bolts? First he had to get the hubcap off, which proved harder than expected. That might explain why one end of the iron rod he held was wide and flat. After a struggle, the hubcap popped loose and he fell on his rump.

"Tell no one," he said as Allison helped him back up again.

"I'll file it away in the blackmail folder," she replied. "Want me to take over?"

"Just show me how you get one bolt off and I'll do the rest. I have to learn sometime, right?"

Allison nodded, taking the tire iron from him. "Not to rub it in, but we wouldn't be in this situation if you had let people help you in the kitchen."

Ben sighed. "I know. I just wanted it to be special. Tim didn't have many good Thanksgivings when he was growing up. His parents had some fancy dinner they would go to and kids weren't invited. Most of the time he had to fend for himself. To this day he insists that pizza pockets are a staple of Thanksgiving."

Allison laughed. "I think he's got the right idea. My dad and I would go out for burgers."

"Like drive-thru?"

"Yup! I remember keeping that from you. I was embarrassed at the time. These days I've embraced the tradition. After the first disastrous Thanksgiving with my new family, I finally understood where my father was coming from. That's all Brian and I usually do. Burgers and fries. Even when we visit his parents, I still have the urge to go out for a Happy Meal or whatever."

The idea went against the mouth-watering spreads his mother

and father put on the table every year, but at the moment, it held a certain appeal. Still, he found his head shaking. "That's not good enough."

Allison shoved the tire iron toward him, the first bolt successfully removed. "Excuse me?"

"I don't mean for you!" Ben said quickly. "Tim and I have done the same thing. We'd go out to eat on Thanksgiving, and that was fine." He strained, leaning his weight against the tire iron until the second bolt finally loosened. "This year is different though. Because of Jason."

"It's not his first year with you," Allison said, sounding confused.

"Right, and he never minded us going out for dinner before. We didn't make him stay at home like the Wymans did their son. I realized though that Jason doesn't care about Thanksgiving because he had so few normal ones. Not until we were at my parents' house last year. You should have seen his face! I don't think he's ever witnessed so much food and family in one place. I wanted to give that to him again, but closer to home. With *our* family, you know?"

"That's sweet of you," Allison said, collecting the bolt he had managed to work free, "but he's old enough to understand the thought behind your good intentions. The meal doesn't have to be perfect."

"No," Ben said, "But there's more on the line than making happy memories. I told you that Jason and William are taking a break?"

"They seemed fine just an hour ago!" Allison said, not hiding her surprise. "Then again, it was getting a little tense right before we left."

"Exactly." Ben handed another bolt to her. "They spent the last two weeks apart because it turns out that William had met Caesar before and they—"

"I remember," Allison said. "Boston, right?"

"Yeah. I guess it all boils down to hurt feelings."

Allison grimaced. "I've seen plenty of those in my line of work. You can show people a logical solution to whatever relationship problem they're facing, but where feelings are involved, it rarely matters. All you can do is encourage them to talk it out."

"That's what I hoped would happen today," Ben said, pausing to look up at her. "I encouraged Jason to invite William over for Thanksgiving, thinking we would all sit around the table and have a gay ol' time while stuffing ourselves. It's hard to stay angry when fighting off a food coma. And yeah, we still have enough to induce one, but I also wanted the setting to be perfect for—"

"Romance?"

Ben laughed and nodded. "Am I that predictable?"

Allison inhaled deeply. "You do tend to make such things a priority, yes. I hate to say this, because I like William, but he and Jason met as teenagers. They were young. You and Tim might be the exception to the rule, but not many relationships survive high school. As much as you want them to be together—"

"It has to be William," Ben said, already shaking his head. "He's the one."

Allison took the tire iron from him and squatted to continue their work. "That's not for you to decide. Don't feel bad. Generations and generations of parents thought they could influence who their child ends up with, but that's rarely the case. Even arranged marriages can't guarantee that the couple will actually like each other."

"No," Ben said, "but William is *nice*. That's so rare! Think of Jason's history. It's not farfetched to imagine him falling for any manipulative jerk who's willing to show him the teensiest amount of affection."

"Give the boy some credit!" Allison scolded. "He's not a pushover!"

"I know," Ben responded, already feeling bad. "It's just the guy he was with before—well, you've met Caesar. Doesn't he remind you of… Never mind."

"I see now," Allison said, a wicked grin spreading across her face.

"No!" Ben shot back. "Don't even go there! It has nothing to do with my past."

"So this isn't about you missing Jace," Allison said innocently, "the *other* nicest guy you've ever met. And it has nothing to do with any second thoughts you're having about being with Tim again."

"It might look that way," Ben said, snatching the tire iron

from her to tackle the last bolt. "But it really isn't. Tim was never a manipulative jerk. Okay, *maybe* in college, but he grew out of that phase. I'm also not deluded enough to confuse William with Jace. You might be on to something though. My life wasn't exactly stable when I met Jace. He became my anchor, and that's when everything started to improve. He kept me on the straight and narrow. After he died, it all started to crumble again. I saw something similar with Jason. He was grateful for a fresh start and a home with us, but meeting William, *that's* when he really started to thrive. He was happy! If you didn't know his history, you would have thought Jason had a perfectly normal upbringing. Then the Coast Guard happened and they spent four years apart, each worse than the previous, because I saw him slowly unraveling."

"And it was like seeing yourself struggle with Jace's loss all over again," Allison said softly. "I'm sorry, but I still don't think the two issues are unrelated."

Ben clenched his jaw. Then he nodded. "You know what? You're right. I don't want Jason to end up on his own. Relationships aren't for everyone, but he's a lot like me, and I was never truly happy unless I had someone to love who loved me back. Maybe that's unhealthy. I'll have to ask my best friend. She's the therapist."

Allison laughed. "I think it's fine. Everyone has different needs, and you're right, Jason is a lot like you. He probably won't feel fulfilled until he's in a long-term relationship, but it's up to him to choose who that's with. If he asks you for advice, fine. Otherwise I think you should stay out of it."

"No promises," Ben said. He moved aside so Allison could set up the jack, watching with interest as the car slowly rose, one crank at a time. He was glad this hadn't happened while on his own, which led to another train of thought. "Do you ever worry about what sort of future Davis will have?"

Allison laughed. "The answer is yes, but if you're going somewhere with this, you'll have to be more specific. When it comes to my son, I worry about almost every aspect of his life."

"I don't want Jason to be alone again. I know Tim and I aren't that much older than him, but hopefully we'll die before he does. When that happens, I want him to have a support network in place."

"You want him to have a family."

"Right!"

The car hoisted now, Allison stood and brushed herself off. "Then why not make it official?"

"What?" Ben said, mimicking her actions.

"All of it! Finally marry Tim, adopt Jason, and find him some brothers and sisters." When she saw how overwhelmed this made him feel, she laughed. "At least the first two. Or don't, because he already has a family. You and Tim. Your parents and— Maybe not the Wymans, but Jason has me. Brian too. When Davis gets older, Jason will have a cousin. Or what about Marcello? Isn't he like an uncle? Then there's Michelle and her family. Jason isn't alone. No matter what happens to you and Tim—and god forbid anything does—Jason won't be on his own. We'll all take care of him. Not because that's what you would want, but because we love Jason too."

Ben felt on the verge of tears. Rather than cry, he opted for a hug, throwing his arms around Allison. "I'm lucky to have you in my life. You know that? I can't count how many times you've talked me down from the ledge. If there's one thing I'm thankful for today, it's you."

Allison squeezed back. "I'm thankful for you too. Don't take advantage of this, but a part of me—a very big part—loves getting to boss you around."

Ben chuckled and released her. "I figured."

"It's not always easy!" Allison said with an exasperated sigh. "Drains the energy and leaves a gal feeling like she's starving. Of course it would help if you'd let me take a few pinches from one of those Cornish hens."

"No way!" Ben said, crossing his arms over his chest. "I still want this holiday to be as picture-perfect as possible."

"Then a slice of lunch meat turkey?" Allison pressed, eyes big and watery.

"Yeah, okay," Ben said, dropping his arms. "Let's do it. I'm starving too."

Five minutes later they were shoving rolled up slices of meat into their mouths, cheeks bulging while they exchanged ecstatic expressions. Then they got back to work. The rest was easy. All they had to do was take one tire off, replace it with another, and tighten the bolts.

"Is that a different kind of tire?" Ben asked as they lowered the jack. "Something is off."

"The lack of air," Allison said. "Please don't tell me your spare is flat too!"

It wasn't, but barely enough air remained to keep the rim from touching the ground. That might change once they were both inside the car. "Think it's safe to drive?"

"Probably not, but we should try anyway."

"We could go really slow," Ben suggested.

"And drive on the shoulder with the hazards on," Allison said, already nodding. "If we get pulled over, the police officer will be forced to help us."

"Yeah! Civil servant, do our bidding!"

They tossed the flat tire (the flattest tire, at least) into the trunk, packed up the rest, and hit the road. Progress was slow. *Very* slow.

"This is good," Ben said, trying to sound upbeat. "Just another hour or two and we'll be home!"

"It won't be that long," Allison said. "Hey, the stereo still works. You know the best response to any emergency, right?"

"Sing-along!" Ben declared.

Anyone standing on the side of the road would have had to make room for a car puttering along the shoulder, all four windows down as the two occupants crooned gleefully at the top of their lungs.

Their spirits were high when he and Allison arrived back at the house. Ben was escorted to the kitchen, Allison blocking him from view so he could smuggle in the groceries without being seen. Not that he could keep his secret for long. Soon he would be forced to reveal that they wouldn't be having a proper turkey this year.

Once safely in the kitchen, he noticed that he had left the oven on and the turkey inside, not that it mattered since it couldn't get much drier. Still, that seemed like a dangerous mistake. What if it had caught fire?

Ben searched for an empty spot on the counter to place the grocery bag, feeling confused. He was certain he hadn't put the turkey back in before he left, and he definitely didn't remember it smelling so darn good. He went to the oven to investigate, leaning over and peering through the window. Inside he saw the bird of his dreams, succulent golden skin still moist with natural juices.

"Don't be mad."

Ben spun around at the sound of that voice. Tim stood in the doorway, looking sheepish.

"I like your cooking," he said hurriedly. "I really do. But I know how hard it can be to balance so many dishes at once. You did the green beans, the cranberry sauce, and the sweet potatoes. You even made the dinner rolls from scratch! But, uh, you've never had the best luck with meat."

Ben opened his mouth to protest, images of previous failed meals flashing through his mind. His shoulders slumped. "You're right."

"I have faith in you," Tim said, still looking guilty. "I really do, I swear!"

"It's fine," Ben said, double-checking the oven to make sure he wasn't hallucinating. "Where did you get such a nice turkey?"

"Caterers," Tim said. "We just have to finish heating it up. I wasn't sure we would need it at all, and if it turned out we didn't, I would have given it to a soup kitchen for the homeless."

Ben stood up straight to consider this. "So basically, because I ruined the first turkey, some poor homeless people aren't going to get a meal."

Tim bobbed his head. "I thought of that too, which is why I also ordered a turkey from each of us. I've got cards in the other room. For every guest here, we donated a turkey."

Ben stared at him, emotion rising.

"Sorry," Tim repeated, taking a step forward. "I just wanted the day to be special for you."

That did it. A few tears managed to slip free, but Ben wiped them away and refused to cry more, because he was happy. Overwhelmingly so. "When did you get so good at us?"

"Us?" Tim smiled, closing the gap between them. "When it comes to relationships, I've burnt my fair share of turkeys. I had to get it right eventually."

Ben welcomed his embrace, and especially his kiss, not mentioning that it tasted like Tim had snuck a few bites from the sweet potatoes. He could have eaten an entire pie while Ben was gone and not have gotten in trouble for it. Not now.

"You saved the day," Ben said, head resting on Tim's chest. Then he sighed wistfully. "I don't know how Eric did it, but I have a newfound respect for the man."

"Caterers," Tim said again.

Ben leaned back to look him in the eye. "What?"

"Eric always used caterers for his parties. He could cook, don't get me wrong, and he micromanaged the hell out of everything that was prepared, but even he couldn't handle throwing a huge party and being the only person in the kitchen."

"We're not having a *huge* party exactly," Ben said, looking tentatively optimistic, "but eight people is still a lot. Right?"

"Absolutely," Tim said with a laugh. "Some situations are too much for anyone, even Benjamin Bentley." His eyes were shining, just in the way Ben had hoped they would. Not for the exact reason he had imagined, but he'd take what he could get.

"What did you do with the mummified turkey?" Ben asked.

"Oh." Tim appeared sheepish again. "Uh, you cooked for nine this year."

"Meaning?"

Tim led him out of the kitchen and pointed through the sliding glass door. In the yard he saw Chinchilla whipping her head back and forth, a very sad looking creature trapped between her teeth. She seemed more interested in playing with the turkey than eating it, but she was definitely having a good time. Jason and William looked a lot happier too. They were on the back patio watching her, William leaning against Jason, who had an arm around his waist as they both laughed.

"It wasn't my idea," Tim said.

"I've got no complaints!" Ben shot him a smile and turned to consider his other guests. Marcello had let himself in at some point, bringing along a few chilled bottles, but those sat ignored on the coffee table. He was too busy bouncing Davis on one knee, Brian talking his ear off about a recent trip to the mall. Allison seemed content to sit back and relax, but she caught him staring and raised an eyebrow questioningly. He knew that look. It asked, *Everything okay?*

He nodded. She was right, as usual. Days like today were all about being grateful for the people in your life. Ben might not be able to cook, but when it came to choosing who he surrounded himself with, he was a master of his trade. He felt thankful for all the love he received, and for having so many people to love back. When he returned to the kitchen to finish preparing the meal, he didn't go alone. He took Tim with him, understanding now that the only way they could make this day special was by being together.

Something Like Ornaments

by Jay Bell

Austin, 2008

One for each year, from now until forever. It's an easy enough promise to make. Or does it frighten you? I know my answer. And I think you know yours.

A voice from the past, one so welcome that it caused Ben's eyes to mist up. He cradled the ornament in his hand, looking at the Christmas tree from his vantage point on the floor and searching for a good spot on a lower branch. Then he grimaced, because another voice was competing for his attention.

"Sleigh bells are great! Won't you listen? In the rain, they sure glisten." Tim grinned between verses, seemingly unaware of just how off-key his singing was. And how badly he was butchering the lyrics. "It's happening tonight, what a wonderful sight, walking in a—"

"Splinter blunder ham?" Ben suggested.

Tim made a face. "Those aren't the words."

"And yet they were probably closer to what you were about to—" Ben's expression became strained, "—sing."

Tim leered at him. "Then let's hear your version."

"You're trolling me, aren't you?" Ben said. "This is all just a ruse to get me singing."

"Can't blame a guy for trying." Tim dug in the cardboard box for another ornament. He was on his knees, pine needles on the floor around him. Tim had insisted on a real tree this year, not the plastic one Ben was accustomed to. He had to admit the smell was nice, although the way Chinchilla kept sniffing it made him nervous. They definitely wouldn't put any presents under the tree until he was sure she wouldn't treat this as an indoor toilet. Samson didn't seem concerned, having already taken up residence beneath the branches so he could nap.

"Hey!" Tim declared. "Look at this one!"

He raised the ornament, holding it by the golden string. The sculpted cat slowly spun in the air, revealing a splattering of color and too many imperfections to count. Regardless, the ornament filled Ben's chest with yearning.

"Yeah," he managed to say. "That's—"

"The ugliest thing I've ever seen." Tim guffawed. "Look at its eyes! They're pointing in separate directions. And why is it attacking a pile of spaghetti?"

"I think it's supposed to be yarn," Ben said, laughing a little himself. "That one's my favorite because it looks like Samson."

"Yeah, it sort of does!" Tim enthused. "Right after someone hit him in the face with a frying pan. Hey, you've got one too! Let me see."

Ben held up the ornament. Another cat, this one standing on its hind legs in an attempt to capture a butterfly. Except the sculptor couldn't figure out how to suspend a butterfly above the cat, meaning the oversized insect was attached to its head, resembling a misshapen hat. The cat's arms were spread wide. This combined with the crazed expression made it look as if was fleeing a burning building in panic while wearing an unfortunate choice of headgear. When first receiving this ornament as a gift, Ben had laughed so hard that he ended up on his side in tears.

Tim still seemed bewildered. "I don't get it," he said, shaking his head. "Why does the butterfly have numbers on its wings?"

"It's supposed to be the year," Ben said. The right wing had a twenty on it. The other a zero and a three. "They got switched around, that's all. Yours has it too, worked into the yarn."

Tim peered closer at his. "Oh yeah! Two-thousand one." With his free hand, he dug around in the box. "There's more? How many of these things do you own?"

"Seven," Ben said with a lump in his throat.

Tim barely heard him. Instead he was carefully laying them on the floor, calling out the years and rearranging them so they were in order. "Two thousand four, two thousand five… That's it, but you've got a complete set going back to ninety-nine. Why'd you stop collecting them?" He looked up when Ben failed to answer, silver eyes searching his. "Are they hard to find?"

"Yes," Ben answered lamely. "They're made by a lady in a small town. She does one every year. I'm not sure how many she produces, but you definitely won't find them sold at Hallmark stores."

"No surprise there," Tim said. "I'm picturing a crazy cat lady, since there's an obvious theme here."

"What about you?" Ben asked, eager to change the subject. "Any goofy ornaments from when you were younger?"

"Nah." Tim shook his head, happy expression fading.

"Your parents must have some, like ornaments you made at school."

"I don't think we kept any, no."

"Your mom wouldn't hang them up?"

Tim focused on unpacking the box. "Yeah, of course she would. They just seemed to disappear before the next year. She's always been particular about how the house looks. You know that. I can't tell you how many times I came home to find my room completely redecorated."

"That's one thing," Ben said, "but throwing away homemade ornaments? You know I try really *really* hard to love your parents, right?"

Tim chuckled. "You and me both. I hope you like my mom though. My dad I can understand hating, but my mom—"

"She's great," Ben said. Not in comparison to his own, but he knew how much Tim loved her and didn't want to hurt his feelings. "And if she's gotta decorate everything her way, at least she has great taste."

"Thanks," Tim said, brightening. Then he hopped to his feet, taking two of the cat ornaments and hanging them on random branches.

That's *not* how it was supposed to work! Ben clambered to his feet, words of protest on his lips. Tears rose along with them, which wouldn't be good, because this was their first Christmas together in a long time. A house of their own. A fresh start. The last thing he wanted was to muddy new memories by dragging them through the old. That wouldn't be fair, but he couldn't just stand there and watch Tim hang these cats one by one, chuckling to himself as he looked at each. They weren't stupid. They weren't funny.

Ben shook his head. Okay, they *were*, but—

Tim turned toward him, offering one of the cats. The very first one. "Your turn. I bet you know the perfect spot."

That was too much. Ben tried to say three different things at once and ended up making a gurgling noise. Then he coughed to clear his throat. "I need something to drink," he mumbled, heading for the kitchen.

"Eggnog!" Tim called after him. "I bought two different kinds. One's got booze in it!"

"Sounds good." Ben intended to chug his.

When he reached the kitchen, he went to the refrigerator, opened the door, and bent over when he didn't find what he was looking for. He didn't see much of anything, his mind drifting to the past, the cool air on his cheeks reminding him of a winter from long ago.

*

"Merry Christmas," Jace said. He refilled the two glasses of wine on the coffee table, then rearranged the candles there, as if stoking a fire. His new apartment in Austin didn't have a fireplace, and it wasn't quite as cozy as the studio he had rented in Houston, but Ben was still thrilled that he had moved all this way just for him. What sort of guy did that? His guy, apparently. "Ready for some presents?"

Ben laughed, patting the empty spot on the couch next to him. "I just want you. And you're early! It's still Christmas Eve."

"Close enough." Jace checked his watch. "Just another hour until midnight."

"Christmas doesn't start until morning," Ben said. "Trust me. If it worked any other way, Karen and I would have been doing shots of espresso so we could stay up that late."

Jace chuckled, moving toward the tree. "Michelle and I tried one year. We went to bed when we were told, because we'd just figured out that Mom and Dad took care of Santa's deliveries. We set an alarm for one minute past midnight, thinking we had discovered a technicality. Our parents weren't happy when we tried to wake them up."

"I bet!"

"That's the nice thing about being an adult," Jace said, stooping to pick up a wrapped gift. "You get to make your own rules. Just a few more years and you'll also be able to!"

"Ha ha," Ben deadpanned, but he was smiling. He loved that he was dating an older guy. It made him feel classy. And yeah, more mature than he might really be. "Are we seriously going to open presents now? If we do, we won't have anything for the morning."

"Just one," Jace said, returning with a small box. "Please. I can't wait to see your face."

The air in his lungs felt thin as Ben accepted the present. It was heavier than he expected. Was it a bracelet? Or a necklace? Ben wasn't really into jewelry, but he appreciated the gesture. Jace snuggled close to him on the couch, candles and twinkling lights on the tree providing the only illumination. What if it was a ring! That combined with the wine and the romantic setup... This could be serious!

Ben's fingers were trembling as he peeled back the paper. The plain white box didn't offer any hints. He opened it and was prepared to gasp. Instead he stared, a deranged creature eyeballing him in return. The cat wore a fake white beard made of cotton, like it was dressed up as Santa, but instead of a red cap, it had two candy canes sticking out of its head.

"What?" Ben managed, working his jaw. "I don't... What is this exactly?"

"A masterpiece!" Jace declared. Then he started laughing. "These suckers are always ugly, but this one is especially weird. Take it out and see!"

Ben did so unwillingly. The cat's head was disproportionately large compared its body, which was naked black fur except for elf shoes that curled at the toes. "Why does it look pregnant?"

Jace cackled, rolling back on the couch and struggling to get himself under control. "We think it's supposed to be fat. Like Santa. Don't ask me why it has candy canes for antlers." He sat upright again. "Look under the beard!"

Ben did so with apprehension, fearing what terror lurked beneath. All that awaited him was a pet collar with four raised numbers. "Nineteen-ninety-nine," he read. "This is from last year."

"Exactly," Jace said. "There's a lady, Mrs. Henderson, who handcrafts these in Warrensburg. My mom has been collecting them ever since I was little, and yes, they're always this good. Some years we were more excited to see what freaky new ornament she dreamt up rather than our actual presents!"

"It's an ornament," Ben repeated, noticing the gold string between the two candy canes. "Seems a little heavy."

"They're branch breakers all right!" Jace still seemed

pleased, but he grew serious again. "Happy anniversary."

Ben blinked. "What?" Then he thought about it. "The flight we met on, that was Christmas morning! Like super early in the morning!"

"Technically, I first laid eyes on you during Christmas Eve. And if you paid attention to my safety demonstration, then you definitely saw me too."

Ben wished he could remember for sure. "But we didn't actually speak until past midnight. Is that right?"

Jace nodded. "Correct. Take your pick. It could be either day."

"Maybe we should count our first date instead."

Jace pretended to pout. "But that's so far away!"

"Just by a few days," Ben said, laughing at his behavior. "I don't want our anniversary to share a day that's already dominated by the biggest holiday of the year."

"My sentiments exactly. Christmas Eve is usually spent waiting for the next day's excitement. Now we'll have something to distract us."

"That's what you consider our anniversary?" Ben asked, still grinning. "A distraction?"

Jace nodded and rested his head against Ben's shoulder. "Yup. I only flirted with you when we first met because I couldn't stand waiting for my presents any longer. Hey! Speaking of which..." He hopped up and returned to the tree, foraging beneath it.

"We agreed on one present," Ben said.

"That's when we were still talking Christmas. This is our anniversary."

Ben hurriedly went through a mental list of the presents he had bought Jace, wondering if he could repurpose one now. Then another box of the same size and weight as the previous was shoved into his hand, and he decided Jace didn't deserve a gift. Not if he was making Ben open another horrific ornament.

"Go on," Jace said, already laughing.

"And here I thought you loved me." Ben braced himself when opening the box and felt lucky at first because the ornament appeared to be a normal Christmas tree, but no. It was a cat dressed as a Christmas tree, and on it—" He shook his head disbelievingly. "The ornaments are little cat heads. It's a cat ornament decorated with cat ornaments."

"Makes you think, doesn't it?" Jace said, reaching over to turn it around. "Look at the back."

Ben choose to ignore that the cat's tail was fitted with multi-colored bulbs and focused on the numbers made out of sculpted snow. "It's from this year," Ben said. "Does that mean what I think it does?"

"Mm-hm!" Jace leaned closer, nuzzling their noses together. "One for each year, from now until forever."

"Forever?" Ben asked. "That's awfully close to being a proposal."

Jace shrugged as if not concerned. "It's an easy enough promise to make. Or does it frighten you? I know my answer. And I think you know yours."

Ben blanched, noticing that Jace's wine glass was much emptier than his own. "You're not serious!"

"Of course not." Jace leaned back. "But maybe someday."

"In Paris?" Ben asked.

Jace nodded. "In Paris. Now then, why don't you hang these on the tree? I bet you'll find the perfect place for them both."

Ben felt a little weak at the knees when he got up. He considered the tree carefully, not wanting to disappoint. Then he hung the ornaments, starting with the one from the previous year before placing the other not far from it. He stood back to consider his work.

"Now I see what you really think of my gifts," Jace said. "Bottom branch, huh?"

"No! You promised me one of these every year, so I have to plan ahead. We'll work our way to the top. I'm picturing an entire tree covered in nothing but freaky cats. When we run out of space, we'll hire Mrs. Henderson to make a star for the top. I figure that'll be our fiftieth anniversary." He turned around to find that Samson had hopped up on Jace's lap, never missing an opportunity for some loving. If only Ben had gotten there first. "What if I'd said yes?"

Jace raised an eyebrow. "To my drunken proposal?"

"Yeah. Say I had taken it seriously and accepted. What would you have done then?"

Jace smirked. "Now you'll never know."

Ben moved closer to him. "Never? I would prefer eventually. Or maybe even soon."

"Did I say never?" Jace leaned forward. "I misspoke."

"Slip of the tongue?" Ben asked, placing a hand on the back of the couch and bringing their faces close.

Jace's eyes sparkled in response. "That's exactly what I had in mind."

*****

"Promises have been made," a voice boomed, "a sacred pact that shall only be satisfied with eggnog!"

Ben spun around, surprised to find himself at the kitchen counter. He didn't remember walking there, or pouring the two glasses. He certainly hadn't heard the doorbell, but that wasn't surprising, since Marcello tended to let himself in. He seemed proud of his grand entrance until he noticed Ben's expression.

"Is everything all right, my dear? I didn't mean to startle you. Well, I did, but not so thoroughly."

"It's not your fault," Ben said, frowning. "I'm just… I don't know."

"Ah." Marcello strode forward, placing a hand on his shoulder. "I can see it now, clear as day."

Ben looked surprised. "You can?"

"Yes, the holidays have their own special sort of melancholy. I find it cuts deeper than the usual fare, and no wonder, considering how hopped up on joy we all are at this time of year. It's only natural that, on occasion, we find ourselves strung out. Peaks and valleys."

"I know what you mean," Ben said. "For me it was always Christmas night. Part of me didn't want the holiday to be over, the rest worried about the people out there who don't have as much as me. Like maybe they didn't get any presents, or were cold, hungry, and alone."

Marcello patted him. "I'm sure such people had other ways of making their holidays special, no matter how much they envied warmer lives full of gifts. The streets have their own little miracles, if one looks hard enough."

Ben blinked. "Who exactly are we talking about here?"

"Ah," Marcello said, focusing on the counter. "Refreshments! Do I smell rum? These glasses are distressingly small, but I suppose they can be refilled. Repeatedly. Could I trouble you for a third?"

"Yeah!" Ben said. "Just a sec." He dug around in one of the cabinets until he found a matching glass. Then he filled it, making sure to choose the eggnog with alcohol. Not that their guest would have let him forget.

"I find company is the best way to maintain holiday cheer," Marcello said, accepting his drink. "I plan on hosting a party for each day of Hanukkah this year. You and Tim are invited, naturally."

"Thanks!" Ben said. "I never realized that you're Jewish."

"I am whatever I wish to be," Marcello said. "I know the staunchest of atheists who still celebrate Christmas. Who wants to suffer through winter without festivities? As for myself, experience has taught me that a week-long celebration is more suited to my needs. One night simply isn't enough."

"No," Ben said with a chuckle. "I bet it isn't. Well, if it turns out a week isn't enough either, you're welcome to join us on Christmas."

"Very kind of you," Marcello said. "Now then, let's see how drunk we can get Tim. Enough for him to stop singing, I hope."

"You and me both," Ben said wearily.

Marcello placed a hand on his back, guiding them out of the kitchen. "If you do find yourself feeling melancholy again, just remember that sorrow has its own special beauty. The other side of joy's mirror, if you will. A reflection stretching from then to now."

"I don't understand."

Marcello tried again. "Sometimes happy memories haunt us, causing sorrowful feelings in the present, but that's not such a bad thing. It simply means that you were lucky once, and once is better than never."

Ben stopped. "I hope you have happy memories too."

Marcello nodded. "More than I could ever possibly count. I make it a point to revisit each, on occasion, but that doesn't mean I'm not eager to make more. Why do you think I invite myself over so frequently?"

"You're always welcome here," Ben said, deciding to focus on the present. By the time he was Marcello's age, he wanted to be able to look back and say the same, that he never took all the good things in his life for granted.

"Merry Christmas!"

Tim said this as he flopped down next to the tree. He was

still in his bathrobe, the dark fabric matching his hair. As he leaned forward to shuffle wrapped boxes around, the fabric draped open, revealing the muscles of his upper torso. "You ready to unwrap some stuff?"

"I'm ready to unwrap something," Ben said. He would have drooled if he wasn't already yawning. The morning was early, the light still cold, and yet it was a good three hours later than he used to wake his parents. Maybe he should call and apologize.

"Where should we start?" Tim asked, not seeming tired in the slightest.

"Stockings," Ben said. "Always start with the stockings."

They began by unpacking those they had prepared for the animals. Chinchilla was torn between enjoying her treats and wanting to see what Samson had gotten. She managed to shove her nose into both stockings, but after some swift parenting, she backed off. Before long, Samson was rolling around contentedly in catnip while Chinchilla worked on a rawhide. Then it was the humans' turn. Ben had stuffed Tim's stocking full of snacks and delicacies, challenging himself to choose only tried and true favorites. As for the stocking Ben received, Tim had gone overboard, which wasn't a complete surprise because he had done the same for Ben's birthday two months back. Instead of candy, his stocking was full of cologne, watches *plural* ("I couldn't decide!" Tim explained), theater tickets, and more luxuries than Ben usually allowed himself in a year.

"This is too much," he said.

Tim shook his head. "I'm making up for lost time. Ready for a real present?"

"Seriously?" Ben eyed the huge pile under the tree. "I'm already happy. We can stop and save the rest for next year."

"Or we can keep going." Tim placed his hand on a large box. "What's this one?"

Ben squirmed. "Only one way to find out. Open it." The wrapped toolbox was basic. They had a drawer full of random wrenches and screwdrivers, but some were really old, and finding what they needed was always a struggle. He had felt proud of the idea, but it hadn't been expensive. Even without needing to pay off a mortgage anymore, Ben's finances were still tight, and he wasn't about to use Tim's own money to buy a present for him.

"Hey, this is great!" Tim said.

"You sure?" Ben asked, thinking of the really high-end set that Tim would have surely bought, regardless of expense, to prove his devotion.

"Yeah! I love it!" Tim stood and lugged it around as he walked in a circle. "Makes me feel manly."

"You do look hot with it," Ben mused. "You should carry it wherever you go. Like a fashion accessory!"

"I might," Tim said, grinning at him. "Okay. Now your turn." He sat on the floor again so he could reach toward the very back of the tree.

The box he handed over was small. Ben hoped it wasn't a third watch, which was still within the realm of possibility. He ripped off the paper, finding a plain cardboard box. Tim crawled nearer in excitement, like he too was curious to see what was inside. Ben opened the lid, pulled away tissue paper, saw gold string, and used it to take out the ornament. The cat was white, and decidedly female. It had luscious red lips, purple eyeliner, and disturbingly large breasts. The feather boa it wore spelled out the year in four numbers. Two thousand eight.

"To go with the rest," Tim said with an amorous expression. He leaned in for a kiss. "Happy anniversary."

Ben leaned back, eyes wide. "That's not funny."

Tim blinked. "What?"

"You know what!" He tossed the ornament aside, scrambling to his feet.

Someone had told Tim everything. Michelle or Allison maybe, but it didn't matter, because today was definitely *not* their anniversary! What the hell did Tim think? That he could take Jace's place so easily? Did he seriously believe he could slip into the empty space left behind? Ben yanked at the sliding glass door, stumbled out into the backyard and sucked in cold air. His cheeks were burning, tears threatening to rise up, but he shoved them back down with anger.

"Benjamin!" Tim grabbed his shoulder.

Ben spun around to escape his grasp. "Who told you?" he demanded, pointing toward the house.

"Told me what?" Tim asked. "You mean the ornament?"

"Yes!"

"Emma! I asked her where to get them, hoping she would know. I wanted to surprise you."

"I know what you wanted," Ben said, "and that's not what I meant! Who told you what today is?"

Tim shook his head. "It's Christmas. I don't get it."

Ben's chin started to tremble. "That's not what you said a second ago!"

Tim seemed perplexed, his eyes darting between Ben's own. Then realization dawned. "Oh man..." He covered his mouth with both hands, turning toward the house and back again. "I think I get it now. You and Jace."

"Damn right me and—" Ben's voice cracked. "Fuck you."

"I didn't know!" Tim said. "You never told me when you met him. I know you said it was around the holidays, but not... not freaking Christmas!"

But that wasn't right. Or maybe it was, but he and Jace had long ago agreed on when their anniversary was, and it wasn't the twenty-fifth. Tim had said the wrong thing, but on the wrong day, so maybe he didn't know after all.

At the moment he had gone pale. Tim took a step forward and reached out, but then dropped his hand again. "I'm sorry," he said. "I didn't know. I swear!"

"Then why did you say that?" Ben asked. "It didn't make sense. You and I met in the summer. That's our anniversary!"

"It *does* make sense," Tim said, studying the patio beneath his feet. "Never mind. Can we just forget this whole thing? Not what you guys had. I just want to rewind and take back that present."

Ben clenched his jaw, forcing himself to calm down. "I need to know what you were thinking. Why you said what you did."

Tim looked skyward in exasperation. "Now is definitely not the time for me to explain!"

"Why not?"

Tim groaned. "Okay. Fine. I was trying to get with you."

"Get with me?" Ben repeated.

"Yeah. Remember our first Christmas together?"

Of course. Tim's parents were out of town, which seemed really coldhearted. Ben's mom had given him a bunch of leftover food and he had shown up at Tim's house with presents. They opened those and the ones the Wymans had left behind. Then they danced to some music, goofed around and— made love. Beneath the Christmas tree, but they hadn't just traded blowjobs.

That had been the first time they tried something different. "Oh."

"Yeah," Tim said sheepishly. "What happened that day was a big deal to me. Not just physically. Emotionally too. I thought we could, um, reenact. I didn't realize that today was your anniversary with Jace."

Ben exhaled. "It's not. Yesterday was. You just caught me by surprise. Those ornaments, he gave me one each year that we were together. That's why they stop past a certain date. I guess there would have been one more, but he... he wasn't around for..." The dam broke and Ben didn't have a choice. He started crying. Tim was there instantly, wrapping arms around him and shielding him from the cold, even though his bare feet had to be freezing. Ben at least had slippers on.

"He would have been there for you," Tim said. "If he had a choice, Jace would have been at that Christmas and every single one that followed."

Ben wasn't sure if that was true, but he'd done enough crying over it and had forgiven Jace long ago, accepting that he had left when he felt he needed to. Ben respected that now.

"I'm sorry I ruined everything," Tim murmured.

"You didn't," Ben said, freeing his arms to hug him back. "Are you kidding? I'm the one who flipped out over nothing." He snorted. "Over a cat dressed as a hooker."

They both mustered a laugh.

"I'm sorry," Ben said. "I should have kept my cool."

"Nah," Tim said. "I understand. It must have been weird for you. I'll get rid of the new ornament. Now that I know the full story, it's a creepy present for me to give. I'll throw it away."

"No," Ben said, but he did so halfheartedly.

"Do you really want to keep it?"

"I don't know. Throwing it away seems wasteful." And mean, since Tim had gone to the trouble of procuring it. Still, the idea of it being there, hanging next to the others, felt wrong. "Let's go inside before we freeze. I'll make you a coffee and me a tea."

"Okay."

Tim let him go alone into the kitchen, which gave Ben the privacy to blow his nose and compose himself as much as possible. He let his thoughts turn fuzzy and shapeless as the coffee percolated and the tea steeped. Then he heard a smashing sound and hurried to the living room. Tim was on the ground, picking colorful fragments off the floor.

"So clumsy!" he said. "I dropped the new ornament and it totally shattered."

Those ornaments were tough. Ben didn't know what they were made of, a solid chunk of kiln-fired clay maybe, but he doubted dropping one would be enough to destroy it so completely. He noticed the open toolbox to one side, a hammer not far away.

Ben smiled. "I love you too."

He went to the kitchen to fetch a dust pan. After cleaning up together, Ben returned to the kitchen for their coffee and tea. Then they sat on the couch sipping, not quite ready to tear into more presents.

"Eric must have had ornaments," Ben said. "I can believe you not having any from when you were young, but surely in all that stuff he owned—"

"They're upstairs," Tim said. "In the attic."

Ben sat upright. "What? Why didn't you bring them down?"

"I didn't want him looming over the holiday," Tim said. "Not that I would mind, but I figured it might be weird for you."

Ben laughed and leaned back. "I bet you regret that decision now."

Tim chuckled in response. "A little. He had some really neat stuff. Do you want to see?"

"Sure!"

Tim raced upstairs. When he came back, he held a battered cardboard box that he set on the coffee table, eyes lighting up when he opened it. Ben had the same reaction. One by one they peeled away tissue to reveal gorgeous ornaments that were the very opposite of kitschy cats. These were elegant and tasteful.

"Some of them are really old," Tim said. "Maybe from his childhood. They belong in a museum."

"Forget that," Ben said. "They belong in our house and on the tree! Don't you ever hide these away again. They're beautiful!"

Tim nodded. "They remind me of him." Then he looked up. "Is that how it is for you? Do those ugly cats make you think of Jace?"

Ben peered at him. "Was that a slight?"

"No! I figure they reflect his sense of humor. He didn't really like them, did he?"

Ben bit his bottom lip. "That's up for debate, but yes, they remind me of him. And I like that these remind you of Eric. I never met him, but this gets me a little closer. I really do want them on the tree."

"Okay," Tim said, cheeks flushed. "Next year we'll hang them."

"This year," Ben said. "I know it's Christmas, but let's decorate the tree."

Tim laughed. "Okay. And then afterwards…"

Ben felt a rush of warmth to his cheeks. "And afterwards we can—how did you put it—reenact."

Tim's face lit up. "I was going to suggest we open more presents, but I like your idea better."

"I bet you do!"

Tim grabbed his coffee mug and raised it in a toast. "Merry Christmas, Benjamin. To the first of many."

Ben raised his tea cup. "From now until forever."

The package came two days later. The mailman apologized for not getting it there sooner, probably due to the festive address label wishing him a happy holiday. Ben took one look at the return address and smiled. Jace's family. They usually sent a package, or on a few occasions, came down to visit Michelle and her family. Then they would always insist on Ben joining them in Houston, and not a year went by that they didn't invite him to Warrensburg for any occasion, holiday or otherwise.

Ben took the package to the kitchen, set it on the table, and used one blade of the scissors like a knife to cut open the tape. He found many of the usual staples inside, such as the stocking Serena packed for him every year and the overspill that wouldn't fit. He noticed a wrapped present too, but focused on the note, scanning past the usual holiday greetings and well wishes.

I was surprised when Michelle called me asking about Mrs. Henderson's ornaments. Emma said she heard from Tim, who was hoping to surprise you with her latest. I hope I didn't ruin that surprise! I'll mail this a little late, just so I don't. I'm encouraged that you feel strong enough to start collecting them again. I know you must associate them with Jace, and I hope this means you've healed enough to focus on your happy memories together and not so much the loss we all suffered. That's why I finally feel comfortable mailing this to you. Jace always asked me to pick up an extra ornament from Mrs. Henderson for him to give you. That final year was no exception. I place my orders early. Believe it or not, she often sells out! So I've been holding on to this, not wanting to hurt you, because this was the year Jace talked Mrs. Henderson into using his idea. I think he had you in mind when—

Ben couldn't take it anymore. He set aside the letter and grabbed the wrapped present, tearing it open. The theme was decidedly French. The cat wore a beret and a black and white striped shirt. A disturbing number of wine bottles were gathered at his feet. Some had spilled, and judging from the inebriated expression and rouge-stained whiskers, many were empty. The vintage on each bottle was two-thousand and six, the year Jace had died. In his hands, the cat held a large baguette that it had twisted, like a balloon animal, into the shape of a Christmas tree. Ben smiled. Paris was the place Jace had finally proposed to him, but he always wondered how much of a joke that first proposal was. Now he had an ornament representing both occasions, and for once, one of Mrs. Henderson's cats didn't seem so random. Maybe the rest of them made sense too, but only for the people whose lives they represented. This strange thought was interrupted when Ben spotted the croissant at the cat's feet, hidden among the bottles. He brought his nose closer in disbelief, noticing a small streak of gold paint that he was pretty sure was meant to represent a ring.

Ben started laughing. So hard that he ended up in tears, but they weren't sad, because Marcello was right. So many happy memories for him to reflect on, enough that he would never run out. He truly was one of the lucky ones.

Something Like Champagne

by Jay Bell

Austin, 2015

I'm trusting you with my heart. You helped keep it safe once before. I'm asking you to do so again.

Marcello gazed across the ballroom, searching for someone who had passed away years ago, and settled on another person by association. Tim Wyman. Life was long—if chance and circumstance were kind—and Marcello had seen numerous wonders in his own. What many would find sensational had long since become passé for him, so he cherished what mysteries were left, always seeking out strange and unusual experiences. This was a tricky business because surprises were, by definition, unexpected. He marveled at each, some long after their discovery, such as how a friendship could transmigrate from one person to another and survive physical mortality. That is what had happened after Eric's death, when he found himself without one of his dearest friends and forced to fulfill a promise. At the time he and Tim hadn't truly been close, and while losing Eric had given them something in common, more had been needed. And it came. The love he felt for Eric took shelter in a six-foot-tall Latino with the most striking silver eyes. As if that weren't miracle enough, the love Tim felt for Eric seemed to seek out a new home too, not quite so discerning when choosing which body to settle in. Then again, what Marcello lacked in appearance, he made up for in… well, everything really.

"Truer words were never spoken," Marcello said to his conversation partner, scarcely hearing what the man had said, but the smug expression suggested the political rant had come to an end. "You've given me much to think about. If I didn't have pressing matters that demand my attention, I would remain your captive audience for the remainder of that night. Perhaps we can continue this another time? Excellent. Excuse me."

Marcello took long strides, pausing only to address one of his waiters. Diego possessed a surprising number of piercings. The discovery of each had provided a delightful diversion some months back. "See he doesn't follow me," Marcello instructed, swapping an empty champagne flute for one that was full. "Get him talking about anything other than politics and you'll get a bonus."

"Proof?" Diego asked, already confident in his chances.

"Two minutes of audio recorded on your phone."

Diego narrowed his eyes in suspicion. "The rules say that waiters can't have phones when on duty. We've gotta hand them in before our shift starts."

"Because few things are less attractive than a person squinting slack-jawed at a text message," Marcello replied. "And it isn't my policy. It's Nathaniel's, which is why you've been giving him your old phone while the new one remains in your pocket."

Diego went wide-eyed. "How'd you know?"

Because not only was Marcello observant—he had spent a lifetime studying the subtle folds of clothing to better understand what hid beneath—but also because Nathaniel was a shrewd man who had already detected this ruse. At the time, Diego had been one of Marcello's fleeting interests, so the boy had been given extra leeway. It certainly didn't hurt that Diego had already proven himself discrete in other ways. Marcello trusted him not to offend any of their generous guests by whipping out his phone each time it vibrated.

"Just keep him occupied." Marcello moved through the crowd again, his progress slow. Everyone knew who he was, and considering that they were here to donate money to a worthy cause, he couldn't afford to be rude to anyone. Correction, there were few things he couldn't afford, but common decency insisted he treat all his guests with the respect their charitable intentions warranted.

By the time he reached Tim, the young man was surrounded by a half-circle of admirers. Many knew him from his previous stints as a waiter, but sadly, today was not such an occasion. Even fully dressed in a tuxedo, Tim cut a handsome figure, enough that Marcello was unlikely to get him alone unless he took drastic action.

"Mr. Wyman!" he declared sternly, wagging a finger for good measure. "I'm very cross with you! In fact, I insist on having a word alone. Pardon me, gentlemen."

Those gathered around Tim appeared more interested than

scandalized. Who didn't love to witness gossip unfolding? His request was respected though, and most of the admirers dispersed. Marcello dragged Tim toward a far corner where they were less likely to be disturbed.

"How'd you know?" Tim asked on the way.

"Know what?"

"That I needed rescuing."

"I noticed one of the men holding a tape measure," Marcello said. "I can only imagine where that might have led."

Tim scoffed. "He wanted me to measure my biceps."

"Ah." The man in question was Troy Markham, a fitness nut and fetishist. Marcello knew through the escort service he owned that Troy enjoyed nothing more than watching naked men using exercise equipment. "And what did the measuring tape reveal?"

"I didn't do it!" Tim said. "What kind of person measures their own muscles?"

Marcello stopped and looked at him, raising an eyebrow expectantly.

"Fourteen inches," Tim said, "but I was barely flexing and this was a few years ago. I've upped my game since then."

"And what else have you measured?"

"Don't start," Tim said, glowering at the increasingly drunken crowd. "This is exactly why I shouldn't have come without Ben. He usually protects me. A wedding ring isn't enough these days, you know? Without a guy on your arm, people think you're on the prowl."

"I was sorry to hear that he couldn't attend. Sick at home on the calendar's final day! Not the best way to end the year."

"Or to begin a new one," Tim agreed. "I should probably head back there soon. I don't care how stuffed up and gross he is, I'm kissing him at midnight. It's bad luck not to."

"Even if you catch his cold?"

"I don't care. It's worth it."

Marcello smiled. "You know, I can never quite decide which of you is luckiest, although most of the time I suspect it's him."

Tim grinned. "You're the only one who thinks so."

"Nonsense. You have more fans than you'll ever realize. Speaking of which, guess who I was just reminiscing about."

"Eric," Tim said instantly. "This time of year makes me think of him too. He always loved it."

Marcello chuckled. "I'm not sure why. All he did was work, especially in December. One party after another."

Tim nodded. "Christmas and New Year's. I thought he was crazy too, but he thrived on the stress. I tried talking him into throwing one really big party instead."

"As did I, but he always felt gay people needed somewhere to go on the holidays. Few of us had traditional families back then, and too many were being shunned by their relatives. I'm almost sad to see that changing. Not the acceptance part. That pleases me, but I always reveled in how different we were. True outsiders! I'm used to seeing Jeff Stryker or Edith Massey on my Christmas cards. Now it's smiling gay couples, dressed for church and holding up toddlers for the camera to see. When did we become so respectable?"

"We?" Tim said. "You're including yourself?"

"Never!" Marcello said adamantly. "I'll be the last stalwart of unscrupulous behavior, if need be. Did I tell you I went to a bath house in Tunisia, and when I asked where the dark room was, the clerk stared at me blankly? He didn't have a clue what I meant!"

Tim made a face. "Why would you go to a bathhouse to have photos developed?"

Marcello sighed. "Your generation is hopeless. Imagine a pitch-black room, fill it with dozens of delightfully desperate men groping around in the dark, slipping on lube and grabbing the nearest body part of their fellows for support."

Tim held up a hand. "How did we get from warm fuzzy memories of Eric to this?"

"You're right," Marcello said, mentally backpedaling. "I do miss his parties, and while I've now taken the burden upon myself, it's just not the same. Say, why don't we pop over there for a visit?"

"To his old house?" Tim said, perking up. "Driving by could be kind of fun, but uh, don't you have a party to host?"

"Nathaniel can handle everything in my absence. He's more than capable. And I don't intend to simply drive by. We'll go inside."

Tim shook his head. "I don't know. It'll be weird with other people living there now."

That was close enough to agreement for him. Marcello was an expert at recognizing the embers of temptation and fanning them into blazing fires. "The couple living there has left town. They won't be back until the end of January."

"For real?"

"Indeed. I have a key. You promised ages ago to accompany me at least once. Don't think I've forgotten!"

"I remember," Tim said, "but I don't think I promised. Did I?"

He hadn't, but clearly wanted to believe so. "Solemnly. You had your hand on a Bible at the time. There were witnesses present! Shall I call Ben? Or Jason?"

"No," Tim said, "but I really do need to get home soon."

"A small detour on the way," Marcello pressed. "Eric's house is just around the corner. We'll be in and out in no time. This will be good for us both, you'll see. It's prudent to reflect on the past before starting anew. With just a few hours left in the year, now is the ideal time."

"Okay." Tim's slow nod gained speed. "Yeah! Let's do this!"

Marcello raised his glass to salute this decision, but discovered it mysteriously empty. Funny how that always seemed to happen. Rarely did he ever regret it, although one occasion did spring to mind from many years ago.

*

"I am so… so very… completely…" Eric's face contorted as he searched for the right word. "I'm really *really…*"

"Drunk?" Marcello suggested. The description was apt for them both. From his summer spent in Corsica, he had brought back a crate of wine as a gift for Eric. Marcello had guzzled plenty while there, but not on an empty stomach and rarely so much at once. During the trip, his thoughts had often returned to Eric—how a year apart from Gabriel had finally brought his friend some semblance of happiness again. Contentment was often a tentative beast, so Marcello had repeatedly invited Eric to accompany him on the trip, taking each refusal as a sign that he was truly back on his feet. Now he had returned to find his dearest friend an absolute mess.

"Done!" Eric declared, finding the word at last. "I'm so *done* with him."

"Clearly," Marcello said, trying to focus, because Eric appeared to be sitting on the floor, clutching papers and photos to his chest. Even with his blurred vision, Marcello could see that most bore either Gabriel's image or his name.

"Cold turkey," Eric replied, swaying slightly. "No more

calls, no more visits, no more presents. Did I tell you that I sent one? For Christmas. Two, actually. One for Gabriel, and one for Zachary."

Marcello made sure he was hearing things right. "You sent Gabriel's new boyfriend a Christmas present?"

Eric nodded. "Isn't that sad?"

"Misguided, perhaps."

"I'm pathetic!"

"You're not." Marcello got down on the floor with him. "Possessing a generous heart is nothing to be ashamed of."

"Thank you," Eric said, releasing the papers so he could swipe the bottle of wine Marcello was holding. One of them, anyway. He took a long swig. After swallowing, he allowed a smile to creep over his features. "Wanna know what I gave him?"

"Zachary? Do tell."

"A butt plug!" Eric cackled.

Marcello considered the idea solemnly. "Had the thought occurred to me, I would have done the same. I just hope you sent an extra-large one."

"You!" Eric slurred, pointing a finger at him. "You're the best. Seriously."

"Thank you. I don't mean to pry—"

"Ha!"

"—but why are you covered in Gabriel-themed paraphernalia? Please tell me you don't plan to set yourself on fire in protest."

"No," Eric said, seeming to have remembered an important task. "No no no." He set down the bottle carefully. It fell over anyway but was empty enough that nothing spilled out. Then Eric scooped and shuffled the papers and photos into one messy pile before standing on unsteady legs.

Marcello did the same, head spinning. What were they doing here? They were in Eric's home. Somewhere. Which room was this anyway?

Eric turned to face him. "I'm trusting you with my heart."

Was he confessing secret feelings? Marcello felt deeply for him as well, but love complicated everything, and he had learned the hard way that it wasn't worth losing a friend over.

"You helped keep it safe once before," Eric continued. "I'm asking you to do so again."

Marcello checked the bottle he was holding to make sure he

hadn't finished it off. Then he looked back at Eric. "I don't have the faintest idea what you mean."

"When Gabriel left me," Eric said, eyes watery. "You protected me from all of it. You made Gabriel leave the house, you packed his things, you insisted he speak to you if he needed anything from me. I know. Gabriel told me later. I know what you were doing. You were keeping me safe."

"I only wish that had been possible," Marcello replied. "The worst had already transpired. Your heart had been broken. All I did was help you gather the pieces."

"You did more," Eric said, staring at him. "Way more." Then he sniffed and looked down at the papers. "Come on."

They walked together, but where? A different room? The same one? Eric stopped in front of a piece of furniture. Or maybe a painting. Perhaps a bookshelf. All Marcello knew for sure was that the papers and photos were put inside a safe before Eric ushered him forward so he was standing in front of a keypad.

"I'm done with him," Eric said. "Maybe I can't bring myself to throw away these things, but I'm not going to look at them again. Ever. You set the combination. Six digits. Only you will be able to get back in."

Marcello could barely see straight. Everything in front of him warped and shifted as if behind a heatwave, so he typed in numbers he knew by heart. His birthday.

"Hit 'pound' when you're done," Eric mumbled "Then do it again. Then hit 'pound' again. Then do it *all* again. Ha ha! I'm kidding. But really. Do it again."

Marcello shook his head, trying to clear it, and nearly fell down. Then he stared at the keypad until it stopped moving and punched in the combination again. After he hit the pound sign a second time, the safe made a chirping noise, a green light flashed, and he heard mechanical bars sliding into place.

"That's it," Eric said. "He's locked away for good."

Marcello carefully turned in a circle. "You don't have Gabriel's severed head in there, do you?"

Eric lit up, like it was an excellent idea. Then he seemed to reconsider. "No. He can keep it."

"Good," Marcello said. "I think he's lost enough, even if he doesn't realize it."

"I love you," Eric said, stumbling forward for a hug. "You're my best friend."

"And you're mine," Marcello said. "Now then, unless we want a crippling hangover tomorrow, I suggest we have a... what's it called? The clear zero-proof drink."

"Water?" Eric said, taking the bait.

"That's it," Marcello said. "We'll have water. And then we'll order a pizza. Not because I'm hungry, but rather I know a place where they only hire the most delicious young men. It's time for you to move on."

"No," Eric said, shaking his head. "I'm done with all of that. I'll never love again."

"Ah," Marcello said, "what a world it would be if such a promise could be kept."

"You'll see," Eric said stubbornly.

Marcello's response was gentle. "One day, so shall you."

*****

Marcello frowned, frustrated that he couldn't recall certain details. No matter how hard he tried, he failed to remember which rooms he and Eric had been in, or how the safe had been concealed. The memory had come to him only recently, rising up out of the hazy depths of time. Eric had kept his word and stayed away from Gabriel for a respectable period, allowing them to kindle a polite friendship toward the end. The mysterious safe and its contents had lost all importance by then. Eric had probably cleaned it out. Even without the combination, he could have contacted the manufacturer and proven his identity to have it reset. If he had chosen to do so. Or known that was an option.

Marcello continued to frown because the passenger seat he occupied was much too small for his liking. "What happened to the Bentley?" he asked.

"I married him," Tim said.

"You've gotten more mileage out of that joke than you did the actual car. What do I have the dubious pleasure of sitting in currently?"

"A Dodge Challenger." Tim grinned proudly. "It was so cute! I wanted it for Christmas, but of course Ben couldn't afford it, so I told him all I wanted was permission. One of my presents under the tree was a card, and all it had written inside was one word: 'Permission!' I was so relieved, because I had already bought the car and driven it into the trees on our land—not literally—like I was hiding it there, hoping he wouldn't see and—"

The sudden silence concerned Marcello. Perhaps Tim had

run out of oxygen and passed out, but no, his friend had spotted Eric's old house, face in awe as if he had stumbled upon one of the seven wonders of the world. "It's been some time for you, I take it?"

Tim nodded. "I used to drive by after I sold the place, but not anymore. Oh man, I'm so excited! You really still have a key?"

Marcello treated the question as rhetorical.

Tim grew increasingly antsy as they left the car and went to stand in front of the door. He continued to fidget as Marcello unlocked it. "Are you sure they aren't home? Maybe we should knock first. What if we took turns? I'll play lookout and you can go in and then we'll swap."

"Calm yourself," Marcello said as the door swung open. "The deed is done."

Tim stared into the dark interior. His curiosity must have overpowered his fear because he stepped inside. "It doesn't smell the same."

Marcello flipped on the lights.

"Wow! It doesn't look the same either."

"No," he said, scrutinizing the front room. "Eric had better taste. Regardless, many of his hallmarks can still be found."

Tim had abandoned all caution, walking through the house and switching on light after light, criticizing and waxing nostalgic often in the same breath.

"They call that a couch? Barely enough room to stretch out on. Eric used to love reading over there by the window. He always preferred natural light. I would read with him, or sometimes pretend to and stare, because I always wanted to paint him like that. I wish I had. Actually, I will!" Tim tapped the side of his head while grinning wildly. "It's all still up there. I just haven't thought of it for a while."

"I know the feeling," Marcello said, still troubled by his fuzzy memory. "Did Eric ever show you his safe?"

Tim looked puzzled. "He didn't own a safe. You mean at the bank? The safe deposit box?"

No, they definitely hadn't drunk half a case of wine while at the bank. "A normal wall safe. I think it might have been hidden somehow."

"I don't think so." Tim froze when a phone on an end table started ringing. Eyes wide, he grabbed Marcello's arm and hissed, "What do we do now?"

"Refuse to answer? I'm more shocked that they have a landline. What's the point these days?"

"They know we're here!"

"They didn't bother to call any of the other times I let myself in while they were gone. No, it's probably some elderly aunt wanting to wish them a prosperous New Year's." Marcello gestured to the next room. "Come. Let's continue."

Tim walked into the kitchen, the ringing phone soon forgotten. "Oh man! They've hardly changed a thing!"

Marcello could understand his fascination. Eric had always made this space feel like the heart of the house. Most parties began with the guests strictly forbidden to enter the kitchen, and ended with the very closest of his friends gathered there. Even on normal days, Eric would often bustle about the room to prepare a meal or sit at the table to sift through his mail and pay bills.

"We should make it a memorial site," Marcello said. "The Eric Conroy Kitchen, open to the public."

"I'd give tours," Tim said, practically leaping with each step. "Here is the breakfast bar, where Eric and I would sit every morning and eat our cereal. We had a strict 'no speaking' policy. Not before the first mug of coffee. Over here is his crazy double oven. This one time when he was making pies, we treated it like a race, trying to see which was faster, cherry or blueberry. Cherry owned that race! And this is the dishwasher that I put liquid dish soap in—the stuff used for washing dishes in the sink. Bubbles went everywhere. I thought he would be pissed, but he laughed so hard that when he called the maintenance man, I had to take the phone 'cause he couldn't get the words out. And over here… What? They changed the refrigerator! Why the hell would they do that?"

Because it had been more than ten years since Eric's passing, making it surprising that *any* of the appliances were still there. Marcello didn't feel like reminding Tim of how much time had gone by, not caring to dwell on it himself. "I remember visiting one spring day," Marcello said. "All the cabinets had been emptied out, cans and dishes scattered everywhere, so Eric could wipe clean the shelves before putting it all back again. The windows were open, the radio was on, and even though he could afford an army of maids, he seemed absolutely content in performing such a menial task. I would rather have torn the cabinets out and had new ones installed, but not Eric. He knew how to take care of things because he understood their value."

"And you don't?" Tim said. "You're not just talking about cabinets. Eric saw stuff in me that even I didn't know was there. I've seen you do the same. What about Nathaniel?"

"Perhaps," Marcello said, "but Eric had a certain loving touch that I'm lacking. He was rather like a mother in that regard. I told him so. It amused him greatly and influenced his Halloween costume that year, although in the spirit of Norman Bates rather than what I had intended."

Tim's eyes were shining. "He was the best, wasn't he?"

"The very best," Marcello agreed. "Shall we continue?"

Tim nodded, looking around the kitchen one more time before they turned toward the door. "I really don't remember him having a safe," Tim said, "but if he did, it would have been upstairs."

"Why do you say that?"

"Because it doesn't make sense to have it on the first floor. Easy access for anyone who breaks in."

"Very well. Let's see what we find upstairs."

They began in the master bedroom. Tim was less talkative here, perhaps because he didn't have as many good memories to relay. Eric's final days had been spent in this room, which made it endearing that Tim chose to sleep there after he was gone. Whatever happy memories he was hoping to cling to had surely been tarnished when Ryan began sharing his bed. Just the little brat's name was enough to rouse Marcello's anger. He siphoned some of this off by beating his fist against the walls of the closet, testing for hollow spaces.

"What are you doing?" Tim asked.

"I believe it was concealed by some mechanism."

"The safe?" Tim knocked on a nearby wall. "How do you know?"

"Because he showed it to me once."

"And you don't remember where?"

Marcello shoved aside a row of dress shirts to check the wall behind them. "I was inebriated. We both were."

"Why am I not surprised?" Tim had his arms crossed over his chest in disapproval. "Why does it matter anyway? Eric wouldn't have left anything important in there. He knew he was dying."

"True, he did make many preparations." Marcello had been

a part of those discussions, and when he recalled which side he had taken, he wasn't proud. He turned to face the person he had once so harshly criticized. "I have reason to believe that he wouldn't have been able to open the safe."

Tim appeared skeptical. "So basically you think he had a secret safe that I never found and that he couldn't open."

The phone started ringing again.

"That's correct, and no, we're not going to answer it."

"Okay," Tim said, sounding exasperated. "If he did have a safe, I would have noticed it when I moved out. Unless it's behind some of the things that were left here."

"Such as?"

"All that stuff in the kitchen, or the baby grand piano, or some of the furniture. Like that dresser over there, but I moved it once when vacuuming. Or there's the weird shelves in my old room."

"Weird shelves?"

"Yeah. In the closet."

They stared at each other a moment, then hurried to the hall. "Which room was it?" Marcello demanded.

"This one. I always hated the closet because the back is taken up by these ugly cubby holes. See? I never asked Eric about them because he designed this house, and I didn't want to hurt his feelings."

Marcello could understand his aversion. The walk-in closet had one small rod to hang clothing. The rest was filled with a system of shelves, two-by-two squares reaching all the way to the ceiling. These were currently full of the usual things that got stored away and forgotten: old winter hats oddly contrasted by the swimming goggles next to them. Dusty framed photos of the two owners or their extended family. A folded inflatable mattress, worn empty briefcases, a roll of bubble wrap… Marcello had no more patience for it. He began scooping these items toward him, allowing them to fall to the floor so he could get at the back wall. He didn't see anything special, and when he knocked, it didn't sound any hollower than the rest of the house.

"I guess not," Tim said. "It was worth a try."

"I thought he slid something aside," Marcello said, yanking on the shelves.

"Did you hear that?"

"What?" Marcello asked.

"Downstairs."

"You're paranoid. Answer the phone the next time it rings, if that helps ease your mind. I look forward to hearing the ensuing conversation. Aunty must be a real nag or they would have told her they were going on a trip."

"I'm serious," Tim said.

"So am I," Marcello said. He pushed at the wooden framework and felt it budge. Was that a click he heard? "Interesting. Here, help me move this... What's in this bag? A bowling ball?"

"Yeah," Tim said with a grunt, lowering the bag to the floor. "Man, how big is this sucker? Feels like it would atomize any pins it—"

"Freeze!"

A lifetime of watching television and movies compelled them not only to freeze, but to put their hands in the air. Marcello heard the crackle of a police radio and some hissed swearing as the bowling ball landed on Tim's foot. By the time he turned around, he felt perfectly at ease. Two officers, both male. One was old and grizzled, the other baby-faced. Guns were drawn, which he wasn't fond of, but he possessed a much more powerful weapon. Words.

"Gentlemen," he said amiably. "Allow me to explain. My name is Marcello and you are..." He peered at the badges. "Forgive me, my eyes aren't as good as they used to be."

The younger officer nearly snapped to attention, which was worrying considering the firearm pointed at them. "I'm Officer Butler of the West Lake Hills Police Department and this is my partner, Officer Duggins. Please state if you are a resident of this domicile." He sounded as if he was reading from a training manual!

"I do not reside here," Marcello began, "but my friend is the former owner, and we were merely—"

"Are the current owners aware of your presence?" Officer Butler yammered, his grip on the gun a little too eager for Marcello's liking. "Do you have explicit permission to enter these premises? Have you obtained, within the last twenty-four hours—"

"For fuck's sake," Officer Duggins growled. "Just ask them what they're doing here!"

"What are you doing here?" Butler repeated, appearing somewhat deflated.

"Looking for lost property," Marcello said. "I assure you, I'm friends with the owners, and if they are unavailable to vouch for me, I'm a close acquaintance of Commissioner Hernandez."

If they'd been playing cards, he would have just set a pair of aces on the table. The only thing stopping it from being three of a kind was—

"Commissioner Hernandez has jurisdiction over the Austin police force," Butler stated. "We are with the West Lake Hills—"

"—I only mention him as a character witness," Marcello tried to interject.

"—Police Department which is led by Police Chief Maxine Adams, who has served—"

Marcello turned to the older officer. "Does he have an off switch?"

"Enough!" Duggins shouted. "Everyone shut up." He pointed at Marcello. "You know the owners?"

"Yes."

"Do the owners know you're here?"

"I imagine they *might* be slightly surprised by my presence," Marcello said. "Let's call them and find out."

"The security company couldn't reach them." Duggins looked him over, which was slightly thrilling, before he gave Tim the once over too. Then his attention returned to Marcello. "You really know Commissioner Hernandez?"

"Yes!" Marcello said. "The commissioner and I are good friends. In fact, he's enjoying a social gathering at my mansion right now, so if you would allow me to call him, I'm sure we could get this all sorted out."

Officer Duggins barked laughter. "The commissioner is at your mansion? All right, Bruce Wayne. You and the Boy Wonder keep your hands up while my partner here frisks you for batarangs."

Butler appeared confused.

"Just check them for weapons," Duggins spat.

Butler lowered his gun. At least that reduced the likelihood of their imminent demise. Marcello did a quick inventory of his person. He was fairly certain the one-hitter was in another jacket, and he had prescriptions to explain anything in the pill case. His phone was encrypted beyond the local police force's capability, so all in all, he should be fine.

"Have you been drinking?" Butler asked after sniffing a few times.

"Only for the last four decades or so," Marcello admitted, noticing that Officer Butler had a decent little body beneath that uniform. His flushed skin was delicious, especially when paired with the ginger hair. "I suppose you'll need me to bend over and spread my cheeks to check for contraband. I only ask that you're gentle, but do know that I'm willing to cooperate."

"Christ!" Tim moaned. "I'd rather be arrested than witness that!"

"I'm about to grant your wish," Duggins said. "Get their IDs."

Tim was frisked too, although he didn't seem to enjoy the process as much.

"You'll notice we're both wearing tuxedos," Marcello pointed out. "Unusual garb for burglars."

Duggins wasn't convinced. "I arrested a guy last week who held up a convenience store while dressed as the Queen of England. If her majesty is capable of petty crime, then I figure anyone is." He took their drivers licenses and eyed them.

"All of this can be resolved with one simple call," Marcello said quickly.

"That's what I intend to do." Duggins grabbed the radio on his shoulder and spoke into it.

He was running their identification, checking their criminal history. Marcello's attorneys had done their best to seal most of his records, but it was astounding the number of laws out there and how easy they were to break. The dispatcher responded with police codes unfamiliar to him. One of them must have suggested a prior record, because suddenly Officer Duggins appeared even grimmer.

"Turn around, both of you. Keep your hands up."

Marcello did as he was told, and as his wrists were grabbed and brought behind his back, he giggled. No surprise there. Handcuffs always had that effect on him.

The West Lake Hills Police Department was one step away from those portrayed in Western movies, where the sheriff sat at his desk in plain view of jail cells in the same room. The facilities here weren't quite that primitive, but Marcello was something of a connoisseur, having been arrested more times than he cared to count. This police station was small. The booking process was familiar to him, a matter of routine really. Identities were confirmed and possessions were logged. They were subjected to a more thorough frisking, but not made to strip—much to his disappointment. Their belts were surrendered, as were their shoes and bowties. A shame that they weren't given orange jumpsuits since the outfits were surprisingly comfortable. Marcello had a few at home for roleplaying. Fingerprints were taken (Oh how he missed rolling the tips of each finger in an ink pad! Digital scans simply weren't as satisfying.) followed by the requisite mugshot. Marcello made sure to scowl during this. Such photos were accessible to the public, and he wanted any business competition investigating him to believe he was a hardened criminal.

Tim didn't share his appreciation for this procedure and its subtle nuances. Instead he alternated between bewildered and hangdog expressions. He was currently wearing the former, which made him appear younger for the camera. "Pardon me!" Marcello said, seated at a nearby desk and ignoring Officer Butler's questions. Instead his focus was on the mugshot station where Tim was taking his turn. "If you could just raise the angle of the light slightly it will help catch his eyes and strengthen the impression of innocence."

Officer Duggins didn't appreciate this advice and glared at him.

Marcello remained determined. "Raise your chin by ten degrees," he advised Tim, "and stop clenching your jaw. Now imagine you see God standing in the distance, giving you a big thumb's up. And he's *naked*!"

Tim's eyes widened even more, just as the camera beeped, confirming a photo had been taken.

"Could I get a copy of that?" Marcello asked, straining to see the display screen.

Duggins ignored this perfectly reasonable request and shook his head. "Is he always like this?"

"Yes," Tim said. "Can I get a separate cell?"

As it turned out, not only would they share a cell, but they had roommates. The two other men were unkempt and didn't smell good. Their ages were difficult to determine due to the grime and hard skin that came from living on the streets. Marcello eyed the wear on the men's clothing, recognizing telltale signs that brought back less-than-pleasant memories. The holes in their hardened socks, the mud caked on the fraying legs of their jeans, and the layers upon layers of shirts, which were worn to stave off the cold, especially at night. Few people realized just how frigid the nights became while they were safely tucked in bed. They might glance at their weather app and adjust their thermostat, but they were clueless as to how a chill could get into your bones and refuse to leave, even after the sun finally rose again.

"I have a call I'd like to make," Marcello said, standing behind the bars of a holding cell.

"You'll get your turn," Duggins said, being no more specific as he left.

"Well," Marcello said, turning to assess the cell again. "I've certainly seen worse."

"I haven't!" Tim said, huffing a few times.

"First time?" Marcello asked.

"Yes!"

"Oh how exciting! Shall I tell you what to expect, or would you rather be surprised?"

Tim glowered at him. "When do we get out of here?"

Marcello gestured to one of the benches, discretely choosing the one farthest from their cellmates. The poor souls were both in need of a shower. "As soon as I'm allowed to call my lawyer, bail will be posted, assuming our purported crime is on the bail schedule. If not, she'll expedite the process with a judge—of whom I know a few—and we'll be out nearly as quick."

"How soon?" Tim said, looking tentatively hopeful as he sat.

Marcello settled down next to him. "An hour, perhaps two."

"But it's almost midnight!"

"Yes," Marcello frowned. "That is a shame. Ringing in the year without a drink in my hand. Hardly seems fair, does it?"

"I don't care about a stupid drink!" Tim moaned. Good lord he was handsome when pouting! "I should be with Ben right now."

Marcello waved a hand dismissively. "He's probably zonked out on cold medicine and unaware of his surroundings."

"Yeah, but..." Tim frowned and shook his head.

"Ah, the crucial kiss." Marcello leaned forward, addressing

the other side of the room. "My friend feels it's bad luck to start the new year without a kiss. How do you feel about the matter?"

The two men looked at each other, sharing suspicion.

"Of course," Marcello said. "How rude of me! We haven't been properly introduced. I'm Marcello Maltese, my companion is Tim Wyman, and you are…"

"Terry," one of the men said.

The other stuck out his bottom lip, as if refusing to answer, but when his bench mate elbowed him, he finally offered his name. "Ralph."

"Terry and Ralph," Marcello said, unable to make either name sound illustrious. "A pleasure to meet you both. What are you in for?" He beamed at Tim, delighting in the opportunity to ask such a question.

"We're homeless," Terry replied.

Marcello raised an eyebrow. "And that is a crime?"

Terry scratched at his beard. "It is when they catch you sleeping in somebody's shed."

"They thought we were raccoons," Ralph added.

"Trespassing," Marcello said, managing to keep a straight face. "Perhaps you weren't aware, but Austin has a number of homeless shelters."

"They're full," Terry said. "Have been for some time."

"Why wasn't I made aware of this?"

Two pairs of beady eyes stared back at him, not understanding.

"Why would you need to know?" Tim asked.

Because the largest shelter belonged to him, but he didn't wish to share that information. "Had I known, I would have had a word with the various owners to see what could be done." He poked Tim in the chest. "It's important to become involved in your community!"

Any response was curtailed when Officer Duggins reappearing. "Okay, who wants to make a call?"

Marcello patted Tim's hand. "I'll take care of everything."

He stood, nodding cordially when Duggins slid aside the barred door for him. He was led to an office area where most of the cubicles were empty due to the late hour and seated at a small desk with nothing on it but a telephone.

"There you go," Duggins said, leaning against the cubicle

wall with a smug expression. "Be sure and tell Commissioner Gordon that I said hello."

Marcello didn't have much of a temper. Similar to a volcano, he remained mostly dormant until environmental factors caused him to explode. Fortunately, it took more than a sarcastic comment to make him do so, but he did have pride, and nothing would please him more than seeing smugness replaced by shock when he really did get the police commissioner on the phone.

He dialed Nathaniel's number, knowing he would be the most efficient at tracking down the commissioner. As the phone rang, he smiled at Duggins pleasantly, as if enjoying himself.

"I don't have time for you," said a gruff prerecorded voice. "Leave a message."

"Nathaniel," Marcello said after the beep. "The West Lake Hills police have kindly invited me to spend New Year's Eve with them, and although it pains me to turn down the invitation, that's what I intend to do. If you could please ask Tom—that is, Commissioner Hernandez—to call me at this number, I feel he could be of great assistance." Marcello put the receiver back on the cradle. "We won't have long to wait."

"You're wasting your time," Duggins said. "He's not our police chief."

"Are you saying he holds no influence here? Or that you have no interest in starting a career with the Austin Police Department? I can only imagine how the higher pay grade and more distinguished work would appeal to one such as yourself."

Duggins looked away, but only briefly. "Doesn't matter. Who'd you really call? Your own cell phone?"

"I called my most trustworthy assistant," Marcello said, "and now I will call my *mansion,* a concept that you seem to believe only belongs to fiction. Then we'll see how amusing you find my claims."

Duggins shrugged. "Knock yourself out."

Marcello picked up the phone again and hesitated. He really did find landlines to be outdated. If someone needed to reach him, they could call his cell phone or leave a message at the studio. Even his secretary used a cell phone these days. This left him without a central number to call, but all he needed was to reach someone—anyone—on the ballroom floor who could go where he needed them to. A face from earlier in the evening sprang to mind, one he was certain had a phone handy.

Marcello dialed the number, grateful he had a good memory for such things, and waited. The line clicked a second later.

"You owe me a bonus," Diego said, "and man was that guy a bore! I couldn't even distract him with my— Go on, say it."

"Your tight little pecs," Marcello said, fondly recalling the nights they had spent together. Then he remembered he had an audience and cleared his throat. "You're familiar with Commissioner Hernandez?"

"Uh... Who?"

"Tall gentlemen, white hair and a mustache."

"Answers to Commissioner Gordon," Duggins said with a snicker.

"Who's that?" Diego asked.

"Never mind. Walk around and see if you can't find him."

"Walking now," Diego said.

As the minutes dragged on, Duggins appeared less amused.

"Listen," Marcello said, "if you happen to see Nathaniel while making the rounds, that's just as good."

"He's busy."

"Busy?"

"Yeah. That guy of his showed up. The really hot one who used to be a model."

"Kelly."

"I don't know. Maybe that's his name."

"No, I'm not asking. I'm telling you that's— Surely you've spotted the commissioner by now. Have you checked the basement?"

"There's a basement here?"

"Yes, but I suppose you wouldn't know since you don't enjoy..." his eyes darted to Duggins. *"Lluvias doradas."*

"What? I don't speak Spanish."

"Well, I'm not at liberty to clarify."

"Just because I'm Mexican doesn't mean I speak Spanish."

"Duly noted."

"That's racist."

"I'm not racist! If that were true, would you and I have spent so much time in the Poconos?"

"What's that place got to do with anything?" Diego said.

Marcello sighed. Diego was a beautiful boy, but he wasn't the brightest, which had cut their love affair short.

"Oh, you mean sex!" Diego said suddenly. "Yeah, I guess that would be weird if you were racist, but then again, it's always the politicians and priests who hate gay people, right? They're the ones who get caught blowing random guys in bathroom stalls, so maybe."

"An excellent point," Marcello said, his patience dwindling, "but I'm very pressed for time. Maybe you could ask anyone around if they have seen the commissioner or—"

Whatever else he had to say was cut short when Duggins put his finger on the button to hang up the phone. "You've had your fun. That's enough. You're finished."

"I'm nowhere near finished!" Marcello shot back. "I intend to call my lawyer next!"

"Fine. Once you've sobered up. For now, it's back in the holding cell."

"I assure you, I'm perfectly—" Marcello hesitated. "Sober might not be accurate, but I am in full control of my faculties."

"And I'm in control of my facilities, so come on. Back in the cell."

Marcello felt more foolish than angry. He had pandered to his own ego rather than choosing the most effective course of action, but it wasn't too late. Tim shot to his feet as soon as he saw them.

"Do I get a call?"

"Fine," Duggins said, opening the door. "But just one. No more games."

Marcello grabbed Tim's arm on the way in. "You need to call Angela Cho. She's my most accomplished lawyer. Her number is—"

"I'm calling Ben."

"Listen to me!"

Tim glared. "That's exactly what got me into this mess! I'm calling Ben. He needs to know where I am."

"Or you can tell him what happened in person. Trust me, she'll have all of this sorted out immediately. Now listen."

He rattled off the number and made Tim keep repeating it to himself. Then he stepped out of the way. Within an hour, two at the most, Angela would have the matter resolved. Or at least he would be released on bail and reunited with his cell phone. From there he could take care of the rest.

"So much excitement," Marcello said, smiling at his cellmates as he waited. "Who did you call?"

"Nobody," Terry replied.

"No one at all?"

"I only got one friend in the world," Ralph said, jerking a thumb at Terry, "and he's sitting right here." He turned to his friend. "Can you bail me out?"

"Afraid not," Terry said. "Can you bail me out?"

"Nope!"

Then they started cackling. Marcello joined them, because laughter was free, and sometimes it's all anyone could afford.

Tim soon returned, which Marcello took as a good sign. Why would the call be long when Angela only needed to know where they were being held? Tim's glum appearance shook any optimism.

"What happened?" Marcello asked, not waiting until he was back in the cell.

"Another of your imaginary friends didn't answer," Duggins said.

"Voicemail message," Tim explained. "It said she's in the Poconos."

"What a coincidence," Duggins said. "All of your powerful friends seem to have skipped town on you."

No coincidence at all. Marcello had raved about his trip, recommending the resort to Angela and her husband. The topic had come up because she was planning a last-minute vacation. Apparently she had taken his advice. "One more call," he pleaded.

Officer Duggins shook his head. "The next person you're talking to is a judge. And a public defender."

"No!" Marcello said, gripping the bars. "Anything but that!"

Duggins rolled his eyes and walked away. Marcello turned to Tim, bracing himself for outrage. Oddly enough, Tim didn't seem to have any fight left in him. He sighed, shook his head, and sat down on the bench.

"I know how bad this seems," Marcello said, sitting next to him. "We might be in for a long night, but as soon as I am allowed to speak with the right people—"

"It's five minutes to midnight," Tim said. "I just wanted to be there for Ben."

"The lucky kiss?"

"Yeah."

"I see." Whenever Marcello felt guilt approaching, such as this very moment, he preferred to find a solution that would keep it at bay. "Does it matter who this kiss comes from?"

Tim looked up, already wary. "I guess not."

"Then I'm happy to be of service."

Tim laughed, then gawped. "You're serious?"

"Why not? I might not be as presentable as your husband, but kissing me is surely better than facing an entire year of bad luck. If I'm not mistaken, from the sound of distant revelry I hear, the moment is upon us."

Tim narrowed his eyes. "Just a peck. Like one you would give your mother."

"Naturally."

"Okay."

The night wasn't completely lost after all! Marcello leaned over and closed his eyes before remembering how handsome Tim was and opened them again, just in time to see his face nearing. Then it happened, a perfectly innocent peck on the lips that—

"Dude!" Tim shouted as he pulled back. "What the hell?"

"I often get that reaction."

"I felt your tongue! Is that how you would kiss your mother?"

"I never met the woman," Marcello said haughtily. "Not formally. I slid right out of her and marched out of the room without looking back."

"I should have known better," Tim said, shaking his head. Then he stopped and stared across the room. "Whoa."

Marcello followed his gaze. Their cellmates seemed to be trying to eat each other's faces. "Now *that*, my friend, is a lot of tongue!"

"And slobber," Tim added.

They continued to watch until this display came to an end. Ralph noticed them staring. "What? We ain't had much good luck. Figured it was worth a shot."

"I feel certain your fortunes will improve," Marcello said approvingly. "Sooner rather than later."

The ability to amuse oneself makes life's tedious moments all the more bearable. Marcello prided himself on this skill, delighting in witty banter or clever observations, much to the benefit of himself and those around him. But even he had his limits. As another hour dragged by, he found himself increasingly sober. And tired. He wasn't exactly young anymore, and if he was honest, getting arrested had been fun only the first ten times or so. He began to long for his bed, or to return home for the end of the party, which was normally filled with quiet conversations, and more often than not, a warm body to chase away the evening chill.

"What was in it?" Tim murmured.

"Hm?"

"Eric's safe. What did he keep inside?"

"The usual. Paperwork and such." He could say more, but he wasn't sure how Tim would react to finding out it was filled with the essence of Gabriel. He knew Tim wasn't fond of the man.

"Oh. You don't think something in there was for me?"

This gave Marcello pause. "Such as? Don't tell me the money has run out."

"No! I blew through a lot, especially when Ryan was around, but after he left I decided to get smart."

"I'm relieved to hear it."

"I just thought..." Tim cleared his throat. "I don't know, he might have left a letter or something."

"Ah."

"Ben's always getting stuff," Tim said, eager to explain. "Jace bought an ornament for him that Ben didn't get until a few years back. Like a surprise present. He also sent a freaking kid to us, and I'm like, did he plan all this in advance or what?"

Marcello chuckled. "As fond as I am of Jason, I don't think he was part of any plan."

"I know, but it's romantic. I've seen how stuff like that makes Ben happy, and I wouldn't mind a little myself. So it would be amazing to find a letter from him or whatever."

Marcello smiled. "Eric was never the sort of person to hold back his feelings. Nor was he in denial about his illness. I know he wasn't forthcoming about it with you, not at first, but he only did that to spare you stress. And because he wanted to feel normal. People like me were hounding him to find a miracle cure. Eric was more interested in planning for the inevitable. My point is that anything pressing would have been communicated personally. He wouldn't leave such things to a chance discovery."

"You're right," Tim said. "I just wanna hear from him again."

Marcello nodded solemnly. "We share that desire."

"Did you guys ever talk about me?"

"Of course!"

"What did he say?"

Marcello looked over at his companion. "Many things. I would have expected this conversation shortly after his death, not all these years later. What's this about?"

Tim shrugged. "Sometimes I wonder, that's all."

"Wonder what?"

"How he felt about me."

"Ha! As if there is any doubt. He loved you!"

"Yeah, but how?"

Marcello took a deep breath. "To the best of his ability."

Tim made a face. "That's not what I meant."

Marcello leaned his head against the cool cell wall and closed his eyes. "I'm not sure what else to say. Every man's heart is a mystery, none more so than his own." That didn't stop anyone from wondering though, so it was only natural that Tim was asking such questions. In fact, it didn't seem so long ago that Marcello had made similar inquiries…

*

"Eric! What a pleasant surprise!"

Marcello stood up from his desk and strode across the office with his hand extended, but only out of habit. He might conduct most of his business here, but he was greeting one of his oldest friends. By the time he reached Eric, both his arms were engaged in a hug that he never wanted to end.

"Okay okay!" Eric said, gently detaching himself. "I'm happy to see you too."

"Something to drink?" Marcello gestured to the wet bar.

"No." Eric reconsidered. "Oh heck, why not? What have I got to lose?"

Marcello normally shared this sentiment, but now it was an unwelcome reminder of mortality. Not his own. He found that thought easier to confront than the idea of Eric's death. "Are we celebrating?" Marcello asked, "or commiserating?"

"Celebrating," Eric said, "but only because champagne sounds better than wine right now."

"Very well." Marcello selected one of his best vintages, opened the bottle with practiced skill, and poured the golden liquid into two flutes. As he did so, he tried to shake the feeling that he wouldn't enjoy today's conversation. He knew that Eric had been to the MD Anderson Cancer Center recently and had received news. He only prayed that it would be good. "To the immutable power of friendship," he said, hoisting his glass.

Eric did the same, and for once, wasn't moderate in the amount he drank. That couldn't be a good sign.

"Have a seat," Marcello said, gesturing to the couches. Then he reconsidered. "You know what I would love? To see my desk from the other side. Please, be my guest."

Eric laughed. "What?"

"Take my usual place. I mean it!"

Eric continued to laugh as he walked around the desk. Then he lowered himself into the big chair, placing his palms flat on the desk surface, as if to feel the raw power gathered there. He nodded approvingly. "I could get used to this."

"So could I," Marcello said, sitting across from him. "It's lonely at the top. You're the boss now, owner and president of Studio Maltese. I mean it! It's all yours. I'm giving it to you today."

"You're crazy!"

"I've never felt so sane. Tell me, what's your first order of business?"

Eric's expression grew serious as he considered the question. "No more photography. From now on, all the models will be hand-painted."

"An excellent idea," Marcello said. "I myself have used body paint on more than one of my models, and I can assure you, the experience in all but one instance was breathtaking."

"What was the exception?"

"He had an allergic reaction and started swelling at every location but the most desirable. The trip to the emergency room was awkward. We pretended he was auditioning for the Blue Man Group, rather than admit the truth."

Eric laughed. "That's not what I meant. I'm talking classical painting."

"A lovely idea," Marcello said. "Beauty captured on canvas. I might just try that."

Eric's expression became demure. "Tim paints."

"Is that why you're here? Don't tell me, he has another young man he's trying to woo and needs to rent a cabin."

"No, but I'm still grateful for what you did."

Marcello was too. Tim Wyman was beautiful, and while he didn't have the makings of a professional model, his photo shoot had proven to be surprisingly lucrative. At the time Marcello had only been doing a favor for Eric, who needed a way to give Tim money indirectly. Apparently the boy had been too proud to accept handouts, but that hadn't stopped him from moving in with Eric and living off his good nature.

"I suppose I'm here for a related reason," Eric said, removing a folded piece of paper from his shirt pocket. "I need your best lawyer to take this and make it official."

Marcello reached across the desk for the paper, unfolding it and instantly recognizing its nature. "A will."

"Yes," Eric said. Then he raised a hand. "I know what you're going to say. I already have one, and it's crazy to change it just because… Well, go ahead and read it."

Marcello did so. Eric was leaving most of his wealth to his sister, with additional trust funds set up for her children. Then came a list of charities that would benefit, many of them Marcello's own. That was flattering, but he already dreaded the confirmation of his suspicions.

"I see Mr. Wyman is to be a beneficiary."

"A small amount," Eric said. "Just to make sure he's okay when I'm gone."

"People as handsome as he rarely need such assurances," Marcello said. "I can't imagine it will be long before he finds some other old fool to take him in."

"Is that how you see me?"

"At times."

Eric took a sip. "Well, you're wrong. Maybe not about me, but about Tim, because he won't need to find another home. I'm leaving the house to him."

Marcello verified this was on the paper and not a joke. Then he shook his head. "I love that house!"

"Are you saying you would rather have it?"

"No. But you and Gabriel built it together and—"

"So you're saying Gabriel is more deserving?"

Marcello wasn't sure what he meant to say, which was an unfamiliar sensation. "Perhaps you should reconsider leaving such a large sum to a person too young to appreciate it. You and I worked hard to get where we are today, and I dislike the idea of seeing that money squandered by anyone."

"He's a smart kid," Eric said. "He won't squander anything."

"You don't know that."

"You don't know him! I'm in a better position to judge these things, and honestly, who cares if he wastes it all on fast cars and pretty faces? Maybe that's exactly what I'm doing. The money is of no use to me now."

"Not true." Marcello stood so he could lean across the desk and reach the computer. He angled the monitor so they could both see it, then grabbed the mouse and started clicking. "I read an interesting article today. They bombard the cancer with protons, but it's nothing like chemo where they flood your body with poisons. This targets specific areas of cancer while leaving the healthy tissue untouched. I strongly believe this is worth your consideration. Please. Tell me what you think."

Eric glanced at the screen. "Send me the link and I promise to look into it. This doesn't change anything though. I still want to change my will."

"There's no need because you *aren't* going to die. God help me, I'll hire people to kidnap you and take you to every experimental treatment there is before I let you go!"

Eric's smile was gentle. "Thank you, but there is no cure for mesothelioma. We've both done the research."

"No solution ever exists until the moment it does," Marcello said. "Someone has to be the first person to survive any so-called fatal illness."

Eric considered him, then stood. "I shouldn't have bothered you with this. I'll make my own arrangements."

"No no," Marcello said, waving him back into the chair and then sitting again himself. "I'm sorry. I do have an excellent attorney on retainer who can help you. But I must ask once more, are you certain?"

"Yes."

No hesitation. No pause to rethink his decision. Just an immediate answer. That wasn't like Eric at all. "Do you love him?"

"Of course! How could I not?"

"Why him?" Marcello asked.

"Why not you? Is that the real question?"

"I was under the impression that you do love me," Marcello answered swiftly, "and you've often mistaken the intensity of my feelings as being romantic in nature, but as you have no doubt noted over the years, I don't hold long-term relationships in high regard. It's possible to love another person without wanting to possess them or demand their undivided attention. All I've ever wanted from you is exactly what you give to me of your own accord. That is love in its purest form, and I do question whether this young man feels the same. What does he want? That's the question I pose to you, because I *know*." Marcello held up the will. "This. This is what Tim wants!"

Eric shook his head. "He doesn't know that I'm dying."

"But you told him—"

"About the cancer, yes, but not the full truth. Who do you think talked me into starting chemo? He did. And you're not hearing what I'm saying. I'm dying, Marcello. It's time."

He shook his head so viciously that he felt his neck might snap, but then Eric told him about the most recent doctor visit and the dire prognosis. Marcello pointed to the screen with a shaking finger, insisting there was hope, but he might as well have been screaming at God and demanding that no one he loved would ever die again.

"I plan to enjoy the time I have left," Eric said, remaining calm, "and part of that is ensuring the people I love are taken care of. I know you'll be fine. We've both been through this before. Tim hasn't, and it's going to be hard enough on him without losing his home. You're right that he's awfully young to come into so much money, which is why I have another request. I want you to keep an eye on him, and if need be, intervene."

"Since when have young people ever listened to previous generations?"

"We never did," Eric said, "but please try. If anyone can guide him, you can. Tim has a good heart. You'll discover that for yourself."

Marcello studied him. "You didn't answer the question to my satisfaction. Do you love him?"

"Yes."

"But how?"

"To the best of my ability." Eric laughed, a coughing fit interrupting him. Marcello refilled their glasses and urged him to drink. When the fit had passed, Eric shook his head. "I don't know. That's the honest truth. If I was younger or healthier... What you said earlier, about not expecting anything from the other person, I suppose that's where I'm at right now. I want nothing from him, but I want the best *for* him. Please."

Marcello sighed. "Have I ever been able to deny you? When we first met, and you urged me to invest my money in computers, of all things, I thought you were crazy. And when you suggested that I be patient... Had that come from anyone but you, I would have walked out of that office."

Eric smiled. "Thank you. And just to follow up on what you said earlier, the impression you are under is correct. I do love you. With all my heart."

"You've made me a rich man," Marcello said, emotion rising, "and I don't just mean the money. I won't enjoy this world half as much when my dearest friend is no longer in it."

Eric wiped at his eyes. "I want you to enjoy this world twice as much! Do all the things I couldn't. And make another friend." Eric's hand moved toward the will resting on the desk's surface. "For me."

Marcello knew that he would never be able to replace the person across from him, but he would try. What choice did he have? Despite all of his capabilities, refusing Eric was beyond him.

*****

Marcello jerked awake. He had nodded off and was leaning to one side, but lucky for him, Tim was there. His chest was surprisingly comfortable, considering it was so firm, and the arm wrapped around Marcello felt nice too. No wonder Ben smiled so easily. "I'm sorry," he said, sitting upright. "I never intended to get you into trouble. I feel as though I've broken a promise."

His arm free now, Tim rolled his shoulder to work away the stiffness. "What do you mean?"

"Just that I'm slightly older than you, and thus should be the one guiding you away from such mistakes. I promise to make amends. As soon as I'm able, I'll set all of this right. This evening won't appear on your criminal record, and as for Ben, next year

I'll make sure you're not only together for New Year's Eve, but in an ideal position to celebrate. I promise to keep our little kiss a secret too."

"Oh he's hearing about it!" Tim said. "From me! Somehow I doubt he'll fly into a jealous rage. In fact, I'm pretty sure he's going to laugh."

"He has a kind heart," Marcello said. "As do you. I didn't see that initially. When you and Eric first met, I had my doubts, but I'm more than happy to admit that I was wrong. I'm very grateful to you."

"For what?" Tim asked, clearly taken aback.

For being there until the very end. Marcello hadn't expected that. A hospice nurse was charged with taking care of Eric, but she had other patients and a family of her own. The true burden fell on Tim. In the final weeks of Eric's life, Marcello had stopped by often. Tim was always there, caring for Eric and seeing to his every need. Even when Eric was no longer responsive. The money might as well have been in Tim's pocket at that point. Eric was comatose, but Tim still treated him with the utmost dignity. Marcello never announced himself. He often made his way up the stairs as quietly as possible. Day or night, Tim was at Eric's side. Few comforts were found in such a tragic situation, but knowing that Eric hadn't been alone when he died, that he was with someone he loved—and who from all appearances loved him back—helped make his passing slightly less painful.

"I'm grateful that you were such a good friend to him," Marcello said. "As to your earlier inquiry, Eric did love you. I don't think he ever limited that love to any one category. He simply loved you. I hope that's enough."

"He said that?" Tim asked, his chest heaving.

"Yes. Unequivocally."

"Okay." Tim nodded, as if reassuring himself. "Thank you."

"My pleasure. Now then..." Marcello stood, ignoring his body's soreness. "Time for me to set all of this right."

He looked for a metal cup to rattle against the bars. Failing to find one, he walked over and started shaking them. "I demand to speak with a lawyer, ANY lawyer, right this instant!"

Officer Duggins appeared, already weary. "Okay, okay! Enough with the theatrics. It looks like you really do have friends in high places."

"Commissioner Gordon?" Marcello asked innocently.

Duggins glared at him. "Judge Matthews. He called to set your bail at the same time someone else showed up to pay. Funny coincidence."

"Old Mickey Mathews! Why didn't I think to call him earlier? Oh, that's right, I was denied making any further calls, a detail I'm sure he'll find of particular interest."

Duggins yanked open the cell door. "Hey, I was only doing my job!"

"Said the scorpion to the frog. My friend is free to go as well?"

"Bail has been posted for you both, yeah."

Marcello turned to consider their cellmates, who were slumped against each other and sleeping. "And those two?"

"What about them?"

"I would imagine trespassing is on the bail schedule. No need to see a judge to determine the amount. Am I correct?"

Duggins shook his head, but answered to the contrary. "Right, but they're better off here than on the street."

"We'll make a humanitarian out of you yet!" Marcello said. "I'm more than happy to post bail for them both. They can stay in my mansion until the shelter gets a much-needed expansion."

Duggins stared. "You're not kidding, are you? Everything you've said tonight is true."

"Only the most fantastic of my claims," Marcello said. "Now then, I'd like my shoes and belt please, *and* my bow tie. It's important to maintain appearances!"

The process for leaving was nearly as tedious as their arrival. Marcello was exhausted by the time they were allowed into the reception area, but he felt revitalized when he saw who was waiting for him. Nathaniel. If only he had been around when Eric was still alive. They could have compared notes, because Marcello had a greater understanding now of how love could compel a person to do all they could for another.

"Sorry," Nathaniel said, cracking his knuckles and glaring at their surroundings. "I didn't get your message until—"

"After you and Kelly had finished celebrating?"

Nathaniel blinked. "How could you possibly know about that? You were gone! And in jail!"

Marcello tapped his nose. "I'm not so different from Santa Claus, except I'm only interested in when you've been naughty."

"Implants," Nathaniel said. "You've got implants and they let you tap into the security cameras, but no, I made sure to turn them off for the room we— Oh! Hi, Tim."

"I don't know how he does it either," Tim said, shaking his head. "So how do I get out of here?"

Marcello leapt into action. Reunited with his phone, he summoned a taxi to take Tim home immediately so Ben wouldn't have to worry any longer than necessary. He took the key to the Dodge Challenger from him first, which they had parked discretely down the street from Eric's house, and promised to have it delivered to Tim's home the next day. Then he finalized arrangements for Terry and Ralph, instructing Nathaniel on what to do with them. They would be his guests until he could find a way of improving their situation permanently. Once everything was in order, he called another taxi for himself.

"You're not coming with us?" Nathaniel asked.

"No," Marcello said. "I have unfinished business. Thank you! You're an absolute blessing, as always."

"No problem," Nathaniel said. "An explanation would be nice. Why did you and Tim break into that house?"

"A story for another time," Marcello said, patting him on the arm. "Don't worry. I've learned the error of my ways. I won't make the same mistake again."

"I hope not!" Nathaniel said, sounding overwhelmed.

Marcello noticed his taxi arriving outside, said his goodbyes, and got into the car. He breathed out a sigh of relief after giving the driver the address and the police station faded into the distance. His New Year's resolution was an easy one. Don't get arrested again. Ever. That didn't mean he would change his ways. It simply meant he would work twice as hard not to get caught.

The taxi pulled out of the driveway and backed into the street. Marcello waved as it drove away, then turned around to consider the house. It wasn't his own, but at times it had felt like a second home. Eric had made everyone who visited there feel welcome. Marcello walked to the door, inserted the key, and opened it. The trouble with a silent alarm is that it didn't scare away potential intruders. He didn't know if the security company had reset it after the police left, or if he had all the time in the world, but he didn't plan on sticking around to find out.

Marcello hurried up the stairs, then paused at the top to catch his breath, realizing he could have taken them slowly and not needed to rest. He blamed this on a lack of sleep rather than age, and made himself continue to the guest room. Tim's old room. He wasted no time entering the closet and pressing where he had thought he heard a click. It did so again, but felt more secure. Marcello pressed once more, moving his hands away. Four of the cube shelves moved with him, swinging open. Behind them was a safe, the indicator light still lit. He entered the numbers of his birthday, checking over his shoulder to be absolutely sure nobody saw, and held his breath as the inner mechanisms whirred. Then the door popped open, and he was confronted by a time capsule. The papers and photos were all still there, a messy pile shoved carelessly inside by drunken hands. He could almost smell a hint of wine in the air.

Marcello gathered up the pile and used his elbow to shut the safe door and the shelves that concealed them. Then he hightailed it out of there. He was puffing as he ran down the drive, glancing back occasionally to make sure he hadn't dropped anything. He reached the Dodge Challenger, clutching the papers to his chest as he struggled to get Tim's car unlocked and open. Once he squeezed inside and tossed the papers in the passenger seat, he started the car and gunned it the short distance to his own home. He paused when stepping out of the vehicle, hearing the distant sound of police sirens. Hopefully they would assume it was a false alarm. If not and they came looking for him, well, they'd have to drag him naked out of a bubble bath, because that was his next destination.

Marcello sat at the kitchen table. The morning was late, creeping its way toward noon. His new guests had been bathed and fed, and now they were out with one of his assistants shopping for decent clothes. As charming as he found their company, he was eager for silence so he could look over what he had gone to such great lengths to acquire. That he was seated at the kitchen table was no coincidence, since Eric had often done the same, preferring it to a desk. This made the situation feel more like a séance, as if this location and these papers had the power to summon back his spirit.

In a way, they did. Very few of the photos were of Gabriel

alone. Eric was in most of them, smiling at his side or making silly faces for the camera. Marcello organized these into themes, traveling with them on vacations or catching glimpses of their holidays at home. He was even in one photo, standing between them like a gleeful third wheel. Then he turned his attention to the written material, savoring Eric's elegant handwriting more than the content itself, which mostly took the form of love letters, some of them never delivered. Those were the hardest to read, since they painted an intimate portrait of the pain Eric had suffered during the separation. One letter puzzled him more than the others until he realized, to his utmost joy, that it was intended for him. The penmanship wasn't quite so orderly, implying it hadn't been written while sober, but that only meant it would be more honest.

If you're reading this, I made you open the safe. I'm sorry. It's not your fault that I was weak. Don't feel bad. I take full responsibility. It's just hard when you feel so much for someone. Love makes you powerless, which is odd, because it can also be so empowering. You're no stranger to addiction, and yet it always surprises me how you've been able to resist the most addictive drug of all. Please don't look away now, even though I'm probably blubbering over these stupid photos and letters that you've reunited me with. I want you to learn from this. Let my pathetic state act as a cautionary tale. Don't be like me. Remain strong, because people like me need people like you when we fall apart. Thanks so much for your infinite patience. I'd like to think that someday I will return the favor. Somehow.

With love,

Eric

Marcello reread the letter a few times, chuckling occasionally and near tears at others. Then he fetched his own stationary and composed a response.

My beloved Eric,

Oh how I miss you! I take comfort in the fact that, before too long, you and I will be reunited. I can't imagine we will end up at the same place, but I'm fond of the idea that Hell has visitation rights. Or that my connections can get me to wherever you are, because if there's one thing the Devil likes, it's a good deal. Your words moved me, if you even remember them anymore, but I must contest some of what you said. You are *strong, because to have loved and lost is much harder than to have never loved at all. Those who have gone without don't truly realize what they are missing. I don't count myself among them. When have I ever resisted intoxication? I have known love in many forms and paid the inevitable price, none so great as when I lost you. To be there, to provide any sort of comfort in your time of need, was always the greatest of honors. I would do it all a thousand times over again if need be, but in truth, I'd rather you never have need of me than to see you suffer. Any debts have long since been repaid. You demonstrated how opening your heart to a stranger and trying to instill them with your wisdom could not only bring comfort at the end of a life, but also better this world. You would be proud of what Tim has achieved, how he has grown and used what you gave him to help others: countless artists in need of representation or education, a young man who didn't have a family of his own, and even one as heartbroken as you once were, who now never seems to stop smiling. Had I not seen what your generosity could accomplish, I might not have opened myself to the same possibility. I wish you could meet Nathaniel. I think you would like him very much. Then again, I choose to believe that we will all be reunited someday, so with that in mind, I will save any other heartfelt words for when I can speak them to you in person. Just know that I love you.*

Yours,

MM

Marcello wiped his cheeks dry, took Eric's letter, and placed it with his own. After some consideration, he added the photo of him standing between Eric and Gabriel. Fastening this together with a paperclip, he walked through the house to a safe, this one not hidden. The combination wasn't his own birthday, but that of another person. Unlike Eric, Marcello wasn't quite so forthcoming with his feelings, and there might come a day when Nathaniel needed to hear what he hadn't managed to say in person. Or want to understand his reasons a little better. He added these letters to everything else he had placed there, then walked to the nearest window. The sun was high above the Austin skyline—the first noon of a new year. The past was never far behind, but at the moment, the future beckoned. Life was for the living, and Marcello still counted himself among them. Time to rejoin their ranks and fill his days with stories that he hoped, one day, to tell his dearest of friends.

Something Like Hearts

by Jay Bell

Austin, 2015

"I'm ready for anything. That's what these rings will be. A promise. As long as it involves you, I'm game."

Kelly tore his eyes away from the ring on his finger to look over at his... What? Boyfriend? Fiancé? While they hadn't discussed titles, or the rings since they had first put them on, one thing was absolutely certain: He loved the man sitting at his side. Nathaniel was currently scowling at the contract he was holding, brow knotted up in concentration. His jaw was probably clenching too. The beard made it hard to tell. Kelly liked it. Nathaniel had always been scruffy, but a recent trip to Alaska had encouraged him to grow it out. Kelly had done the same, albeit on the top of his head instead of the bottom. His normally short-cropped hair was longer now and currently sticking up in playful twists. Not a major change for either of them, but they often touched each other in these places, Kelly rubbing his palm along the beard when they kissed or Nathaniel reaching up to tug his springy coils.

Now they were seated in the office of a studio where they both had once worked, trying to decide what their future held. The last few years had mostly consisted of them traveling together, Kelly taking photos or arranging the occasional exhibition. Nathaniel had seemed at peace too, but only at first. They toured around in their RV, Nathaniel planning the best route between stretches and stubbornly refusing to use the GPS. When not in motion, he would distract himself by performing maintenance on the vehicle, or by ensuring Zero got enough exercise and affection, or by cooking for them all. Even this wasn't enough. Whenever they decided to stay in one place for an extended period of time, Nathaniel sought out work, unselective about what kind. During the brief spells when they returned to Austin, he would make his way to the very studio where they now sat. Marcello invariably had need of him, most recently during the New Year celebrations. Now that they had agreed to settle down here again, there was no question as to where Nathaniel belonged. The ink on his contract was already dry. Kelly, on the other hand, was less certain. Not about who he loved but rather what he should do with himself.

"Looks good," Nathaniel said, handing the contract to Kelly. Then he appeared apologetic, glancing across the table to Marcello. "Not that I don't trust you."

"A perfectly reasonable request," Marcello trilled. "I read through it myself. My favorite lawyer once drew up a contract that promised a young man a position here as a 'mold' instead of a model, although this did make me ponder all the ways that mold could be filled."

Kelly chose to ignore this visual image and turned his attention to the finely printed legalese instead, but only briefly. "My one lingering concern is the sort of work I'll be doing. Photography, yes, but I'm not sure I want to be stuck in the studio all day. I had enough of that when modeling. I also don't want you paying me to take photos you'll never use, but I prefer to be out in the field. For me, half the fun is trying to document life as it happens."

"Capturing spontaneity?" Marcello said, a twinkle in his eye. "That was your first assignment with Nathaniel, if I'm not mistaken. The beginning of it all! If you'd be willing to repeat the experiment on occasion…"

Kelly leaned back. "As in me modeling again? I hope that's not what you mean."

Marcello waved a hand. "No! No, of course not. Those days are firmly behind you. While I'll never agree with your decision, I respect it. Although, seeing as how you've chosen to broach the subject, it *has* given me an idea."

"Here we go," Kelly murmured.

Marcello rose, walked across his office to the desk and picked up a manila envelope. "Now that the laws have changed and same-sex couples can marry, clients are no longer tiptoeing around sexuality by asking for vaguely homoerotic imagery. Instead they crave blatant images of support: happy gay couples wearing the latest fashion trends, shopping for their new hybrid vehicle, or holding the hand of their adopted child while pondering which life insurance policy would be best for their family. Companies have gone from fearing they'll scare away conservatives with a pro-gay stance to recognizing that the scales have tipped—all that disposable income pouring in one direction. Naturally, they hope to be on the receiving side."

"It's more than just gay people having extra money to spend," Nathaniel said. "What's really changed is the number of supporters and allies. The more people who come out, the more straight people there are with gay siblings, coworkers, or friends, and that makes them less likely to tolerate homophobia or even silent neutrality."

"Precisely," Marcello said, sitting across from them again. "All of this is wonderful news for civil rights *and* this studio. We're struggling to keep up with demand. There's one client in particular—" He placed the folder on the coffee table and tapped the cover. "—I've been chasing down for years to no avail. Now they've not only come around but have approached me. I'm eager to provide them with a result beyond their expectations."

"Sounds like a good challenge," Kelly said. "One I would be happy to accept. But only if I'm taking photos and not featuring in them."

Marcello's face fell. "What a pity. I thought it would make a fitting grand finale. Just think of the publicity!" He moved his hand in an arc, as if willing a rainbow to appear in the air. Or a headline. "'Famous model Kelly Phillips comes out of retirement one last time to show his support for marriage equality.'"

Nathaniel cleared his throat. "That *would* be an excellent PR angle."

Kelly's only response was to raise an eyebrow at him.

"What?" Nathaniel said. "You've mentioned more than once that you regret not using your fame to support more causes."

"Former fame," Kelly stressed. Then he mimicked the hand motion and created his own headline. "Kelly Phillips shows his support for marriage equality by starting a new chapter in his illustrious career. *Behind* the camera"

Marcello tsked. "I prefer my version."

"As do I," Nathaniel responded. "Yours sounds vain."

Kelly sighed. "I knew coming here was a bad idea."

"Now now," Marcello said, "it was only a suggestion. This advertisement will be in all the big magazines and on the most trafficked web sites. I've even heard whispers of a Super Bowl commercial. I simply wanted to give them our best, and when it comes to the hundreds of models who have passed through these doors, only one person meets the criteria. You."

Kelly exhaled. "I appreciate the compliment. And the offer, I really do, but I'm a photographer now, not a model. I'd still like to be involved, but I understand if you want someone with more experience on this assignment."

"My apologies," Marcello said. "I shouldn't have put you in such an awkward position. Never fear! I'm sure we'll find some crucial role for you to play. I had already selected a model for the job anyway. He's rather gifted. I think you'll like him. Perhaps you worked together previously? I simply can't remember." He flipped open the folder, revealing a photo.

"Cameron Herman?" Kelly said disbelievingly. They had indeed worked together. The guy was a dick. A very photogenic dick, but still. Kelly's rise to the top had been accompanied by snobbery and jealously from the models he surpassed, but most chose to talk trash behind his back or silently seethe. Cameron had found something nasty to say between each shoot, his pièce de résistance being, *"You sure are getting a lot of jobs these days. Makes me wish I was missing a leg so people would feel sorry for me too. Can't blame you for not turning down pity work!"* Once Nathaniel caught wind of this, he had offered to remove one of Cameron's legs for him. Personally. Had it been anyone other than Cameron, that person would have been fired, but he really was one of the studio's best models. Not *the* best. At least not at the time. "If I remember right, he's not even gay."

"No matter," Marcello said. "He's to be commended for showing his support to an issue that has no personal impact on him. Say, perhaps that could be the PR angle! We'll peddle him as a hero. An ally to our cause!"

"Could work," Nathaniel said, nodding slowly. "We'll book him on talk shows, make him an icon for the gay community. Worked for the Jonas brothers."

Marcello appeared delighted. "I like it!"

"But with a contract this important," Kelly said, "shouldn't we consider our options?"

"I don't see why," Nathaniel said.

"Nor do I," Marcello agreed. "We're on to something good here. If we play our cards right, Cameron Herman will soon be a household name."

"Wait!" Kelly said. "Just give me a minute to think about this." The last thing he wanted was snotty Cameron Herman getting famous, or having to see him on the cover of every fashion magazine. What was the alternative? Accept this assignment and take his place? Was he really going to accept this job out of spite? Yes. That's exactly what Kelly would do. "I'm in. Forget about Cameron. This is the last time though!"

"Wonderful!" Marcello said, his hands gripped together in glee. Then he reached for the folder, pulling out papers held together by a clip. "If you would just sign here, we can start discussing details."

A contract had already been drawn up, his name right on it. Kelly's mouth fell open. Then it snapped shut again. "I hate you."

"Nonsense. And before you arch those eyebrows at Nathaniel, he had no part in my scheme. I'm sure my tactics will be forgiven when you see how generously you'll be compensated. If not, you can be angry at me later. We're on a tight timeline and need to start shooting this weekend. On Saturday, to be precise."

That didn't give him much time to prepare! He checked the calendar on his phone, surprised when he saw the date. "Valentine's Day?"

Marcello blinked. "I suppose it is! How appropriate."

"Appropriate for romance," Kelly said, "not for work."

"Ah." Marcello looked between them. "Will this be an issue? Did you have plans?"

"No," Nathaniel said. Then he noticed Kelly's expression and shrugged. "What? We've never made a big deal out of it before."

True. A number of bad experiences had resulted in Kelly feeling an aversion to the holiday, starting way back in junior high when all his friends were pairing up with girls. He had done so too, suffering through an awkward relationship that lasted three days. Once he joined the gay youth group, he repeated the same experiment, accepting any offer because it was better than being single on a day dedicated to love. Or so he had once believed, but that philosophy had proven false on more than one occasion. Even the time he and Jared had vowed to have fun on Valentine's Day despite both of them being single, the holiday had still been miserable. Jared spent most of the night talking about unattainable girls he wanted, leaving Kelly more heartbroken with each name because none of them were his. Then there was the terrible restaurant date with William. The less said about that, the better. Now that he was with Nathaniel, romance happened without prompting. They never needed to plan it, or schedule it for one specific day. Not that they hadn't tried. Way back during their first year together, in fact…

*

"Here."

A heart-shaped box was shoved beneath Kelly's nose. He was sitting on the bed, pulling on his leg. *The* leg. The brand-new X2, which had made it possible to walk again, and with a little practice, would allow him to run. He loved it so much that he was tempted to cuddle with it and give the prosthetic a ridiculous pet name. Had he still been sleeping alone and not in Nathaniel's bed every night, he probably would have, but he didn't want to get kicked out of this little apartment. He cherished it too much.

Kelly accepted the box of chocolates, and when he looked up to express his thanks, a bouquet of flowers was thrust in his face.

"Roses!" he said, leaning back to avoid being poked by thorns. "Wow."

"Take it," Nathaniel said, sounding impatient, "or I'll beat you over the head with them."

"Happy Valentine's Day to you too!" Kelly said, not hiding his trepidation.

"Sorry." Nathaniel's arms dropped to his sides, the gifts lowering with them. "I don't do romance."

"Nobody said you had to." Kelly reached for his jeans. He hesitated, wondering if he should leave them off, but the vibe wasn't exactly sensual right now so he put them on. "You seem tense."

"Because I had to go to the florist. Again. I picked up a dozen roses yesterday and hid them so you wouldn't see. While I was making breakfast for you, Zero found the bouquet and tore it up."

"The mutt probably thought they were for him," Kelly joked.

Nathaniel didn't smile. "By the time I got back from the florist, Zero managed to drag most of the food off the counter and, well, just don't expect a big breakfast."

"It's the thought that counts," Kelly said, extending a hand. "Show me what you've got."

The roses looked a little sad and probably would have been discarded if flowers weren't in such high demand today. The box of chocolates was still nice, so long as he ignored the puncture marks left by dog teeth.

"I had to wrestle Zero for them," Nathaniel explained.

"Your efforts are appreciated." Kelly's stomach growled. "You really made breakfast?"

Nathaniel averted his eyes. "Technically."

Kelly fought down a smile and went to investigate. He smelled eggs on the way, and soon noticed an oily frying pan on the counter and a cutting board decorated with curls of onion skin and discarded tomato stems. Omelets! The bottle of maple syrup implied pancakes would be included too, but when Kelly glanced at the table, all he saw were two small plates with one slice of toast each. "I don't know if I have room for all that," he joked.

"Shut up," Nathaniel grumped.

Kelly stared at the meal, trying to find something more positive to say. "It looks good! Toast *and* jelly. Already spread too! You spoil me. Um… Is the jelly supposed to be in the shape of a heart?"

Nathaniel clenched his jaw a few times. "Maybe."

Kelly imagined Nathaniel trying to glare the jelly into assuming the correct shape. Then he laughed. He wasn't trying to be cruel. He thought it was cute, but Nathaniel took it the wrong way, crossing his arms over his chest and frowning.

"I love it," Kelly said, lifting the flowers and chocolates. "All of it."

"You don't have to pretend," Nathaniel said. "I know you probably expected the day to be special but—"

"I hate Valentine's Day."

Nathaniel peered at him to judge his level of honesty. Then he appeared hopeful. "You do?"

"Yes!" Kelly said with a laugh. "It's a ridiculous money grab. I don't need flowers or candy to make me feel loved. If wooing me was that simple, I'd still be with all sorts of guys." Oops! Not the best way of phrasing it, because Nathaniel tended to get jealous.

"Like who?"

"Doesn't matter," Kelly said. "None of them compare to you. And hey, look what I got you! Nothing! What kind of a jerk boyfriend does that on V-day?"

This made Nathaniel smile. "So technically, I did better than you."

"Exactly! You tried, and I appreciate it, I really do." Kelly nodded at the snoozing dog on the couch. "You made Zero happy. Assuming he ever comes out of that food coma, this is going to be the best Valentine's Day he's ever had."

Nathaniel's posture relaxed. "Not bad for my first time."

"Really? So you and Caesar never…"

Nathaniel shook his head. "He wasn't into flowers. Neither am I. You like them though. Right?"

"On occasion," Kelly admitted. "But it doesn't have to be today. Actually, that'll be my gift to you. From now on, you never have to worry about Valentine's Day again. It'll be a normal day like any other."

"You sure? Sounds good to me, but is that really what you want? Be honest."

Kelly shrugged. "When I was a kid, I liked the idea of this being a romantic day. I had a lot of fantasies, most of them hokey, but experience has taught me that such things can't be forced. They happen when they happen. That you even tried is enough for me. From now on, don't worry about it. Being with you is all I need."

Nathaniel puffed up his chest. "I think I can manage that."

"Good. Now let's eat our toast before Zero wakes up and decides to steal that too."

They had just sat down when Kelly's phone rumbled.

"Don't tell me you have another valentine," Nathaniel joked.

Kelly checked to see who it was from. Layne. "Definitely not!" He scanned the text message. "A friend of mine is having a party next week. It's his birthday. Do you want to go?"

Nathaniel poked at his toast with a fork. "I like our alone time."

"So do I, but I want you to meet more of the people I know." Kelly winked. "And who knows, it might turn out to be romantic."

Nathaniel abandoned the fork and picked up the toast to take a bite. While chewing he nodded and said something. Kelly couldn't be sure, but it sounded like, "How bad could it be?"

* * * * *

Kelly stood at the altar and fidgeted. He was getting married! That had come as a surprise. When he had agreed to this assignment, he hadn't expected the marriage aspect to be so literal. He had visualized himself and another guy picking out rings together in front of the camera, or one of them kneeling for a staged proposal. Presumably all those preliminaries had already happened in this scenario, because now he was about to take his vows. Kelly's nervousness was real but easy to banish. All he had to do was turn his head and look at the studio, where a crew made final adjustments to the cameras and lights. When he looked the other way again, the illusion of a church returned.

He had to admit the effect was impressive. Finding a real chapel and shooting on location would have been cheaper than building a set, but that would have made controlling the environment difficult. Lighting levels could be easily adjusted this way without any unpleasant surprises, such as congregation members showing up unannounced, or time limits that forced them to pack up and leave before they got their required shots. They also wouldn't have to cover up crucifixes or anything religious to guarantee the resulting advertisement was secular.

Marcello had clearly spared no expense. To all appearances, Kelly was standing in a rustic church. An arch had been constructed with an alcove beyond, all of it treated to look like worn stone. The altar was stout and hewn from dark wood. An older man dressed in clerical robes stood in front of it and appeared nervous too. The wedding officiant. He might have been a priest or pastor or something else entirely. Kelly couldn't tell which denomination, but he supposed that was the point. Behind the altar was a stained glass window, artificially lit from behind. Tall candelabras flanked the window, wicks lit and wax dripping.

The officiant noticed him taking it all in, turning to do the same before approaching. "Impressive, isn't it?" he said. "Or is this normal? I don't know. It's my first time. I'm Perry."

"Nice to meet you. I'm Kelly, and yes, it's an impressive set. For this studio. I've seen fake blizzards, artificial hurricanes, and just about any other weather you can imagine recreated inside studios twice this size. My favorite was an underwater scene, at least until they dangled me from a wire so it looked like I was swimming. That was fun for about five minutes. But five hours?" He grimaced, remembering the discomfort.

"Wow!" Perry said, clearly impressed. "So you're a professional?"

"I used to be. And so are you! If you're here and getting paid, you're the real deal."

Perry laughed. "I don't know about that."

Kelly smiled in response. "Even pros have a first day."

"That's kind of you to say. It makes me feel better that—even with all your experience—you still get nervous too."

Was it that obvious? Kelly was only partially nervous about the shoot. Sure he was out of practice, but he still remembered the basics. He was confident he could deliver. So why was he feeling so antsy? His attention returned to the scenery, which was a little too convincing, making it easy to believe he really was about to get married. Would that be so bad? As soon as the Supreme Court had made its ruling last year, ensuring marriage was available to anyone regardless of their sexual orientation, no end of family and friends began asking when he would be getting married. The pressure kept building for them both. Nathaniel got quiet whenever anyone broached the subject. That brought back a few bad memories. The last thing Kelly wanted was to scare him away again. Besides, why bother? They were good how they were. Right?

"You look amazing."

He was surprised to find Nathaniel standing in front of him, eyes amorous as he looked Kelly over. That had everything to do with the tuxedo—the very product this advertisement would sell. The suit's cut accentuated his shoulders and hugged his hips just right. Even the pants managed to show off his package nicely. The black fabric shimmered just enough to catch the light without appearing too glitzy. The finer details were there too: buttons made of tarnished metal and engraved with a delicate leaf pattern, silk lapels a darker shade than the rest of the suit, and charcoal gray thread that revealed the skillful tailoring. The photographer would have his work cut out for him when attempting to capture these details.

"You all right?" Nathaniel asked.

"Yes," Kelly said. "A little overwhelmed, that's all."

"I'm not worried." Nathaniel nodded toward the cameras. "I remember your first shoot in this same studio. Marcello had you grilling under the lights all day, but you performed like you were born to do this. I couldn't keep my eyes off of you then, and now…" He moved closer, placing his hands on Kelly's shoulders. "Now there are other things I can't keep off you."

"Places, please!" Someone shouted. "Where's the groom? No, the other one!"

Nathaniel stepped back. "It's your big moment. Want me to

walk you down the aisle and give you away?"

"Shut up!" Kelly said, tittering. "Actually, who *am* I marrying?"

Nathaniel froze. "Marcello didn't tell you?"

"No. Who?"

Nathaniel was already hurrying away. "I better get out of the shot."

"Thank you," the photographer snapped, approaching with his light meter. He checked it and looked around. "Cameron, into position, please."

Cameron? As in Cameron Herman? No! Anyone but him! Kelly's worst fear was confirmed when he was faced by his polar opposite. Blond hair, pale blue eyes, pink pouty lips, tan skin, and a body that made him wish he had lifted weights to prepare for this gig.

"So you're my bride-to-be," Cameron said with a deep Southern drawl. He laughed and shook his head, addressing the crew. "Don't y'all think I can do better?" He looked at Kelly again. "That's what everyone is going to think when they see this ad."

"Hey, you're the one wearing white," Kelly said, eyeing Cameron's tuxedo with disdain. "You know what that means, right? You're my bitch. *That's* what people are going to be thinking. And imagining."

"If they even notice you."

"The only reason they wouldn't is if your massive ego is blocking the shot." Kelly glared. "You haven't changed a bit."

Cameron looked him over with feigned disinterest. "Sorry, have we met before?"

"Seriously?"

"Gentlemen," Marcello said, hurrying forward. "While normally I would allow the camera to transmute aggression into sexual tension, this is supposed to be a tender moment. The ultimate expression of your love."

Kelly scoffed. "For him?"

"Unrequested love," Cameron shot back. "No way would I fall for someone like you!"

"It's *unrequited*, you idiot, and I can't think of anything more abhorrent than the idea of spending my life, or even another minute, with you!"

"I see," Marcello said, shaking his head sorrowfully. "I had thought myself in the presence of professionals, but perhaps I was mistaken. You're merely handsome faces, not performers. I'll find more qualified—"

"Oh I can do this!" Kelly snarled.

"So can I!" Cameron shot back. "I'll do a better job than he ever could!"

"Excellent," Marcello said, appearing pleased. "May the best man win."

Cameron narrowed his eyes with new determination. Kelly rolled his own because they were being played. Not that he would let that stop him from obliterating the competition. They scowled at each other as the makeup technicians brushed powder on their faces. The instant the photographer clicked the first photo, their expressions shifted to pure adoration. As the hours dragged by and they switched from one position to another, Kelly convinced himself that he was facing the love of his life. This illusion was shaken when they were told to hold hands, Cameron squeezing his painfully tight.

"Great job!" the photographer said. "Love those watery eyes, Kelly. I can feel the emotion!"

Kelly could feel the pain. He squeezed back, and was gratified to see Cameron's features straining.

"You look like you've got cold feet, Cameron," the photographer complained. "Come on now! You've been waiting for this day, not dreading it. Let's move on to the rings. Perry, move forward two steps and present them. No, pick up the box first. That's right. Go ahead and open it."

Perry's hands were shaking slightly as he opened a box swathed in red velvet. Kelly braced for Cameron to make a snide remark about this nervousness. Instead he laughed. Without cruelty. They both did, because the box was empty.

"Call off the wedding," Cameron drawled. "Someone done stole the rings!"

"You've got to be kidding me," the photographer said, spinning around to face his crew. "Where the hell are the rings?"

Chaos ensued, which was good for Kelly, since it allowed him to relax and take a breather. He moved back a few paces to get out of the hot lights and away from Cameron. Three hours down, who knew how many to go. He had a feeling this was going to be a very long shoot.

"We've got a problem," Nathaniel said as he approached. He held the red box in one hand, the lid open.

"Looks like you found one of them."

"That's my ring. Wardrobe forgot to order the props. You have yours?"

"Yeah," Kelly said. He had slipped it into his pocket before the shoot began.

"Do you mind?"

"Of course not." Kelly glared in Cameron's direction as he pulled out the ring and placed it into the remaining slit inside the box. "But if he puts your ring on, even for a second, I'll break his damn finger!"

Nathaniel chuckled. "I love it when you get mean. As long as it's not directed at me. You're doing great, by the way. You've still got it."

"Thank you," Kelly said, voice softer now. "I just wish it was you standing there with me instead."

"I'm not pretty enough."

"I disagree." Kelly leaned forward for a kiss, but Nathaniel had already turned, intent on delivering the box to Perry. "Okay," he murmured to himself. "Keep it professional. Back to work."

He held on to his urge to kiss Nathaniel, directing it toward Cameron instead. As far as the camera was concerned, Kelly only loved one person in the world, and they were about to tie the knot. He was doing a lot better than Cameron, who seemed increasingly uncomfortable with the situation. Was he worried they would have to kiss? Maybe he wasn't such an ally to gay people after all.

"Just pretend you're looking in the mirror," Kelly suggested. "That should get your libido going."

"My what?" Cameron mumbled.

That's it? No biting back? A lack of comprehension had never stopped him before.

"Makeup!" the photographer shouted. "Mop up that sweat on Cameron's brow. He looks like he's about to bolt!"

That's exactly what he did. After twenty more minutes of gasping and perspiring, Cameron ran from the room without an explanation. Kelly allowed himself to bask in the moment. He didn't know what was going on, but he had just proven who was more professional.

"Everyone take ten," Nathaniel shouted. "I'll find out what's going on."

Kelly shook his arms loose and walked in a circle to get his blood circulating. He wanted nothing more than to sit, but that would wrinkle the tuxedo.

"This is harder than it looks," Perry said. "Do you think it's possible to get a sunburn from those lights?"

"No," Kelly said with a chuckle. "It just feels that way. Come on. Let's grab some water so we don't dehydrate."

He loitered in the breakroom until their ten minutes were up, mostly because the temperature was a lot cooler in there. When he returned to the studio, the vibe was tense. He approached Marcello and Nathaniel, who were in a huddle with the photographer. "What's going on?"

"Cameron is in the restroom," Nathaniel said. "He's glued to the toilet."

"Please tell me you mean that literally," Kelly said, not hiding his amusement.

"Figuratively," Marcello said, "but from what I was able to gather, he can't make it far before needing to return." He wrinkled his nose. "I don't recommend venturing in there."

Kelly would have laughed if it wasn't Nathaniel's job to manage this project and make sure everything went smoothly. As amusing as Cameron's severe diarrhea was, this client was too important—and impatient—for any delays.

"What do we still need?" Nathaniel asked.

"In terms of shots?" The photographer massaged his temples. "All the over-the-shoulder angles and close-ups of them wearing the rings."

"The hands are out of focus for the latter," Marcello said. "Aren't they?"

The photographer nodded in confirmation. "To focus on the suits, yes."

"So all we need is another pair of hands," Kelly said, "and as long as you're shooting me over someone's shoulder, nobody will know it isn't Cameron."

"That could work," Nathaniel said musingly. "We'd need to get another model in here."

"And the proper paperwork drawn up," Marcello said. "When the advertisement goes national, I don't want a lawsuit from a greedy temp."

"How long will that take?" the photographer demanded.

"Depends how quick we find someone who is willing," Nathaniel replied. "And how far away from the studio they are. We need to get one of the lawyers in here too."

"How long," the photographer stressed, seeming on the verge of a heart attack.

Nathaniel shrugged. "It's the weekend. And it's Valentine's Day. I'm guessing most models have plans already."

"Wait just a moment," Marcello said. "What if you took Cameron's place?"

"Me?" Nathaniel scoffed. "I'm not a model."

"Nor am I, but you have a similar build to Cameron, and as we've established, you won't really be in the shot. We just need a body in the right clothing. Am I correct?"

"You're not wrong," the photographer said, latching on to the idea. "I'll have to be creative with some of the angles, but it could work."

"Do it!" Kelly said, already loving the idea. At least he wouldn't have to pretend to love the person he was with. He grinned at Nathaniel. "Let's get hitched!"

"Ladies and gentlemen," Marcello declared. "We have a solution. And a proposal!"

They all laughed before Nathaniel was whisked away. Kelly amused himself by imagining Cameron passing his tuxedo beneath the bathroom stall so Nathaniel could put it on. Hopefully they would steam clean it first. He felt a lot more chipper when told to take his place, and absolutely thrilled when Nathaniel returned.

"Hot damn," Kelly said, barely able to breathe. "You look fine!"

The tuxedo fit Nathaniel perfectly, and while he didn't have Cameron's toned-to-perfection body, the strong shoulders and impressive chest had Kelly salivating.

"Let's get this over with," Nathaniel growled.

The crew sprang into action. Lights were adjusted, and the photographer started moving around them. They were instructed to hold hands. That went on for a while before Kelly was told to place a palm on Nathaniel's arm. After another series of photos, they were asked to move closer and angle their bodies toward the camera so the contrasting colors of the tuxedos would be captured. He couldn't believe he was being paid for this! It really was amazing how well the suit fit Nathaniel, and thank goodness it didn't stink. At all. Nathaniel smelled like the cologne Kelly had bought him as a gift. Funny how the suit wasn't too tight around his stomach, especially considering that Cameron lived for sit-ups while Nathaniel had just enough paunch to make Kelly giddy. Had he lost weight? The buttons weren't straining, and even though he was certain Nathaniel's shoulders were broader than Cameron's, the fabric wasn't taut there either. In fact, it looked as though it had been tailored to fit him. Probably because it had.

"That's not the same suit," Kelly said.

Nathaniel's eyes met his. "What are you suggesting? That I had myself fitted for the same tuxedo and slipped Cameron a dangerous amount of laxatives earlier to make sure I'd have an excuse to wear it?"

Kelly stared. "Did you?"

"Maybe."

"Why?"

"Okay," the photographer said. "Time to put on the rings."

Kelly's eyes widened. "What's going on here?"

Nathaniel turned his attention to the room. "Everybody out!"

That's all it took. The crew, the photographer, even Perry scuttled from the room. Marcello was the last to go, expression pleased and cheeks rosy.

"I have something I need to say." Nathaniel moved toward the lights, turning off the most intense. The studio became much darker, but the candelabras still flickered with warmth. Nathaniel walked toward him again. "A question."

"Yes," Kelly blurted out. Then he covered his mouth.

Nathaniel paused, then continued until he was close enough to take his hands. "You don't know what I was going to ask."

Kelly laughed nervously. "I have a pretty good idea."

"You don't, because I'm not asking you to marry me someday."

His stomach dropped. "What?"

Nathaniel sighed and looked past Kelly at the church backdrop. "I don't do romance. I was hoping the environment would carry this for me, because I don't know the right words to say. I feel so much for you. Too much to express how good it is going to bed every night, knowing you'll still be there in the morning. Or how in Colorado, I saw you picking burrs out of Zero's fur, and when you were done, you rubbed his neck affectionately before you stood. That might sound stupid, but you loving him like that..." He shook his head and scowled at the floor. "You do this thing whenever we eat somewhere new and you take your first bite. You chew for a really long time and your eyebrows either shoot up if you like it or down if you don't. Jesus, Kelly, I love you! Everything about you! I want what we've got to last the rest of our lives, so that's what I'm asking. I want you to marry me, and if you say yes, I'm not waiting. I want it to happen right now."

A jumble of thoughts romped around in Kelly's head, a tangle of words jockeying for position—too many to be useful—so he abandoned them all. Instead he placed a hand on Nathaniel's cheek. Then he leaned forward and kissed him.

"Is that a yes?" Nathaniel asked, pulling away.

"It's a give-me-a-second," Kelly said. "I'm still trying to make sense of everything. Help me out. You're saying this client, this entire shoot, was just a ruse to get me dressed up and in front of a priest?"

Nathaniel shook his head. "It's all real. The client and everything. I simply saw an opportunity and took advantage of it. And he's not a priest, or a model. Perry is the county clerk. He can issue a marriage certificate. We don't need a judge to marry us because Marcello is an ordained minister. I know, it's like finding out that the devil gives communion in his free time, but it's true."

"Okay. Wow." Kelly took in the church set, then turned and imagined pews filled with the people they knew and loved. "What about our families? Our friends?"

"We can still have a ceremony," Nathaniel said. "If that's what you want. But I know myself. I'm not a patient man. Not when it comes to needing to be with you. If we're getting married, the last thing I want is to suffer through opening presents, making toasts, and cutting cake. That's not what we're about." He gestured to the studio. "This is where we fell in love. We did so while working together, so it seems appropriate that the ceremony would happen here. While we're working. Honestly, even if you say no and it turns out you hate the idea of marriage, all I'm asking is to spend the rest of my life with you."

"Oh is that all?"

"Yeah," Nathaniel said, jutting out his chin. "That's what I want."

Kelly considered him and sighed. "You're wrong about not doing romance. It might be the strangest variety I've ever encountered, but you're definitely romantic."

Nathaniel grinned. "So? What's your answer?"

"I already gave it. I didn't have to think and I still don't, because it's what every fiber of my being desires. I'm so in love with you!" Kelly laughed, feeling on the verge of tears. "I don't think you realize how much you've given me. The strength to walk away from a bad relationship, hope when I thought I had none. Hell, you even gave me back my leg, and now you want to give me your heart?" He swallowed, overwhelmed by emotion. "I don't deserve you."

"That's where *you're* wrong, but don't worry," Nathaniel took hold of him, bringing their faces close, "I've been told that marriage is mostly about correcting the other person."

Kelly would have laughed if his lips weren't so preoccupied. They kissed long enough that he felt like hopping up on the altar and continuing things there. Only the idea of the crew being pressed up against the studio door to listen made him stop. "So how does this work?"

"There's a piece of paper we have to sign," Nathaniel said, refusing to let go. "That's it. The rest is up to us. We can exchange vows, if you want."

Kelly chuckled. "I think we already did."

"And I've done way more than kiss the bride."

"Not today you haven't, but there's still time. So that's it? We sign a piece of paper and that makes us married?"

"No," Nathaniel said. "That's just the beginning. A marriage isn't forged by signing papers and trading rings. It requires a lifetime of dedication. We'll get old, passions will cool, and chances are we'll have doubts along the way. Plenty of arguments too."

"Ha! You know me so well."

"The real trick to is to survive all of those bad times, to make it past the doubts to certainty again, to invent new ways of falling in love, and to find forgiveness when there seems to be none."

"You paint a bleak picture." Kelly leaned against him, resting his head against the strong chest. "And yet somehow, it still sounds like perfection."

"Yeah." Nathaniel's voice was a rumble against Kelly's ear. "It does to me too. I love you, Kelly Phillips."

"Kelly Courtney," he corrected.

"You sure?"

"It has a nice ring to it."

"Mm-hm. It's also two girl names in a row."

"You're such a bastard!" Kelly pushed away as if offended, but he didn't struggle when Nathaniel pulled him close again. "I suppose that's why I love you."

They heard the studio door squeak open and turned to see Marcello sticking his head in. "If you're not decent," he said, "just tell me and I promise to look away. Eventually."

"It's fine," Nathaniel said. "You can bring in the champagne."

"Oh." Marcello's eyes widened as he stepped into the room. "About that. The funniest thing happened last night."

"I told you not to drink it!" Nathaniel growled. "I had it imported from—"

"France, I know," Marcello said as he approached. "What do the French know about champagne anyway?"

"They invented it!"

"And the Chinese invented pasta, but you don't go to Beijing when craving a plate of spaghetti, do you? I have some wonderful champagne from a local manufacturer." He squinted. "Don't I? No, I'm afraid I drank that too. Well anyway, I'm certain I have a bottle of vodka upstairs. Mix it with little seltzer water and apple juice and you'll never know the difference."

Nathaniel released Kelly so he could turn toward his boss. "I refuse to believe that you, of all people, have run out of champagne."

"You'd be surprised how much a troupe of acrobats can drink, especially when holding certain positions for so long. Ahem."

Marcello was close enough to punch now, if Nathaniel chose to, but instead he sighed. "Please tell me you're kidding."

Marcello winked. "Would I ever fail you?" He clapped his hands. In an instant, waiters began pouring through the door carrying chilled bottles and polished glasses on each tray. The crew followed them. Corks popped, booze was poured, and

Perry oversaw the completion of their marriage license, the altar doubling as a desk. Then they placed the rings on each other's fingers, just as they had done years before. Afterwards they returned to work, which was perfect, because it meant they spent a long time holding hands as more photos were taken. Kelly kept laughing during this, overcome with joy. Nathaniel was right. This is where—and how—they had fallen in love. They belonged here, which is why just days ago, they had both signed contracts ensuring they could stay. They were bound to this studio and Marcello's crazy world. A marriage of another sort. Kelly stared into the eyes of the man he loved, not surprised when he saw that Nathaniel's happy tears matched his own.

"What's next?" he whispered. "A honeymoon?"

"We've done enough traveling," Nathaniel murmured. "I keep thinking of our house, how we've barely spent any time there, and how good it would be to hide away for a few weeks. Or months. Or years."

Kelly grinned. "You can get anything delivered these days. Even groceries."

"You're really okay with this?" Nathaniel said. "If you want the traditional ceremony, a Niagara Falls honeymoon, or anything like that—"

"I'm sure," Kelly said, all traces of doubt chased from his heart. "I've already got everything I've ever wanted."

"That's a wrap!" the photographer declared.

"Not quite," Marcello said. "We've forgotten one crucial element, and I would hate to disappoint our client. How do they always put it? Ah yes. You may now kiss the bride. Or groom. Oh forget the semantics! Just kiss!"

They were all too happy to comply. Luckily for them—as with all modeling shoots—they were required to reenact the moment over and over again, just to make sure they got it right.

Something Like Shamrocks

by Jay Bell

Austin, 2009

"My milkshake brings the boys to the—" No. "Hit me baby one more—" Uh uh. That wasn't it. "This love has taken its toll on—" Nope. "I'm your biggest fan, I'll follow you until you—" Yeah. Maybe!

Layne Jenkins' leg bounced up and down to the rhythm in his head, shifting with each song as he tried to find one guaranteed to give Stella her groove back. He studied the door as he mentally worked himself up, waiting for his Prince Charming to walk through. Any minute now. Any minute… Ugh! He turned his attention to the circle of chairs, looking at each seated person just in case he'd missed any potential suitors. He quickly decided that happy couples shouldn't be allowed to attend the gay youth group. Or lesbians. Or gay guys who weren't interested in him. Basically it should just be him and his soulmate sitting in a church classroom that was used for daycare on the weekdays. If not his soulmate, then at least someone good-looking and fun who wanted his body. Or just someone tolerable who didn't hate him. At this point, anyone would do!

"Okay," said Keith, the group leader. "Everyone ready to begin?"

"No," Layne said, glancing desperately at the door. If the lecture started, all hope was lost. He'd have to wait until the next meeting in *two weeks* to see if anyone new showed up.

"Why not?" Keith asked, moving to shut it.

"I'm expecting someone."

"You are?"

"Mm-hm." He stared at the entryway, leg bouncing at hyper-velocity. He could hear the other kids grumbling but didn't care. This was the day. It had to be!

A distant door squeaked open and closed. A stretched shadow appeared in the hallway outside. Then a figure filled the doorway. He was short and stocky, but in a way that made him look strong like a… whatever the football position was where the guy acted like a wall. The brunet hair, the pug nose, the sprinkling of freckles. This was true love!

"Told you so!" Layne said, hopping to his feet and extending a hand in greeting. He walked right up to the newcomer and decided he was more interested in squeezing one of those bulging biceps. "So glad you could make it! I'm your future husband. We're out of chairs but you're welcome to sit on my lap. Or vice versa? No. I'm definitely not getting that sort of vibe, but wait until you feel *my* vibration! Ha ha!"

His soulmate—whatever his name was—had gone pale. With wide eyes he looked Layne over, considered the rest of the room with a panicked expression, then pulled his arm free and fled. The room was silent as the door to the outside squeaked open and closed again. Then someone started laughing.

Layne already knew who before he turned around to look. Katsu, or as many in the group called him, Kat. He did have a somewhat feline appearance. Like a lion. Asian eyes sparkled in amusement, the thick black hair gelled into a frozen wave. Defined cheekbones and luscious lips only made him more striking. Layne had about died the first time Katsu showed up and had been absolutely determined to win his affection. Then Layne had opened his mouth and made some stupid comment about defying Asian stereotypes. He hadn't meant it in a bad way. Katsu was tall! His tight jeans had been cupping a decent bulge too, rumors later confirming that it wasn't a pair of socks down there. Yes, perhaps Layne had chosen his words carelessly, but Katsu wasn't a saint either, never letting him live it down. Such as now.

White teeth flashing, Katsu put two muscled arms behind his head and shook it. "Looks like you scared away another one. And in record time! You know what, Layne? You'd make an excellent bouncer."

"Ha ha," Layne said, returning to his chair. "Very funny."

The rest of the group laughed at his expense. Layne rolled his eyes and ignored them. He didn't embarrass easily. In fact, he didn't care what anyone thought. Mostly.

"That's enough," Keith said, clapping his hands. "Let's get started. Today we are discussing respect, which is obviously a quality lacking in this group. Now then—"

Layne tuned out most of the lecture, alternating between feeling despair and shooting glares in Katsu's direction. He was such a jerk! A hunky, very popular, and lucky-in-love jerk. The chairs nearest Katsu were filled by his friends, all but the one to his immediate right where Thomas, a scrawny guy with blond hair, gleefully gripped Katsu's hand. Layne was a scrawny blond guy too! Slightly better looking and with way more personality. So why had Katsu chosen Thomas instead of him? Not that Layne would ever date Katsu. The guy would need a personality overhaul first. Or a full-blown lobotomy.

"With that in mind," Keith declared, "let's partner up! Try to choose someone you don't always see eye to eye with. Layne, Kat, I want you working together."

What the hell? Could this day get any worse? Layne stubbornly remained where he was, arms crossed over his chest, and refused to budge. Katsu strolled over to him, plopping down in the freshly vacated seat next to his and stretching out. He always took up a lot of space, and he always put his dumb hands behind his head. Either his deodorant smelled really good or it was his cologne because— No! Layne might be boy crazy, but even he had standards. "Let's get this over with, Kitty."

Katsu shrugged. "Fine. You go first."

"Oh. Um… What are we doing?"

"Seriously?" Katsu huffed, slowly sitting upright. "You weren't paying attention."

Layne pursed his lips. "I didn't hear a question mark at the end of that sentence."

"There's a reason for that."

"I *was* paying attention."

"Then go ahead."

Layne prodded at his subconscious, hoping for a little help. None. Nada. He knew respect was the topic, so he tried to build on that. "Respect. You want to find out what it means to me? Just a little bit? It's all I'm asking for. Just a little bit. I ain't gonna do you wrong. So all I'm asking for, is respect."

Katsu started laughing again. "You're an idiot."

"I'm not!"

"Then let me ask you something. Why do you come to these meetings?"

Layne scoffed. "To meet guys. Not to listen to dumb lectures."

"And how's that working out for you?"

"Great!" Layne said, his voice choosing to crack. Wonderful. Seventeen years old and puberty wasn't finished with him yet? He cleared his throat and tried again. "Really great."

Katsu leaned back. "That's what I thought."

"Hey, my love life is *extremely* active. Don't assume you know everything about me, just because I don't kiss and tell."

Katsu's attention was on Thomas, shooting a wink to him across the room. "You don't kiss anyone at all. That's why there's nothing to tell."

"I do too!"

Dark eyes moved to meet his, cool and confident. "Prove it."

"Okay," Layne said defiantly. "I will! Um… How?"

"Photographic evidence."

"You want a photo of me kissing a guy?" Layne asked, reaching for his phone.

"New photos. Not you making out with the old group leader. Everyone knows about him."

Damn it!

"If your love life is so active," Katsu continued. "You shouldn't have trouble producing a few new ones. Let's say… five?"

"Make it seven," Layne said. "It's my lucky number!"

Katsu appeared delighted. "Fine. Photos of you kissing seven different guys."

Wait, seven *different* guys? Layne thought he meant seven photos of the same guy! Still, he wasn't about to back down now. "No problem. I might need a little time though. A week for each one?"

Katsu laughed. "I'll give you seven months! In all the time I've been here, I've never seen you hook up with anyone. I'm really not worried."

"Then let's make it interesting," Layne said. "The loser has to stop coming to group."

"Exile?" Katsu raised an eyebrow. Then he nodded. "All right. You've got a deal."

He held out his hand. As Layne shook it, he hated how warm and strong it felt. This action delighted their group leader, who had come to check on them.

"Looks like things are going well here!" Keith said.

"They are," Katsu replied, oozing charm. "Layne and I are going to interact more and update each other about our personal lives. We're hoping an exchange of information will put an end to any unresolved issues."

"That sounds like a very mature conclusion," Keith said. "I'm proud of you both!"

When they were alone again, Layne resumed glaring. This didn't seem to faze Katsu, who stood and checked his watch. "Seven months," he said. "Better get started." After he sauntered away, Layne dropped the tough guy act and did a panicked inventory of the room, trying find anyone as single and hopeless as he now felt.

In the colder or wetter months, youth group members would hustle inside the church building and wait for the meeting to start. But with summer not yet giving way to fall, the outdoors still offered plenty of warmth to enjoy. That meant loitering in the parking lot until the very last minute. Layne arrived at the next meeting with new determination. He had a plan, starting with conducting a survey of who was with whom. Every car that pulled in, he would approach, using deductive reasoning to find out if any single men were inside. If they were, he added them to the list of potentials. If not, he fought down frustration before moving on.

He reoriented on the sound of another engine. The red hatchback belonged to Bonnie, but she had passengers. One of whom he hadn't seen for quite some time. Jason Grant stepped out of the car, then rushed toward the church building, as if he had urgent business. Funny! And also interesting, because there was a bounty on his head. Layne sent a quick text message to Kelly Phillips, who had been asking about Jason recently. He provided the location and kept his eyes on the scene. Emma got out of the car next, Bonnie soon pressing her up against it and putting on a show that demonstrated just how much they loved each other.

Why couldn't Layne find something like that? Even for a brief second so he could take a photo. "Aren't they adorable?" he said when he heard crutches approach and stop next to him. Forget adorable, Kelly was hot! Way out of his league, not that he hadn't tried once when he was younger. As usual, no luck. What was he missing that everyone else had found? He stared enviously at Emma and Bonnie, who continued mashing mouths. "Geez, look at those two go! Do you think lesbians are better kissers than gay guys? Maybe I should go undercover—dress in drag and find some butch beauty to rock my world."

"Sounds like a plan," Kelly said without much interest. "Where's Jason?"

"He had to use the little boys' room. I guess the ride was too long for him." Layne pulled his attention away from the PDA. "Hey, I wanted to ask… Is he single?"

Kelly thought about it. "Ever see that movie about the dog who kept waiting for his dead owner to return home, even though years had gone by?"

"Oh my gosh! That's so sad!"

"Yes, it is. Hopefully he gets a happier ending, but for now, don't waste your time."

"Oh. Are you single?"

Kelly laughed. "What exactly is this about?"

Finally! A sympathetic ear! "You wouldn't believe me even if I told you. Actually, it would make a phenomenal television drama, starring Robert Pattinson as yours truly. It all started when—"

"Excuse me." Kelly said, moving toward the church.

Layne turned and saw Jason leaving the building. That seemed to be the only reason Kelly had been coming to group lately. He wasn't sure what that was about. Were they in love? Layne didn't have time to worry about it. Not with his own problems, which he still felt like talking about, so he continued. Let people think he was crazy, he didn't care. Talking helped him organize his thoughts. He paced as he did so, reaching the end, which at least he had an audience for, because Kelly had returned with Jason in tow.

"—so basically, Katsu thinks he's going to humiliate me and force me away from this group, when really, I'm more determined than ever to find the love of my life. I should probably thank him!"

"Don't let Katsu get to you," Kelly said. "It wasn't cool how he made fun of you at the previous meeting."

"Who's Katsu?" Jason asked, shaking his head.

"Super-hot Asian guy," Kelly replied.

Jason's face lit up. "Oh! You mean Kat? Yeah, I've had a few impure thoughts about him!"

"You're not alone," Kelly said. "Too bad he joined the group after William and I met, because man would I love giving a saucer of milk to that cat!"

Jason chuckled. "You're so bad!"

"Neither of you is helping!" Layne complained.

"Fine, fine," Kelly said, still grinning. "Tell us what's wrong."

"I already did, but if you insist. It all started when—"

"The condensed version," Kelly said.

"Katsu and I have a bet. He thinks I can't find anyone willing to kiss me. Care to prove him wrong?"

"Taken," Kelly said instantly.

"Too heartbroken," Jason said just as quickly.

Layne sighed. "There's got to be someone."

"What about Danny?"

Layne wasn't sure which of them said it. He was too shocked by the suggestion. His eyes moved unwillingly toward the far end of the parking lot where an old matte-black muscle car was parked, its windows so tinted that seeing inside was impossible. Even from a distance the muted thud of pounding bass could be heard.

"Danny Darko?" he said incredulously. That wasn't really his last name. Probably. Too many legends surrounded Danny to be sure of anything. Normally he never left his car. He'd show up for each meeting and just park there. Layne had heard that he liked cruising and was gifted with an insatiable twelve-inch cock. He'd also heard that Danny was really a woman dressed as a man, or that he was elderly and only posing as a teenager. Cannibal, serial killer, escaped psych patient... The rumors went on and on, none of them good. Except that first one, but honestly, Layne wasn't into casual hookups. He was too fond of romantic movies, especially the kind that ended with him surrounded by sopping wet tissues. He wanted a heart-wrenching love story, not a quick fix in the back seat.

"He's single," Kelly said. "Probably."

"Have you ever seen him?" Layne asked.

"Yes. I talked to Danny before he was old enough to drive. Back then he would drag a chair into the far corner and just sit there."

That eliminated him being some creepy old guy. The group leaders made sure to check IDs for ages.

"Might be worth a shot," Jason pressed.

Layne bit his bottom lip, looking back to the grisly car. "Is he hot?"

Kelly paused tellingly long before he answered. "They say opposites attract."

Another vehicle pulled into the parking lot, a blue BMW. Layne already knew who was behind the wheel. The car parked and Katsu stepped out. So did Thomas. It didn't take long for Katsu to spot him. He looked at Layne, then the two guys he was with, and gave a thumbs-up with a questioning expression. Asshole. Layne didn't have a chance with Jason or Kelly, but he wasn't about to lose this bet without a fight.

"Wish me luck," he murmured. "If you never see me again, tell my mom I love her, and that yes, I was the one who stole her favorite china doll. I thought it would be fun to put makeup on it, which honestly went really well. Then I decided to pierce its ears. A hammer was involved, as were nails, and when it all went wrong, I was just as broken up as the doll."

When his friends didn't laugh, he turned to discover them already halfway to the church. He could only hope that Danny had a higher appreciation for his wit. Steeling himself, he walked toward the car, putting a little swing into his hips. No doubt Danny was eyeing him in the rearview mirror and sharpening a knife— No no. Start over. No doubt Danny was eyeing him in the rearview mirror and rubbing his crotch hungrily. Actually, that wasn't much better, but Layne was out of time for revisions, because he had reached the car.

He went to the window on the driver's side, unable to see much of anything beyond, so he knocked on it. The glass slid down just a crack. Loud music leaked out, sounding dark and industrial. The kind of music angry killer robots would prefer. A pair of sunglasses stared out at him as the volume lowered.

"Hi!" Layne said. "Care for some company?" Great! Now he sounded like a prostitute.

The window rolled back up. No surprise there. He was about to walk away when he heard a click, the passenger side door now ajar. An invitation? Or a trap! Layne supposed that, if he was about to be murdered, the reason he had put himself in a dangerous situation would come out and Katsu would get the blame. Not a bad consolation prize, even though he would be dead and unable to enjoy it.

Resigned to his fate, Layne walked around the car and got inside. He noticed the interior first. Voodoo seemed to be the theme. A shrunken head hung from the rearview mirror, the shift stick was topped with a skull, and a cone of pungent incense burned in the ashtray. All of this was illuminated by a red roof light. "Neat," Layne manage to squeak, turning to the driver. His hair was long, dyed black, and shoulder length. It seemed to blend in with the black clothes, which themselves were lost against the black seat cover. Layne detected a theme!

"Don't you just love black?" he asked, attempting to make conversation. "They say it's slimming, but try telling that to a killer whale, am I right?"

Danny's head nodded. Probably. It was hard to tell. He didn't move much.

The Silence of the Lambs came to mind, especially the part where the victim tried to make her kidnapper recognize her as a human being by saying her name. "I'm Layne, by the way. I like rainbows, grandma hugs, and not being murdered."

Danny reached out to lower the volume on the stereo further. Then he spoke. "My grandma died yesterday."

"Oh! I'm sorry."

Danny shrugged. "Doesn't matter. We're all going to die."

"Hopefully not today," Layne said. "Especially not right now. I *really* like my life."

"So do I."

Really? Wow. Common ground! "You've got a nice car," Layne said. "I'm assuming it's not your mother's. That's what I'm stuck driving. It's a minivan. Yuck!"

"I really hate minivans."

"Me too!"

"Almost as much as I hate people."

"Oh. Why's that?"

Danny's shoulders rose and fell. "Doesn't matter. Nothing does."

The guy was a barrel of laughs, but Layne tried working with him anyway. "I know, right? I'm always saying that. 'Who cares' is pretty much my motto. Why let people, or minivans, or dead grandmas get you down?"

Danny was quiet. One song came to an end, the pause before the next one feeling like an eternity. Was this when the stabbing would begin? "Are you here on a bet?"

"Who me?" Layne asked, hand casually inching toward the door handle.

"Yes. Are you in my car because someone dared you?"

"Would it matter if I was?"

"No."

Wow, the guy was exceptionally apathetic! Maybe he could use that to his advantage. "Um. I know this is sort of random, but do you want to make out?"

"Okay."

Danny remained stationary. That meant it was up to him. Layne turned in his seat and leaned forward, lips wanting to pull back as they neared that face. It's not that Danny was ugly. Between the sunglasses, hair, and gloom, he couldn't see enough to decide. Layne just found the whole situation creepy. He closed his eyes as the kiss began. Half a minute later, they shot open again. This felt good! Really good! Danny's head was barely moving, but his mouth, lips, and tongue had a life of their own. Layne was struggling to keep up. He nearly forgot why he was there, but a bet was a bet. He pulled out his phone and strained to see the screen.

"Souvenir photo," he took a break to explain.

"Whatever," Danny responded.

They resumed kissing, Layne trying to use one hand to hold his camera and hit the right button. After a few minutes of this, he pulled back, short of breath. "That was incredible!"

"I like kissing," Danny said, voice devoid of enthusiasm.

"I noticed."

Danny leaned back, making his crotch available. "I also like other stuff."

Layne was sorely tempted to find out if the twelve-inches rumor was true, but that really wasn't his style. The goal was to prove he wasn't hopeless, not sleep with a bunch of strangers. "I gotta run," he said, grasping for a more elaborate excuse.

"That's cool."

He should have known an explanation wasn't needed.

"Thanks for… um. Thanks!" he said, opening the door and letting daylight in.

"You know where to find me."

In a fantasy later tonight, most likely. Layne stumbled out into the parking lot, realized he was rock hard, and tried covering himself. Then he noticed that everyone had gone inside for the meeting and stopped worrying about it. Checking his phone, he saw a bunch of dark blurry images. Only one of them had turned out well, him wide-eyed while someone else's tongue filled his cheek. Good enough! One down, six to go!

*****

Layne lay on his stomach in bed, staring at the most recent yearbook and wondering if depression was contagious. Maybe he had caught it from making out with Danny. The pages currently open featured rows of smiling faces, his own among them. He'd made sure to tan before the photo was taken. His blonde hair had been highlighted naturally by the sun. His parents wouldn't let him get his teeth bleached, so he had used a whitening toothpaste and worn lip gloss for extra shine. He'd even worked golden glitter into his bangs. The other kids had teased him mercilessly, calling it metallic dandruff. Maybe he was ridiculous. Layne tried not to care. What was the point in being gay if it meant being subjected to the same narrow limitations that straight guys were? He didn't want to play sports or wear boring clothes. Layne wanted to have fun! He just wished someone wanted to have fun with him.

Phil liked him. The former group leader hadn't made the first move. That had been Layne. After watching *Pretty Woman,* he had decided he needed an older man and started flirting. To his delight, Phil had reciprocated. Sure he was married and abusing his position and probably just longing for his lost youth, but someone had actually given Layne attention. That had been worth all the problems and complications. At first, anyway. Layne eventually had to choose between continuing an unhealthy relationship and rescuing his self-esteem. Now he wished he had abandoned his pride, because boy was he tired of being alone!

He could only assume that he himself was the problem. Layne wasn't totally oblivious. His sense of humor wasn't for everyone, and his parents had always complained about his energy, calling him hyper. He did tend to wear people out. Only someone with the patience of a saint seemed capable of putting up with him. Speaking of which…

Shutting the yearbook and rolling over, he grabbed his phone and dialed a friend.

"Hello!" Lisa said, sounding chipper. "Are you excited about the first day of school tomorrow?"

Layne groaned. "Don't remind me. Can I come over?"

"Sure! You can help me clean my lizard pit."

Layne glanced at the phone. Lisa was the perfect straight man to his comedy routine, innocent and oblivious, but sometimes she seemed to be feeding him lines on purpose. Rather than responding to this one, he hung up the phone, left his house, and walked across the street. That's all it took to reach Lisa. They had been neighbors their entire lives, standing silently at the bus stop together for most years. Only when he started going to the gay youth group and she showed up a few months later did they realize they had something in common.

The similarities began and ended there. Their rooms attested to this. Layne's was draped in colorful fabrics and was full of exotic garage sale finds. Old lamps, hand-painted cabinets, postcards sent from people long since gone... Anything different. Lisa's room looked like it belonged to an eight-year-old boy. Wildlife posters covered the wall, plastic dinosaurs filled the window sill, and the top of the dresser was taken up by the terrarium home of Madam Ruby the iguana. At times, being in Lisa's room made Layne feel like he had a little brother. He wouldn't be surprised to discover that she thought of him as an older sister.

After being let in by Mrs. Holmestead, he found Lisa sitting on the bedroom floor next to a trashcan and a terrarium. Madam Ruby sat on the bed, tongue flicking out occasionally while her eyes bored into his soul, like she could see all of his previous sins.

"A little help?" Lisa said. She didn't want him to lift the giant glass container, even though he was nearly twice her height. No, his job was to hold open the trash bag while she tilted the terrarium contents into it. He studied her as she worked. Lisa was small and had brown hair nearly devoid of style, the ends curling inward just above her cheeks. If her hair was any shorter, her head would have resembled a giant mushroom. Layne never left the house without styling product in his hair. He fussed over fashion while she was a T-shirt and shorts kind of girl. Neither of them were particularly lucky in love.

"What are we doing wrong?" he asked.

"I want to put fresh plants inside," Lisa replied. "Little potted ones that don't die after just a few weeks."

"I mean with our lives," Layne said. "We're not getting any younger. How many proposals have you gotten this year? It's time you settled down, young lady!"

Lisa's cheeks grew rosy. "Angie asked for my phone number."

"Seriously?" he whined.

"Sorry."

"Maybe I should ask Danny for his."

Lisa brightened at the idea. "Maybe you should! Do you love him?"

Only she could make such a ridiculous question not sound sarcastic. "Yes, but alas, our differences are irreconcilable. Besides, you know I need to kiss six more guys before I settle down with anyone. I guess you could say I'm playing the field before I make a final decision."

"You're such a stud!"

Was she making fun of him or trying to be encouraging? Either way… "Thanks. But between you and me, I'm already out of ideas. Nobody else at group is willing to kiss me, and I'm not old enough for a gay bar."

"I've got an idea!" Lisa set down the tank. "Let's ask Madam Ruby!"

Oh boy. The iguana's name came from some old movie. He didn't remember which. Lisa had convinced herself that the lizard had psychic powers, although she did get disturbingly good ideas from playing this game. She went to the bed and picked the creature up, waving it around in the air. "Let's see what Madam Ruby sees!" She said that every single time. When she spoke again, she used a croaky voice that seriously creeped him out. "You must try the online dating. There you will find a man willing to kiss you."

Like he hadn't thought of that. "Nobody ever looks like they do in their photos."

Lisa opened her eyes. "Does that matter for your bet?"

"No," he admitted. "I guess it doesn't."

She set down the iguana. Layne helped her put the terrarium back on the stand. His interest was piqued when it came time to decorate the interior. He amused himself with dreams of a lizard-sized house with a little couch and beds. And a long dining room table for entertaining company! Maybe he should get a lizard of his own. Monsieur Rouge!

He noticed Lisa staring at him. Probably because he was giggling to himself.

Layne sighed. "I'm a freak, aren't I?"

"No! Well… No!"

"Be honest. That's why no guy wants me. I'm not bad-looking, right? It's not that, so it's got to be my personality."

"I like you," Lisa said, eyes brimming with innocent affection.

"Thanks. I like you too. But if you had to guess why guys don't like me, what would the reason be?"

"Ummm...." Lisa put on a big show of thinking about it. "It's important to be a good listener?"

He ran that through his niceness decoder. "You think I talk too much?"

"Maybe a little."

He did love to talk. Who didn't love the sound of their own voice? Still, if that was the only problem...

"And you're kind of silly."

That took him by surprise. "What's wrong with silly?"

Lisa pressed her lips together. "Hmmm. I don't know."

"Then what did you mean?"

"Well, all the movies you watch, are they full of funny guys?"

She meant romances. Most of the guys were brooding and misunderstood. Only the women were allowed to be funny, laughing their way through the world and encouraging their men to lighten up. "So basically I'm the girl."

Lisa shrugged. "I think you're sweet."

"Because you're a lesbian. I'm trying to attract men who like men." No fats, no fems. That's what many of the classified ads made sure to state. No overweight people, and nobody feminine. Layne didn't consider himself that way. Maybe he was a little flamboyant, but he didn't lisp or swish. Still, he could try to man up. That couldn't hurt his chances.

"You're the best," he said, kissing Lisa on the cheek. Or should he punch her arm instead? No, too late. Maybe next time. Right now he had to find a man and *be* a man!

His date's name was Stewart the College Boy. Presumably that wasn't his legal name, but it's how Layne thought of him. Madam Ruby's advice—or was it Lisa's?—had paid off! Layne had gone home, taken a shower, and didn't style his hair. He simply brushed it to one side with his fingers. Then he took a photo while glowering at his phone's camera and used the image in a new dating profile. He limited his answers to just five words or less per question, no exclamation points or adverbs. Instead of "I totally love to dance, especially if we're talking Lady Gaga! Little monster here. Heeeey!!!" he wrote "Dancing is fun." or "Movies are great."

Soon he had a profile that only vaguely represented who he

was, but the results were promising! At the moment he was sitting in a restaurant. Without his parents! Stewart was a handsome man with ebony skin and small gold-framed glasses with round lenses. He was a philosophy major, which made for stimulating conversation that Layne was working very hard not to dominate.

"—and that's why the Third Republic French labor movement was doomed to fail. Political motivations might be borne out of social schisms, but only cross-demographic solidarity can propel an ideology into becoming a broadly accepted virtue."

"You're absolutely right," Layne said, trying to make his voice sound deep. "I've never heard anyone put it so—" What was the word? Not sassily. Sussysink? Succinctly! Wait, did that mean what he thought it did? Better not risk it. "I'm just blown away."

Stewart smiled. "I'm enjoying our discourse too, although if I didn't know better, I'd think you were much younger than your profile says."

"Nope, I'm twenty-one. Get carded all the time when buying cigarettes."

Stewart frowned. "You're a smoker?"

"No! I just buy them for friends. Or as presents around the holidays." Oh god, Lisa was right! The more he talked, the more he screwed things up! "Tell me more about schisms."

Stewart narrowed his eyes thoughtfully. "Well, if you think about it, each of us is born into one and are prematurely influenced by societal architypes belonging to extinct generational philosophies that were themselves the product of political propaganda. It's crucial then to liberate ourselves from—"

Layne nodded along, not understanding half the words or even wanting to. He felt relieved when the waiter brought their food, since eating would help keep his mouth occupied. Unfortunately, the meal involved tiny beads that might be fish eggs, and for whatever reason, the potatoes were covered in black sprinkles that smelled like feet.

"Don't you just love truffles?" Stewart enthused.

"The quality is irrefutable," Layne responded, feeling proud of himself for using a fancy word.

Stewart smiled. "You're a strange guy. Tell me more about yourself. What are you studying?"

College things! Think of college things! "I guess you could say that I'm studying to help others study, because I plan on becoming a professor."

"Interesting! What are your thoughts on tenure?"

"Well," Layne said, not having a clue what that meant. "I think you can guess my feelings on that subject."

Stewart studied him. Then cracked a smile. "You're biased! That's what I think!"

"Guilty as charged."

"My personal stance is that a middle ground approach of reform is required to—"

Layne resumed nodding. Is this what having a serious conversation was like? If so, he wanted out! He also never wanted to eat anything but fast food again, because when the meal came to an end, his half of the bill was fifty bucks, which was most of his current savings. Cheap burgers tasted better anyway. Still, he felt a sense of accomplishment for having made it this far into the masquerade. Maybe he had a future as a secret agent.

"Have you taken in the view from the back patio?" Stewart asked after they paid. "It really is breathtaking. Come see it with me."

At this point he expected the view to be a bunch of dry and dusty books filled with boring stuff that dead people had once believed. He was surprised then to find a small garden path that led to a view of the Colorado River.

"Very nice," he said, turning and putting his back to the rail. "Dare I say… romantic."

"Dare away!" Stewart came close, pressing their bodies together. This was it!

"Just a sec," Layne said, pulling his phone free.

Stewart looked over at it and smiled. "For posterity?"

Whatever the hell that meant! Layne just nodded and leaned forward. He was smarter this time, recording a video that he could later take a still frame from. Stewart was no Danny Darko when it came to kissing, but he wasn't bad. Layne was just getting into it when Stewart pulled away, chuckling under his breath.

"*Erasthai!*"

Layne shook his head. "Sorry?"

"The Greek word for eros. You're determined to prove Plato's theory correct, aren't you? If transcendental beauty is understood as—"

"You know what I like?" Layne interrupted. "Hats."

"Hats?" Stewart repeated.

"That's right. Hats. I like putting them on, taking them off, or throwing them like a Frisbee. Women's hats, men's hats, even those made for dogs. I don't think I've ever met a hat that I didn't like. I also eat peanut butter on canned pineapple slices, and you know that technology they used in *The Lord of the Rings* movies to make people look small like Hobbits? I think they should use that on elephants. Preferably in a music video."

Stewart shook his head. "I don't understand."

"Good. Now you know how I felt all through dinner. I'd like to thank you anyway, because you've made me realize that I'm perfectly happy being who I am. Now if you'll excuse me, I need to call my mother."

"Your mother?"

"She's got the minivan. Duh! I'm only seventeen. I don't have my own car yet."

"Seventeen?" Stewart repeated.

Layne nodded happily. "You're going to love my mom. Just wait until you meet her!"

That did it. Stewart stammered an excuse and left. Layne breathed out, turned to consider the river, and then looked down at his phone. Number two was out of the way. He prayed that bachelor number three would be more fun.

Online dating sites? Those were for old people. Deception? Only fools bothered with such things! Layne had streamlined his approach, thanks to a phone app called Grindr. It was fairly new, and from what he understood, most people used it for casual encounters. That's what he was looking for. Sort of. When he created a profile, he made sure to be very clear about his intentions:

I'm into kissing other guys while taking selfies. Usies? Groupies! No… Let's stick with selfie and do away with any drama. Just kiss me *while I click* us.

He was especially pleased with the last line. That little lure would net him all the boys. Before the next group meeting, Layne would have the remaining five photos he needed, no doubt about it. He activated the app after school one day, disappointed with how far away all potential make-out partners were. This problem was easily solved. He took the minivan downtown and caught his first fish. Layne checked the man's profile. *xxHeadbanger87xx* was the user name, and while he had a buzzed scalp instead of long hair, the piercings were definitely metal.

Deciding he was cute enough, Layne shared his location in more detail. He was standing outside of Starbucks, sipping coffee. Technically he was only sipping tap water out of a paper cup he had begged one of the employees to give him. His recent date had drained his funds too much for real coffee, but such things were mostly about appearances anyway. xxHeadbanger87xx showed up mere minutes later. He was tall and lanky. And a little ripe. No deodorant in the heat of summer? Really? Convincing himself it was part of the punk-rock appeal, Layne smiled and held out a hand. Then he tried holding his breath. Definitely ripe!

"Tell me how this works," xxHeadbanger87xx said, all grins as they shook. "We just get right to it?"

That had been the plan, but Layne quickly decided a little prep was in order. "Gum?" he asked, setting his water down to frantically pat his pockets.

"Sure. So what's this all about?"

"I read that kissing is a great way to burn calories and I'm hoping to slim down."

"Ha!"

That laugh was carried on a gust of breath, one that smelled like raw onions and… feet?

"Had lunch recently?" Layne asked, nearly crying out with joy when his patting hands detected a small rectangle in his jeans. Gum!

"Sorry," xxHeadbanger87xx replied. "My girlfriend makes the craziest limburger sandwiches. She's from Wisconsin. Cheese head!"

Girlfriend? Cheese head? Was he mentally disturbed? And why did people enjoy eating things that smelled like feet? No matter. Layne popped a stick of gum in his mouth, then offered one that—thank everything holy—was accepted. They chewed in silence. Awkward but necessary. When satisfied, Layne spit his gum into the wrapper. xxHeadbanger87xx swallowed his.

"Okay!" Layne said, making sure his phone was ready. "Let's get started!"

xxHeadbanger87xx didn't waste any time. He was all tongue in his technique. Was that a barbell Layne detected? Sixteen gauge, if he wasn't mistaken. With a hint of pickle. Yuck. He already regretted the gum, since spearmint and limburger apparently didn't mix well, or cancel each other out. He winced while taking photos until he felt certain he had enough. Then he pulled back.

xxHeadbanger87xx followed, licking all the way from Layne's chin up to the tip of his nose. "So, what's for dessert?"

"Something smelly," Layne wagered.

"You want me to eat your ass? I'm game!"

Oh boy. "I would!" Layne said, sidling away. "I really would, but I have curfew."

"It's not even six yet!"

"I have very strict parents. We're Scientologists. Tom Cruise calls every night to make sure I'm in bed before dinner. It's easier to just combine the two. Talk about crumbs in the sheets! Yeah, so… Bye!"

He hurried down the street to the minivan. Then he sped all the way home, deciding any police officer would accept this situation as an emergency. As soon as he arrived, he rushed through the house to his bathroom and grabbed the bottle of mouthwash with shaking hands. He guzzled the contents until his cheeks bulged and his tongue burned with antiseptic. Then he spit it out. Rinse, repeat, and brush brush brush! A thorough face washing was required too, along with more gargling. By the time Layne went to bed that night, the inside of his mouth was sore and red from excessive hygiene, and yet somehow, it still managed to feel dirty.

No more strangers. That was Layne's new philosophy. He would still flirt shamelessly with any cute guy he saw mere seconds after having met him, but when it came to kissing and more, he wanted to be comfortable and certain that he actually liked the person. Besides, he'd gotten a good head start. He had months to find another four guys to kiss. He'd probably have that many boyfriends over the coming winter. His dry spell couldn't last forever. Right?

For the most part, Layne tried putting the whole stupid bet out of mind. Tried, because Katsu never let him forget. At every group meeting, he made sure to bring it up. Even worse, it turned out that the last day of their bet was on March sixteenth. Layne had until midnight. That meant the photos were due on St. Patrick's Day. Katsu incorporated this into his teasing, keeping tally on how many days remained and always letting Layne know. "One hundred and seventy-eight days to get lucky!" "One hundred and thirty-four days to get lucky!" "Ninety-three days to get lucky!"

They were down to the double digits and Layne hadn't been on a single date. He still refused to lock lips with a total stranger. He also remained clueless as to what he should do until a chance encounter at the grocery store. Layne was in the cosmetic aisle, fondling things he couldn't afford, when a guy caught his eye. A familiar one, because Harold had often frequented his fantasies. Brown hair, dark eyebrows, and an easy smile—he looked like he'd stepped off the page of a men's fashion magazine. Funny then that today he was wearing an old T-shirt and cut-off jean shorts, natural tassels created where they frayed. How did he make that look good? Then again, Harold had always looked good, which is why Layne had spent so many gay youth meetings committing every detail of him to memory.

Harold noticed him staring and gave an upward nod. Layne took this as an invitation to approach.

"Hi! Long time no see!"

"Hey…" The bright-toothed smile remained, as did the adorable dimples in his cheeks, but Harold's eyes narrowed slightly as he struggled to remember. "Lance, right?"

Close enough! When a guy that hot speaks to you, there's no point in splitting hairs. "You remember me!" he said, refusing to feel pathetic. "I never see you in group anymore."

"Got too old."

"Too big for your britches?" Layne said, eyes treacherously darting downward without his consent. "Aren't you cold wearing those?" He asked in an attempt to cover. "Or does your natural hotness keep you warm?"

"Laundry day," Harold said, looking decidedly less comfortable. "You still go to meetings?"

"Yup! Still gay, still young."

"Say hi to the guys for me. Okay?"

"Will do!"

Harold nodded again. "See you around."

"I wish!"

Layne watched him push a shopping cart away, and decided the encounter had been no more embarrassing than most conversations he had with single guys. Not that Harold was likely to be available. Then again… As Layne turned his attention to the nearest shelf, he remembered a rumor. Harold was available to anyone with enough money because he was some sort of high-class escort. Scandalous! And sexy. He wondered if he could empty out his college fund early. Although he might not need to.

Layne ran through the store, looking down each aisle. Harold wasn't a stranger! They were on a first name basis! Sure, only one of them had that down completely, but they did sort of know each other. He found Harold looking between two different brands of orange juice, reading the labels and trying to decide which was good enough for him.

"Fancy meeting you here," Layne said.

Harold chuckled nervously. Or was he terrified? Either way…

"I've heard things about you," Layne said, wagging a finger. "You have a very interesting profession."

"I have no idea what you're talking about," Harold said without missing a beat.

"Professional companion?" Layne pressed. "A gentleman of discretion? A lady of the night?"

"I'm definitely no lady!" Harold protested.

"Rent boy?"

Harold glared. "What do you want?"

Layne batted his eyelashes. "How much would a kiss cost?"

Harold set both juice containers back in the cooler and turned to leave.

"Wait!" Layne said. "It's not what you think." He launched into his story, Harold less insulted and more amused as it progressed. By the end of the tale, he was smiling and shaking his head. "So all I need is one little kiss, Layne explained. "I figure that can't be *too* expensive."

Harold looked him over. "Fifty bucks."

"Oh." Layne pulled out his wallet. It was fabric and Velcro. A T-Rex roared on the outside. Lisa had given it to him as a present. "I've got twelve dollars," he declared after peering inside.

"Close enough," Harold said, holding out his hand. Once the crinkled bills were placed in his palm, Harold pocketed them and looked around. "Does the backdrop matter?"

"Nope!" Layne said, hoping his breath was still minty fresh from the last time he had brushed. "I'm in your capable hands!"

Harold smirked and stepped forward. One strong hand grabbed Layne's hip and pulled him near. The other was on the back of his neck. Harold's lips were soft. The kiss started gently and built slowly, tongue only coming into play toward the end, and even then it wasn't overwhelming. Just enough to tease him and make him desire more, which Layne definitely did!

"There ya go," Harold said, withdrawing. "Happy?"

"Yes," Layne confessed. "Although I forgot to take a photo."

Harold rolled his eyes, made sure Layne had his phone held ready, and kissed him again. This time it was merely a firm peck held in place, but it made for a convincing enough photo.

"Thanks," Layne said, heart still fluttering. "Can I get a receipt? One with your phone number on it?"

"No," Harold said. "In fact, tell no one about this or— Uhhh." His expression became strained. "My pimp will cut you."

"Your secret is safe with me," Layne said, already fawning over the photographic evidence.

"You're good," Harold said, just as he was pushing away his cart. "The other three guys you're going to kiss? They're the lucky ones. Just remember that."

"Aw!" Layne said, twirling around happily. "Thank you."

Harold shot him a wink. "My pleasure."

He probably said that to all of his clients, but Layne still felt lighter than air as he left the grocery store, too broke to buy anything but feeling a lot richer in other ways.

"Fifty-one days to get lucky!"

These words had haunted him ever since Katsu spoke them recently. Time was running out, and unless Layne thought of more hot escorts he happened to know and a pile of cash he'd forgotten, he was officially screwed. He really did need luck, and when returning home from school one day in late January, he was walking across the lawn when he found his solution. A patch of clover, half of it dead, but the winter had been mild and the plant was already showing signs of new growth. Layne fell to his knees. Katsu was right. Luck is exactly what he needed!

Twenty minutes later, he was still weeding through the clover, trying to find one with four leaves, when someone spoke.

"What are you doing?"

He looked up to discover Lisa standing there.

"What are *you* doing?" he said accusingly. "You disappeared from school. Hiding from your gambling debts?"

"Dentist." Lisa pointed to a sticker of a smiling tooth that she wore on her shirt. "Hey, I don't gamble!"

"Maybe you should start. I've always wanted to stage an intervention. Give me something to work with!"

"Are you looking for bugs?"

"Four-leaf clovers. The more, the merrier."

Lisa got on the grass next to him and helped with the search. She wasn't very determined and gave up a few minutes later to offer an alternative. "I have a rabbit's foot."

"Gross! Can I borrow it?"

"Yup! It's in my room."

That's where they ended up. Lisa dug around in her closet, opening an old shoebox and pulling out a turquoise rabbit's foot.

"You can keep it," she said. "My uncle gave it to me. I find it disturbing. I was thinking of burying it."

"We'll hold a funeral *if* it does a good job and lands me a man. Three men!" Layne rubbed the foot experimentally. Then his shoulders slumped. "I'm so going to lose."

"You just need to start dating," Lisa said. "No more yucky guys."

"You think all guys are yucky."

"I mean no more weird people you don't care about. Find a guy you love and kiss him. Who cares what Katsu thinks?"

He sighed. Her advice was sound. If he could find someone he loved and who loved him back, he wouldn't care about winning the bet. "I've tried."

"Once. You went on one date from that site and met one person on Grunter."

"Grindr," he corrected, keeping his teeth clamped shut and intentionally not pronouncing any vowels. "You think I should try again?"

"The dating site, yes. And don't worry about kissing anyone. Just use it to meet guys and get to know them."

"And if that doesn't work?" Layne said. "If on Saint Patrick's Day I'm still single *and* I lose the bet?" He shook his head. "I won't be able to handle the humiliation."

"It's a silly game," Lisa chided.

"I just wish it was over. And that I'd won."

"Me too. I'd kiss you if I was a boy."

He looked over at her. The sentiment was sweet. And the scheme was brilliant! Layne tossed aside the rabbit's foot. Forget luck! He'd use cunning! "Excellent idea! You'll become a boy and then you'll kiss me!"

Lisa frowned. "Transitioning takes a very long time. I'd have to start with therapy and—"

"Shut up and follow me!"

A few seconds later, he was standing in her older brother's bedroom. Alone. Then he had to go back to Lisa's room, apologize for telling her to shut up, and return to her brother's room. Once there, Layne started raiding the dresser drawers. That would have been a lot more exciting if her brother was hot, but he wasn't. Layne soon had an outfit picked out. All he needed was a ball cap, which he found hanging on the back of the door.

"Are you trying a new look?" Lisa asked.

"No, you are. To the bathroom!"

Lisa rarely wore makeup, so she had none to wash off. They repurposed some dark eyeshadow her mother had bought her, applying a dusting to Lisa's cheeks to create a five o'clock shadow. After putting her in a Polo, popping the collar, adding the ball cap and Layne's sunglasses… She looked like a sexual predator who wanted to remain anonymous. Close enough! Layne grabbed her hand and dragged her back to the bedroom. She stared as he lowered the blinds, making the room suitably dim. Then he turned to face her.

"I don't really want to kiss you," Lisa said.

"I know. The feeling is mutual. But this is how it's done in Hollywood. All the gay actors need a fake wife or they get crappy roles. I need you to do this for the sake of my career."

"But you aren't a—"

"Shhhh," Layne said, placing a finger to her lips. "The time for words is over. I've seen the way you look at me, how you watch as I put on powder and base, your loins catching fire as you blur your eyes and pretend I'm a girl."

"Could you dress up like a girl now?" Lisa said, moving his hand away.

"Sure, but we'd have to go back to my place, since you only own boy clothes."

"Oh. Right."

"Just use the power of make believe. Think of someone really pretty. Like Ellen. I'm just a very butch version of Ellen DeGeneres."

"Actually you're more feminine than—"

Layne kissed her, trying to utilize some of the tricks he had learned from Harold, but he stopped short of using tongue. Then he broke away and looked Lisa in the eye. "Well?" he said, voice husky.

"I'm definitely gay," she replied.

"Yup! Me too. This is a good look for you though. It's very *Boys Don't Cry*. If you want to mislead straight girls, now's your chance. See?"

He showed her the photo, and even Lisa had to admit it was convincing. Five down and two to go!

Birthdays were magical. Layne couldn't remember one that hadn't been successful. When he was young, this meant getting the presents he most desired. As he grew older, the parties mattered more since his social life—despite all its imperfections—meant the most to him. His parents had always been generous, but they went overboard on his birthday, all because he was a miracle baby. After struggling for years to conceive, his parents consulting doctors and getting nothing but bad news, it shouldn't have been possible. And yet, here he was! Maybe that gave him superpowers and explained why, on his birthday, everything seemed to go just right.

The party was already shaping up to be epic. Layne had invited everyone from group *except* Katsu and his boyfriend. Layne had also invited friends from school. Everyone was allowed to bring a plus one, and most did. Kelly showed up with his new boyfriend, Nathaniel, who looked like an absolute brute. Layne was already envious, and a little peeved when Kelly threatened to steal the spotlight just because his crutches were gone. He had some sort of bionic leg now or something. Layne was happy for him, but it was *his* birthday, and that's where the focus should remain. Still, a good host was a generous host.

"I think it's fabulous," Layne said, looping arms with Kelly and guiding him toward the party. He used this as an excuse to take hold of Nathaniel's arm too, which felt strong and hairy and probably tasted like sweat. Geez, he really needed to find a man!

Or get wasted. "Speaking of which, did you bring my present?"

With his free hand, Nathaniel held up a gift-wrapped present with an unmistakable outline. "You mean the bottle you're still three years too young to drink from?"

"That's the one!" Layne released them both so he could nab it. "This should liven things up!"

Kelly nodded toward the inflatable castle. "You might want to think twice about getting people drunk and shoving them in your ball pit."

"It's not a ball pit," Layne corrected. "It's a bounce house, and it happens to be my most ingenious plan yet. Just imagine me and a handsome boy jumping around in that thing, bumping into each other and getting all handsy until he falls on top of me and… Well, paint your own picture."

"So who's the lucky guy?"

That was the million-dollar question, but he had it narrowed down to three. His guests of honor! He nodded to one corner of the yard where they were still clustered together, having arrived half an hour earlier. Layne had taken Lisa's advice and was searching for someone he was willing to date. He spent a lot of time in chat rooms. That's where he'd met Rico, his spicy Latino, but if that wasn't enough, he came with a spare. Rico's twin brother Tito was also present and also gay. They had brought along a friend too, a yummy redhead named Noah. Three choices, and with two guys left to kiss—on his birthday!—Layne was in for a very interesting evening.

"Which one are you after?" Kelly asked.

"Any of them will do," Layne said. The twins could singlehandedly win the wager for him. "Or all of them. I'm hedging my bets. I figure I'm tripling my odds by inviting all three here."

Kelly looked impressed. Or entertained. "Are they from the youth group?"

"Imported. God bless the internet!"

"Hungry," Nathaniel muttered.

"If you'll excuse me," Kelly said, moving to guide Nathaniel away. "I have to go feed my man-beast."

"Have fun, you lucky bastard." Layne watched them head toward the buffet, feeling a pang of jealousy. Then he remembered that he had options. By this time tomorrow, he might be taking turns popping grapes into Tito's and Rico's mouths. He was headed toward them when his mother made an appearance. What the hell? She was forbidden to be here! His father too, who was already inserting himself into conversations without being invited. Layne quickly stashed the bottle amongst his pile of presents, hiding it from sight. Then he went to the cake, where his mother was lighting candles.

"What are you doing?" he growled under his breath.

"Making sure my baby's wishes all come true," his mother said, summoning up a few emotional tears.

Oh fine. Considering they were paying for everything—not just the bounce house but the DJ and the fire jugglers who would show up later—he *supposed* his parents could enjoy a little fresh air. But once the candles were blown out, that was it! Layne watched his mother work, giving her a squeeze in thanks. Then he made a big show of blowing out the candles. This was a crucial part of birthday magic. The wish had power! He knew what he wanted, but it paid to be as general as possible, so he wished for everyone present to fall madly in love with him.

Perhaps he was pushing his luck, because the gods grew angry. Before he could enjoy a single bite of cake, he noticed his bounce house was deflating. Something had gone wrong on his birthday! This was unthinkable! A travesty! He rushed toward it, crying out. The bounce house was in the shape of a castle, but one of the towers had flopped over. He wedged himself below it and tried to lift. When this didn't work, he let it go, clutched his hands to his chest, and turned around, expecting Rico to rush past him and somehow save the day. Instead it was Nathaniel who came to the rescue. That was no good. Nathaniel was already taken. What was the point in being distressed if it wouldn't attract the attention of a handsome and emotionally available boy?

The party had already resumed, so Layne decided to rejoin it. That's when Noah walked over to him. Gosh, he was cute! Noah was taller than Layne, his hair crimson, the freckles minimal. At least from what Layne could see. Maybe beneath the clothes he had all sorts of freckles. And fiery pubic hair! Wouldn't that be adorable?

"Hi," Noah said, seeming a little shy. "I wanted to thank you for letting me be here. We don't really know each other but—"

"Any friend of Rico's is a friend of mine!" Layne declared.

"You *are* just his friend, right?"

"Huh? Oh! Yeah, we're just friends. Why? Are you interested in him?"

"Maybe," Layne said coyly. "I'm considering my options. I can't decide if he's cuter than his brother or not."

"They're identical aren't they?" Noah asked, seeming puzzled. Then he understood it was a joke and blushed while laughing at himself. Definitely cute! "Duh. I don't know which of them I like better myself. They might look alike, but their personalities are totally different."

"Oh really?" Layne said. His chat sessions had been mostly with Rico, who flirted shamelessly and enjoyed sending photos of himself. "What's Tito like?"

"Serious. He's really smart, reads a lot of nonfiction. Tito can be picky about who he's with too."

That didn't sound good. "Picky?"

"Well, I've seen him shoot down plenty of guys. I had a small crush on him when we first met, but I don't think he likes me much." Noah reconsidered. "Actually, I'm pretty sure it's just my boyfriend he hates."

The smile slid off of Layne's face. "Your what?"

"My boyfriend. He's—"

Layne held up a hand. "—misunderstood but has a heart of gold? I'm sure it will all work out. If you'll excuse me."

Layne stomped away. Noah was seeing someone? How thoughtless of him! He was supposed to be a potential suitor! Now Layne's options were limited to two, but the twins were all he really needed. At the same time? The idea made him lightheaded. He took stock of where they were. Tito was flipping through a crate of records the DJ had brought, brow creased in concentration. The serious type! Rico was by the cake, grinning from ear to ear. While flirting with Kelly Phillips. That wouldn't do at all! Layne accepted the blame. He shouldn't have invited anyone better-looking than himself.

He was walking toward them to interrupt when things got crazy. Rico kissed Kelly, which was heartbreaking, and then Nathaniel charged and started swinging, which was deliciously dramatic. They were rolling on the grass when Layne hurried over to help. Or to get a better view. A little of both? He grabbed a napkin from the buffet, ready to dab distraught tears from his eyes just as soon as he could force a few out. The fight was too short-lived. Kelly and a friend pulled Nathaniel off Rico, who hadn't been faring well.

"My poor Rico!" Layne cried. "What have you monsters done to him?" He swooped in, recognizing an opportunity. Rico had covered his nose and was glaring. Layne gently moved his hand away, saw blood, and patted at it with the napkin. This was good! An injured nose and injured pride. Who would be there to pick Rico up, both physically and metaphorically? "Don't worry, baby, I'll make sure they don't hurt you again."

"I guess that's our cue," Kelly said, voice terse as he struggled to keep his hunky beast in check. "Happy birthday, Layne. Sorry about all of this."

Layne was stroking Rico's cheek, and while pretending to do a medical assessment, turned Rico's head so he couldn't see. Then he looked up at Kelly and mouthed the words, "You're a genius!" Or maybe this was birthday magic in action. Layne would care for the injured object of his affection, nurse him back to health, and the two of them would slowly fall in love during the process. Not too slowly though. He had less than a month to kiss two guys, but still, it sounded like the beginning of a very romantic story!

"I'm fine," Rico said, shoving his hand away. Then he started swearing in his native language.

The only Spanish that Layne knew came from menus, but some words communicated their meaning by sound alone. "The bad man is gone now. You're okay."

"I would have waxed the floor with him!" Rico snarled.

"Wiped the floor," Layne corrected automatically, but the Spanish accent was sexy as hell. He quickly looked around to make sure his parents had already gone inside and hadn't witnessed any of this. They were the kind of people who called the police if the mailman rang the bell after dark. Fortunately, they were nowhere to be seen.

"Shit!"

This brought Layne's attention back to Rico, who was sitting up and looking down at his shirt in disgust. More blood had dripped from his nose, staining the fabric. Perfect!

"Come to my room," Layne said. "You can borrow one of my shirts."

"I don't want a different shirt," Rico grumbled, getting to his feet. "I need a drink!"

"I can help with that," Layne said, standing up with him.

Rico went still and met his eye. "Yeah?"

Layne smiled. "Mm-hm! But not here. In my room."

Rico jerked his head upward. "Let's go."

Could this get more exciting? Layne turned toward the house and smiled. He passed by the table with presents, grabbing the bottle from its hiding place. They would go to his room, do a shot together, and then sit on his bed while making out. So hot! He noticed Lisa on the way and pulled her aside.

"If anyone asks, tell them I'm in the bathroom. It might be a while."

Lisa's expression was sympathetic. "Diarrhea?"

"No!" He glanced back at Rico. Pitch black hair, bronze skin, and a face still handsome despite the piece of birthday-themed napkin shoved up one nostril. "You know what? Sure. Tell them whatever you need to."

His next challenge was sneaking Rico into his bedroom without his parents seeing. They were both standing at the kitchen sink, the radio playing golden oldies that his father loved singing along to. Hardly any stealth was required to slip past them undetected. Before long, Layne had his back to a closed door while watching a hot Latino guy pace his bedroom and swear.

"¡Pendejo!" Rico growled, getting himself worked up again. "That guy thinks he can mess with me?"

"Obviously not," Layne said. "That's why he jumped you when you weren't looking."

Rico pivoted to face him. "Hey, that's true."

"It's also why he ran off afterwards."

"You're right!" Rico boxed the air a few times. "He knew he couldn't take me. I still don't get why he wanted to fight."

"You kissed his boyfriend."

"Oh."

"Kelly is taken. But I'm not." Layne made sure the door was locked and tore away the gift wrap from the bottle. "Let's see what we've got here."

Vodka. The vanilla-flavored kind. God bless you, Kelly and Nathaniel! Normally he liked to drink it mixed with orange juice, or at the very least on ice, but he couldn't imagine risking a trip to the kitchen. "It's not chilled…"

"No problem," Rico said, striding toward him. "Go ahead, birthday boy. You first."

What a gentleman! After opening the bottle, Layne took a sip. Then he handed it to Rico, who swallowed two hearty swigs before passing it back.

"So," Layne said, feeling the need to make conversation. "How do you like Austin so far? Is it very different from San Antonio?" He'd been there plenty of times and knew that it was. He just wanted to hear more of that accent.

"It's good," Rico said vaguely, walking around the room. "This is a nice place you've got here."

"Thanks! I'll have it all to myself soon."

Rico looked over. "Yeah?"

"Mm-hm. I'm thinking of putting my parents in a retirement home. It's time, especially seeing as how I'm eighteen now and they're… old. Make room for the next generation, you know?"

Rico shook his head. "My mom will live with us until she dies. I love her."

Adorbs! "Mine too," Layne said, quickly backpedaling. "What I mean is that this house will be like a retirement home to them."

Rico came back for the bottle, his Adam's apple bobbing as he guzzled more. He sure could drink! Layne tried his best to match him, the two small sips making his eyes water. "So…" he said. "About that shirt."

"Oh man," Rico said, looking down at it sullenly. "It was my favorite."

"I think I have one like it," Layne said, handing him the bottle and moving toward his closet. He returned with a shirt that had long sleeves instead of short but was generally the same color. Then he stopped in his tracks because Rico had taken off the old shirt. His muscles were small, but what he had was toned to perfection.

Rico noticed him staring and smiled. "Do you think I'm hot?"

"*Muy caliente,*" Layne tried, hoping he'd gotten it right.

Rico's smile got bigger. "Like, do you think I could be a model?"

"Probably." Layne moved closer, performing a professional critique. "You have a nice body, but…"

"What?" Rico asked, his expression leaping to insecurity.

"Can I feel your muscles? For quality control purposes."

Rico took another swig, lips wet. "Sure."

Layne's hands were shaking as he reached out. They got a whole lot steadier when placed on that hard chest and then down one arm, Rico flexing in response. "What do you think?"

"You could definitely be a model!" Layne said, nearly gasping for breath. Now would be a good time to make his move. He pulled out his phone. "We could take photos; see how they turn out."

"Yeah!" Rico said, stumbling back a few paces and spreading his arms wide. The liquid in the bottle sloshed, almost spilling out.

"Let me take that from you," Layne said, grabbing the bottle and setting it aside. Then he pulled the napkin from Rico's nostril, the blood having dried up. "Great, now just act natural."

Rico licked a finger, then traced it down his chest to his bellybutton. Okay. Layne starting taking photos—one of him flexing, with both arms this time, or one of his back, Rico looking over his shoulder. Then Rico undid the top button of his jeans, tugging them down lower on his hips.

"Very nice," Layne said, feeling dizzy.

"Yeah? Let me see."

Rico came close, putting a hand over his to angle the phone in his direction. He left it there as Layne swiped from one image to the next. Rico made happy noises. Then he looked over, face just inches away from Layne's.

"¿Tienes ganas?"

He had no clue what that meant, but Layne nodded, feeling it was the safest response. He must have gotten it right because Rico grinned. Then he grabbed Layne's shoulders and shoved him toward the bed. He fell into it, flipping over onto his back to see what would happen. Rico was already crawling on top of him.

"Okay," Layne said. "Wow. Um..."

"You're a very cute boy," Rico said, an arm to either side of him now. "I like you."

"I like you too."

"Good." Rico started grinding against him, a hard lump in his jeans.

"Kiss me," Layne breathed, rising up to meet him, but he

was knocked down again as Rico pressed his full weight against him, still grinding.

"¡Que rico!" he was moaning, staring into Layne's eyes. "¡Que rico!"

"Okay," Layne said. "I'm not sure why you're saying your name over and over. Me Layne? You Rico?"

"¡Que rico!"

"Can we just... Um." He groped around for his phone. Where had he put it? "Could we kiss?"

Rico smiled, pushing himself up on his knees. "You want something to kiss?" Without waiting for an answer, he opened his jeans the rest of the way, yanking them down. His cock was brown and uncut and just as handsome as the rest of him.

"Wow," Layne said. "That's really *really* nice. But I was hoping we could—"

Rico hobbled closer, flopping forward with impressive accuracy to take advantage of Layne's open mouth. Not that it stopped him from speaking.

"Mrrrph glllm blllrg fffnng," he tried, nose hitting pubic hair. It was hard enough to breathe, let alone talk! Deciding they could kiss afterwards, Layne went to town, encouraged with each strange Spanish word he got Rico to moan. And of course there was plenty more "¡Que rico!" Was he fantasizing about himself? Like blowing himself? Or wait, was this actually the other twin? God, that would be kinky! Layne was just getting into it when a chorus of "¡Ay papi!" along with faster pumping preceded warm liquid shooting into his mouth. That was quick!

Rico groaned and pulled out. He shuffled backward, looking down at Layne with glazed eyes. Then he flopped over, pressing his full weight against Layne again.

"You're so good, baby," he murmured.

"Thanks," Layne responded. "Sooo..."

Rico squeezed him closer. Maybe he just needed a second to recover before they could do more. As it turned out, he needed roughly one minute to fall asleep and start snoring.

"I thought guys only did that in the movies," Layne said. "Or is it the vodka? We could drink more if you want. Hello?"

Rico didn't budge.

Layne sighed, still pinned down and resigned to his fate, until he noticed his phone on the nightstand. After a lot of squirming and struggling—some of which felt pretty nice—he managed to reach it. Now what?

"Hey," he tried again, jostling Rico. No good. Sex and booze had finished what Nathaniel had started and knocked him out cold. Enough that he could do anything with Rico that he wanted. Layne tried to remember the lecture on ethics that Keith had given them during one of their meetings, but all he could recall was trying to get the attention of a new guy. Oh well! He set down the phone, turned Rico's head so that their cheeks were pressed together, and then puckered up while taking a photo. Rico's mouth was hanging open, so it would make for a weird-looking kiss. That inspired Layne to stick out his tongue, part of it reaching Rico's mouth. Then he closed his eyes too. There. That would look *way* more convincing! Mission accomplished!

His task completed, Layne went slack, wishing Rico had been polite enough to return the favor before passing out. Eventually his hormones gave way to boredom. Layne kept squirming and shoving until he was finally free, Rico waking up briefly to grab a pillow for his head before losing consciousness again. Layne rolled his eyes, then decided to return to his party, gorge himself on cake, and speak about this to no one for the rest of his life.

Final day to get lucky. Send me those photos!

The text message from Katsu had arrived on Layne's phone the day before. How did he have his number? What a creeper! Katsu had given him hell during the most recent gay youth group, Layne tempted to show him the six photos, but he didn't want to even hint that he'd been successful until he had all seven. At the time he'd had over fifty hours left. Now he had none. The bet was lost. Layne could have used Grindr again, or found a willing partner in a chat room. That wouldn't have been too difficult.

So why hadn't he? Because everything he'd been through had shown him what he really wanted: someone who liked him. The casual encounters, Danny and the headbanger guy, hadn't taken the time to get to know him. Layne was equally to blame for that. Stewart had been an actual date, but Layne had pretended to be someone else for most of it. Lisa was his friend, Harold had been paid, and he was pretty sure that Rico only liked himself. So basically, even though Layne had kissed plenty of people and blown a guy, none of his partners actually cared about him. Except for Lisa. She was awesome. Too bad she wasn't really a boy. He'd date her. Wishes, fishes, etc. If you boiled down the entire sea, he still wouldn't find anyone for himself at the bottom. Not even in the slimy muck.

So he gave up. Katsu could have the gay youth group to himself because he was right. Layne wasn't getting any action there. With the exception of an older guy who had probably taken advantage of him. All wasn't completely lost, however. He no longer had to stress about kissing anyone, school was over for the day, and he had half a bottle of vanilla vodka hidden in his room. Layne opened the closet door to retrieve it and paused when the doorbell rang. If Lisa had come over, she was welcome to join him. They were lightweights. Half a bottle was more than enough for them both.

He heard his mother talking to someone, and sure enough, knuckles soon rapped on his bedroom door. Layne opened it, then almost shut it again because a very attractive Asian guy, one who made him feel like a complete loser, was standing there.

"Time's up," Katsu said.

His smirk was all it took to get Layne's blood boiling again. Give up? Never! "What do you want?"

"Did you forget? We had a bet. You promised me photos. I'm here to see them."

"Fine," Layne said, stepping aside and gesturing for him to enter.

Katsu walked in, inspecting Layne's room, which thankfully wasn't too messy. "So, this is where the magic happens?"

"Wait and see," Layne said, his mind racing. He was one photo short, but if he was clever, maybe he could still win this. He grabbed his laptop, asking Katsu a question to stall for time. "How did you get my phone number? And my address?"

"Oh. Keith has a notebook with all our contact information inside. He's not very careful with it."

"I'll be sure to let him know!"

"Please don't."

Layne looked up, surprised by the gentle tone.

Katsu shrugged. "I don't want to get in trouble."

"You won't be going back anyway," Layne said, working feverishly. "Not once I win the bet."

"What are you doing?" Katsu asked, straining to see.

"Nothing." Layne angled the laptop away. "I'm just putting the photos in one directory so we can cycle through them." Eight total, by the time he was done, because one was needed to support the other. "Okay. I'm ready."

Katsu sat on the bed next to him. "You're bluffing."

"I'm not! For the consideration of the court, I present... Exhibit A!"

He brought up the first photo.

Katsu stared. "Danny Pinkerton?"

Was that his name? Pinkerton? "That's right. Things got hot and heavy in his car. He's a very dark soul, you know. He might even be a vampire because I was enthralled."

Katsu fought down a smile. "He lives with his grandparents."

"Does he?"

Katsu nodded. "I've been there. His grandpa collects California Raisins merchandise. It's everywhere. Danny works part time at Babies"R"Us. You know that, right?"

"Oh. Still... That's number one." He pushed the arrow key, bringing up the next image. "Who's the handsome college guy, you ask? Is that Layne Jenkins that he's kissing? Yes. Yes it is."

"Very nice," Katsu said. "I'm a little surprised though."

"Why's that?"

"No reason."

Feeling smug, Layne hit the arrow key again. "Bachelor number three!" Otherwise known as xxHeadbanger87xx.

Katsu stared. "Is he homeless?"

Layne squinted at the screen. "Maybe. Still counts!"

Katsu laughed. "Fine. I guess it does."

"You won't find this one so funny," Layne said, switching to the next image.

"*Harold*? The guy who used to be in our group?"

"Yup! Want me to zoom in? Those lips are locked! Somebody get the combination because I can barely breathe!"

Katsu managed to laugh, but he was clearly impressed. "Are you guys in a grocery store?"

"No."

"I can see chocolate milk. And juice."

"Okay, yes, it is a grocery store, but everyone knows that's a great place to pick up guys. What?" he demanded when Katsu chuckled. "It's true! You're looking at proof!"

"I can't argue with that. Show me the next one."

Layne glared at him and moved to the next image. Lisa. As a boy.

"This one is awfully dark," Katsu said, leaning closer. Why did he have to smell so good? "And blurry. Who are you kissing? He... This person looks familiar."

"His name is Larry," Layne said, hurrying to the next photo. "Boy next door. We're close. Obviously."

Katsu didn't respond. He was too busy trying to make sense of the next image which, granted, was pretty weird. An unconscious Latino guy had his face pressed against his, Layne stretching his tongue out as far as he could to reach his mouth, eyes clenched shut in concentration.

"We were pretty wasted," Layne explained. He pointed to the half-empty bottle of vodka. "I'm a bad kid."

Katsu looked between him and the screen a few times. "You're definitely full of surprises."

"Get this," Layne said, switching to the next image. This one was a lot more innocent. It simply showed Rico and Tito standing side by side. "They're twins!"

"Wow!" Katsu said, taken aback. "That's hot!"

"You have no idea."

"And you do?"

"Yup!"

Katsu's eyes widened. "So you've... With both of them?"

Layne grinned. "Yes, I have."

"Got proof?"

Kind of. He hit the arrow key, summoning the next image. "There you go!" He tried shutting the laptop, but a hand got in the way.

"Wait! Let's see that again."

Layne sighed. Then he allowed the laptop screen to be raised.

Katsu leaned forward to inspect it. "This is the same photo as before. And the same twin. You just mirrored the image and drew a mustache on him."

"They're *identical twins,*" Layne stressed. "Of course they look the same! And before you ask, they kiss the same too."

Katsu spluttered laughter. "Unbelievable."

"It's a very unusual technique, I agree."

"But in the photo of the twins together, neither had a mustache."

"He shaved it off," Layne said, putting on a lewd expression. "They wanted to keep me guessing!"

Katsu laughed again, wiping at his eyes. "You're ridiculously funny. You know that?" The way he said this didn't sound demeaning.

"I am?"

"Yeah!" The happy expression faltered. "Too bad that you're racist."

"What? I'm not racist!"

Katsu's brow knotted up. "Really? What's the first thing you said to me?"

Ugh. The comment about not fitting stereotypes. "That was supposed to be a compliment."

"*A compliment*?" Katsu repeated in disgust.

"Look at these photos!" Layne said, cycling through them. White, black, brown… My love is blind."

"That surprised me, I'll admit it. No Asian guys though. I wonder why?"

"Are you kidding me?" Layne demanded. "You have no idea how attractive I find you!"

Katsu froze. Then the corner of his mouth twitched. "Oh yeah?"

Layne groaned. He set aside the laptop and stood so he could pace. "Fine. Yes. It's true. Tell everyone and make a big joke out of it, I don't care, but I'm *not* racist. I just say really stupid things sometimes. I open my mouth and words come flying out before I can stop them."

"Most of the time they're funny," Katsu said.

Layne turned to face him. "You really think so?"

"Yeah! You're one of my favorite things about the group. It would be boring without you."

Katsu always laughed after Layne spoke. He just assumed he was being laughed *at* instead of *with*. "So you'll miss me?"

"The bet. Right." Katsu pulled the laptop close, cycling through the photos and counting under his breath. He paused once or twice, shoulders shaking with mirth. Then he looked up. "I count six. You definitely didn't kiss both twins."

"I know." Layne sighed. "I could have won if I really wanted to."

"You still can."

"What?"

Katsu smiled and got to his feet. "I'm a good sport. I'll give you a twenty-four-hour extension."

So Layne could find another stranger to kiss? No thanks! Then again, he really would miss going to the meetings. Poor Lisa would have to carpool with someone else from—

Lips touched his, unexpected but warm and welcome. They belonged to his greatest enemy who, when Layne thought about it and rearranged his perception a little, was actually his biggest fan.

Layne pulled back. "You actually like me?"

"Yes!" Katsu replied. "Can't you tell?"

"You tried banishing me from the group…"

"Because I hated being attracted to a racist jer— To someone I *thought* was racist. Every time you made me laugh, I kicked myself for not staying true to my convictions."

"And that's why you rolled your eyes?"

Katsu thought about it. "Some of your jokes *are* pretty bad."

"One or two," Layne admitted. "But so long as you like me as a person…"

"Yes," Katsu said, moving in for another kiss.

"What about Thomas?" Layne asked as he dodged.

"Ancient history. We broke up. He wasn't any fun. Not like you are."

"Do you like me enough to wait? Seriously. I wouldn't mind taking things slow. I've done a lot of rushing lately and it's not good."

Katsu looked over at the laptop. "All those hot guys and none of them did anything for you?"

Layne shook his head. "I guess I've got a thing for Asian guys. Oh wait, is that—"

A kiss interrupted him again.

"We can take things slow," Katsu said. "I'm fine with that, but any time you say something stupid, I'm going to shut you up."

Layne thought about it. "That'll work. In exchange, I'll still let you go to group meetings, even though I totally just won the bet."

Katsu laughed. "That's very generous of you. Considering we've had our first kiss and I've already met your mother, I'd say we're overdue for a date."

"Yes please! Wednesdays are sample day at my favorite

grocery store. I always ask each person if I can bring an extra sample to my wife, and they always say yes. If you do the same thing, that's a lot of food. For free!"

Katsu shook his head ruefully. "Sounds like a good start. Let's go."

They went outside to a blue BMW parked in the driveway. Suddenly the vehicle seemed cool rather than snobbish.

Katsu escorted Layne to the passenger side door, opened it, and looked him over as he climbed inside. "When you say you want to take it slow," he said, not shutting the door yet, "are you saving yourself for marriage or…?"

Layne took in the stylish hair, the tasteful clothes, and eyes filled with amusement rather than annoyance. "A couple weeks should do. Why?"

Katsu smiled. "Fourteen days to get lucky!"

Something Like Bunnies

by Jay Bell

Warrensburg, 1987

My future revolves around my family. Here's what happens: After graduating from college, I travel the world until I'm well into my thirties. While visiting Dublin, I get lost and ask a beautiful blind woman for directions. Deirdre! She's Irish. Deirdre and I stand there talking for half an hour, and it goes so well that we decide to spend the rest of the day together. Then the rest of our lives! Deirdre moves back to America with me, and after getting married, we have six children. They might be a financial burden, but we do okay, because she's a doctor and I'm—

Jace Holden took a break from writing his school essay, his attention drawn to the brownies sitting on the kitchen table. Maybe the sugar rush would help him get the paper done faster. This was just an excuse, because if he was honest, Jace didn't know what sort of career he wanted. How could he? At fourteen years old, he was expected to plan out his entire life? That's why he had focused on the easy part. Wife and kids. Jace knew he wanted those. Maybe he could be a stay-at-home dad?

He bit into a brownie and retched, which had nothing to do with thoughts of being a family man. The brownie tasted like it was made from dirt and salt! Definitely not his mother's baking, or even his father's. No doubt these were the work of—

"What do you think?" Michelle asked, padding into the room, eyes big and vulnerable. She was taking a home economics class and had apparently forgotten half the ingredients. The brownies were an abomination! Still, she was his little sister so…

"They're good," Jace lied. "Although they could be sweeter."

"Like frosting?" Michelle asked, reaching for one.

"Yeah," Jace said. "Lots of frosting."

He watched his sister take a bite and chew thoughtfully. Then she gagged and tossed the remainder at him. "These are shit!"

Jace dodged. "Don't blame me!"

"You could have been honest!"

"I was! I said they needed to be sweeter."

"An entire bag of sugar couldn't save these." Michelle bent down to pick up the brownie she had thrown. "Think we can get dad to eat more than just a bite?"

Jace grinned. "If you give him the whole, 'Look what I made for you, Daddy!' act."

Michelle nodded. "I'll do it."

He returned his attention to his homework, his sister attempting to read over his shoulder. Jace let her, feeling pleased with what he had written.

Michelle snorted. "Deirdre?"

"It's a pretty name!"

"Sounds like an old lady. Are you married to an older woman?"

"Yes," Jace said, just to gross her out. "She's forty years older than me, but it's her wisdom and experience I find so attractive. That, and the way her dentures slide around when we kiss."

Michelle stuck out her tongue. "Grody!"

"Revenge for your poop-flavored brownies. Hey, what do you think I'll do for a living?"

"You mean aside from Deirdre?"

"I'm serious."

Michelle rolled her eyes, then narrowed them thoughtfully and sized him up. He expected her to say construction worker or something equally manly. After all, he had armpit hair and everything now. Or maybe he'd be a professional basketball player, since he had shot up four inches in the last year alone. Jace continued to grin, awaiting her answer.

Michelle nodded, having reached her conclusion. "Accountant."

"*Accountant,*" he repeated incredulously.

"Yup! You'll probably wear glasses by then like Dad and have a pocket protector for all your pens. When did Mom's hair turn gray? Never mind, you'll probably start balding like Dad too. Good thing Deirdre is blind or she'd probably leave you."

"She's not blind!"

"That's what you wrote."

Jace double-checked the essay. "Oh. It's supposed to say blonde."

"Blonde or blind, you better hope she loves you for who you really are, because the looks aren't going to last."

Jace corrected his mistake, then ignored his sister as she put in her favorite Bon Jovi tape and started crooning along to it. He forced himself to imagine his future again, how he would wake up to a big breakfast and excited children who were eager to tell him what they had dreamt about the night before. Then he would kiss Deirdre goodbye and head off to his job as…

Dolphin trainer! Yeah! Jace wasn't the best swimmer and didn't know anything about marine life, but swimming around with dolphins the whole day had to be fun. And good for his body! He was tempted to sneak away to the bathroom and check his progress in the mirror. But first he forced himself to finish his paper, writing about how he and Deirdre would open their own Sea World franchise in Canada, not far from where his grandparents lived. Then he grudgingly pulled his math assignment near, breezing through it and getting a few incorrect on purpose, just to prove Michelle wrong about his future career. By the time he finished, the light had mostly gone from the day. That was odd, since his parents usually returned home and started dinner by now, depending on whose turn it was.

"They've finally abandoned us," Michelle said, returning to the kitchen and opening the refrigerator door. After peering inside, she shut it again and turned. "You're oldest. That means you're in charge. Make me something to eat."

"Peanut butter and jelly," Jace suggested.

Michelle groaned.

He rose to switch on lights in the living room. Then he returned to the kitchen, wondering if he really should cook something. How impressive would that be? His parents would arrive home to find the table fully set, a hot meal ready and waiting. The only problem was that he didn't know how to cook. Michelle was learning, but if her brownies were anything to go by, they were better off starving.

The day was saved when his mother finally arrived carrying brown paper bags stained with grease. Burgers and fries for dinner! Jace smiled his gratitude, his mother's expression remaining somber. Serena looked as though she had walked through gusts of wind to get home, her usually tidy hair frayed, the silver braid trailing behind as she hurried to the kitchen table and dropped the bags of fast food there without ceremony.

"Family meeting!" she declared.

Jace and Michelle exchanged a look.

"Where's Dad?" he asked, approaching the table with apprehension.

"This is it," Michelle said, plopping down into one of the chairs. "She finally left him."

"Stop it, both of you," their mother said, fetching plates for them. "A broken marriage is the last thing I feel like joking about. Now eat. I don't have time for…" Serena spun around, considering the house. Then she sighed, sat, and started unpacking one of the bags. "You heard me. Eat."

Jace took a burger for himself and passed one to his sister. He studied his mother as he unwrapped it. She noticed, taking another deep breath. "Everything is fine," she said. "We just have an unexpected guest coming, that's all. You know the Talbots? Their daughter is nearly your age."

He shook his head.

"Well anyway, they're going through a rough time." Serena laughed humorlessly. "That's putting it mildly. I've never known a couple who actually throws dishes at each other. What's next, hitting each other over the head with frying pans? Sarah—Mrs. Talbot—works with me at the university. Mr. Talbot is one of your father's dry-cleaning customers. I've been meaning to have them over for dinner but…"

"Deep breath," Jace suggested.

His mother nodded. "They're getting a divorce. Sarah is taking the kids to her mother's house in Kansas City, and Mike is drinking himself silly, so their home is no place for an exchange student. That's where your father is now. He's picking up Gia… Giano? Whatever his name is, he's coming here to stay with us." Serena put a hand on her cheek, looking toward the two stairwells. One led down to the family room and his sister's bedroom, the other upstairs to a hall and more bedrooms, including his own.

"Where's he going to sleep?" Jace asked.

"On the couch downstairs for now," his mother said. "We'll get the office turned back into a guest room, but until we buy a new mattress—"

"Is he cute?" Michelle asked.

Serena looked at her sharply. "I have no idea, and you are much too young to concern yourself with such things."

Michelle shrugged. "How old is he? And where's he from?"

"Did you not hear what I just said?" Serena shook her head. "I suppose it wouldn't be appropriate for him to sleep downstairs. No. Jace, you'll have to take the couch. We'll put our guest in your room."

"What?" he said, not hiding his disgust. He turned a glare on his sister. "You suck!"

"Don't blame me!" Michelle said. "It's not my fault I'm irresistible."

"Mom!"

"It's just for tonight," Serena said. "We'll go shopping for a new mattress tomorrow and… Eat your food, please. I should probably put fresh sheets on your bed."

"You just did the other day," Jace said, pushing one of the burgers toward her. "It's fine. You need to eat too."

His mother smiled at him, then relaxed a little. "You're right. This is the last private meal we'll have together for quite some time."

"What's he like?" Jace asked after she had gotten a few bites down.

"I honestly have no idea. Your father is helping him pack and will take him to dinner, then we'll find out."

That made him nervous. Jace was already imagining someone his own age who wanted to talk sports, or even worse, actually participate in them rather than go somewhere quiet in the woods to read, or play video games and watch movies like he did with Greg. That led to another thought. Greg was much more athletic than Jace was. What if this new guy and Greg got along too well? What if his best friend was stolen away?

"Can't we just get him a hotel room?" Jace asked.

His mother frowned. "I expect better from you. Consider how he must feel, far away from home and having to leave his host family! Put yourselves in his shoes for a moment, then ask yourself what you would want to happen."

"I *love* staying in hotels," Jace replied.

"Good idea!" Michelle said. "I volunteer. Jace can stay in his room, the foreigner can stay in mine, and you and Dad can put me up in a hotel."

Serena sighed. "Or maybe your father and I will go stay at a bed and breakfast. Enough silly talk. Finish eating. We've got a lot to do before our guest arrives."

Thanks to Michelle being boy crazy, preparation mostly involved Jace straightening up his room. He took some satisfaction in her having to clean the upstairs bathroom, even though she never used it. Serena concerned herself with the rest of the house. Jace was hiding clutter in his closet when he heard his father's car. Feeling apprehensive, he went down to the kitchen and joined his sister near the door that opened from the garage to the house.

Beyond it, they could hear their father chatting happily. Bob didn't stop when he opened the door and saw them, too eager to finish his story. "—and really, who in their right mind would drop off an entire couch to be dry cleaned? How would we fit it on one of the conveyer belt hangers? Ha ha ha!"

Jace craned his neck to look past his father, already having heard that anecdote more times than he cared to count. The person behind Bob was definitely not his age. He was a man, probably in his early twenties. His skin was brown like he came from a land of eternal summer. The stubble on his cheeks matched the ruffled black hair. His eyes were like onyx marbles, sparkling with amusement at the story or just the situation in general. Jace's apprehension increased. This stranger was going to be sharing their home?

His sister didn't share his reservations. "Tall, dark, and handsome," she murmured before skipping forward and offering her hand. "Welcome home! I'm Michelle."

The man ignored her hand, choosing instead to kiss one of her cheeks, then the other. "I am Gianni," he said. "*Piacere.*"

What was that? Italian?

The man stepped back and noticed him. "You must be my new brother," he said with a thick accent. He walked right into Jace's personal space to greet him with the same ritual. A scruffy cheek pressed against his, accompanied by a smooching sound. He could smell cologne and a hint of fast food—the taco place his father was so fond of. Jace froze, unsure what to do, the face of another guy passing mere inches from his own as Gianni went for the other cheek.

"He did the same thing to me!" Bob declared, laughing gleefully.

Jace didn't think it was funny. The kisses made him feel weird, but he wasn't sure why.

Then his mother appeared, all traces of agitation gone as she played the perfect hostess, making sure their guest felt welcome, was comfortable, and had something to drink. The rest of his family behaved like they had gotten a new television, gathering around Gianni in the family room. They asked him questions and listened with rapt attention to his answers. Jace listened too, although he didn't participate. He didn't like how quickly a stranger had won them all over, or how he had to fight against mirroring his family's happy expressions.

He paid close attention to everything Gianni said regardless. This was his third year in college and his first time in the States. He wanted to be a doctor, had three brothers, one sister, and…

"I miss my donkey very much," Gianna said, expression pained.

"You have a donkey?" Bob asked.

"Yes. He is always jumping on me when I get home and licking my face."

Michelle was the first to figure it out. "Do you mean a dog? Bark bark?"

Gianni squinted thoughtfully. "A dog! Yes! I am stupid. But they don't make bark bark. We say *bau bau*!"

This led to a conversation on which words were used to describe animal noises in different languages. Onomatopoeia. Jace was proud to know the term, but he couldn't seem to get it past his lips to show off. Instead he keenly listened to the rest of the conversation, almost enjoying it enough to lower his guard.

"It's late," Serena said. "We haven't even let you get unpacked yet. Jace, could you help him carry his belongings to his room?

My room. He didn't say it, but he still seethed as he lugged one of the suitcases upstairs. Judging from the weight and number of them, Gianni planned on living here permanently. Maybe that was the real truth, and the reason the Talbots had foisted him off on them. They had a guest they couldn't get rid of. Until now.

The second they entered his bedroom, Jace let the luggage fall. He was tempted to hold his hand out like bellboys did in movies, but he was forced to move deeper into the room so their guest could come inside.

"Nice home!" Gianni said, more careful with setting down the suitcases he carried. "You have a room all alone? I had to share with my brother. Very smelly guy. Always…" Gianna searched for the word, making a farting noise when he couldn't find it.

Jace smiled. But against his will!

"Ah! What's this?" Gianni moved to the far wall where Jace had pinned a map of the world. Greg had teased him about it, saying that boring things belonged in a classroom. Jace enjoyed looking at the map anyway, usually while dreaming of the places he'd like to go. "Here! This is my home!"

Gianni was pointing at the south of Italy.

Jace moved closer to see. "Salerno," he read out loud.

"You can speak!"

"Huh?" Jace said, looking over at him.

"The whole night you not say a word. I think maybe he can't talk."

Jace swallowed, turning back to the map, because for some reason he found it difficult to look at Gianni when they stood so close together. "What's it like there?"

"Very different. Not like here. I have photos. I think you would enjoy. Salerno is very busy."

Busy? That seemed a strange word to describe a place. Warrensburg could never be described that way, which was enough to pique Jace's interest. He followed Gianni to the bed, watched him open one of the suitcases on it, and noticed tangled clothing that had clearly been thrown in at the last minute. Including black skimpy underwear. Did they belong to a woman? Or is that what Italian men wore?

"Here," Gianni said, pulling out a small photo album. Each clear plastic page was only large enough to hold one photo. "Ah! There is my donkey!" He smiled, showing the mistake was intentional this time as he tapped a photo. In it, a scruffy mutt was being hugged around the neck by Gianni, who looked a little younger and was cleanly shaven. "His name is Baffi." He flipped through more pages. "And here are my parents. My brothers. Sister. She's pretty, no?"

She was okay, he supposed. Unlike Greg, Jace wasn't all that interested in girls.

"Here you go. A nice view of the gulf. That's my Salerno!"

The photo could have been used for a postcard. Green mountains and blue sky filled the distance. In front of them nature gave way to a clutter of beige buildings, a crowded harbor, and azure waters.

Jace stared. "If that's where you're from, why did you come here?"

"I like the USA," Gianni said. "Although I thought it would

be bigger. The buildings, I mean. Sky scratchers?"

Jace fought down a smile. "Skyscrapers. You need to go to New York for those. Why'd you choose Warrensburg?"

"Ah. I make mistake. My brother kept saying I need to enroll early. I didn't listen. Now I'm here."

He could relate to that. Jace also felt stuck in this town against his will. He watched as Gianni finished flipping through the photos, paying more attention to the backgrounds and wishing he could walk down the narrow streets and spend a weekend on the beaches. Isn't that how an exchange worked? Shouldn't Jace be on his way to Italy right now?

"We are both sleeping here?" Gianni asked, closing the suitcase and moving it off the bed.

"No. I'm on the couch."

"But it's your room! You can sleep on the bed. I sleep on the floor."

"It's fine," he said. "I don't mind."

"We share the bed instead? I promise I don't..." He stuck his tongue between his lips and blew out.

"Fart," Jace said with a chuckle. "It's just for tonight. I want to sleep on the couch. Really!"

He did? Looks like he had fallen under the same spell as the rest of his family.

"*Grazie.*" Gianni hooked an arm around his neck and pulled him near. "It's good to have a brother again."

"Okay," Jace said, feeling like the dog in the photo. "Good night."

"Good night," Gianni said. Then he held up a finger. "Don't let the bed bugs bite you. Right?"

Jace laughed. "That's right."

The stupid smile remained on his face even after he'd shut the door behind him. He supposed Gianni wasn't so bad. Having a guest stay with them would probably be fun. He still wanted his room back, but for now, he had to admit he liked the guy. Jace went downstairs to find that the couch had been made with blankets and pillows. He was just settling into them when the door to his sister's room opened.

"Hey!" she whispered, sounding excited.

"What?"

"How'd it go? Did he mention me?"

Jace scrunched up his face. "Gianni? Why would he?"

Michelle glared in response. "Seriously? You're so dense."

"Good night," Jace said pointedly.

"Did you at least see him get undressed?"

"Go to sleep!" he snarled, pulling a pillow over his head. When he heard the muted sound of a door closing, he uncovered his head and found himself alone. As if he'd stand there and watch Gianni get naked! What a stupid idea! And yet, as he tried to find sleep and failed, this image was the one his mind kept returning to.

Jace woke the next day with a sore back. A hot shower made it feel a little better, but the relief was short-lived, since he kept worrying that Gianni would need to use the restroom. He hurried as much as he could, then realized that he didn't have fresh clothes to change into. With a towel wrapped around his waist, he peeked into the hallway. Empty. The door to his bedroom was open, meaning Gianni was probably downstairs eating.

Jace darted across the hall and into his room. But he wasn't alone. Gianni was there, wearing a red bathrobe that seemed three sizes too small because it didn't cover much. Their guest was preoccupied with making the bed, but before Jace could escape unseen, he finished and turned around.

"Good morning!" Gianni said, walking toward him.

Jace turned toward the dressers before more weird cheek kisses could occur. "I need clothes. I'll just be a second."

"Of course! Are you finish with the shower?"

"Yeah. Go ahead." He scurried to collect the basics: shirt, socks, and underwear. He was fine wearing the same jeans. When he turned back around…

Gianni was bent over, digging through a suitcase on the floor. The robe was short enough when he was standing. Now it was close to showing his ass or… Jace stared. He couldn't look away. The legs were muscular and covered with the same dark hairs he'd briefly glimpsed on the chest. The robe fabric inched higher, Jace able to see a fraction of two perfect ass cheeks. In the shadow between the legs, he thought he could see more, but Gianni stood again.

Jace was hard. Not completely, but still enough to notice. He turned and ran for the bathroom, slamming the door behind him.

When he met his own gaze in the mirror, he shook his head at himself. He'd had thoughts like these before and tried to ignore them. Now would be no exception. He got dressed, mentally chastising himself for losing control. He knew the cause. It had begun just over a year ago, when Jace was lying in bed, on his stomach, while reading. The fantasy novel had featured a female thief and a male barbarian, and during one part, they had to swim across a river to escape being tracked by an enemy. After their swim, they had stripped down to dry out in the sun. Jace had moved against the sheets as he imagined this. That had felt good, and when he rolled over and started using his hand…

Panic had followed pleasure. Jace worried he had injured himself or sprung a leak. That didn't stop him from doing it again the next night. Or the next. For the first year, he felt guilty each time. Recently he had been shameless, sometimes indulging more than once in the same day. He knew now that it was called masturbation, and that it was supposed to be natural. The thoughts it conjured up—those couldn't be. Whenever he jacked off, he imagined all sorts of weird things, but his twisted fantasies used to go away as soon as he was finished. Lately though, such thoughts seemed to be seeping into normal life too.

Not for the first time, he promised himself to stop. Maybe almost getting caught with a boner would finally give him the motivation to do so. Jace got dressed, shoving his concerns aside. Then he went downstairs, ate breakfast, and worked overtime to convince himself that everything was fine.

"Does he smoke?" Greg asked as they walked from one class to another.

"No," Jace answered, keeping his reply short because his friend kept asking one question after the other.

"Weird," Greg said. "I thought all Italians smoked. Is he with the mafia?"

"No."

"How do you know? Did you ask him?"

"No."

"Can I ask him?"

"No!"

"Can I meet him?"

Jace sighed. "Sure. But only if you promise not to ask any more questions."

"I'm done asking you! I'm going straight to the source."

The image of a slinky bathrobe popped into his mind, making Jace want to growl with frustration. He looked over at Greg, who had definitely changed in appearance. He wasn't as tall as Jace, but his shoulders were broader, and lately he seemed to put on muscle without effort. He wasn't manly like Gianni, but he was on his way. Jace hoped he was too. Maybe what he felt was nothing more than envy. His own body was changing, but not in the exact way he would have liked, so he admired guys like Greg and Gianni. He probably just needed to do pushups and eat more meat to catch up to them.

"You all right?" Greg asked, noticing his stare.

"Yeah. No. I don't know. Can I ask you something personal?"

Greg shrugged. "Since when do we have secrets?"

Jace stopped, looking up and down the hall and waiting for three girls to pass them. "Do you ever do stuff? Like in the shower."

"In the shower?" Greg asked, expression confused. "You mean singing?"

"Or right before you go to sleep."

"Huh? Oh! Uhhh…" Greg peered at him suspiciously. "Do you?"

"I don't know," Jace said, casting another glance around. "I might."

"You might what?"

He sighed. One of them had to be the first to say it. But if he was alone on this, it would be embarrassing, so he made a pumping gesture with his hand instead.

"Are you saying you do that?" Greg asked.

"Yes," Jace hissed, cheeks flushing. "Do you?"

Greg grinned. "All the time. Well, not *all* the time. I'm not doing it right now. Obviously. Ha ha! In the shower, huh?"

"Yeah! You don't?"

"No! You're supposed to be getting clean, not getting dirty." Greg laughed again. "I can't believe we're talking about this."

"Me neither." Jace felt relieved, but not entirely, because the most difficult question was yet to come. "And when you're uh… *busy*, do you ever think weird thoughts?"

"Oh yeah!" Greg said without hesitation. "Is that what you're worried about?"

"Kind of. What sort of things do you think about?"

Greg's eyebrows shot up. "You're asking for details?"

"No, I just… How weird does it get?"

Greg exhaled. "Pretty damn weird!"

"Like what? I mean, what's the general subject matter?"

"Sex," Greg said. "Obviously."

Jace nodded. "I figure that's normal."

"Right, but sometimes…"

"Sometimes," Jace said, "the fantasies get really strange. Then what are they about?"

Greg rolled his eyes. "Ugh. Fine. I'll give you an example, but don't freak out."

"I won't. I promise."

"This one time, I had a fantasy that I was in your house. In your room. In your bed."

Jace's heart started thudding. He'd had a similar fantasy about Greg once. So it *was* normal!

"Then your mom walked in and found me. This made her mad, because I wasn't supposed to be there. She made me get out of bed, and when she saw I was wearing your clothes—don't ask me why—she made me take them off. You can guess the rest."

Jace's mouth dropped open. "My *mother*? You think about my mother while you—"

"Shut up!" Greg huffed. "I don't want anyone else to know! Besides, you promised not to get mad."

"Yeah, but…" He shook his head. "I guess I shouldn't have asked."

"I guess not," Greg said, sounding defensive. "You're the pervert whacking it in the shower every morning."

"Don't knock it," Jace said. "Shampoo feels really good. Conditioner is even better."

Greg looked puzzled. "In your pubes?"

"Nope." Jace made the hand motion again. "To keep things slick."

They both laughed, then continued walking to class. Jace felt reassured. Greg having fantasies about a mom proved just how strange thoughts could be while masturbating. That Jace thought of guys occasionally no longer seemed like such a big deal. It sure beat fantasizing about Greg's mother!

Despite the promises made, he didn't find a new mattress

when he got home, and the office hadn't been converted to a guest room. Those plans would wait until Saturday, which his parents pointedly reminded him was tomorrow, but then neither of them had to sleep on the couch or wake up with a sore back. Still, the evening wasn't a complete disaster. Easter was on Sunday, which meant it was time to color eggs.

Jace sat at the dining room table, inhaling vinegar fumes while surrounded by bowls filled with liquid of various colors. Currently he was writing his name in wax on a hardboiled egg and trying his best to ignore the man seated across from him, who was tsking and saying strange things with an accent.

"My mother always use onions. You take the paper and boil it to make color. Yellow or red. Or the little berries. Americans always putting them in muffins."

"Blueberries," Serena said from next to him. "What a lovely idea!"

"I bet it makes the eggs taste strange," his father chimed in.

"They smell nicer," Gianni countered.

Bob laughed. "I bet they do!"

Jace pulled the yellow dye bowl closer, planning to repeatedly dip his egg, let it dry, and dip it again to get the deepest hue. "Where's Michelle?" he asked. "She's missing out."

"Staying with a friend," Bob said. "Your sister thinks she's too grown up for Easter. We'll see how she feels about not getting a basket on Sunday."

"Basket?" Gianni asked.

"The woven things," Jace's father said, craning his neck to check the microwave clock. Then he turned to his wife. "It's about to start!"

"Oh." Serena eyed all the undyed eggs. "You boys can finish up here. Right?"

Jace shot an uneasy glance at Gianni—a bad idea, because his eyes were narrowed in an effort to understand, making him look… Cute? Could another guy look cute? "Where are you going?"

Bob was already getting to his feet. "They're rerunning the most recent episode of *Dallas*, which we missed because of the PTA meetings."

"You could join us," Serena said. "We can always finish up later."

Jace shook his head. Even feeling uncomfortable around a house guest was better than the glorified soap opera his parents couldn't get enough of.

"Gianni?" his mother asked.

"Television?" the Italian man asked. Then he too shook his head. "We stay here and do our work together. Right, Jace?"

He made the name sound cool—exotic!—putting extra emphasis on the front. Jace nodded and kept his head down, dipping one end of an egg in blue, the other in purple to give it two different colors.

"What is a basket?" Gianni asked eventually.

Jace took a deep breath, trying to figure out the best way to describe it. "You can put things inside and it has a handle. It's what you get Easter morning. It's full of candy?"

Gianni's mouth turned downward as he shrugged.

"Okay," Jace said, trying again. "You know what birds live in?"

"Yes."

"It's like that, but with a handle. So you can carry it." Jace pantomimed doing so.

"Ah!" Gianni declared. "A *cestino*!"

"I guess," Jace said. "It's what the Easter bunny brings."

"Bunny? What is bunny?"

Oh boy. Jace put both index fingers above his head and curled them to simulate bunny ears.

Gianni pulled back in shock. "The devil?"

"No!" Jace started laughing. "A bunny is an animal. It brings us Easter baskets and hides our eggs."

"That's not very nice," Gianni said, frowning as he worked.

Jace supposed the tradition did sound a little odd, now that he thought about it. He dyed two more eggs in silence, occasionally shooting a glance across the table. Gianni seemed so calm and collected, even though it must be hard to be so far from home. "What's Easter like in Italy? Is it different?"

"It's a big party!" Gianni said, his dark eyes lighting up. "Many days of celebration. Good food and lots of special walks."

"Walks?"

"The holy men. No? Come outside. I'll show you."

Jace knew how to walk, but he was getting bored with dyeing eggs, and the weather had been a lot warmer lately. The idea of being outside sounded nice. He followed Gianni to the front door, noticing how his T-shirt didn't hang off his shoulder blades like Jace's did, but instead curved over rounded shoulders and hugged his sides, a V-shape leading down to his hips. Did all Italian guys wear such tight clothes?

"The holy men come out for the walk," Gianni said once they were outside and heading toward the street. "Very many. They wear cloths. Robes? And they carry fire through the city. Sometimes they are quiet. The best times have music. In the front of the walk..." Gianni fell back a few paces. Jace felt strong hands grab him beneath each arm before he was hoisted up.

"Hey!" he protested while squirming, but it was no good. He was being held aloft as Gianni went into the street and started walking down it. Good thing they lived in a sleepy neighborhood!

"Usually we have Virgin Mary, but you can be the Jesus. This is our Easter *parata*."

"Parade?" Jace guessed, starting to laugh as their speed increased.

"That sounds right. Easter parade. Usually they are slow. I think they should go fast."

Gianni started running, Jace amazed that he was strong enough to do so while carrying him. They didn't get far before he was set down again. Jace kept laughing. Gianni grinned as he tried to catch his breath. Then he threw an arm around Jace's neck just as he'd done the night before and left it there, guiding him farther down the street. Should he do the same? Jace's arms remained limp at his side, but the urge to do something with them—anything that increased their physical contact—remained.

"Good times," Gianni was saying. "My mother can cook. I always look forward to her *pizzagaina*. Best food of Easter. My brothers always take too much, so one night I get up early and eat almost half. Then I get sick."

"You have pizza for Easter?" Jace asked.

"Not like American pizza. It's a pie. Lots of eggs and pig meat."

"Sounds like quiche."

"Maybe. We also have chocolate eggs."

"Cadbury?"

Gianni moved his arm away, patting Jace on the back a few times. "I don't know. Sorry. My English is bad."

"Your English is great!" Jace said, maybe a little too enthusiastically, because Gianni ruffled his hair like he was being silly.

"You're a good guy. I'm youngest in my family. It's nice to have a little brother."

"I'm the oldest." He refrained from saying more, because he didn't like the idea of Gianni being his big brother. Jace liked *him* though! A lot! Too much to be considered family.

"Where is everybody?" Gianni shouted suddenly, grinning and spinning around. "In Salerno, the nights are alive with drinking and talking. Here? Everyone is inside watching television."

"It sucks," Jace agreed. "I want to go to Italy."

"You're smart. I know you can do it. When you're older, come visit me. You'll be exchange student, and I give you my bed."

That sounded incredible! And why not? He probably just needed to get good grades and fill out the right forms. His parents would agree, now that they actually knew someone from Italy. He hadn't paid much attention to the country before, but Jace became filled with the desire to know everything about it. As they continued their walk, he asked any question that sprang to mind, sometimes helping Gianni find the right words in English. That felt good. Like they had a partnership, something that until now, Jace hadn't realized that he wanted. Nor could he explain why that desire burned so deeply in the center of his chest.

"Are you done with the shower?"

Gianni was wearing his skimpy robe again. Jace noticed this after turning around from the dressers. Once again he had forgotten to choose an outfit before showering, only a towel providing him with cover.

"The bathroom is all yours," Jace said, feeling a lot more confident than he usually did. "I hope I didn't use all the hot water!"

"It's fine," Gianni said, reaching for the belt of his robe. "In Italy, we only take ice cold showers. It puts hair on our chests."

As if to demonstrate, he undid the belt's knot, the robe billowing open before it fell from his shoulders to the carpet below. Jace stared, first at the chest that was indeed hairy. Then his eyes moved down the naked body, which was tan and muscular and… Another man's dick! He hadn't seen one, not since playing doctor with a neighbor boy who had moved away years ago, but they had been children then. The game had been innocent, neither one of them having much to show or understanding what to do. This was different. Gianni's cock was huge, his balls pendulous, with a bush of hair above it all that put Jace's to shame.

"I like the way you look at me," Gianni said, coming closer. "Please. Let's share your bed." He reached a hand out and snagged the towel, which fell away to reveal Jace's erection. More than that. Jace was ejaculating. He couldn't help himself! The situation was too exciting, but Gianni didn't seem to mind. He smiled, expression calm and understanding. "I love you," he said. "I love my little brother."

Jace shot awake, cheek sticky with drool. That wasn't the only thing sticky. He shifted, back aching from sleeping on the couch again and realized that his underwear was damp. He definitely hadn't peed the bed. Jace remembered the dream, feeling a mixture of embarrassment and shame. Not quite as potent was another emotion. Stubbornness. Part of him was sick of feeling ashamed. Part of him liked the dream and wanted more, preferably in real life. There was a word for that…

He shook his head. The only reason he'd had a wet dream—and such an odd one at that—is because he lacked privacy, making it impossible to jack off. The family room where he slept was right next to his sister's bedroom, and the idea of her potentially catching him killed the mood. He had to hurry in the shower too, so it hadn't happened there either. Pent-up sexual frustration. That's what Dr. Ruth would call it. Jace had secretly tuned in to her radio show more than once at night, fascinated by her frank discussions on sex and the way she made everything sound so normal. One show in particular caught his attention, when a caller asked about a gay friend. Dr. Ruth had insisted it was natural, and that young homosexuals should go to a big city or university to find support. Then she had moved on from the topic, dispatching further sexual wisdom in a German accent.

So maybe Jace wasn't experiencing sexual frustration. Maybe he was gay.

This wasn't the first time he'd entertained such an idea. Jace had wondered the night of that particular radio show and also the first time someone at school described what gay meant. Usually he dismissed the thought as neurotic, but his fascination with Gianni was different. Impossible to ignore. These thoughts were on his mind as he showered. He didn't want an older brother. He didn't want to be Gianni. What did he want then? To lie naked together in bed? To do even more? Yes. Exactly that. Jace's heart thudded as he allowed himself to face the truth. Good or bad, if he was really honest and stopped playing games of denial, he knew he wanted last night's dream to come true. Ideally he wouldn't blow a load while standing there, but he did want to share a bed with Gianni.

Jace finished his shower and dried off. A towel was wrapped around his waist when he walked across the hall to his bedroom. The space was empty. Gianni must be downstairs in that robe, no doubt giving Michelle the thrill of her life. Jace decided he wouldn't mind another peek either, so he hurried to get dressed. Once downstairs, he found only his mother.

"Your father and Gianni got up early," she explained. "They're out buying a mattress right now, don't worry."

Jace wasn't concerned. He almost felt disappointed. Maybe they could have shared his room, Jace taking the floor or even squeezing into the small bed, like Gianni had offered. He'd probably been joking when he suggested that, but if not…

"Did you sleep well?" Serena asked, setting a box of cereal and a carton of milk on the table.

"Fine." Jace left it at that. He might be starting to accept who he truly was, but he knew his parents never would. Ever. Neither would Michelle, Greg, or anyone at school. The truth had to remain a secret. But what about Gianni? Maybe people were cooler about such things in Italy. Everything else there sure sounded better!

Jace finished eating breakfast, listening for the garage door to open and growing more frustrated by the second. He wanted to see Gianni, if only to confirm his feelings. "How much longer are they going to be?" he complained to his mother as she cleared the table.

"Buying a mattress is complicated. If you're bored, you can help me with the dishes."

"Can't," he said, shooting to his feet. "I have a business meeting I need to get to."

His mother didn't find this amusing. Only after helping her clean up in the kitchen was he free to go. Jace took his backpack from his room and his bike from the garage and pedaled into town. He didn't have a lot of money. His parents never gave him an allowance, although if he really wanted to buy something, they would usually come up with some task for him to complete so he could earn the money. Luckily he still had cash from his recent birthday. He used this to buy an Easter basket, which unfortunately was pink because that was all the store still had in stock. He also picked up fake grass and the cheapest candy. He needed to save his money to splurge on the most important item—a chocolate bunny. He got the largest and nicest one he could find, the kind with candy eyes and a nose. It even wore a real cloth bow! After paying, he carefully tucked most of this into his backpack but was forced to hang the pink basket on the bicycle's handlebars. If anyone had suspicions about him being gay, this surely wouldn't help.

When he returned home, the garage door was up and his father's van was in the driveway. Jace hid his purchases behind some old boxes, then went inside. He found Gianni in the kitchen guzzling water, adam's apple bobbing in his brown neck, a drop of water racing toward it. Jace stared. Yup! He was a homo! He didn't exactly feel like celebrating, but some part of him was a little thrilled. He had a secret now! Keeping it wouldn't always be easy, but he did feel it made him a lot more interesting.

"Did you guys buy a new mattress?" he asked, just to make conversation.

Gianni nodded toward the stairs. "Go see."

Jace did as he was told, letting himself smile once his back was turned. Why? No idea. Something about Gianni just made him want to. He walked down the upstairs hall to what had been an office. It still looked like one, except now in the middle of the room was a basic metal frame with a box spring and mattress. His mother was putting fresh sheets on it.

"That's way bigger than mine!" he complained.

"All part of the plan," Serena said, taking a step back to consider her work. "You've outgrown your bed, so when Gianni leaves, we'll put this one in your room. I just hope it fits." She sized it up, then went to a desk drawer, pulling out a tape measure.

Jace helped her write down the dimensions. Then they went to his room. Sure enough, the mattress would fit. Good thing too, because he was sick of his feet hanging off the old one. That only happened when he stretched out, but still.

"It'll look nice in here," his mother said. "You're growing up!"

"Must be all the steroids Greg and I take."

She shook her head at his joke. "I'll get your sheets washed so you have clean ones for tonight."

Jace looked at the bed, at a pillow still indented from Gianni's head. "It's okay!" he said quickly. "You already washed them earlier in the week."

"Are you sure?"

"Yeah." Extremely sure. He wanted to slip beneath those sheets, bury his face in the pillow, and inhale. That was messed up, but again, he was finished denying what he truly wanted. He'd make sure nobody found out what that was, but if anyone was on his side, it should be himself.

When he went downstairs, he found Michelle bugging Gianni, making a weird face as she talked with him, like she'd been presented with a delicious cake that she couldn't wait to eat. Then Greg showed up for their plans to go fishing. They invited Gianni who, as it turned out, had plans of his own. That sucked, but Jace didn't despair too much. They lived together! It wouldn't be long before they saw each other again.

Turned out to be a little longer than expected, since Gianni still wasn't home when Jace returned. He didn't ask where Gianni had gone, deciding to be subtle. Instead he took the basket and backpack from their hiding place and went to his room to get it ready. An hour went by. Still no Gianni.

Boredom drove Jace to walk across the small valley to Greg's house. They played video games together, made fun of people they both disliked at school, and talked about their Easter plans. Greg and his family were going to visit relatives in St. Louis. Jace's nearest relatives were in Canada, so he didn't share that problem.

Dinnertime was inching closer when he returned home. He followed voices to the kitchen table, which was covered in textbooks. A woman who looked to be in her twenties was seated next to Gianni. Her cheeks were glowing as she smiled at the man next to her, and she kept tucking her long blonde hair behind one ear, but she didn't seem like a ditz. Her eyes were sharp and alert when she noticed Jace standing there, her expression friendly. Jace hated how pretty she was. She didn't have the glamorous sort of beauty that models had, but something more natural. The kind of beauty that would be impossible to dismiss as artificial.

"There he is!" Gianni declared. "We were just talking about you."

"You were?" Jace said, feeling a little more cheerful.

"Yes. Hannah, this is my new little brother, Jace."

"Aren't you handsome?" Hannah declared, like she was truly impressed. "Come sit with us."

Okay, maybe she wasn't so bad. Jace moved forward, eyeing the table suspiciously. "This looks like school work," he said disapprovingly.

Hannah laughed. "We were hoping you could finish our assignment for us. I'll pay you five bucks!"

"It'll cost you more than that," Jace said, taking a seat and flipping through the nearest book. Math. Except with lots of letters and weird symbols, none of which made sense.

"Right there," Hannah said, pointing a pencil at him. "I know that's how my face looked all of freshman year!"

Jace grimaced. "If this is my future, then I think I'll drop out now."

"Drop out?" Gianni asked.

Jace opened his mouth to explain, but Hannah got there first. She spoke in rapid-fire Italian, Gianni laughing and responding in a similar fashion. He was so much more animated when speaking his native tongue. And talkative! Jace couldn't help but wonder what he was missing.

Hannah noticed and translated. "His oldest brother ran away from home once just to avoid an important exam. When he came back the next day, his mother marched him to school and sat in the desk next to his until he had completed the test."

"Wow." Jace looked to Gianni, whose eyes were still shining at the memory. What other stories was Jace not hearing because he couldn't speak the language?

"Hey," Gianni said, addressing him. "What was the word you try to tell me? Remember?" He mimicked the bunny ears motion.

For whatever reason, Jace didn't want Hannah to translate. He wanted them to have something private together that no one else knew. "The devil?" he asked, playing it off as a joke.

"*Diavlo*?" Hannah said.

Gianni responded to her in Italian. They exchanged a few sentences, but in the end she shrugged, not figuring out what he meant. Gianni said something else indecipherable, rose from the table, and left the kitchen.

"Where's he going?" Jace asked.

"Little boys' room," Hannah said.

"Oh. I wish I could talk to him like that."

"In Italian? You just have to learn."

"Yeah, but they don't teach it in junior high. The only language elective is Spanish, and that's just for half a year."

Hannah nodded. "I remember. I took it and forgot almost everything by the next semester." She sat upright. "Hey, if you're serious about learning Italian, I can teach you! I could use the experience. And the money."

"I've got about six bucks," Jace said, not bothering to get excited. He was sure it would cost more than that.

"Maybe your parents would be willing to pay. I won't charge much. Just a little for pizza and gas."

Jace eyed her. He wanted to like Hannah, but he still had reservations. "How do you know Gianni?"

"I was part of the welcoming committee for the Italian students." She laughed. "All three of them!"

Jace continued to scrutinize. "So are you guys…"

"We're just friends." Hannah looked toward the stairs. "Sadly."

They had that much in common. Still, her being nothing more than a friend was welcome news. Deciding to like her, he said, "I bet my parents would let you tutor me. Especially if I promise to take Italian in high school, which I will because I want to go there as an exchange student."

Hannah's face lit up. "You do?"

"Yeah!" They discussed this until Gianni returned. Then, to Jace's delight, he received his first lesson. Just the absolute basics, like how to say hello and goodbye. *Ciao! Arrivederci!* Or please and thank you. *Prego! Grazie!* Best of all was Gianni's approval of Jace wanting to learn. He kept smiling and helping Hannah coach him on the proper pronunciation. Dinner interrupted their fun. Hannah left, returning to her dorm on campus, but Jace made sure to show off what he had learned while they ate. When his parents seemed impressed, he hit them with his sales pitch. A successful one, as it turned out, because Hannah was going to be his tutor. Jace would learn Italian! He was already looking forward to being able to converse with Gianni like she could.

Jace bugged the man for more vocabulary after they finished eating, his appetite anything but satiated. They even took another walk together when the rest of his family decided to watch TV. By the time he tumbled into bed, his cheeks hurt from smiling so much. Jace pulled the sheets up to his neck, rolled over, and let his face sink into the pillow. His hope was proven right. The scent was faint, but it was there. His bed smelled like Gianni. Jace closed his eyes, intending to bask in it. A few minutes later they shot open. He had privacy again. Might as well take advantage of it!

Jace went downstairs to the living room as soon as he woke up. Normally he was excited about getting his Easter basket. It was there in front of the fireplace, his father having spelled out his name in jelly beans. Michelle's too, which never seemed fair, since hers had so many more letters. This year he barely cared. He was more interested in giving someone else a basket. He brought it with him and set it next to the others.

"How thoughtful of you!" Serena said. "I'm sure he'll be thrilled when he wakes up."

Jace unpacked the basket his mother had prepared, looking repeatedly at the stairwell and hoping to see a handsome Italian guy descending. Eventually his wish came true. Gianni showed up in that wonderful robe of his, Michelle letting out a little gasp. Jace glared at her. Then he rose, grabbed the basket, and met Gianni halfway, wishing they had privacy.

"*Buongiorno,*" Jace said carefully, making sure to pronounce it right. "Happy Easter."

"What's this?" Gianni said. "For me?"

"Yeah." Jace handed it to him. "Basket."

"Basket," Gianni confirmed with a smile. "*Cestino.*"

Jace repeated the word, trying to commit it to memory. Then he led the way to the couch, sitting next to Gianni as he rifled through the contents. Why hadn't Jace bought more? Suddenly it didn't seem like enough. The best was when Gianni took out the chocolate bunny. He stared at it, then looked to where Jace's basket still sat ignored. "Is this… What is the word?"

"Bunny," Jace said, already grinning.

Gianni laughed. "No devil! I see. But this is a rabbit, no?"

"Oh!" Now Jace laughed, because he could have simply used a different word the entire time.

"What's the difference?" Gianni asked.

"Um." Jace looked to his mother for help.

"A bunny is a baby rabbit."

"I see! *Coniglio, conglietto.*"

"We'll take your word for it," Bob said, still yawning himself awake. "How about some coffee-etto?"

He went to fetch it, Jace tempted to ask for a mug too when he saw that Gianni intended to partake. While they waited, Serena asked about Easter in Italy. Jace listened eagerly to see how many details he already knew. He even tried adding a few facts himself. Apparently he had become an expert overnight. The rest of the morning passed slowly, which was fine with him. He wished they could sit around chatting like this forever, but eventually everyone went in separate directions. Almost everyone.

"Come to my room," Gianni said. "I want to show you something. A secret."

That sounded intimidating, but Jace followed him upstairs, averting his eyes as they climbed. Not in denial, but because it seemed the decent thing to do. Besides, maybe his other dream would come true when they were alone in the new guest room. Gianni shut the door once Jace was inside and started digging around in a suitcase. It was on the bed, so no bending over required.

"My mother send me this, but I want you to have it. I don't have extra for your sister, so please don't tell." Gianni found what he was looking for and turned around. It was huge! At the bottom was an egg-shaped item nearly as large as Jace's head. This was wrapped in orange and white foil, which was cinched at the top before it kept rising, doubling its height. "Do you know this?"

"No," Jace breathed, still not sure what he was seeing. "I've definitely never seen one of these!"

Gianni smiled. "Open it."

Jace sat on the edge of the bed to do so, feeling a thrill when Gianni joined him. He was too distracted to focus much on that, unwrapping the foil to reveal a giant chocolate egg.

"*Kinder Sorpresa,*" Gianni explained. "There is a surprise inside."

"I'm supposed to break it open?"

"You supposed to eat it!"

Jace felt a little bashful as he broke the chocolate shell and tried a piece. It was much sweeter than the chocolate he was used to. He practically swooned when Gianni growled like a dog and used his teeth to steal a bite straight from Jace's hand. Inside the chocolate egg was another made of yellow plastic instead. Once he rescued and opened it, he found a bunch of plastic parts. They puzzled over these together, Gianni insisting they couldn't cheat and look at the included instructions. Eventually they figured it out and assembled a small toy steamboat.

"This is great!" Jace said, spinning the paddles in the rear. "I really like it. Thank you. *Grazie*!"

Gianni smiled at him and ruffled his hair again. "You're my little Easter bunny."

Jace searched his eyes, an urge rising that he struggled to understand. Then it came to him. He wanted to kiss Gianni. Never had he wanted to do that before, but now it made perfect sense. Touching his lips to another person's would somehow articulate his feelings more effectively than words ever could.

Gianni shoved him playfully. "Now go away. This bed is too nice. I want to sleep more."

Jace stood, cheeks flushed, and gathered up his gift, murmuring his thanks. For more than just the chocolate or the toy, even though he couldn't say so. Jace had known for years that he was gay, the thought banished to the outer edges of his mind, but not until he met Gianni did it feel okay. More than just okay. Because of him, it now felt good.

Time flies, but only when you don't want it to. The realization of his feelings for Gianni was accompanied by a bittersweet awareness of just how few days they had together. Less than a month, but Jace was determined to make the most of it. When not in school or asleep, his hours were spent with Gianni. Often this was at a pizza place downtown, one of Hannah's favorite hang-out spots. There she tutored Jace. Gianni was always present, his patience seemingly infinite, even though it must be tiresome for him. Jace imagined it would be like teaching a baby to speak, but Gianni always sat there coolly, smile subtle. Jace did his best to make him proud.

This was hampered somewhat when Greg started tagging along. After meeting Hannah during one of the rarer home sessions, he had developed a crush of his own. His seemed much more superficial. Greg knew almost nothing about Hannah. Still, comparing notes, going through this together, would have been nice. Jace kept his crush secret though. He was too smart not to. As for his best friend, Jace was beginning to doubt his intelligence.

"I'm so glad you agreed to share a basket of breadsticks with me." Greg nearly panted this, pushing the plastic tray toward Hannah. "Please. Help yourself. And if you need more marinara sauce, I shall procure it for you."

He would *procure* it for her? Had he been reading his mother's romance novels or something?

"I think we've got more than enough," Hannah said, appearing amused.

Greg nodded fervently. "I'm here for you! I mean it."

Jace cleared his throat, hoping to stop his friend from humiliating himself further. "So anyway, *scusi* is how you say you're sorry to someone?"

Gianni shook his head. "Only if you knock them."

"Bump into them," Hannah clarified.

"Bump into," Gianni repeated. "Okay. If you bump into them, you say *scusi*. If you are late, you say *scusa il retardo*."

"Scuzzy I'm retarded?" Greg said, guffawing laughter. He glared at Gianni when no one else joined him, having decided the Italian man was his only competition.

"If someone's mother die," Gianni continued, "you say *mi dispiace*."

Jace asked for more examples to be sure he understood. He could feel Greg getting restless next to him, leg bouncing beneath the table. Eventually his friend couldn't take it anymore and Greg declared, "Hannah, *tu es belle!*"

The table went silent. Jace waited for some sort of a response. When one didn't appear, he asked, "What's that mean?"

"I don't know," Hannah said.

Gianni shrugged. "It's not Italian."

"It's supposed to be," Greg muttered under his breath.

Only later did Jace learn that Greg had meant to say, "You are beautiful." And he had! Just in the wrong language. He'd been trying to speak Italian and managed French instead, having gotten bad advice from a fellow student. Greg didn't show up for any tutoring sessions after that.

Just as well, because Jace loved his time alone with Gianni and Hannah. He liked having college-age friends. Considering he was still in junior high, this made him feel exceptionally mature. Jace did everything in his power to please them both—especially Gianni, who could be difficult to entertain. American television was too fast for him to follow comfortably. Instead they took walks together at night, but their little neighborhood didn't offer many sights. Gianni showed up in Jace's room more than once, wanting to look at the map again, as if already planning his next trip. Or maybe he wanted to get away from Warrensburg. Not a bad idea! Jace begged his father to drive them to Kansas City during the weekend, wanting to show that his country was more than just this small town.

They explored the rough but artistic Westport area first, shopped and dined at The Plaza next, the city's glitziest and most expensive district. Then Bob dragged them into the World War I museum, which Jace was ready to complain about until Gianni expressed interest. Afterwards they strolled through Penn Valley Park to the Kansas City Scout—a statue of a Native American on his horse, hand shading his eyes as he looked to the city skyline. The vantage point on the hill afforded them an excellent view.

"Skyscrapers," Bob declared proudly. "That's what you came here to see, isn't it?"

Gianni smiled. "Of course! How beautiful."

Over the last couple of weeks, Jace had gotten to know Gianni fairly well. Especially his expressions. He had a certain smile he used when humoring people. Jace's father especially.

Bob pointed out the more significant buildings, passing on what he knew about each. It was during this he got a little wild-eyed. "Boys, you'll have to excuse me. The burritos we had for lunch aren't agreeing with me. I'm going to hightail it back to the museum. Meet me there in ten?" He puffed up his cheeks and exhaled. "Actually, better make it twenty!"

Jace shook his head in embarrassment as his father ran

off. Then he turned back to Gianni, who was still studying the horizon. "Why did you really come to the US?"

Gianni sat on one of the flat rocks next to the Scout and raised his face toward the sun. "My sister."

"Your sister?" Jace asked, sitting next to him.

"Yes. She speak lovely English. No mistakes. She win prizes. My brothers are good too, but my sister was exchange student. Chicago. I was jealous when she come back. 'When do I get to go?' I ask. She tell me never because I don't speak English and I am too stupid to learn." Gianni grinned. "She know what she's doing. What a bitch!"

"Do you like her?" Jace asked.

"I love her!"

"Then she's a brat. Not a bitch."

"Oh. Too strong?" Gianni stuck his lips out, like he always did when committing something to memory. "Yes, so I wanted to prove her wrong. And I did. That's why I'm here." He looked over, bumping shoulders with Jace. "Don't let anyone tell you never. You dream it, you do it. Understand?"

"I think so."

"Any life you want, you make it happen. You want a pretty wife? You want to be a dolphin trainer? Okay. You do that."

Jace stared. Then he groaned. "You read my essay."

"It was a good paper!" Gianni said. Then he started laughing.

Jace did too, out of embarrassment. "That's not really how I want my future to be. I don't know what I want."

Gianni shrugged. "I also don't know."

"Do you like it here?" Jace asked, tempted to ask if he'd stay permanently. Why not? People immigrated all the time. "I know Warrensburg is boring, but do you like the US?"

Gianni thought about it, then looked him right in the eye. "I fall in love."

With the country? Or with him? That seemed too good to be true. Jace managed to hold Gianni's gaze, wishing his Italian was already perfect and that they didn't have any barriers between them. Language, distance, sexuality… He wanted to tear down every obstacle so they could be together. Even if Gianni didn't love him and couldn't, Jace still wanted him to remain a part of his life.

"Yes," Gianni said, looking away at last. "I like it here very much."

"I do too," Jace said, but he meant the rocks they sat on, the moment they were sharing. If it were up to him, they would stay there forever.

Each minute they spent together seemed to multiply what Jace nurtured in his heart. He was surprised any space remained inside! Surely his heart would eventually buckle and burst, his feelings spilling out for everyone to see. Or at least one person. Jace had to tell him. Only a week remained. If there was any chance that Gianni felt the same way, then at least they would have that time together.

Jace was in his bedroom after school when he reached this conclusion. He rose, feeling shaky, and went first to the bathroom to brush his teeth. Just in case. Then he walked with legs made of rubber down the hall. Gianni often took a catnap after getting back from class, showing up at the dinner table while yawning and stretching his arms. The door was open slightly. Not wanting to wake him if he was still sleeping, Jace placed his hand on it and gently pushed. The door swung open, silent thanks to his father's love of WD-40. Jace peeked inside.

That's when he saw them—Hannah and Gianni sitting next to each other on the end of the bed. Just like he and Greg did when playing Nintendo. Except their attention wasn't on a television screen or pixelated figures. Their heads were turned toward each other, slightly tilted as they kissed.

Anger. The emotion hit Jace unexpectedly, numbing the gut-punch of pain that he'd felt momentarily. He growled and slammed the bottom of his fist against the door frame, causing enough noise for the two lovers to jump. They blinked at him, as if coming out of a dream. Gianni was the first to speak.

"Jace! What are you… I did not see…" Words failed him.

That made two of them. Jace turned and stomped back to his room, slamming the door behind him. He continued stomping while in there, pacing in an effort to let off steam. Soon he started grasping desperately for anger again, because the more it slipped between his fingers, the more the hurt returned. Real physical pain! He hadn't expected that. All those cartoon illustrations of hearts cracking in half were more accurate than he ever expected, because as he threw himself on his bed and curled into a ball, he felt sure his heart was breaking.

* * * * *

No more Italian lessons. No laughing over pizza or walking around a nighttime neighborhood, the chaos of the world reduced to a few quiet streets for two. Jace spent all of his off hours either in his bedroom or at Greg's house. He didn't have long to hide. The week came to an end. As did Gianni's time at their house.

"Wanna ride with us to the airport?" his father asked, oblivious to all that had transpired.

Jace's stupid head nodded before he could stop it. Maybe this was for the best. He probably needed to see Gianni leave. That would provide closure. Maybe it would also help seal the invisible hole in his chest. Jace sat in the backseat, ignoring any opportunity to join the conversation. He still listened though, loving Gianni's accent, or the creaking "ehhh" noise he sometimes made when searching for a word. Even the dark waves of hair and profile of his face, which was all Jace could see from the backseat. He loved all of it. He couldn't help himself, otherwise he wouldn't be in this predicament.

Regret kicked in when they parked at the airport. This was it. They would never see each other again, and Jace had squandered these final days together feeling sorry for himself when they could have shared more conversations and made new memories. That would have been better than nothing. He felt like apologizing. Jace insisted on carrying one of Gianni's suitcases to make up for being so petty. The process went much quicker than he would have liked. Soon they were standing in a curved hallway, just outside Gianni's gate.

"Be sure to say hello to your family for us," Bob was saying. "I bet it'll feel good to sleep in your own bed again! You said you had a dog, didn't you?"

"Baffi," Jace said automatically. "That's his name. It means mustache."

Gianni smiled at him.

Jace wanted to return the gesture. He truly did. He just hurt too much inside.

Gianni turned to Bob. "Can I have a moment? Just for your son and me."

"Oh! Of course. I'll be over there browsing the magazines."

Jace's heart was already pounding. It shifted into a higher gear when Gianni placed a hand on his shoulder. Looks like his heart wasn't completely destroyed after all. He just hoped this conversation wouldn't cause it to break again.

"I knew a girl at my church," Gianni said. "Very beautiful. I was always watching, but she was older. I was your age. Old enough to feel, but to her, I was a baby. I tried anyway and…" Gianni shook his head and laughed. "She say no. Many times. She never say yes to me. I was sad. Then the next year I meet her little sister. My age. She said yes." Gianni gripped his shoulder tighter, shaking him slightly. "You don't give up! You find that girl!"

The words were well-meaning, but they weren't what Jace needed to hear. He didn't want a reminder that Gianni was only interested in women, or worse, that he thought Jace was upset because of a crush on Hannah. That wasn't it at all. He wanted Gianni to recognize Jace's feelings without him having to voice them, because doing so was too dangerous. Or did it not matter? His father was too far away to hear, and Gianni would be on a different continent by this time tomorrow. Why not tell him the truth?

"I really…" Jace choked on the words, his throat raw, tears already spilling from his eyes. He continued anyway, voice shaking. "I really *really* like you."

"I like you too," Gianni said, pulling him close for a hug. It wasn't subtle. No distance remained between them. Gianni clutched Jace, muscular arms squeezing painfully tight. His body felt good. Warm. Reassuring. Then he brought his cheek to Jace's, voice soft in his ear. *"Avrai sempre un posto speciale nel mio cuore."*

Jace didn't understand the words, but they sounded like a promise. He felt panic, repeating them mentally so he wouldn't forget. Then Gianni released him, an announcement on the intercom informing them that boarding had begun. The world was a blur. Jace wiped at his eyes. His father reappeared to shake a hand. Jace sniffed and tried to get himself under control, watching as Gianni joined the queue. The best thing that had ever happened to him was leaving, and Jace was powerless to stop it.

"Should we go?" his father asked.

Jace shook his head. He wouldn't budge until there was nothing left to see. Past the other passengers he could only spot a strong arm in a black T-shirt, the skin of the hand brown and perfect. He only hated the boarding pass that it held, and how this was handed to a flight attendant. Time was up. One step through that door, and he would be gone forever. Before this happened, Gianni turned, leaning to see past a line of impatient passengers. He spotted Jace, dark eyes sparkling for him one last time. Then he smiled, waved goodbye, and returned to the world he had come from.

Bob put an arm around his shoulders, guiding him away. "Gosh, you really liked him, didn't you?"

Jace nodded glumly. "I still do."

Hannah. She was a lifeline. Getting in touch with her had been embarrassing. No doubt she had also reached the same conclusion about Jace's angry outburst, assuming he had a crush on her. He needed her though, not just because she could translate Gianni's parting words, but because she was the only other person who understood. His parents might say they missed Gianni, and Michelle acted pouty the first night, but they didn't care in the same way. Not like Jace did, and as he came to discover, not like Hannah did either.

She cried in front of him. They had just sat down to begin a tutoring session at the usual pizza place when she looked around and shook her head as tears streaked her cheeks. "It's not the same, is it?" she asked.

"No," Jace admitted.

"We'll have to find somewhere else to do this."

"Yeah."

She blew her nose, Jace wishing he could let his emotions show like that because keeping it in made his throat ache. "Can you help me translate something?"

"Sure!" Hannah said, seeming eager for the distraction.

He passed her the piece of paper. He had written the phrase on the back of a dry-cleaning receipt as soon as they were back in his father's van. He wasn't great at transcribing the sounds to written form, which is probably why Hannah looked so confused.

"*Avrai sempre un posto…* um… *speciale nel mio cuore,*" Jace said, hoping he had gotten it right.

Hannah looked up. "Where did you hear that?"

He hesitated, unsure if it was supposed to remain a secret. Then again, where else would he have heard it?

She had the same realization. "Oh. It means 'You'll always have a special place in my heart.'"

Jace swallowed. Then he glared and rubbed at his eyes

because he really didn't want to cry in front of her. Not that it did much good, but he managed to hold most of it in.

Hannah's expression was pure sympathy. "You really love him, don't you?"

Like a brother? Is that what she meant? Or did she know? Jace was too emotional to care. "Yeah."

Hannah nodded. "So do I."

They sat there in silence, sharing their misery. After enough of this, Hannah pulled out a pad of paper, setting it on the table with a thunk. "Ready? You've got a lot to learn if you want to write him a letter."

"A letter?"

"Yeah! He's not gone forever! Maybe if we write him a bunch, he'll get annoyed enough to come back. Just to shut us up."

Jace laughed at the idea. Then he sat up. "Okay," he said. "I'm ready to learn."

The letter came three years later. At one time they had come more frequently. Jace wrote Gianni primitive messages, the responses requiring Hannah's assistance to translate. Then high school had started, and he found himself distracted by all sorts of things. The tutoring sessions with Hannah occurred less and less often, a teacher at his school taking over. The last time Jace had seen her, Hannah had just gotten back from a winter trip to Italy, bringing with her photos that he had obsessed over, an old familiar ache returning to his chest. They had lost touch after that. It all seemed so long ago, which is why Jace was surprised to get a letter with both of their names on it. Gianni and Hannah. And it was from Italy!

The only reason he didn't open it right away was because he wanted privacy. There hadn't been a lot of that lately. He sure didn't mind though! Nor could he wait any longer. Jace picked up the envelope from his dresser. He considered again the writing on the outside. Then he opened it.

The card inside was long, half of it a photo, the rest of it text. He didn't need to read the words to know it was a wedding announcement. The photo gave that away. Gianni was wearing a black suit, his smile proud. He looked much the same. A little older maybe, the scruff on his cheeks thicker. Hannah was next to him in a white dress, her happy expression like sunshine. Most telling was the little boy between them—still just a toddler, but he had his father's dark hair and his mother's generous smile. Jace turned the card over, reading a handwritten note that promised they still thought of him—still *talked* about him—and that they wanted to see him again if he ever visited Italy. Then he flipped over the card to look at the photo once more, tears coming, but this time they were happy.

"Is that from another college?"

Jace turned. On his bed was a guy with mismatched eyes, a punky fauxhawk, and scruff of his own that Jace had felt pressed against more places than just his cheek. Unlike Gianni, Victor never needed long to figure out what he was thinking. Or feeling.

"You all right?" Victor said, sitting upright and pushing himself out of bed. "A ghost from the past, huh?"

Jace shook his head and laughed. "How do you do that?"

Victor didn't answer. He just took the card from Jace and examined it. "Can't say I blame you. He's cute! A little young though. What is he, two years old?"

"Shut up!" Jace pushed him playfully. "This was the first guy I ever had feelings for."

Victor's eyes were probing as he moved closer. "But not the last?"

"No, definitely not the last."

Arms wrapped around him, Jace leaning back before they could kiss. He looked with wonder at the handsome face before him. He had once thought, been certain, that secrets would keep anyone from truly knowing who he was. And they had, but not any longer. His parents, Michelle, Greg, and everyone else—they all knew the truth and accepted him. Best of all was the persistent guy with a crooked smile, squeezing him and refusing to wait any longer. Love was more complicated than he had ever imagined, full of communication barriers that went far beyond words, but as a kiss silenced the laugh burbling forth from his lips, Jace decided it was the language most worth learning.

Something Like Flowers

by Jay Bell

Austin, 2015

Don't let go, darling. Press hard, like each guitar string is a snake that you must hold down or it'll bite. You don't like that? Okay, each string is a mouse's tail, and you can change how they squeak depending on where you squeeze them. Up here are the ears, and if you twist them just so... No, you won't hurt the mice. It's more like they're being tickled. There! Perfect. Now then, don't let go. Hold on tight, and I'll show you how to make music.

Jason Grant finished tuning his guitar, positioned his fingers over the right mice tails, smiled, and played a few chords. Satisfied, he opened his mouth to sing. The voice he heard was dry and tuneless. The words were wrong too! He clamped his mouth shut, but the singing continued.

Of course. His roommate.

Jason shook his head and gently set the guitar next to him on his bed. Then he went to the living room where Emma was sitting on the floor in front of the coffee table. She continued crooning, Jason grimacing as he tried to figure out what song she was singing. Was it from a Western? The lyrics were about being wanted dead or alive. When he realized that it was Bon Jovi, the grimace etched even deeper into his features.

"I will pay you to stop," he said over the noise. "I mean it."

"No deal," Emma said, not looking up from her work.

What was she doing anyway? Jason moved closer to see. The coffee table was a mess of construction paper, glitter, scissors, glue, markers, and metallic stars. "Working on your thesis?" he asked.

"Ha! I wish. That would be so cool."

He sat on the couch so he could watch. "Seriously, what is this?"

Emma's tongue was sticking out of the corner of her mouth. She sprinkled more glitter onto a swirl of glue, shook off the excess, and held it up for him to see. A homemade greeting card. In the center were flowers, the petals created from haphazardly arranged star stickers. The stems and leaves were made out of glitter and glue, the vase purple construction paper that had been cut into a rounded shape. Written in marker above and below were two lines:

Roses are red.

Violets are blue.

"Ready for this?" Emma asked, opening the card for him to see. The inside was still fairly plain except for two more lines of questionable poetry:

You're the best mom.

Girl you know it's true.

"Girl you know it's true?" Jason asked incredulously.

"Ga ga ga girl!" Emma declared. "Ew ew ew, I love you!"

Jason made another face. "Milli Vanilli?"

"Yup!" Emma said shamelessly. "I've been listening to my mom's favorite music for inspiration."

He thought of Michelle, his former caseworker, and tried to imagine her rocking out to Bon Jovi or Milli Vanilli. He was pretty sure she had better taste than that and felt the need to defend her. "There's a difference between the music you grow up with and the music you actually like."

"Not for most people," Emma said, setting the card on the table. "For music snobs like you, there's a difference, but the rest of us roll with it."

"I'm not a snob!"

Emma looked over at him, eyebrows raised.

"Maybe just a little," he admitted. He nodded at the card. "What's the occasion? Does she have a birthday coming up?"

"Mother's Day."

Oh. He didn't know a lot about it. Jason possessed exactly zero memories when it came to the holiday, aside from always feeling left out. The same with Father's Day, although he supposed that would be different this year, now that he'd officially been adopted. In another month, maybe he would be sitting where Emma was now, making a card for Ben and Tim. He tried to imagine their reaction if he handed them a piece of folded construction paper covered in bad poetry and glitter. "Aren't you worried she won't like it?"

Emma shot him a confused look. "Why wouldn't she?"

"Because it's uh… Never mind."

"What?" she demanded. "Say it!"

"No way."

"Be honest! I can take it."

Jason exhaled. "Fine. The card is sort of doofy."

He expected Emma to be angry. Instead she seemed confused. "She's my mom! Of course she's going to love it! Are you crazy?"

"Sorry," Jason said, shooting to his feet. "I don't know what I'm talking about."

Wishing he had never pried, he went to his room. This wouldn't be an adequate escape. Emma wasn't the type to let things slide. Normally he liked that about her, but today he wanted to forget the subject completely. The best course of action was to leave the apartment and let it all blow over. He was pulling on his shoes when Emma appeared in the doorway.

"Sorry," she said. "I wasn't thinking."

He shook his head. "I'm the one who's sorry! It's a fun card. You're right, maybe I am a snob."

"I don't think so." Emma walked into the room. "You just don't know what it's like to have a mom."

She meant well. Emma was never malicious or deliberately cruel. Not with him. But this time she was wrong. "I do know," he said, looking to the guitar on its stand. That's where all the good memories were, like his mother teaching him how to play the instrument. At the time it had felt like learning magic. Real magic. He had always been amazed when she made her own music and had become jittery with excitement when she agreed to show him how.

"All moms care about is the gesture," Emma continued. "Yeah, the card is dumb, but it will remind her of all the stupid ones I made as a kid. To her, it'll be the best card ever, or at least she'll love me enough to say it is."

"It's a fun idea," Jason said as he stood, still feeling embarrassed. "You're right. I didn't get it."

"Where are you going?"

"I have a few errands to run. That's all."

Emma remained in his way. "Are you mad at me?"

"Never," he said, giving her a quick hug. "You're my best friend. I can never stay mad at you."

"I am pretty awesome," she said, hugging him back. Then she stepped aside. "You could come with me to Houston tomorrow. I'm driving out to see Mom. I don't mind sharing."

"Thanks," he said. "I might have plans, but we'll see."

Once in his car, he sat in the driver's seat and wondered where to go. This weekend was a rare one for him. He had two days off from both his day job at the pet store and the animal shelter where he volunteered. Instead of reveling in his freedom, he struggled to find direction. Hanging with his best friend was out, now that he'd made things awkward. What he really wanted was to see William, who now lived halfway across the country, having returned to saving lives in the Coast Guard. Jason thought about driving to the airport spontaneously, just to see what would happen. The idea sounded glorious until an old fear clutched at his stomach. What if he liked Oregon too much? What if he never wanted to return? Any potential happiness was ruined by the thought of leaving Ben and Tim behind, their affection for him wilting like an abandoned houseplant in need of water.

Then again, maybe they could be the solution! They were his adoptive parents now, and that meant they were supposed to provide comfort whenever he needed it. Jason grinned at the thought. Then he started his car and drove to the outskirts of Austin.

He already felt better when cruising down the long drive to the house he used to live in. After parking in front of the separate garage, he walked to it and stood on his toes to see in the window. Both cars where there! That alone made him happy. Jason walked to the house and let himself in the front door. Chinchilla was the first to greet him. She wasn't exactly a young dog anymore, but she still had spirit. She hobbled toward him, wearing what resembled a wide smile. Jason got down on the entryway tiles to pet and kiss her. This attracted the attention of someone else.

"Hey!" Tim said. "What are you doing here? What's that you say? You came to mow the lawn? That's so nice of you!"

Jason rose to give him a hug. "I will if you want me to."

"I love my riding mower too much," Tim said, putting an arm around his neck and guiding him toward the living room. "Benjamin will be happy to see you. I am too. The grass can wait."

Jason found his other father on the couch, a phone pressed to his ear. Ben's face lit up when noticing him. He stood and held up a finger. Then he rolled his eyes and spoke into the phone. "Yes, I'm sure Karen can't wait to see me. Right. Jason is here. We'll talk tomorrow. Okay. Love you. Bye." He tossed the phone on the couch, then opened his arms wide. "My real family! Get over here!"

Jason laughed, his troubles already distant. "Who was that?"

"Your grandmother," Ben replied, studying him. "No? Still seems weird?"

Jason nodded. "I love her, but—"

"I get it," Ben said.

Jason believed him. Ben might not know what it was like to be adopted, but he was one of the most empathetic people Jason had ever met, and on more than one occasion, seemed to know what he was feeling without him having to speak a word. "Does she *want* me to call her Grandma? I'd hate to hurt her feelings."

Ben chuckled. "My mom has waited a very long time to become a grandparent. I'm sure she can wait a little longer. Whenever you're comfortable is fine. Or never at all. She'll love you either way." He nodded toward the kitchen. "I'm going to make tea. Do you want some?"

"Or," Tim interjected, "we have some of that neon-green poison you love so much."

Mountain Dew! Jason followed them to the kitchen and cracked open a can. "How's everyone in The Woodlands doing?" he asked.

"Fine," Ben said. "Mom and Dad have started marriage counselling, Karen is out of rehab, and the roof above my old bedroom caved in due to all the rain this year. Wait, did I say fine? I meant to say wine, because that's what I need." Despite his joke, he started boiling water for tea. "I'm driving out there tomorrow, if you want to tag along and see everyone."

"Don't you want to be alone with your mom?" Jason asked.

Ben blinked. "Because it's Mother's Day? Not really. The more, the merrier!"

"Don't listen," Tim said, leaning against the counter. "He just wants to use you as a human shield."

"I do not!" Ben said. Then he looked sheepish. "Although it *would* be more bearable with you there."

Jason laughed. He sat at the breakfast bar and looked to his other father. "What about you? Are you also visiting your family?"

Tim's expression became strained. "Nah. I called, but Mom's got plans already."

The Wymans. Jason wasn't crazy about them. They reminded him too much of the bad sort of foster parents he'd been stuck with before. The kind who, on paper, liked the idea of kids, but didn't actually have the time or patience for them. Still, the good news is that not everyone would be busy tomorrow. "In that case, we should catch a movie or something."

Tim shook his head. "I'm going to The Woodlands too. Someone needs to drive Benjamin home when he's an emotional wreck."

"He's not kidding," Ben said, dunking a teabag repeatedly. "When did they get so crazy?"

"Around the time Karen joined that cult," Tim supplied helpfully.

Jason laughed. It had only been a fringe religion, but even once the preachy lectures had dried up, Ben's sister still had a talent for making everyone miserable. Suddenly he didn't feel so bad about not having a traditional family. He took a swig of Mountain Dew when a grumbling from below attracted his attention. He looked down to see Chinchilla raise a paw and put it down again, like she was stomping a foot. Then she grumbled again, the noise similar to a harrumph. Jason prided himself on being able to read the body language of animals. They had their own way of communicating that didn't rely on words, and he considered himself a student. His reward? When most animals noticed how quickly he reacted to their needs, they tended to treat him as their personal servant.

"Ignore her," Tim said. "She's already gone potty."

"That's not good enough," Jason said, hopping down. "She thinks I'm here just to visit her."

Chinchilla's butt started wagging when he reached down to pet her, then she bounded toward the living room and no doubt the back door. Maybe she wasn't so old after all! Jason laughed and followed. Ben joined him. Tim went to start mowing the lawn. Jason was soon sitting in the backyard, rump on the patio stone so that Chinchilla could lean against him. Ben plopped down too. For a few minutes, they were content to enjoy the sun in silence. On the surface, Jason felt just as warm and content as his skin. Deeper down he was still conflicted, and it was into these depths that Ben seemed to see.

"What's wrong?" he asked.

"Nothing," Jason said automatically. All those years of hiding how he truly felt from foster parents had become a bad habit. He sighed. "Sorry. The day started rough. That obvious?"

"A little," Ben admitted. "When you first got here, your smile seemed sad. Is it William? Have you—"

"I'm sure he's fine," Jason said, looking skyward.

"You know, it's never too late to—"

"Not today," Jason pleaded. "I don't have the energy."

"Okay," Ben said easily. "We don't have to go down that road, but if that's not what's bugging you, then what is?"

Jason took a deep breath, hoping the truth wouldn't hurt. "I'm grateful that you adopted me, so please don't take this the wrong way, but—"

"Mother's Day?"

Jason looked over at him in surprise. "Yeah! How'd you know?"

"Experience," Ben said, "but not my own. Allison lost her mother when she was young, and I saw how difficult this day was for her. Eventually she found a way of celebrating. She uses the day as a memorial. Have you thought about approaching it like that?"

Jason shook his head. "What do you mean?"

"Why not visit your mother's grave tomorrow? When's the last time you did?"

"Never," Jason said.

"*Never?*" Ben seemed shocked. "Why not?"

Because he didn't know where she had been laid to rest, or if she even had a grave. Jason felt too embarrassed to admit that, so he just shrugged.

"A trip to her grave might make you feel better," Ben said. "I know it won't be the same, but it *is* a way of spending time with her."

"Do you visit Jace's grave very often?" Jason asked.

"No," Ben said. "He doesn't really have one. Jace was cremated, and the place where his ashes were scattered isn't in Texas. When I want to reconnect with him, I drive by our old house, or visit the park where we got married. Those are the places that make me feel close to him, and that's fine too. You could visit your childhood home instead. Just standing outside of it would bring back a lot of memories. Do you still know the address?"

Jason strained to remember. "I think so. At least, I kind of know where it is."

"Then come with us tomorrow," Ben said. "While I'm stuck with my family, you can take the car wherever you need."

"I already got an invitation from Emma to drive with her."

Ben smiled. "Once she finds out Tim and I are headed that way, I bet she'll want a ride. From what I understand, her father is making her pay for everything now, gas included. Something about her grades last semester?"

Jason winced in sympathy. "Yeah. That was a bad situation." He thought about it some more. "It's really okay if I tag along?"

"Are you kidding?" Ben put an arm around him and squeezed. "I love every second I get to spend with you."

The feeling was mutual. Jason realized he *did* know the address of his childhood home. He might have been in his late teens when he first moved there, but he had returned often enough since then. His home was right here, with Ben and Tim, and he prayed nothing would ever change that.

The ride to Houston always stirred up memories. This was inevitable, considering that Jason had lived there for nearly two decades. He chose to focus on more recent memories, such as the time he and William had raced to Houston in the dead of night to witness the birth of a child. Those happy times were especially difficult to think back on, now that they were apart.

Jason didn't have to face any old ghosts just yet. First they stopped in The Woodlands. He liked the Bentleys. June and Adam were always welcoming, even though he might not think of them as his grandparents yet. Karen was okay too if you kept her on the right subjects and shrugged off any nasty comments. All three of them treated Jason like he was family. For better or worse.

Adam answered the door. He glanced over his shoulder before addressing them in hushed tones. "I hope you brought flowers."

Ben sighed. "Did you forget? Again?"

"Hey, this holiday is supposed to be you kids paying tribute. She's your mother, not mine!"

Tim snorted. "Somebody's sleeping on the couch tonight. Pro-tip: get an extra blanket, fold it a couple times, and use it to cover the cushions. It's almost as good as a mattress."

Adam finished hugging his son, then took Tim's hand to shake it. "I've got a pro-tip for you. Watch TV until you get tired, then sneak into the guest room. That way you'll have a real mattress!"

Tim's mouth dropped open. "Why didn't I think of that?"

"Because you haven't been married as long as I have." Adam noticed him standing there and opened his arms wide. "Jason! Come here! How's my little guy doing?"

The problem with being the only grandchild was being treated like he was still a kid. Adam was nice, but if he did that damn trick again…

"What's this?" Adam declared, sounding surprised. "I think there's something behind your ear. Let's see!"

Jason took one look at the quarter that was being held mere inches from his face and shook his head. "Like I said last time, you really need to figure out how to pull more than just coins from my ear."

Adam wasn't the least bit discouraged. "Maybe we should try the other one!"

"Yay," Jason deadpanned. "Then I'll just have to find a vending machine from the eighties and maybe I'll have enough for—" He stopped, a fifty dollar bill appearing out of thin air and waving before his face. A second later, he snatched it away. Okay, sometimes it was awesome being treated like a kid. "I love you, Grandpa," he said.

"Sell out," Emma whispered from next to him. Then louder she added, "Hey, do me next!"

"This ATM is out of money," Adam said. "Jason, would you mind sharing with her?"

"No problem," Jason said, handing Emma the quarter.

"Where's my cut?" Tim demanded. "I drove you both here."

"I can't pull a beer from your ear," Adam said, "but I was smart enough to put a six-pack in the fridge this morning."

"You're the man!" Tim said, leading the way inside.

"Nice trick, Dad," Ben said as he passed by.

Emma didn't seem as impressed, glowering at the quarter in her palm as she went inside.

That just left Jason. The nature of the day had him feeling shy, so as they moved deeper into the house, he hung back, preferring to watch events rather than be part of them. June entered the living room at the same time they did, Ben walking over to give her a hug. Then he took a step back, extended a hand, and began singing. He didn't have to ask the room to be silent first. Ben's voice was too pleasing to interrupt. Jason wasn't familiar with the tune until Ben had begun listening to it frequently so he could practice. *Danny's Song* by Anne Murray. Ben had explained how it was his mother's favorite song when she was pregnant with him. Jason had to admit there was a certain poetry in him singing it to her now. Everyone stood still and listened. By the end of the song, June had covered her mouth and her eyes were filled with tears. Then she rushed forward to hug her son. The scene was moving, and Jason couldn't help but wonder how many times he would have behaved similarly, had his life taken a different course.

"I gotta admit," Emma said from next to him, "that's *way* better than a homemade card! Speaking of which, ready to go?"

"Sure," Jason said, tearing his eyes away from the scene. Ben was telling his mother how grateful he was for all that she had done for him. There was no questioning his sincerity. Having a mother must be awesome. Jason was already regretting coming along today, since it would probably just be one big reminder of what he was missing.

Not wanting to ruin the festivities for anyone, Jason put on a happy face, spent a few minutes talking to June, and asked Tim for the car keys. Then he and Emma went outside to the car.

"You owe me twenty-five bucks," she said.

"You owe me twelve and a half cents. You'll get yours when I get mine. Exact change only."

By the time they were on the road, she was on her phone and searching the internet to see if half-pennies had ever existed in the United States, and if she could get one cheap enough to be worth it. Knowing her, she wouldn't mind breaking even or losing money just to make him cough up his half of the dough.

Jason kept his attention on the highway. He took an early exit by mistake, but he wasn't lost. Not by far. He recognized his surroundings. Twenty-four different foster families had taken him in, so he had lived in most areas of Houston. Some were more memorable than others. As they drove toward an affluent area, they passed a street that would have led him to where the Hubbards lived. He wondered if Caesar was there now, trying to appease his parents. If not, his former foster brother Peter would surely be visiting home to kiss butt. Jason was tempted to crash the celebration in the spirit of revenge horror movies. *"Remember me?"* he'd declare before revving the chainsaw. The thought made him laugh. In truth, he didn't harbor any anger toward them anymore. Those events felt too much like ancient history.

The house they eventually arrived at was still part of his present. Jason had never lived there, but he'd stayed the night on a few special occasions, such as when he and Emma first became friends. That was before she had moved to Austin. Back then she had been an ornery teenager with incredibly awesome parents, one of whom was responsible for introducing them and so much more. Jason felt a swell of affection when she appeared at the door.

Michelle Trout, his former caseworker, the person who had done the impossible and found him a family. She hugged her daughter first, but when she turned to Jason and did the same, the embrace was just as loving. He enjoyed the sensation for as long as it lasted, then followed her inside, feeling more comfortable here than he did at the Bentleys. Jason wasn't sure why. Maybe because he and Michelle shared more of a history.

They wound through the house to the backyard, where Michelle's husband, Greg, was manning the grill. Their two teenage sons were there as well. Preston was... Punk? Goth? Emo? Jason wasn't sure what the right term was. Half of Preston's head was shaved, the other covered by long purple hair. He had a number of piercings and wore enough makeup to make his gender uncertain at first glance. His brother, Sylvester, had his father's muscular build and was doing his best to live up to the action star he was named after. Considering that Emma was a big beautiful lesbian, and Michelle relatively normal in appearance, most people wouldn't immediately assume they were a family. Aside from Sylvester and Greg perhaps, who looked like younger/older versions of each other. This made Jason feel even more at ease. He was just one more misfit mingling with the rest!

He made the rounds, saying hello and engaging in the usual small talk. Then it was time for lunch. They all squeezed onto benches attached to a picnic table. Greg served them burgers and roasted veggies before sitting too. At the end of the meal, Jason witnessed more Mother's Day rituals.

"We don't get to choose our parents," Preston said, rising and walking over to his mother, "but I suppose I could have done worse. I want you to have this." He handed a small book to her, the cover black and without a title.

"Your poetry?" Michelle asked, pressing a hand to her chest. "How wonderful!"

Preston grunted. "Promise to burn it after you've read it."

Michelle looked aghast. "What? No!"

"Swear you'll burn it!" Preston growled.

"Great present, son," Greg said, standing to gently usher him away. "Who's next?"

Sylvester jumped to his feet, went to his mother, and plonked a tall present down on the table. "I got you this," he said, all grins.

"Thank you," she gasped, careful as she unwrapped a statue of a female angel, covered in cherubs. They were in her arms, on her shoulders, at her feet, in her hair… "My goodness!" Michelle said, expression difficult to read. If Jason was a betting man, he would guess she was trying to hold back laughter.

"It's from the Hallmark store," Sylvester said proudly. "It was really expensive!"

"I can tell," Michelle said, turning the statue to view it from different angles. Not that it helped improve the appearance. "Thank you so much!"

Sylvester hugged her, then strutted back to his seat. Emma was close enough to remain seated. She pushed the homemade card toward Michelle, who took it, read it, and laughed.

"This certainly brings back memories! Wait, is this from that song?"

"Milli Vanilli," Emma said. "Sometimes, when I miss you, I listen to the cheesy old music you like."

Greg laughed.

Michelle pretended to scowl but was soon smiling again. "What a cute idea! I love it."

Sylvester strained to see, expression unhappy. "Seriously, Emma? Could you get any cheaper?"

"Hey!" she shot back. "I'm not still living at home like you. I've got bills to pay."

"I work my ass off!" Sylvester shot back. "Unlike you, I don't expect Mom and Dad to pay for everything!"

"You better burn it," Preston said, still focused on the book of poetry. "I mean it!"

"Quiet!" Greg shouted. "All of you!" Then he leaned over to

kiss his wife on the cheek. "Honey, I'll give you my present later."

"Please tell me it's a hysterectomy," she murmured. In a louder voice, she said, "This is the best Mother's Day ever! Thank you all. I'm so proud of my babies!"

And she was. Even Jason could see that. The presents might not be what she would have chosen for herself, but she did love her children, despite their flaws. After more conversation, Greg instructed everyone to help clean so Michelle wouldn't have to. Of all the gifts, this seemed to be her favorite. Jason rose to help, but Michelle gestured that he should sit again.

"Keep me company," she said. "It feels like ages since we've seen each other!"

"It's been a while," he admitted.

"How are things with—"

"The same," he said, easily guessing the topic. Everyone wanted to talk about William. What was there to say? Nothing had changed.

"And how are you feeling today?"

Jason scrutinized her. "Emma told you."

Michelle nodded. "She said you were having a hard time because of Mother's Day. That's why we used to distract you guys in the group home."

He snorted. "Really?"

"Yep. Remember those ice cream outings? The first one was always in May, supposedly due to the warm weather, but really it was because of Mother's Day. We made sure not to mention that, and you know how rare any sort of field trip was."

The ice cream trips had felt really special at the time. Jason had looked forward to each, even making sure to get kicked out of a foster placement once just so he could participate. "Now that you mention it, I do remember the year Shirley Packard was crying into her orange sherbet, and how another guy asked if he could eat it."

Michelle laughed. "I don't think I was there for that one."

"So somewhere in Houston right now, a bunch of orphans are gorging themselves on ice cream?"

"Mm-hm! Next month is my turn. Father's Day. You're welcome to join us, but I'm guessing you'll have plans."

Jason grinned. "I've got two dads, so I'll be twice as busy." He nodded to the angel statue. "Hopefully they won't sell out of those before then."

"Hush," Michelle said, turning the statue to view it again. "Sylvester is a sweet boy. He *does* need to stop equating love with price tags. You should see how much he buys his girlfriend."

"Not the worst trait for a guy to have."

"No," Michelle said, eyes darting to the house, which wasn't exactly small. "He gets that from his father. So you're doing okay despite it all?"

He nodded. "Yeah. Actually, there's something I wanted to ask. How much do you remember about my mother?"

"Nothing," Michelle said. "I was probably still in college when Child Protective Services took you away."

"True, but I thought there might have been more information about her somewhere."

"I gave your file to you, remember?"

He nodded. "But there's nothing in it about my mom. Just her name on different forms, and a little of my history with her."

"That sounds normal," Michelle said. "What sort of info were you after?"

"I uh—" His throat went dry. He had to clear it to continue. "I don't know what happened to her after she died. Like if she was buried or…"

"Oh!" Michelle's brow creased in concentration. "If that wasn't in your file, I think I might know where it is."

His heart leapt. "Really?"

"Yeah. I'll have to check at work."

His elation plummeted. "Oh. Okay. Well, let me know if you find anything."

"We'll find out together," Michelle said. "Let's go!"

He didn't budge. "To your work? I don't want to ruin your day. I'm sure you're sick of being there and—"

"Jason. This is important to you, isn't it?"

He took in her earnest expression and nodded. "Yeah."

Michelle stood. "Then let's go."

He felt a surge of affection for her. "I really appreciate it," he stammered. "I honestly wouldn't have asked if I'd known it would inconvenience you."

"Inconvenience," Michelle repeated, shaking her head. "It doesn't. Not at all. You're family now, and even if you weren't, I'd still want to help you. Just don't get your hopes up, okay?"

"I won't."

Michelle made sure their eyes were locked. "Do you promise? I can't stand seeing you sad."

He nodded. "I promise."

Returning to the group home was a bittersweet experience. Jason had despised his first months there. After discovering how much more he disliked foster placements, he eventually came to think of the group home as a sanctuary. Not as good as turning back the clock and being with his mother again, but way better than pretending he belonged with a family that wasn't his own. Little had changed in the years since his absence. The place was mostly empty, thanks to the ice cream outing, so he could tour the facility in peace. This included one of his old rooms. The posters on the wall were different, as were the scant possessions, but the rest looked the same. He paused in the television area, remembering long forgotten faces and conversations. The same with the dining area, where a tall man with a warm voice and a name similar to his own had helped soothe his broken heart. And offered him a place to live, even though Jason hadn't accepted. Little had he known that, years later, their conversation and a phone number written on a cereal box top would eventually lead to a new family and so much more. That still seemed like such a miracle.

He looked over at Jace's sister, who was patiently waiting. "Ready?" Michelle asked.

Jason nodded, then followed her to a small office space. He was quiet as she booted up and checked her computer, watching Michelle for any indication that they had succeeded. None came. She shook her head in frustration, then led him to a room that wasn't familiar at all. The sign on the outside said *Archives*. This turned out to be a long closet full of filing cabinets. Jason stood back, wanting to help but unsure what to do. The minutes ticked by, and just when he accepted that they wouldn't find anything there, Michelle spun around, a document in hand.

"Copy of the death certificate," she said.

"Can I see?"

"Of course!"

She handed it to him, Jason's hand shaking a little when he took it. The certificate was full of information that most people would find boring, but he studied each line eagerly, wanting to learn more. *Helen Gladys Grant*. He had forgotten his mother's middle name—if he had ever known it—and sometimes wondered if he had the first one right, since to him she had always been Mom. Her date of birth was there (more news to him) along with her birthplace. Colorado, a state he'd never known he had a connection to. Then he noticed an important line on the form. *METHOD OF DISPOSITION*. Beneath this, a box for "burial" was checked.

"She was buried," Jason said excitedly.

"Does it say where?"

He looked again. "No. There's some empty lines they could have filled out, but they didn't."

Michelle took the document from him to double check. Then she swore.

"It's fine," he said. "Thanks for trying."

"I'm not quitting yet!" Michelle marched back to her office.

Jason hurried after her, his promise broken, because his hopes were way up now! Michelle sat at her computer, typing and clicking. Jason was too scared to ask what she was doing. That might break her concentration and cause her to miss something. Eventually she grumbled, picked up the phone on her desk, and started making calls. From the sound of it, Michelle was calling funeral homes. She kept providing them with his mother's name and social security number. Then she would wait, say, "Thanks anyway" and try another number. Some funeral homes weren't even open. Jason would have given up long ago, but she kept at it. After ten or so calls, instead of a "Thanks anyway" she said, "Really? Yes, please!" and started writing down information. His heart thudded as he waited for her to end the call. Once she had, she held up the piece of paper victoriously. "Got it!"

"That's great!" he said. He wasn't entirely sure if that was the truth, because now he was faced with a different predicament. For the first time in nearly twenty years, Jason was going to visit his mother.

Death places a firm punctuation mark at the end of every life. Most people's stories are written by the second, new details constantly added to the narrative, no matter how trivial. When someone dies, that process halts. Their story is complete, and others can only go back and reread what has already occurred.

The final mystery is what form that final punctuation takes. Is the person's life summed up by a humble period, or perhaps saluted with an exclamation mark? Or, as in the case of Jason's mother, sometimes a question mark is most appropriate.

That's what made the impending visit to her grave so difficult. When Jason thought of what he wanted to say, he mostly had questions. Why had she allowed that abusive jerk into their lives? Was it loneliness? Desperation? Did it break her heart when Jason was taken away? Did she fight to get him back? Was there something he should know that would make her actions more forgivable?

The car turned, bringing them to a strip mall parking lot. Jason was glad Michelle had offered to drive. He was much too distracted to do so safely. They parked in front of a flower shop.

He looked around, not a cemetery in sight. "What are we doing here?"

Michelle nodded to the window display. "I thought you might like to put flowers on her grave."

"Oh. Right."

They went into the store together, the florist eager to help them. The man seemed in high spirits, probably because this must be one of his most profitable days.

"We're just looking," Jason said when the florist asked, wanting privacy. He considered the flowers on display, most of them colorful and cheerful. Was that appropriate? Maybe something somber would be better. Did they have black roses? He walked back and forth between the displays, unable to decide. Eventually he turned to Michelle. "I don't know. What do you like?"

"Well, orchids are my favorite, but they're kind of expensive."

"This is the first time I've bought her flowers in my entire life. Expensive is fine."

He underestimated just how expensive. The florist created an arrangement of six pink orchids, which ended up costing him almost one hundred dollars.

"I can chip in," Michelle said.

Jason shook his head. "I'm not as broke as I used to be. Besides, they really are beautiful."

He couldn't think of anything to say during the drive to the cemetery, still distracted by his memories. He divided them into two categories: before the drinking started and after. Not all the memories in the after category were bad, but fewer of them were good. He greatly preferred what little he could remember from the before category. His grandmother had still been around, providing a sense of stability and security, even if Jason hadn't been aware of it at the time. So much of what he thought he knew came later, when he looked back and tried to interpret events, but he was certain that at one time his mother had laughed more and had patiently taught him to play the guitar. Once he had gotten the hang of it a little, she would sometimes dance and sing while he played, crooning out the words to classic rock songs. He remembered laughing too, and falling asleep in her bed more often than he did his own. When he pictured her, she was still gigantic, a large warm presence he could snuggle up against. Even though he was a grown man, when Jason dreamt of being with his mother again, he could still fit comfortably in the crook of her arm.

"Ready?" Michelle asked.

Jason looked up to find they were stopped in a parking lot, a cast iron fence separating them from rows of graves. He nodded wordlessly and got out of the car. Michelle seemed to know what she was doing. She led the way, sometimes stopping to consult the paper, or to look around and get her bearings. They passed the correct grave and had to backtrack to find it. He was surprised when they stopped in front of not one, but two headstones.

"Lauren Grant," Michelle read out loud. "Did she have a sister?"

"I think that's my grandma," Jason said, nodding when he saw the dates. "Yeah." He looked to the grave next to it. Helen Grant. The birthdate matched what he had seen earlier. This was it. The headstone was simple, just a block of stone with rounded edges. The graves themselves were covered in trimmed grass. He frowned, hating that this was all that remained of his mother. Somehow it didn't seem fair.

"I'll give you privacy," Michelle said. "When you're ready, I'll be at the car."

He nodded his appreciation, waiting until Michelle was gone before he looked down at the grave. He thought he should cry, or feel more than he did. Maybe he was doing it wrong. Jason got down on his knees over the spot where he assumed a coffin must be. He felt cool moisture soaking into his jeans, when what he wanted to feel was some sort of energy, or a sign that she knew he was there. When he felt neither, he decided to speak.

"Hi, Mom." His throat constricted, his body shaking a few times in an effort to fight back tears. When had he last let himself speak those words? "It's me. Jason. I'm not sure if you recognize me. Maybe you've been watching me this whole time. Um. I don't know what to say. I miss you." Jason bit his bottom lip, not wanting to cry. Then again, screw it. If you can't bawl at a cemetery, where could you? He sobbed as he forced himself to continue. "Why'd you let them take me away? I wanted to be with you. I don't care about the bruises. I would have preferred getting hurt more if it meant I could stay with you. I didn't like what happened. You shouldn't have let them take me." He swallowed against the pain. "I guess you didn't have a choice. Sometimes I wonder… Why didn't you put me in the car and just start driving? Why didn't you tell that asshole to fuck off? I mean—" His voice cracked.

Jason shook his head, looking around at the silent graves. His sorrow was shifting to anger, and as it turned out, he did have a lot he needed to say. "It's all your fault. I don't want it to be, but you could have stopped drinking. I saw other kids return to their parents. Do you know how bad that messed with me? I saw that there was hope, that if you got your life together, we could have been reunited. So I made sure none of the families wanted me. I fought everyone who cared about me, just so I would still be there if you came back. But you never did. Then you fucking died."

Jason wiped at his eyes. "I'm sorry. I shouldn't… I bet I didn't cuss this much when I was little, did I?" He managed a laugh. "I'm not mad at you. Maybe I should be, but I don't care. You're my mother and I love you, and I want you back. Part of me is still waiting. I know it's impossible and it'll never happen, but I have this fantasy that you'll show up out of the blue, that it will have all been some crazy misunderstanding."

He looked at the stoic headstone—undeniable proof that this would never happen. The past couldn't be changed. All he could do was deal with it. He never doubted that his mother loved him. Regardless of how badly she had messed up, he was certain she'd felt terrible about it, and that drinking herself to death was probably due to losing him. If she could hear him now, he didn't want to leave her thinking that he was still angry, or that he hated her. "I did okay," he said. "It wasn't easy, but I'm doing good now. I have a family. New parents. Two dads. They're gay. Oh, so am I. Surprise!" He chuckled. "That's not such a big deal these days. The world has changed a lot since you were here. I even fell in love. I managed to make a mess of it, but maybe it's not too late. We'll see. I work with animals and— Hey! Remember the guitar? The one you taught me to play on? I still have it. Damn… I should have brought it with me. I could have played you something."

He thought of Michelle's children, how they had each given her a part of themselves, be it homemade or something they had worked hard to earn. He didn't have a guitar to play, but he could still sing. Not as well as Ben, but he tried. Jason chose a song, one of his mother's favorites. *Wild Horses* by The Rolling Stones. He let the tune play in his mind, singing the lyrics he could remember and humming the rest. When he was finished, he found he had little else to say. Jason got to his feet. "I love you," he said. "Tell Grandma hello from me."

He thought about promising to come back, tempted to say that he would visit as often as possible so they could stay connected. Then again, past a certain point, she hadn't done that for him. She had let go. He didn't understand how or why, but she had. He looked down at the flowers in his hand, perfect and delicate. Then he thought of a woman who had been there for him time and time again, even though she had no reason to be. Jason turned and walked back the way he had come, pace picking up as he neared the parking lot. He saw Michelle standing next to the car and hurried to her before he lost the guts to say what he needed to say. When he was close, he held out the bouquet.

"You're the closest thing I've had to a mother in a long time."

Michelle stared at the flowers, then him. "Jason, I—"

"I know you're not my mom, and I don't really need you to be. I'm fine with the way things are. But I love you, and I'm so—" He sobbed, desperate to get the words out. "Thank you for saving me."

Michelle's face crumpled. Then she started crying. Before he knew it, Jason was wrapped in her arms.

"Happy Mother's Day," he managed to say.

Michelle didn't let him go. She just squeezed tighter. "Happy Mother's Day. I love you too."

*****

Jason stood in a large kitchen. On the counter was a vase filled with pink orchids. It sat next to an angel statue, a homemade card, and scrawled poetry. Somehow that felt right. Michelle kept herself busy, unloading the dishwasher or wiping down surfaces that looked perfectly clean. Jason helped, both of them feeling sheepish from the emotional outpouring earlier. They had stayed in the parking lot and cried together. Jason had talked about his mother a little, but he mostly focused on everything Michelle had done for him. He wanted her to know that she was appreciated. Hearing events from her perspective was interesting too, especially the difficulties of her job. He could relate. When working at the animal shelter, sometimes he developed attachments. His duty was to provide a new home for animals, not take them into his own, and that could be difficult.

"With you, I kept trying to cheat," she had told him. "I wanted Jace to adopt you so you would be a part of the family. You have no idea how happy I am that my little plan worked. Just not how I expected or when."

She talked more about Jace, and how for her, sometimes the lines blurred. Jason had always reminded Michelle of her brother. This only made it more crucial to her that he was okay. And he was! The greatest proof of that was when Ben and Tim walked into the kitchen. Emma had gone to pick them up, tired of arguing with her brothers and eager for an excuse to get away. Now they were here, and if Jason's whole face didn't hurt from crying, he would have shed more tears when Ben hugged him. As usual, his adopted father could tell how he felt.

"Aw," Ben said, rocking him back and forth. "It's been a hard day for you, hasn't it?"

"Yeah," Jason said, enjoying the feeling of being pampered, and that the hug showed no sign of ending.

"I'm sad too," Tim said. "Look."

They did. His face was wet, but he had clearly splashed water on it.

"Come here," Ben said, opening an arm. "There's room for you too."

Tim joined them. With his big arms embracing them both, it was hard not to feel safe. And loved.

"My two boys," Ben said, sighing wistfully. "You might be larger than me, but when you get down to it, you're both really tiny, aren't you?"

"Yup," Tim said instantly.

"Definitely," Jason agreed.

As nice as it would have been, they couldn't stand there hugging forever. Eventually they had to return home to Austin. Jason said goodbye to everyone, saving Michelle for last. He asked Ben and Tim to wait in the car for him. Emma was there already, her brothers elsewhere. After a look from his wife, Greg mumbled an excuse and disappeared too, leaving them alone on the front porch.

"Well," Michelle said. "That was quite a day."

Jason laughed. "I made everything awkward, didn't I?"

Michelle shook her head. "You made it one of the best Mother's Days I've ever had. Although…"

He tensed up. "What?"

"I like white orchids even better than pink."

Jason grinned. "Next year?"

Michelle nodded happily. "Next year. Of course there's a fair chance that I'll be taking a bunch of kids out for ice cream. Care to join me?"

"I wouldn't miss it for the world!"

Jason hugged her again. Then he went to the car. His parents were in the front seat. Waiting in the back for him was his best friend. Considering that her mother's brother had once been married to his adopted father, they might be cousins. In law. Or something like that. If Jason started calling Michelle his mother, that would make him and Emma siblings too. After thinking about it, he decided his family tree was already complicated enough. That didn't change how he felt though. He still loved his real mom, but when it came to the most special woman in his life, there was no contest. The person waving goodbye to him from the front porch, a tissue squeezed in one hand, would always occupy that most precious place in his heart.

Something Like Memories

by Jay Bell

Austin, 2016

Hey baby. It's our big day! Or at least the anniversary of it. Probably. I figure it's around here somewhere. I know we disagree, and today definitely isn't the right time to argue. I just want you to know that I love you bunches. Ha! Instead of two peas in a pod, we're two bananas in a bunch. That's not supposed to be sexual. Unless you want it to be. So uh… Yeah.

Tim Wyman looked up as the door to the Eric Conroy Gallery opened. He was grateful for the interruption, the greeting card he had been writing in already ruined by his clumsy efforts. Romantic prose didn't come easily to him, which is why he had bought five more of the same card. Just in case. They were currently spread out across the desk, but only two of them were untouched, the rest having been marred by bad poetry or blundering declarations of love.

"Just let me know if you need anything," Tim said to the couple who had entered.

He offered a smile and looked down at the card again, pretending to be busy. As soon as the couple had moved to the first painting, he covertly sized them up. They had sales potential. The man was in his late fifties or early sixties, the slacks and Polo shirt implying he needed to be prepared for emergency business meetings at the nearest country club. His wife was a good ten years younger, maybe more, her taste refined. The clothes she wore were stylish. Her jewelry and makeup popped without being excessive. The couple moved from one painting to the next, giggling and finding excuses to touch each other. The afternoon was still early. Tim could imagine they had eaten lunch down the street and gotten tipsy while doing so. Time to move in for the kill.

"That's a great piece," he said, nodding at a painting of a disembodied head—a self-portrait of the artist, whose red nose and downturned lips gave the impression of someone with a cold. The sickly pink color that filled the backdrop only helped reinforce this. "The artist is just starting out, but I can promise you that he's a name to watch. A self-portrait of Rembrandt was valued at fifty million recently, and one of Van Gogh sold for seventy. All we're asking is five hundred bucks, so it's a real bargain."

The man laughed appreciatively, then turned to his wife. "What do you think, honey?"

"I don't know," she said. "It's kind of… icky."

Tim couldn't argue with that. Whenever he looked at the painting he thought of cough syrup and days spent in bed surrounded by sopping wet tissues. That's why he was so eager to sell it.

The wife turned to Tim, perhaps noticing him for the first time, because her eyes took a stroll over his body. "Do you have anything cuter?"

"Cute? Let's see… There's a new exhibition in the west wing you might like. Right over there."

"Thanks!" She smiled demurely and then walked in the direction he had indicated.

The husband chose to stay behind. "Roy Miller," he said, offering a firm handshake. "We do this each year for our anniversary."

"It's your anniversary?" Tim asked. "Wow! I was just working on a card for mine when you came in."

"Then it looks like we chose the right gallery! A card, eh?"

Tim grimaced. "Yeah, I know. It's a lame gift. I'll figure something else out. I made a mess of it anyway."

"Is this your gallery? As in, do you own it?"

"It belongs to a foundation, but I'm the man in charge."

"Excellent," Roy said approvingly. "Then why don't you give your man one of these paintings?"

His man? Tim tried to remember if he and Roy had met previously. He was certain they hadn't. "You're not wrong, but how do you know I have a husband and not a wife?"

Roy grinned. "I'm good at reading people, and most guys are a little more excited when my gal checks them out."

Tim laughed. "Busted! So you buy your wife a painting every year?"

"We're not married." He elbowed Tim playfully. "Get with the times! And yes, we have a hall in our home with eight paintings. Today we'll be adding a ninth."

"Congratulations!" Tim said. "This calls for a toast!"

He had already smelled alcohol on Roy's breath. Not an excessive amount, but enough to know that the man drank. Tim hurried to the back room where champagne from the most recent opening was still in the refrigerator. A bottle or two less than he remembered, not that he couldn't guess who was responsible. After popping the cork and filling two glasses, he returned to the front room. The couple were together again, examining a painting.

"Happy anniversary," Tim said, presenting them with the glass flutes. "Here's to the best-looking pair to ever walk through those doors."

The flattery worked. The couple laughed, and Cheryl—as she introduced herself—kept looking at him with half-lidded eyes, seeking his opinion on various pieces.

"What about this one?" Roy asked, pointing at a painting of a fat baby in pilgrim clothing. "Maybe it will be lucky for us."

"I don't think it's a good fit," Cheryl said. She turned to Tim. "Do you?"

"That depends on the other eight paintings."

Cheryl squinted in an effort to remember. "We've got one of a monkey eating grapes. The little circus dog. Oh, and the two kissing doves!"

Animals. Tim thought of another possibility in the east wing, this one of a rooster depicted in thick strokes of acrylic paint. He liked the piece enough that he would be sorry to see it go. The artist's expression when handed a check for three thousand dollars would more than make up for that. Tim escorted the couple to the painting and left them there, giving them privacy so Roy could make the obvious joke about giving her a big cock. Sure enough, a few minutes after Tim was back at his desk, he heard Cheryl tittering. This made him think warmly of Ben. Usually their relationship was easy. Tim could just be himself, make dumb jokes, and reap the rewards. Anniversaries though, they were special. Especially this one, even if they didn't agree on the milestone. If only Ben would admit that their history was more than just a handful of—

Tim shook his head. Now wasn't the time to angst over his relationship. Not with potential customers in the gallery. "How's it going in there?" he called. "Need a refill? How drunk do I need to get you before you'll buy something?"

He heard laughter. A few seconds later, Roy reappeared, wallet in hand.

"You've decided?" Tim asked.

"She's still thinking about it," Roy answered. Then he leaned closer and whispered, "Might as well ring it up. I know when she's fallen in love with a painting. Just like with me, she needs a little time before she's willing to commit."

"Smart woman," Tim said. "We have customers who don't take their time, and while I love an impulse shopper, it's when they come back the next day for a refund that I wish they had thought about it more."

"Don't worry," Roy said. "Once she's decided, I've never seen her change her mind. We aren't leaving here empty-handed. Not when we both have anniversaries to celebrate! That way you can give your husband some good news along with that card."

Ugh! The stupid greeting card. Tim insisted on refilling Roy's glass before he ran the transaction, wishing he shared the man's expertise in gift-giving. Maybe he was right. Art would be a better present than a card. Not one from the gallery, but a painting Tim created himself. Then again, he had already done that twice previously: once when they had reunited, and once back when they were teenagers and had just met. Their *true* beginning. This made him frown. All that really mattered is that they were happy and together. Who cares that they couldn't agree on one little detail?

"Mind if I ask you something?" Tim said. "If you guys aren't married, then how do you decide which day is your anniversary? First date?"

"Nope. The first time I rear-ended her."

"Is he telling that story again?" Cheryl said, walking into the room.

"Yeah," Tim replied, "but I'm not sure I should hear it!"

"It was a car accident," Cheryl explained. "This idiot can't walk and chew gum at the same time."

"It was my first smart phone," Roy said in his defense. "The headset wasn't working, and I was trying to send a text—"

"—while driving," Cheryl said. "Then he slams into my car and—"

"—fell in love. The second I laid eyes on her."

"What about you?" Tim asked.

Cheryl scoffed. "I threatened to sue! The next day I get a call about meeting with his lawyer for a settlement."

"He asked you to meet us at a restaurant," Roy chided. "That should have been your first clue."

"I thought you were trying to wine and dine me! Of course when I show up, there's only this fool sitting there." Cheryl put an arm around Roy and squeezed. "You're lucky I was hungry."

"You're lucky I'm a bad driver," Roy retorted. "Are you done looking? Have you decided if you want my—?"

"Technically it's my big cock you've been looking at," Tim said, feeling daring. "At least until you sign this receipt."

They were tipsy enough to laugh, Cheryl giving him another once over. Then delivery details were discussed. Tim poured the giggling duo another glass of champagne and joined them at their insistence. By the time they left, he was grinning and longing for his own other half. Few couples seemed happier than he and Ben were, although he supposed Roy and Cheryl had a slight advantage, since they agreed on one *tiny* little detail of absolutely no consequence that drove Tim so freaking crazy that he might hire someone to brainwash Ben into sharing his opinion!

No big deal. Really.

Okay, so the issue needed to be resolved before it turned into a big dumb argument. But how? Ben believed their anniversary began when they had reunited in this very gallery eight years ago. That was fine, but it ignored all of their history before that day. They had dated for a year in high school. Their time together in college had either been mere days or an entire month, depending on if they included when they had tried to be friends. The problem, Tim supposed, was that he had been living with Ben in his heart since he was seventeen. Even during all the years of separation, Ben had remained a part of his life, popping up in his thoughts, fantasies, even his dreams. Tim's love for him hadn't died out only to be rekindled later. It had been constant, sometimes torturous. Screw the facts! They had been together way longer than eight years!

Then again, maybe the facts were relevant. If he gathered enough of them, he could prove his case. After nibbling on his nails and pacing the length of the gallery, he reached a decision.

He knew who to ask. Better than a private detective, this person had been with them every step of the way. She was practically the third member of their merry little relationship. As soon as the gallery closed, he would go see Allison Cross.

Tim stood on the porch of a small ranch-style house and was about to ring the bell again when the door opened.

Allison took one look at the bouquet of flowers he held, crossed her arms over her chest, and raised an eyebrow. "What have you done this time?"

Boy did he know that look! The tone was disturbingly familiar too. "I just need to sleep on your couch for one night," he pleaded, feeling retro. "Ben's angry at me because I refuse to come out to my parents."

Allison studied him. Then she smiled. "Get in here!"

Once he was inside her home, he enjoyed a hug and followed her to the kitchen so she could fill a vase with water. She was arranging the flowers when she looked over at him. "Whatever you really want from me, you're a lot more likely to get it now."

"I just want to talk. How are things going? Where's Davis?"

"With his grandparents," Allison said. "He's spending all of June there. I miss him, but I've also been doing this crazy thing where I sleep for eight hours and don't wake up exhausted. It's amazing. You should try it!"

"Having a kid isn't easy sometimes," Tim said, trying to make himself sound weary when really he loved that he could count himself among the fathers of the world.

"Oh please," Allison said. "Jason was eighteen when he came to live with you. I only wish I could have started out with Davis at that age. It would have taken a lot more pushing, but the rest would have been easier."

"You're just as full of it as I am," Tim said, nodding to his favorite photo on the refrigerator. In it, Allison was holding Davis, who had decided to smoosh an ice cream cone into one of her cheeks. Allison's expression in the photo wasn't angry. Instead, her eyes were filled with laughter.

"He is pretty awesome," Allison said wistfully. "Better change the subject before I get weak and go pick him up. Quick, tell me what you're really doing here. You're not actually in trouble, are you?"

"No."

"But…"

"I did have a question," he said.

Allison looked victorious. "I knew it! Should I make some coffee? Or is this more of a beer conversation?"

He opted for the former, but only because he would need to drive. Soon they were sitting in her living room, which was cleaner than he had ever seen it. Where were the toys, or the pulverized Cheetos stomped into the carpet?

Allison took a sip from her mug. "Is this about your anniversary?"

"Yeah," Tim said. "Except we don't agree on how long we've actually—"

She held up her hand. "I already know what you're referring to. Ben and I discussed it."

"You did?"

"Yup!"

"Was he upset?"

"No." Allison set her coffee mug on the table. "This was years ago, so my memory is a little hazy. I think it just came up in conversation. He definitely wasn't upset. Ben explained your different viewpoints, and I remember seeing where you're both coming from. You're both right, in your own way."

"I think so too," Tim said, "but it bothers me, because I feel like he's shoving half of our relationship under the carpet."

"Is this a therapy session?" Allison asked. "Just let me know so I can start the clock."

Tim chuckled. "Don't worry. I'm not going to make you listen to me whine, and I don't expect a pep talk. I need your help in another way. If I can prove to Ben there's a better anniversary for us, then maybe we can finally agree."

"What date are you going to suggest?"

"That's the thing," Tim said. "Whenever I press Ben on the subject, he asks me what day it would be. When we first hooked up? I was still with Krista then. When I dumped her? I don't want him thinking of that whole mess every anniversary, so if I could figure out the first time we talked to each other… I was kind of hoping you're one of those people who can hear a date and describe what the weather was like then."

"Hyperthymesia," Allison said instantly. "Or some types of autism."

"See?" Tim said, getting excited. "You're brilliant! I knew you could help me!"

Allison's eyes widened. "I didn't say that! I suppose we could attempt a little memory regression. Mind if I hit you over the head with a frying pan?"

"I'm willing to try anything," Tim said.

Allison shook her head. "I don't have much faith in head traumas or hypnotic regression. It shouldn't be too hard though. We were in junior year when you guys met, so that was… Ninety-seven? Is that right? Better look it up. School had just started, making it September. Somewhere in the middle of the month, if I remember right. Just say it was the fifteenth and call it a day. No, call it *the* day."

"I was hoping for something a little more specific," Tim said. "I know Ben. He's going to need solid proof."

"He's not in denial. He knows you were together back then."

"Yeah, but… Hey! What about medical records? When he crashed into me and sprained my ankle. That would give us a date."

"Sure, if that's when you feel like it began."

Tim made a face. "Huh?"

"It sort of goes back to your original argument. You both have basically chosen when you want your anniversary to be. For Ben, it's when you were reunited. For you, it's when you first spoke. Either choice is arbitrary if you think about it. You have more history together than that. Ben knew who you were before the school year began."

Tim let these words sink in. Then he laughed. "I don't see how! I had just moved from Kansas."

"Never mind," Allison said quickly. "I'm being silly."

Tim sat upright and snapped his fingers. "You're not! I remember Emma talking about this once. She said that Ben saw me jogging a bunch of times, but when I asked him about it later, he said she was exaggerating, and that he *might* have seen me once."

"That must be it," Allison said, taking a sudden interest in the couch fabric.

Tim grinned. "He went out looking for me, didn't he?"

Allison exhaled and made eye contact again. "If he did—and I mean *if*—then it makes your job harder. How would you ever figure out the first day he saw you? Would you even count that?"

Tim thought about it and nodded. "Yeah! Who knows, maybe I said hello, or it could be that our arms brushed when I jogged past him. That's important, right? It would be the first time I touched my future husband!"

"Trust me, if you guys spoke, or touched, I would have heard about it. Or more likely, he would have made me read his—" Her smile disappeared, hidden behind her hand.

"What?"

"He's going to kill me." Allison shook her head, debating within herself. "Oh lord… You can't tell him I told you this!"

"I won't, I swear."

"He used to have a diary."

Tim nearly shot to his feet. "Really? And you think he would have written about the first time he saw me?"

"He wrote about everything. Especially if it involved cute boys and how none of them liked him. Then he would make me read each entry while he sat there on the bed with those big sad eyes of his."

"Do you know what happened to it?"

"The diary? Sorry, journal. He always called it that, but we both knew the truth. And no, I don't remember the last time I saw it."

"He never went crazy and burned it or anything like that?"

Allison laughed. "Sounds like something he would do. Chances are he would have gotten me involved for that as well, so I bet it's sitting in a box somewhere in your house."

"Man!" Tim said, hardly daring to hope. "You really think so?"

Allison just smiled. "It's really adorable how excited you get about him. I wish he could see this. Wait! I know, I'll make a video. You don't mind, do you?"

She picked up her phone. Tim pounced to grab it from her. They scuffled briefly, Allison laughing as she pushed him away.

"Okay, okay," she said. "Fine. I'll keep this a secret. For now. You know I've got to tell him eventually."

Tim nodded his understanding. "Just give me a decent head start. Any clues about what it looked like?"

"One of those generic composition notebooks. The kind with the black and white marbled pattern. And if you don't find it, just remember that you love each other. Nothing else matters."

"You're right," he said. Then he shot her a wink. "As usual." He also knew that Ben rarely took her advice, stubbornly needing to learn his own hard lessons. Tim wasn't any better. He had started this quest, and now he was determined to see it through.

The search commenced the next day after Ben left for work. Tim began in their bedroom closet, which was stuffed with more than just shoes and clothes. After peeking inside every storage container there, he rifled through the dresser drawers on Ben's side, and when that didn't turn up anything interesting, Tim decided to check the garage. Then he realized he was being foolish and returned to the second floor. The attic! That's where they kept things from their past that they couldn't let go of but didn't need to see every day.

The attic was a mess, and after emptying three boxes and tripping over the contents, he decided to organize it all. This meant sorting, repacking, and labeling. He kept all of Ben's things, but threw away some of his own. The most difficult decision involved a painting of Ryan. Looking at it brought back memories, not all of them bad. Tim had painted it during the early part of their relationship, when their love had him feeling alive and inspired. Later, when Ryan kept making snide remarks about Tim's art, he had returned to hiding any creative impulses. Most of Tim wanted to throw away the painting. Past the initial rush of nostalgic feelings, the image only reminded him of dark times. Unfortunately, the painting was one of his best, a perfect mixture of realism and artistic license. Ryan looked adorable in a pink bathrobe. Tim still remembered him trying it on in the women's section of a department store. He had strutted around proudly, even wearing it to the register.

The memory made him smile, but this soon faded. Tim swore he could feel his scar itch where the bullet had passed through his shoulder. Hopefully he hadn't developed some sort of Harry Potter powers. Did his scar itching mean that He-Who-Must-Not-Be-Named was close by? But no, Ryan was still rotting away in prison. Tim turned the painting around so that only the back could be seen and leaned it against a wall. Then he resumed his work, taking a short break for lunch. He neared the end of this task without finding what he was seeking. He hadn't seen much from Ben's teen years at all, which was depressing. Maybe those days didn't mean as much to him.

The afternoon was wearing on when the stairs behind him creaked. He turned to find Ben standing there, looking around in wonder.

"Wow!" he breathed. "This is great! I've been meaning to do the same thing."

"It was overdue," Tim agreed. "Took lots and lots of hard work. I'm exhausted. Come reward me."

Ben smiled and strolled toward him slowly, making him wait. The anticipation was worth it. Few things in the world were better than Ben kisses. Except for Chinchilla kisses. Maybe. It was a tough call.

"Find anything cool?" Ben asked, looking around again. "Hey, all those boxes have my name on them!"

"Exactly," Tim said. "And look over there."

A small stack carried Jace's name on each box. Figuring out what belonged to him wasn't difficult. Ben didn't read biographies, and the clothes were too tall to fit either of them. All the airline memorabilia was obvious too.

Ben walked over to the stack, placed his hand on it, and then turned around, eyes watery. "You're the best," he breathed.

"I try." Tim puffed up his chest. "I even made extra room by throwing out some of my stuff."

"Nothing important, I hope."

"No, just old clothes and paperwork. I kept what matters to me, like my sketchbooks." He was purposefully steering the conversation. "Some of them I should call journals instead, because I wrote in them. Did you ever have anything like that? A journal or maybe a diary?"

Ben looked him square in the eye. "Nope."

The little shit was lying! Or Allison had been messing with him, but he didn't think that was true. "You're lucky," Tim said. "My sketchbooks are full of all kinds of embarrassing things, although I suppose it's that way for everyone. A diary or whatever is nothing to be ashamed of."

Ben shrugged. "I wouldn't know. Hey, what do you want for dinner? I'm kind of over that soup I made. Two nights in a row is enough."

Tim studied him. Then he turned around, continuing his work. "We could order pizza."

"Deal!" Ben said, heading for the stairs. "I'll take care of dinner, you keep doing what you're doing."

"Take your time," Tim called after him. Then he focused on the task at hand, twice as determined. Ben *did* have a diary, and while being married still meant giving the other person privacy when they needed it, he now felt morally justified. Ben had lied, which gave Tim every right to snoop and find out why.

Tim parked at the house where Ben had grown up, feeling nostalgic. Not only was he back to driving a black sports car—a Dodge Challenger instead of a Mitsubishi 3000 GT—but he was sneaking around again, skating a line between fact and fiction and praying he wouldn't get caught. The official reason for this trip to The Woodlands was to see his mother. Tim had arrived yesterday and taken her to lunch. Then they spent a leisurely afternoon shopping. Tim had seen his father too when they returned home. That was always a downer, but Tim had planned ahead, giving his Father's Day card early and apologizing that he couldn't be there on the actual holiday. Not that his father seemed to care. That made two of them. Tim did his best to avoid him for the remainder of the evening, which wasn't difficult.

Now it was a new day, and with his visit over, he could start the drive back to Austin. Considering that his mother-in-law lived just a few blocks away, it would be rude not to stop by. Tim grinned on his way to the door, remembering a time when he had wanted Mrs. Bentley to steer clear so that she wouldn't discover his secret relationship with her son. What a joke. These days, seeing June was a highlight of any trip to the Woodlands.

To his surprise, she looked equally glad to see him. Or at least relieved.

"Thank goodness it's only you!" she exclaimed.

"Thanks," Tim replied. "I think."

"I don't mean it like that." June reached up to hug his neck and kiss his cheek. "I'm just in the middle of an emergency. I was worried that Adam had forgotten something and had come home early."

"What's wrong?" Tim asked, following her inside. "And why wouldn't you want your husband here?"

June spun around, looking miserable. "I clogged the toilet."

Tim shrugged. "So?"

"It's clogged with—" She chose to whisper the last two words. "Poo stuff."

"Poo stuff?" Tim repeated, unable to resist a laugh.

"Yes!"

"Okay, that's embarrassing, but how long have you guys been married? Half the time these days, I forget to close the bathroom door when taking a dump. That's how much I love your son."

June swatted his arm, cheeks turning red as she smiled. "I know you'll think I'm crazy, but Adam has seen me give birth, he's seen me puke when I'm sick, and he even had to pull over once so I could pee in a stranger's yard. Poo is where I draw the line. Something has to remain a mystery in this marriage!"

"I guess that makes sense," Tim said. He certainly hadn't expected such a frank conversation when arriving here.

"Are you thirsty? Have you eaten breakfast? I'll fix you something, but first I need to call a plumber."

"For a clogged toilet? Don't you have a toilet plunger?"

June was already on the way to the kitchen. "We do, but the water is up to the brim. If I put anything in, it'll be Niagara Falls." She consulted a magnet on the fridge, phone in hand and finger poised to dial.

"Don't call a plumber," Tim said. "They're expensive. I'll take care of it."

"I don't want you seeing it either!" June exclaimed.

"What's worse?" Tim asked. "Me, or a stranger?"

June bit her bottom lip, looking just like her son. "If you tell anyone about this, at least I know where to find you."

"Exactly. I just need a wire hanger. Trust me, the same thing happens at our place sometimes."

"I can pay!"

He didn't need the money. Tim was happy to be of use. June had been nothing but kind to him since he was a closeted teenager. If need be, he would fish her poop out with his bare hands, but he really *really* hoped it wouldn't come to that. A few minutes later, he was standing in front of a closed bathroom door.

"Don't look!" June said, blocking the way. "You don't need to see, right? You can just feel around?"

"Sure," he said.

"Or I can guide you! I'll tell you where to stand and you work your magic. We just need a blindfold."

"Actually," he said. "Would you mind brewing some coffee? I still need to drive home, and I didn't get much sleep last night."

He had been too excited about this visit. Mostly he wanted her out of the way. Just like old times. June grudgingly returned to the kitchen. Tim unwound the hanger near the hook's neck until he was left with a long wire. Then he took a deep breath, held it, and went inside. The toilet wasn't the disaster he had expected. Poop looked like poop, and the water had gone down a little. That made it easier to insert the hanger into the drain hole at the bottom and stuff it in enough to work at the clog. Less than a minute later, the toilet was flushing again. Disposing of the hanger without touching the part that was contaminated took some finagling, but he managed to get it curled into the trash can.

"I forgot to open the window!" June said, reappearing.

"Ta-da!" Tim said, stepping back so she could see. Then he explained what he had done and advised her about a tool she could buy—a plumber's snake—that would do the same trick with less hassle.

"I love my son-in-law!" June declared. She kept thanking him as they shared a cup of coffee, laughing through her embarrassment.

Tim pretended that he had managed to do the job without looking. She didn't believe him, but he could tell she wanted to. With the crisis averted, he turned his attention to the original reason he had shown up here.

"I organized our attic the other day," he said casually. "We have tons of space now. When I was at my mom's house, I picked up the last of the stuff they were storing for me, which wasn't much. Does Ben have anything here?"

"I believe so, but we have room enough. It's not a problem."

"I figured it would save him a trip if he needed anything. Or maybe you prefer it that way so he's forced to visit."

June laughed. "He's a momma's boy. I'm never worried I won't see him."

"Then I'll load up the car."

"Are you sure? I really don't mind."

Tim nodded. "I'm really excited about the attic. It feels good having it so organized."

All true. He was proud of himself for being honest. He really had picked up some old possessions from his parents' house, and he did enjoy organizing his home. Soon he was standing in Ben's former room, June digging through the closet. "He brought these boxes over when he moved out of his old house. I thought your new one must be really small, but I guess he didn't realize how much space you both would have." She hesitated. "Unless there's a reason he wanted them here instead."

Tim shrugged. "I'll let him figure that out when he's home."

Also not a fib. Tim planned on handing over the boxes, but not before he had a chance to go through them. As it turned out, there were only two. One was half empty, making him wonder if Ben had slowly brought pieces of the content back with him. Like all those photos he showed up with once, most of Jace. Had he been trying to spare Tim's feelings? The other box was full, but nothing more than a casual inspection was possible without revealing to June just how desperately he wanted to dig through it all.

He waited until he had said goodbye and had driven a short distance. Then he pulled over in a nearby neighborhood. Tim got into the backseat with the heaviest box and soon hit the jackpot. Inside were yearbooks and other typical pieces of nostalgia. Beneath these was the really good stuff, such as a ticket stub to a movie they had seen together. Or a roller coaster photo from their date to Six Flags, the image a total blur and not worth the money, but Ben had insisted at the time. Tim found more souvenirs from their past, like a rough art experiment he had done on a napkin using nail polish that Allison had left at Ben's house. The end result was hideous, but he adored that Ben had kept it. There was even a brochure for the haunted house they had visited together. That had turned into a night to remember. He kept digging, heart swelling with every discovery: a pocket-sized English-to-Spanish dictionary, a piece of the cast that had once been on his ankle, and a T-shirt that he barely remembered owning.

Tim reveled in each new find, less interested in the objects themselves than what they implied. Ben had been crazy about him. The realization was tinged with sorrow, because he could only imagine where they would be now if he hadn't made his biggest mistake. If somehow he had managed to grow up without meeting and losing Eric and everything else he had gone through, then he and Ben would have had years of history together—decades—and the start of their relationship would never have been debated.

These thoughts vanished when he reached the bottom of the box. There it was. The fabled journal. Before any moral concerns could trip him up, Tim grabbed it, opening it at random. His trembling hands grew steady as he read, the breath that had caught in his throat coming out as a yawn, because Ben spent paragraph after paragraph complaining about his sister. Really dumb stuff that only seemed like a big deal to the young. Karen had refused to give him a ride home once and called him a dumbass. Oh no. It's the end of the world.

Tim started flipping through the book, only half of the pages filled, but the handwriting became more refined. As Allison had promised, the topic soon fixated on boys, such as a lifeguard who had caught his eye, or a fleeting crush on one of Allison's boyfriends. Or a grocery store bagger who Ben was certain had flirted with him just because he had held up a bunch of bananas and grinned before sacking them. Seriously? Maybe the guy just really loved potassium.

Tim chuckled through many of these entries, but when he reached one in particular, his body went rigid, the jukebox of his heart choosing a song with a faster beat.

I met him. The man of my dreams. I know I've said that before. Five different times. I just counted. I mean it though! This is the one. Allison and I had stolen a real estate sign, the kind that says house for sale, and put it in Jessica Trotter's yard. We want her to move away so bad! Maybe someone will make her parents an offer they can't refuse. Anyway, we split up when it was time to go home, and I got this urge to stay out, so I kept walking. I was by the lake when I saw him. He's got everything I've ever wanted! Here's a checklist:

Muscles

Eyes

Ass

Package

Smile

That last one is a guess. As soon as I saw him coming, I sat on a bench. Real casual, right? I didn't want to just stand there and stare, so I figured it would make more sense to sit. The upside is I got a nice look at his body when he ran by. He was jogging, because that's what my future boyfriend does. He's probably on the track team, and I bet he has a sexy name like Blake or Carter. Or maybe both! Blake Carter! Oh, and I should have added fashion sense to the list above, because he was wearing the most amazing blue shoes. The little jogging shorts were nice too. I bet he didn't have anything on beneath them. Something big sure was bouncing around in there! I need to go back. Not just to look. Next time I'm going to introduce myself. Then he'll probably pick me up and keep running, because he's that much of a stud.

That was the end of the entry. Tim's eyes darted up to the top of the page. Thank every star in the sky that Ben was dorky enough to date each entry, because he finally found the magic number. The first time they had laid eyes on each other—the beginning of it all.

Ben Bentley sat on the edge of the couch in his pajamas, attention glued to the television. In front of him, on the coffee table, a bowl of cereal had grown soggy, absorbing so much of the milk that it was starting to dissolve. A mug of tea had cooled next to it, unable to offer warmth or any comfort at all, because the world no longer made sense. Strange how that could happen. When Ben had woken up that morning, he had felt cheerful aside from missing Tim, who had stayed overnight with his parents in The Woodlands. The day was bright. Fluffy white clouds drifted through a blue sky. Everything was as it should be, or so it had seemed. Ben had been optimistic enough to make plans. A little house work, grocery shopping, and maybe a stop at his favorite place for lunch. All of it seemed shamefully frivolous now, because at least twenty people had lost their lives.

The Pulse nightclub in Orlando. Ben had found the news upsetting enough before he heard that it was a gay bar. That made it feel more personal, his insides aching for the victims and their loved ones. As the details kept coming and he learned of the killer's intent—how a coward had armed himself with a ridiculous amount of firepower so he could murder defenseless people who were out celebrating—there was no settling on one emotion. Ben felt anger, wishing the killer was still alive so he could answer for his crimes, or that the killer had taken his own life instead of those of so many people. He felt anguish, knowing firsthand how difficult it was to lose someone without warning, and how the void left behind would never fill again. Not completely. He also felt afraid. Ben hated to admit it, but he feared this attack wouldn't be the last, that more lives would end, and for what? Because people wanted to find someone to love? Or go out to drink, dance, and have fun?

Fifty lives. Not twenty. The headlines had changed, breathless reporters declaring it the deadliest mass shooting in United States history. Ben watched in horror, crying with each new detail, with each final text sent to a parent, with each victim's name revealed along with their photo, taken at a happier time when they were still healthy and whole. So many had black hair and brown skin. It had been Latin night at Pulse. Too often Ben saw glimpses of Tim in those photos, wishing more than anything that he was here now.

Ben sat there until his butt was numb, his back ached, and his throat was parched. Then he rose, taking the bowl of cereal back to the kitchen. He was setting it on the counter when he looked down at the tile floor, eyes moving to one spot in particular. He knew what it was like to be in a safe environment and to have a madman enter with a gun. He knew what it felt like to be powerless to stop the violence, to want nothing more than to shield the people he cared for regardless of his own vulnerabilities. Love was powerful, but it wasn't invincible.

The front door opened. Ben spun around, muscles tensing as fear shot up his spine. He reminded himself that Ryan had come in through the back door, and that he was still locked away in prison. Logic has little influence over fear, so he remained guarded until a figure appeared in the doorway. Then Ben ran toward it and threw himself into strong arms.

"I heard on the radio," Tim said, clutching him close. "I knew you would be upset. I am too."

Ben couldn't respond, tears overtaking him, but he forced the words out that he most needed to say. "I don't want to lose you. Ever." He never wanted to experience that pain again. He didn't want anyone else to either. "There has to be something we can do!"

"There is," Tim said. "I'm just not sure what. Maybe a fundraiser or—"

"Or we could go there," Ben said, pulling away. "I've been through this. We both have. Maybe it would help if the victims' families had someone they could talk to. Someone who understands."

"Maybe," Tim said, eyeing him with concern.

Ben knew what he was thinking. When conflict reared its ugly head, all Tim thought about was Ben. Even at the expense of himself. Maybe he was overcompensating for the past, or maybe that's just how he loved, but they couldn't afford to be selfish now. "We should go there. It's important. We've been through this and can help."

"What happened to us was different," Tim said, looking hesitant before he forced himself to press on. "We were attacked in our home, not a club, and yeah, I took a bullet and nearly died. That's nothing compared to some jackass firing round after round into a crowd and then—" He shook his head, jaw clenching. "Your heart's in the right place, Benjamin, but the families of the victims might want privacy."

"Then we'll be there for the vigils."

"There's one in Austin. Tonight. We'll start there, okay?"

Ben nodded. Then his chin trembled. "I wish Jason was here."

"I know," Tim said, drawing him near. "I called. He's okay. Why aren't you answering your phone?"

"I don't know where it is," Ben said, pulling away to glance around. "What time is it?"

"Past lunch, and unless this is your new look, you haven't even showered."

Ben gestured toward the living room. "Because—"

"I get it," Tim said. "You need to take a deep breath. I'm worried about you."

"I'm fine."

"Hey! Come look. I brought something that might cheer you up."

Ben couldn't imagine that happening, but he followed Tim to the entryway where two cardboard boxes sat on the floor. He recognized them from his parents' house. At least one was full of memories, little tokens that he had kept from the first time he and Tim had dated. Unfortunately, the contents made him seem like a crazed stalker. "Did you go through those?"

Tim shrugged. "I thought you would want to."

"Maybe later." Ben wiped at his nose. "How's my mom?"

"Good, but she hadn't seen the news when I left. I bet she has now. She's probably as worried about you as I am."

Ben turned toward the living room. "I'll find my phone and call her." A hand on his shoulder stopped him.

"I'll send her a quick text. You go take a shower and try to calm down."

Ben spun around, temper rising. "Calm down? Seriously?"

Tim raised his hands, showing his palms. "I'm not saying you shouldn't feel sad. I'm messed up over this too. I just need to know that you're not going to have a breakdown or whatever."

Ben exhaled, the anger ebbing away. "I feel a lot better now that you're home."

"We'll face this together," Tim said. "You and me, like always. Get cleaned up. I'll call Marcello too. I'm sure he's already got fundraising plans. Hey, maybe you could sing something at the vigil tonight."

Ben nodded glumly and returned to the living room so he could go upstairs. He glanced back once and saw Tim with his head down, attention on his phone, no doubt fulfilling his promise to text his mom. Ben tried to imagine if they hadn't been lucky, if Jason hadn't acted quickly enough to stop the bleeding, if yet another life had been lost to gun violence. Something had to change. The atrocities that had been committed couldn't be undone, but Ben prayed that this time people and politicians would take the steps necessary to prevent such butchery from happening again. Otherwise, what was the point? He wasn't sure if anything happened for a reason, or if events were guided by the hand of some distant deity, but he did know that people could create order out of chaos, hope out of despair. Maybe this time, those who valued guns more than the lives of their fellow man would finally open their minds enough to listen.

"Surprise!"

Ben leaned over to peer into the trunk that his best friend had just opened. Allison stood next to her car, still grinning like she had revealed piles of golden coins. Instead he saw Tupperware containers held together by a thick rubber band, a rolled-up blanket, and a bottle of wine.

"A picnic?" Ben asked.

"Very observant," Allison replied, reaching into the trunk. "I knew you would figure it out on your own."

Ben glanced around at their surroundings. The park was officially closed and shrouded in darkness. They were the only people there because, as he explained to his friend, "It's night. Who has a picnic at—" He checked his watch. "—ten? For real. It just turned ten."

"It's all the rage these days with the younger generation. Jason told me about it once. He said it was fun."

Ben remained skeptical. "Really?"

"Yes. Now if you're done wringing your hands, you can use them to carry some of these fine delicacies I prepared for you."

"But we already ate."

"One taco. That's more like an appetizer." She thrust out the stack of Tupperware. Ben accepted them, still puzzled. The night had been odd, Allison dragging him out later than usual. They had stopped by a food truck for tacos, saw a terrible action movie that they enjoyed making fun of, and now this. He supposed she was celebrating her last few days of freedom before Davis returned home. Or she was trying to keep their spirits high. Two weeks since the Orlando shootings, and he still found himself haunted. His mind often drifted to the victims and their families. He wished he could do more.

"I feel guilty," he blurted out.

Allison put the rolled blanket under one arm, grabbed the wine, and shut the trunk. Then she looked at him. "For having fun? For living? You can't. It would be letting that piece of shit in Florida win. He wanted gay people, minorities, and anyone he deemed unworthy to hide ourselves away or— You know what? I've given up trying to understand what he was thinking, but I have a son who has to live in this nutty-ass world, and I'm going to teach him to be brave. He's going to love whoever he wants and live his life as he sees fit, so long as he's not hurting anyone. You know who I learned all of that from?"

Ben shook his head. "Please don't say me."

"Damn right I learned it from you! And myself, because why deny how fabulous I am? I've even seen that man of yours conquer his fear. Did the shootings shake us all up? Yes. We're still nursing our wounds and trying to make sense of it all. I pray every night for the victims and their families. But I have to believe—if only for my own sanity—that we'll come out of this tougher and wiser. Anyone who doesn't, we'll help along as best we can. Now can we please go have some fun together? Because I love you, and if anything ever happens to either of us, I want to be able to look back and say that we lived our lives to the fullest. Okay?"

Ben remained solemn. "I love you too."

"Good. Let's go."

They walked along an abandoned path, the light of the parking lot soon behind them. The shadows were thick. Ben tried not to flinch at every sound he heard but failed. The world had seemed a much safer place just a couple of weeks ago, but Allison was right. Giving in to fear would mean letting the haters win.

"Loosen up!" Allison said, no doubt noticing how tense he was. "We used to do this all the time on the bike paths."

The Woodlands had a network of paved trails, which they often treated as a sanctuary. "That's because we never had enough privacy at home. All the best gossip was saved for the paths. God those were good times!"

"Tonight can be too. Just pretend we're sixteen."

"If only," he said with a sigh. "I would love to be that age again."

"Really?" Allison snorted. "Not me. Do you honestly want to go back to high school, put up with the bullies, or be told when to go to sleep and what to eat?"

"When you put it like that… Wait, would I be able to keep my brain?"

"You wouldn't be much good without it."

"No, I mean my current brain. All my memories and experiences. That would make it a lot more interesting."

Allison considered him. "What would you do differently?"

Ben thought about it. "Tell off different people. Or go after some guys who, in retrospect, I *know* wanted me. Like Ronnie Adams."

"Shut your mouth!" Allison said. "That's my boyfriend you're talking about!"

Back then he was, but if they were pretending to still be teenagers… "Ronnie wrote those lyrics for me when Tim and I split up. Are you telling me a straight guy could understand what I'm going through? He totally has a secret crush on me. That's the only reason he's dating you. To get at me."

Allison was scandalized. "What about my feelings? You know I love him. Ronnie is the only man for me. Allison Adams! Tell me that's not a name written in the stars!"

"You keep watching those stars. I'll be in the backseat with Ronnie."

Allison glared. "If I could go back in time, I'd choose a

different best friend." She nudged him to show she was only kidding. "For real though, I wouldn't change much about my childhood. Maybe I'd have a few conversations with my father that I can't have now, and I'd spend extra time with my mom. Everything else played out fine. What about you?"

"The lake," Ben said instantly. "When Tim and I almost got caught by the police. Instead of running away, I'd make sure we weren't at the park that night. That way—" His voice faltered. They had rounded a curve, the trees giving way to a small lake. It wasn't the one from that fateful night. That lake was back in The Woodlands, and this was Austin, but in the dark of night, it easily could have been the same place.

"That was spooky," Allison said, sharing his impression.

"Yeah. Anyway, that night was the beginning of the end. The police caught us— Um."

"On a jungle gym, if I remember right," Allison said with raised eyebrows.

"We were at a playground," Ben said sheepishly. "Mostly by chance. It's not like we were trying a new position by hanging from the monkey bars. Anyway, if the cops hadn't interrupted us, Tim and I wouldn't have broken up, and I could have had more time to work on him."

"I bet."

"Not like that! Okay, lots more of that, but I also could have kept easing him out of the closet. Of course then I might not have met Jace so… I guess I wouldn't do anything differently. Or I'd make sure to break up with Tim before I went to college. That way I could still be with Jace. Don't ever tell him I said that! I'd only do so knowing that we'd be together again eventually." Ben clamped his mouth shut, already feeling he had said too much. He still had one important question though. "Am I horrible?"

"No," Allison said. "You'd want to maximize the time you and Tim could have had together while still having your relationship with Jace. That makes perfect sense to me."

"Thanks."

"You're not right about everything though," Allison said, tone lighter. "Ronnie Adams was *not* gay for you!"

"Not even a little?"

She narrowed her eyes. "He did like hearing you sing a little too much."

"Only because you were singing with me," Ben said, feeling warm as a slew of memories came rushing back. He remained lost in them until Allison chose a location for them to sit.

"This looks like a good spot," she said, shaking out the blanket.

"In the middle of the path?"

"Nobody out here but us. That's what makes night picnics so trendy."

"Yeah, but on the concrete?"

"Fewer bugs," Allison said, already sitting. "Hurry up, I'm starving!"

Ben sat next to her. The blanket was thicker and more comfortable than he'd expected. Bound with the Tupperware containers was a baggie of eating utensils. He placed a set on the blanket for each of them and noticed that something crucial was missing. "Corkscrew?"

Allison swore. "It's in the car!"

Ben shrugged. "We'll be okay. Let's eat. Hey, you made deviled eggs!"

"I learned how in my home economics class," she said, continuing with the theme of them being young again.

"Yeah? Well my mom made us her famous—" He opened a lid. "—tuna salad."

"Thanks, Mrs. B!" Allison said. "The last one just has veggies. I'm trying to minimize my carbs."

"Fine with me." Ben patted the small tummy that he was always fighting against. "It's just as well we can't drink the wine. Calorie city!"

"I was looking forward to it," Allison grumbled. "You can't be a teenager without some irresponsible drinking." She stood suddenly. "I'll run and get it."

Ben shot to his feet. "I'll go with you!"

Allison shook her head. "Stay here and guard the food."

"There's no one out here."

"Animals," she replied. "Raccoons, armadillos, maybe even crocodiles."

"What?" He glanced at the water in panic. When he looked back again, she was already deep in the shadows. "Wait!" he called after her. When she disappeared completely, he muttered a few curse words. Then he started rubbing his arms, even though the summer night wasn't chilly. He thought about sitting again and trying to eat, but that would make it hard to run if a crocodile did—

Ben froze when he heard a noise up ahead. A steady thumping sound. For a second, he thought Allison might have gotten spooked and was running back to him, but this was coming from the wrong direction. It definitely sounded like feet. A jogger? Great! Their picnic was in the middle of the path. The jogger would probably step right into those eggs he loved so much if he didn't salvage them. Ben fell to his knees, trying to gather the food, but the sound was louder now, the person near.

He looked up, stunned to see a vision from the past. A handsome guy with jet black hair, an incredible body and— His eyes dropped lower and he gasped. Neon electric blue shoes! Ben really was sixteen again. This lake was magical, or Allison was secretly a witch. He didn't understand how, but Ben had slipped through time and space. The jogger came to a halt and was all heaving chest and a winner's smile.

"Tim?"

"Nah," came the reply. "My name is Blake Carter, and I'm your dream guy."

Before Ben could fully understand what was happening, Tim helped him to his feet, scooped him up, and then broke into a run.

"Somebody put magic mushrooms into that taco I ate," Ben mumbled.

"Smells more like garlic to me," Tim replied.

"Oh my god." Ben covered his mouth, then decided that talking was more important than his breath. "What are you doing? Put me down!"

Tim slowed and stopped, setting him on his feet and bending over to pant. Ben took the chance to check him out. The outfit, the setting, and especially those shoes! He didn't know what the occasion was, but he loved it!

"Now I know why you haven't gotten a haircut recently," Ben said, grinning uncontrollably.

"I think it was a little longer back then," Tim said, standing upright and ruffling his dark bangs. "Best I could do on short notice."

Ben looked to the shoes again. "Those are exactly how I remember them."

"Good. I wasn't completely sure. It's amazing what you can find on the internet. They must have discontinued these— Well, a long time ago."

Ben laughed. "What is all this?"

"I'll show you." Tim reached behind his back, pulling a folded piece of paper from the band of his shorts. It was damp with sweat when he handed it over.

Ben unfolded it, and when he was unable to make out the words, remembered the flashlight app on his phone.

"Here," Tim said, gesturing for it. "I'll hold the phone. You read."

Able to see now, Ben noticed from the gray haze around the paper's edges that he was looking at a Xerox copy. When he focused on the text, he groaned. "Is this from my journal?"

"No idea."

"Seriously, where did you get this?"

"Just read," Tim said, nodding at the paper.

Ben did so, and it was both humiliating and wonderful. He knew he had previously written about Tim, but he had forgotten the finer details long ago. This entry described the first time he had spotted a hunky guy jogging at night, an encounter that had led to Ben going out almost every evening after in the hope of seeing him again. Many attempts later, he figured out Mr. Blue Shoes' routine, which only fueled his obsession more.

"Check out the date," Tim said.

Ben did so, confused when he saw it was from today. Then he noticed the year. He looked up in awe. "Ten… No! Oh my gosh!"

"Six, twenty-six, ninety-six," Tim said, pulling him close with a sweaty arm and kissing him on the cheek. "It's twenty years today."

Emotion welled up, tears streaking down Ben's cheeks. He wasn't sad, just overwhelmed that they shared so much history. Not all of it had been spent together, but from that moment forth, Ben had never stopped thinking of Tim. A day hadn't gone by without that name popping up in his mind.

"I love you, Benjamin," Tim murmured against his neck. "You're the best thing that's ever happened to me. I know you don't consider it our anniversary, but this was the most important day of my life. At least until you broke my ankle."

"I didn't break it!" Ben said, pushing him away playfully,

but he was used to Tim teasing him about this aspect of their past. "Please tell me you didn't read the rest of my journal. I was young, and sometimes very angry or hurt—"

"I stopped reading there," Tim said. "I just wanted to know the day that we first laid eyes on each other."

"Do you remember seeing me?"

"Honestly?" Tim shook his head. "I wish, but I must have. I'm aware of my surroundings when I jog, and the bench was right next to the path. I had to see someone sitting there, even if I was too in denial to admit how cute he was. And still is."

"Stop," Ben said, wanting him to do anything but. "Twenty years! I don't feel that ancient."

"Neither do I," Tim said. "You keep me young."

"And you make it fun to get old," Ben said, shaking his head at the journal entry. "I can't believe you set all this up."

"I invented time travel for you," Tim said. "No big deal. I thought while we're here, we could correct a few mistakes of the past. There's a jungle gym over there."

Had he overheard the conversation with Allison? The playground was where they had starting doing it before the cops interrupted them and— He noticed the leering smile. Tim hadn't overheard. He was just horny. "Correct mistakes of the past, huh?"

Tim nodded eagerly. "Can we?"

"Sure," Ben said. "We got caught having sex back then, so I guess we should correct that mistake by avoiding sex now. That makes the most sense."

"No!" Tim said, sounding panicked. "I meant that we shouldn't get caught this time. Allison has already gone home, and unless Daniel Wigmore is out here setting fires…"

Ben pretended to mull it over. "We might get away with it. Think you'll last long?"

Tim shook his head. "Huh-uh."

"Me neither." Ben grabbed his hand, pulling him toward the playground. He slowed when halfway there. "Twenty years," he said, still marveling.

"That's just according to me," Tim said casually. "I know you don't like to count that far back. Still… Six, twenty-six, ninety-six. It has a nice ring to it."

"It does," Ben admitted. "I like it. A lot."

The hand holding his squeezed in excitement. "What are you saying?"

They reached the playground, Ben pulling him close. "I'm saying that you win."

"I like what I'm hearing," Tim said, his grin wide. "Keep going."

Ben laughed, kissed him gently, then considered the face that had caught his attention so long ago and had managed to move him ever since. "Blake Carter, Mr. Blue Shoes, Tim Wyman, or whatever your name is, I love you. I always will."

Tim smiled, leaning near for another kiss, but first he placed his forehead against Ben's, silver eyes shining with unbridled joy. "They can't stop us from loving each other, Benjamin. There's not a soul in the world with that power."

Ben fought against tears and failed. "Are you sure?"

"I promise. Happy anniversary, baby."

Ben bit his lip. Then he smiled, giving himself over to love. While it might not be invincible, he was pretty sure love was eternal. Look how long it had lasted already! Their story had begun twenty years ago on a dark path not unlike this one, and they had been chasing after each other ever since, slowly making their way toward the light.

Author's Note

The first drafts of this story were written in early June. At the time I had no idea what awaited us later in the month. When it came time to prepare this story for publication, the world was a very different place, and it seemed wrong to ignore what had happened. While I would love for Ben and Tim to celebrate their anniversary without it being tinged by sorrow, I would love even more for those forty-nine stolen lives to still be here with us today. It's easy to feel powerless in the wake of a tragedy like the Pulse nightclub shootings in Orlando, but in truth, there is much you can do. Here are but a few suggestions:

Donations – The easiest and also one of the most crucial for short-term relief. Consider giving to the National Compassion Fund, where one-hundred percent of funds raised go directly to supporting victims of mass crimes and their families. Please visit this site for more information:
http://nationalcompassionfund.org/

Campaigning – This is more of a long-term solution, and while I'm not here to tell anyone what they should believe in terms of politics, if you want to make a difference, start writing letters. Physical letters get more attention than emails do. Write your local representative, the mayor of your town, the president and other Federal and/or state officials, police chiefs, or anyone you can think of who has influence over laws and the way crimes are prevented and responded to. Be polite, passionate, and concise. You don't need to write poetry. Just express what you would like to see changed, why you believe these changes are important, and how their responses can affect your future votes. These sites contain useful information on how to write and where to send:
http://usgovinfo.about.com/od/uscongress/a/letterscongress.htm
http://www.house.gov/representatives/find/

Donate blood – The current policy banning sexually active gay men from giving blood is fucking stupid, pardon my French, but if you don't fit these parameters or have a good poker face, why not give blood? Not just in the wake of this tragedy, but later too. If something like this should happen again, at least blood banks will be better prepared to save lives:
http://www.redcrossblood.org/

Be vigilant, be true, and be kind – The Orlando shooter decided that the best response to what he perceived as violence against innocent people was to induce violence against innocent people. He was a fucking idiot (My French is getting a lot of practice lately!) and we should learn from the disgustingly poor example he set. Hate is not an effective response to hate. Reason, compassion, and understanding are. It's not enough to go around hugging everyone, although that is indeed a worthy enterprise. We should stay vigilant in the hope of preventing another attack. Keep your eyes and ears open while educating yourself as much as possible. We need to stay true by remaining open and proud of who we are and who we support. Don't let anyone get away with making hateful comments. (Even French ones.) Reply to them with calmness and logic. I promise you they'll find this more infuriating than insults, and who knows, you might get lucky and change someone's mind for the better. Most of all, we need to remain kind by keeping our hearts open. Don't stop loving or trusting. Don't give up on your fellow man. There's more good in this world than evil. Pledge to treat those in your life with love and respect. If everyone decided to be kind to everyone else… Well, hopefully we'll find out together what sort of world that would be. Until then, love is the only answer.

-Jay Bell
July, 2016

Something Like Sparks

by Jay Bell

Titus County, Texas
2014

Hi, Momma. It's me again. You always said that people in Heaven get to watch those of us stuck down here. Hey, remember the old television you bought me before I went off to college? The other day it finally broke. The picture still works, but the speakers fizzled out, and I started to worry that Heaven is the same way. Maybe all you see from up there is my mouth moving, so just in case you can't hear me, I decided to write this letter because I have important news. I need to tell you about the man I love, and why I want to marry him.

"There it is!"

Harold Franklin looked up from the letter he was reading, the paper in his hands soft from age and frequent handling. As he folded it and put it back in its envelope, he wondered how many other people his mother had shown it to. He knew she took it out during key anniversaries, his father grinning dopily as she read aloud the list of everything that made him the perfect spouse. A soundtrack wasn't needed to reinforce how perfect they were for each other. That was plain to see from the way they rarely stopped laughing, or how they always seemed to be touching whenever they were together, from grocery store trips to doctor appointments. Harold guessed that most people thought of their parents as a package deal—assuming they were still together—but with his mom and dad, even their friends always treated them as a single entity instead of two separate individuals. Doing otherwise would be like requesting a taxi without wheels or searching for a beach without sand.

"Not impressed?"

Harold shook his head to clear it, then finally saw what his eyes had been staring at. A lake house. Before making this trip, he had envisioned a squat cabin with a small bedroom, a living room with a cast iron stove, and an outhouse to dash to in the middle of the night. The reality was completely different. The narrow road they were traveling twisted around the lake shore, ahead of them a two-story house big enough for a family of four. Or more. The solidly built dock led to a series of steps that zigzagged up a small slope to the house, lush green tress shielding it from the elements. The setup was nice, but his line of work regularly brought him into contact with extravagant properties. In other words, Harold had seen bigger. And fancier.

Then he looked over at the driver and felt a lot more impressed. Calvin was a handsome guy, to say the least, and even though the comparison always made them both groan, more than one person had remarked on his resemblance to Justin Bieber. While they had similarities, they also had differences. Calvin didn't have the questionable tattoos or the attitude. The dark blond hair and eyes like pools of milk chocolate? Yes. The youthful face that ensured he was still carded for alcohol, even though he was nearing thirty? Definitely. Calvin couldn't sing, and dancing was definitely out too. He also had a better body than Bieber, thanks to near-daily trips to the gym, but Calvin wasn't too pumped up. In fact, he was pretty much perfect! Yeah. That summed him up nicely. More than once, Harold had wondered how he'd gotten so lucky. Oh sure, their clients were always going on and on about Harold's chestnut brown hair, or the dimples that appeared when he smiled. He tried to keep himself presentable, but Calvin, he was always beautiful, whether he made an effort or not.

"You've got that look on your face," Calvin said. The car slowed, gravel crunching beneath the tires. "You either forgot something at home, or it finally clicked that we have an entire weekend just for us."

"Four-day weekend," Harold corrected. "Five if we count today. That's almost a week!"

Calvin grinned, his teeth a testament to modern dentistry. Those perfectly aligned pearly whites had probably put someone's kid through college. He wondered momentarily if Marcello had footed the bill, or maybe he had simply taken over from Calvin's mother, because only a lifetime of care could result in such a photogenic smile.

"We're going to have a good time," Calvin said, misreading his stare. "Total privacy. No work or clients. Just a house full of food, fun, and booze."

"And weed," Harold said helpfully. His boyfriend wasn't a

smoker and had never been high, but Harold intended to correct that this weekend. "I'm making you brownies."

"You'll probably get the munchies, eat them all, and overdose."

"You can't overdose on weed," Harold said, but this went unheard as they pulled into the driveway, his boyfriend looking up at the house with a strained expression. "Did you come here a lot when you were little?"

Calvin, as he so often did when the topic of his family came up, made a joke instead of addressing the subject. "I didn't come here at all until I was thirteen. Then I came here a lot. Enough that the maid started washing my sheets every other day."

"Ha ha," Harold said, unsure if it was even a joke. Their upbringings couldn't have been more different. A maid? Harold's parents did all the cleaning, his father insisting on natural solutions instead of chemicals. To this day, he associated the scent of a clean house with diluted vinegar. Luckily the acrid smell evaporated quickly. As for his mother, she tackled chores by singing, and when he was old enough, encouraged him to do the same. Harold still found himself humming along to The Door's *The End* whenever he took out the trash. In other words, his parents were old hippies. As for Calvin's parents, no intimate details had been shared, although surely this trip would help Harold learn more about them.

They left the car together, stopping again before a large door made of dark wood as Calvin fiddled with his keys.

"Does she know you're here?"

"Mom?" Calvin laughed bitterly. "Not a chance. Maybe I should tell her. That way she'll avoid the place just in case some wandering tourist takes a photo of her and me together." He finally found the right key and unlocked the door. "Her website says she's campaigning all weekend, giving speeches to slack-jawed yokels about how great this country is."

Harold was silent, unsure how to respond. Calvin became distressingly bitter whenever his mother was brought up. Once in the entryway, his boyfriend poked at the alarm system and swore under his breath until the high-pitched warning tone finally ceased. With that out of the way, Harold turned his attention to their surroundings. The wood theme continued, exposed beams breaking up the cream-colored walls. Natural light filtered in through tall windows, carpets helped warm the hardwood floors, and large ceiling fans were already stirring stale air. They stepped into a large living room, the furniture tasteful but not too showy. Harold spotted enough cozy nooks and breathtaking views that he knew he would be comfortable here. As a hopeless homebody, he didn't transplant easily, but this place had potential.

"I knew you would like it," Calvin said, dropping his bag on the floor. "I do too. For most people, summer is a season. For me, it's this place."

"You stayed here a lot?"

Calvin nodded. "Every year. As soon as school was out, we'd pack up and move to the lake house until it was time to enroll again."

"Didn't you miss your friends?"

Calvin laughed. "Nope. I'd just bring them along! I was only allowed two. It became a competition at my school. Who would be invited to stay with the Brandt family this year? Especially once Mom bought the jet skis. I can't tell you how many parties that got me invited to."

Different worlds. Most of Harold's summers had been spent building a treehouse with the boy next door, or defending it from imaginary enemies. Not a single kid at school had competed for that privilege.

Harold strolled through the living room, gravitating toward a framed photo. He recognized Angela Brandt immediately, not just because of the no-nonsense hairstyle or power suit that many female politicians seemed to favor, but also because Harold had searched online, curious to learn more about Calvin's family. The photo summed up what he had found out. Dad was out of the picture, both figuratively and literally, and Calvin's two siblings were closer to their mother, flanking her affectionately. A younger Calvin, bucktoothed and gangly, stood awkwardly to one side, his smile less certain.

"Horrible photo," his boyfriend said, laying the frame face-down so the image could no longer be seen. "I'm going to replace it with one of my headshots. I mean it. I have some in my suitcase."

No surprise there. Calvin was an aspiring model. So far without much luck, but surely that would change soon. "What's the upstairs like?"

"Are you asking about the bedrooms?"

Harold grinned. "Maybe."

"Right this way!"

The stairs led to a family room that overlooked the living area below. Beyond this, a short hallway revealed more doors. Calvin opened one and stood aside. "My old room."

Harold expected embarrassing band posters or a forgotten stuffed animal on the bed. Instead, as he entered, he saw that the room lacked any personal touch. The framed prints hanging on the wall were as generic as the furnishings. The room, like those in interior decorating magazines, was innocuous while fulfilling the most basic of needs. "I guess it used to look a lot different than this," he suggested.

"Nope." Calvin strolled into the room. "Bedspread is new. So is that lamp, but the rest is the same."

Harold spun to face him. "There must have been toys and stuff. No kid is this clean!"

Calvin bent next to the bed and pulled. Two storage containers rolled out from underneath. He took off the lids so Harold could see inside. He was greeted by the childhood equivalent of a junk drawer, but taken to a new extreme. Toys, comics, novels, and a ton of music CDs and DVD movies intermingled. "When you've got someone as high-profile as Mom, you can't just leave things around that might offend someone."

"Why not? It's your private room!"

"Private?" Calvin shook his head. "When we had people over to the house, they'd often ask for a tour. I remember this one time, my sister had a 2 Live Crew poster hanging up. Do you remember them?"

"No."

"Me neither. I couldn't name one of their songs, but this politician was touring the house and turned bright red when he walked into her room. I guess he had fought to pass some bill banning explicit music. I think he was with the AFA."

"Who?"

"Professional douchebags. Anyway, even though her room was spotless and my sister was a saint—compared to me, anyway—the guy lectured her to the point where she started crying."

"That's messed up!"

Calvin clenched his jaw. "Yeah. From then on, my mom implemented a policy where we had to keep our personal stuff out of sight. I was little at the time and only upset about having to clean my room again and put more stuff away. When I got older, I accepted it as normal. I would go to other kids' houses, see their rooms crammed full of personality, and think their parents must not care enough about them to make them put it all away."

"Wow."

"Nice message to send your children, isn't it?" Calvin said. "Anything you like, think, or feel needs to be compartmentalized. Otherwise it might alienate a valuable connection."

Harold considered the hidden possessions, shaking his head. "I used to wish my parents were normal. You've met them. They're pretty out there."

Calvin snorted. "Like when your mother tried to cleanse my anus?"

"Your aura, and yeah. When you're a teenager, parents are always embarrassing, so just imagine how I felt about them passing out grounding crystals during a sleepover."

"Grounding crystals?"

"Don't ask." Harold nodded to the storage container. "Now that I see this, I'm glad my parents are so weird. They make it easier to be myself, you know? I couldn't out-weird them if I tried, and that made coming out easy, because I still felt so normal by comparison."

Calvin laughed. "Better than feeling like a freak for doing normal things. I'm glad those days are over." He returned to the hallway and rolled in the luggage they had brought in from the car. "Let's unpack. Then I need a shower. Care to join me?"

Harold had already taken one that morning, and the drive had been only four hours. Neither one of them could be too grimy, but he understood that this was habit. When working, they had to look and smell their best for their clients, and that meant getting cleaned up before dinner. Or maybe Calvin had a big night planned for them. "You go ahead. I'll get everything unpacked and put away. I'll even choose an outfit for you."

"Something comfortable," Calvin said longingly. "I'm fine with sweatpants and a T-shirt."

"You don't own sweatpants. Do you?"

His boyfriend laughed on his way out the door. "I do now,"

he called. "I bought some for this trip!"

No big night out then. Harold was fine with that. He was more interested in exploring this house further and learning about Calvin's past. That was important, now more than ever, because they had a future to discuss. Once the clothes were unpacked and put away, Harold could still hear the trickle of shower water, so he returned his attention to the toys, trying to decipher what sort of child Calvin had been. He noticed more action figures than toy cars. Did that signify a future interest in men? Most of the figures were muscular and showing skin, so maybe. Harold was about to push the storage containers back under the bed when inspiration struck. He scooped up as many toys as he could, then walked around the room, decorating it with the carelessness of an eight-year-old. By the time Calvin appeared in the doorway with a towel wrapped around his waist, the room had been transformed. It now resembled a completely normal—and thus very messy—child's room.

"What the hell did you do?" Calvin said, expression strained. Then it clicked and he laughed. "What a freaking disaster. I love it!"

"You do?"

Calvin hurried forward. "Hey, is that my Prince Adam figure? I *so* had the hots for him! This belonged to my brother until I stole it. I just wish it had a pink vest like in the cartoon." The next half hour was a nostalgic trip down memory lane, Calvin picking up toy after toy and telling stories about each. Harold sat on the bed and laughed through most of this. At times he simply stared because he really loved the guy acting out a battle between two barbarians that soon shifted to a soap opera, complete with an untimely death and a surprise resurrection. Recast of course, a pirate figure taking the place of the fallen lover.

Calvin was the one. He had to be! Harold was tempted to ask now instead of waiting. Then again, he wanted this to be perfect. Whatever moment he chose would be a story they told their friends, family, maybe even their children for years to come.

"Oops!"

The towel had fallen. Calvin was standing naked in the middle of the room, a miniature man in each hand. The body on display was endearingly familiar. The small mole on one shoulder, the pink spot on his left thigh from an accidental burn as a child, even the way his chest hair swept to the left, as if he combed it when really it just grew that way. And of course the muscles Calvin worked so hard to maintain and the big ol' sausage dangling between his legs, these things were familiar too, but Harold's attraction rose above the physical. This was love.

The thought didn't come as a surprise. Over the previous two years, they had spoken their feelings aloud plenty of times. Calvin loved him, and Harold... He was pretty sure he loved Calvin more. It wasn't a competition, but it always seemed like Harold needed him most. Ever since that first awkward encounter, a new client, both of them hired for the same night. By the end of it, Harold had to keep reminding himself that they weren't alone, because he couldn't seem to tear his eyes away. Like now.

"It's been a while," Calvin said, his childhood toys forgotten. "That bed never saw any action. At least, not with anyone else in there with me. Wanna change that?"

Harold nodded instantly. "We can just cuddle. If you want."

Calvin scowled. "Do you think I have trouble getting it up? Because look." He pointed, using the plastic head of the pirate.

Harold looked, even though he didn't need to. He was well-aware of his boyfriend's prowess. "I just like the idea of being in bed and not having to—"

"I understand." Calvin's voice was softer now. "I'd like that too."

When they were at their best, words weren't necessary. While their backgrounds might be vastly different, their present circumstances were very much the same. Not many people understood the life of an escort or had any sympathy for it. Most assumed it was a last choice borne out of desperation. Harold didn't want to think about any of that now. As his boyfriend fell into his arms, Harold happily dragged him toward the bed, dreaming of the future and how drastically this trip might change it.

Harold woke in the middle of the night, as he always did when staying somewhere unfamiliar. He knew from experience that he would need an hour or so to settle down again, so he slipped out of bed, used the restroom, and went downstairs. His backpack was still in the living room where he'd dropped it earlier. After their afternoon nap, he and Calvin had hit the nearest gas station for food and booze. They had mostly drunk their dinner and snacked right before bed, which they normally wouldn't allow themselves, but hey, vacation.

Harold was rifling through his backpack for the cell phone charger when he noticed his mother's letter again. He took it and settled into a worn and cozy chair. His mother had written an address on the envelope. *To Heaven.* Beneath this was further instruction. *c/o Hermes.* Like that made sense, but she hadn't stopped there. She had affixed postage and dropped it in a mailbox. The letter must have been returned to her, because a red stamp declared it undeliverable. The entire exercise summed her up well. Writing a letter to your deceased mother—Harold's grandmother whom he had never met—and then actually trying to mail it? If he asked her what she'd been thinking, she would no doubt insist that she had been feeling instead, something she always encouraged him to do more of.

The letter didn't seem so crazy now. Harold was tempted to write one of his own, although his would be addressed directly to God. *Hey, big guy, I think I've found the one you made for me, but I wanted to double check if I'm doing this right. Some sort of sign would be helpful.* Then again, what would be the point? Even his mother hadn't expected to get a response. Besides, he was fairly confident about his decision.

Harold hooked his backpack with a foot and dragged it closer. Then he dug around inside until he found a ring. He often wore it, although not too often or it turned his finger green. Calvin had bought it for him at a grocery store by the exit where vending machines offered random surprises for spare change. Twenty-five cents had bought them a plastic egg with a simple ring inside. The band of cheap metal was slightly wavy and ridiculously thin, but most surprisingly, it fit. Calvin had dropped to one knee right there in the grocery store and slipped it on Harold's ring finger, declaring it a promise of better things to come. That had been their second date. The gesture was sweet, if not a little juvenile. Regardless, Harold had been careful not to lose the ring. Now he was ready to give it back. Their wedding rings would be forged from a finer material, but for the proposal, Harold felt the little copper hoop was ideal.

He slid it onto his finger, then opened his mother's letter, looking again for inspiration. His eyes darted down to the list of reasons why she had found his father so worthy. Some were ridiculous, like him growing the best turnips in Texas, but others resonated with Harold.

We never run out of things to say to each other.

So true, although to an outsider, his conversations with Calvin probably made it sound like they had a ton of family and friends. In reality, their lives were mostly filled with clients, so that's what they discussed. "Did you hear that Mark's nephew got arrested?" or "I bet Allister would love those oven mitts with the poodles on them!" Some people obsessed over YouTube stars or got hooked on reality television. He and Calvin had their own cast of real-life characters they kept up with. Puzzling Pete was their current favorite. He was good-looking, wealthy, and personable. No strange kinks either. Why he required the services of an escort baffled them both, and they loved coming up with increasingly ridiculous explanations. Harold's most realistic theory was that Pete's fetish was paying for sex, and that one of them should do him for free, just to see if it was a mood killer.

He accepts me for who I am.

Definitely. Harold knew from experience how difficult dating could be in their line of work. Real dating, not the profitable kind. Most people were scared off by his profession, or if not, were eventually overcome with jealousy. He and Calvin never had to apologize to each other for being unavailable most nights, or explain why they couldn't be intimate when they were saving their stamina. They were the same and yet different, the best of both worlds.

It doesn't take long before I miss him.

This line had never seemed so important to him before. People missed people. So what? Now he finally got it. Harold lowered the letter and raised his head, looking toward the stairs. How long had he been down here? Twenty minutes? Already he yearned to be in the same room with Calvin, preferring to lie awake and listen to the sound of him breathing rather than remain apart from him any longer. How ridiculous! They were in the same house, and one of them wasn't even awake, and yet Harold still felt they should be together.

He set the letter on the table, rose, and went back upstairs. Once in the bedroom, he slid between the sheets and nestled close to his boyfriend, already eager for the day he could call him husband instead.

*****

The smell of frying bacon invaded the room, dragging Harold out of bed and down the stairs. He paused in the living room when he saw Calvin sitting in the same worn and cozy chair from last night, the letter in hand. His boyfriend looked up, eyes moving over his bedhead, bare torso, and flannel pajama bottoms. Calvin, as always, had gotten up early and was already dressed in an outfit from Hollister's summer collection. He held up the letter and shook it. "Your parents are crazy."

"In a good way?" Harold asked around a yawn.

"Definitely. I wish either of mine were capable of emotion."

"Having a robot mom would have been cool." Harold yawned again. "Sort of like Rosie the Robot but with missile boobs."

"And now I see where you get it from," Calvin said, returning the letter to its envelope before standing. "Come with me. You need caffeine."

Harold nodded blearily, followed him to the kitchen table, and hardly said a word until he had polished off a cup of coffee and a plate of turkey bacon and eggs. Then he leaned back and sighed contentedly. "Can we keep doing this the entire day?"

"Nope! It's almost the Fourth of July. We need fireworks. As soon as you're showered, we're going shopping."

"Everything is probably closed," Harold said, resting his head on the table. Maybe if he was really quiet and still, he would be forgotten about so he could sleep some more.

"I know of at least one store that'll be open and it's all we need. Get ready, please. Is half an hour enough?"

"An hour is fine," Harold murmured.

"That's not what I said."

"I know." He heard a foot tapping on the floor and opened his eyes. Calvin's arms were crossed and he was attempting a stern expression. It didn't work. He was too cute! "Forty-five minutes?"

"If I had missile boobs, I'd be launching them right now."

Harold laughed, then forced himself to sit upright. "Okay. Half an hour. But no rushing after that. I want to feel like I'm on vacation. And I want to see you lounging around in those sweat pants again."

Calvin grinned and nodded. "Tomorrow. Assuming we have a house left by the end of the day. We've got a lot of stuff to blow up!"

Harold got to his feet and trudged toward the stairs, deciding he should at least look presentable for the fire department when it arrived to put out the flames.

"Over there is where history's greatest mudball fight took place. Kids are always having snowball fights on TV, and we were sick of feeling left out, so we took matters into our own hands. Oh, and see that house? First time I ever got drunk. Her parents were out of town and she was still pissed at her dad for ruining her sweet sixteen, so we drank everything we could find. A friend of mine even drank the mouthwash. Barfed up his guts, but he still swears he's never been drunker since. See that pizza place? Used to be a—"

Harold's head was on automatic nod. They had parked in the quaint downtown shopping area, but something in a nearby neighborhood had caught Calvin's eye. They had been walking ever since, seemingly in random directions. Wherever the next memory pulled his boyfriend, that's where they went. For Harold it was a case of being careful what you wished for. He had wanted to learn about Calvin's childhood, but maybe not in so much detail.

"—never shoplifted again. Not after that. Oh, and over here…"

Harold was yanked down the sidewalk. Then they veered off into a yard, Calvin leading them around the side of the house to a privacy fence that stopped them short.

"This wasn't here back then," he said, peeking over the pointed wooden slabs. "My friend Andy and I were camping out back in a little tent one night. Playing truth or dare."

"Uh oh," Harold said. "How old were you guys?"

"Eight. Maybe nine."

"Oh. So nothing too interesting could have happened."

Calvin grinned. "That's what you think! First time I ever kissed a boy was right over there."

Harold made a face. "Whatever."

"I did!"

"Okay, but no way does that count. A peck on the mouth between two kids? In that case, I probably had my first kiss when I was two and don't even remember it."

"I'll show you." Calvin opened the wooden gate, then

grabbed Harold's hand again and dragged him forward.

"What if someone's home?" Harold protested. "Do Andy's parents still live here? Hey! Someone will see!"

"I don't care," Calvin responded.

They had reached the center of the yard. Calvin wrapped his arms around Harold, who tried to pull away to check the house. Those gym muscles had him trapped. He was better off giving in. That way it would be over soon. In theory. He wasn't sure how long the kiss lasted. Long enough for the hum of an airplane overhead to disappear.

"Like that," Calvin said, finally stepping back.

"Your first kiss?"

"Yup!"

"When you were eight?" Harold asked incredulously. "That much tongue?"

"No. I only wish! Andy was hot. For an eight-year-old."

"Gross!"

"We were the same age! And you're right, it was just a peck, but it meant something to me."

Harold nodded his understanding. "What did he think?"

Calvin laughed. "He hated it. Kept spitting and eventually went inside to brush his teeth. I was convinced I was a bad kisser until Bobby Donaldson, who come to think of it, lives just down the street. Wanna see where?"

"Are we going to do it in his backyard?"

"Maybe."

"Sounds exciting, but you promised me shopping. I need souvenirs."

"Oh. Right." Calvin spun in a circle, as if reorienting. Then he led the way. "Let's see if Janice is still around."

"Shopping," Harold reminded him helpfully.

"I know. Janice owns the old general store."

Harold snorted, thinking it was a joke. General store? Someone had been watching too much *Little House on the Prairie*. They returned to the downtown area, and sure enough, on one corner a wooden sign painted with the words *General Store* hung above a door. The interior was just as he pictured it, narrow and deep. Most surfaces were made out of stained wood, including the floor. Shelves were filled with preserves, canned goods, and other traditional groceries. A long counter stretched the length of the room. In its glass case, he saw a number of humble products for sale, like chunky bars of homemade soap or bottles with handwritten labels. Standing behind this was a burly woman with a cowboy hat perched on her short hair.

"That's Janice," Calvin said, nodding in her direction. "Most of the shops around here are only open during the summer and close once all the tourists leave. Janice's place is always open, which is good, because the nearest grocery store is a twenty-minute drive. Have a look around and see if there's anything you want. Then we'll get down to business."

Whatever that meant. Harold focused on selecting gifts, already knowing that the handmade stuff was perfect for his mom. A rack of retro pranks and novelties would take care of his dad. He even found something for himself—small mason jars that would be perfect for keeping his stash fresh. He carried all of this to the counter, Calvin joining him.

"Don't try giving me any of your tourist prices," Calvin said with a grin. "I'm local."

Janice sized him up with narrowed eyes. Then she nodded as if satisfied. "You're one of the Brandt boys."

"That's right. Do you still sell bomb bags?"

Janice shook her head. "I don't know what you're talking about."

"Perfect. We'll take two."

Janice retreated to a back room and returned with two brown paper bags that had been stapled shut. Drawn on the front of each was a cartoon bomb, fuse lit and sparking. Then Janice started poking at an antique cash register while muttering to herself. "Front of store stock is eighteen, the bomb bags are twenty-five each."

"They used to be twenty."

Janice stopped with her hand on the crank. "Inflation. Take it or leave it."

"You're robbing us blind," Calvin said with a sigh, but he seemed to be having a good time. At least until an older man walked up to him and clamped a hand on his shoulder.

"Is that little Davey Brandt?"

"You're thinking of my brother," Calvin replied.

"Calvin? Can't be! You're just a baby!"

Calvin shrugged, like he couldn't help that he had grown up.

The hand on his shoulder moved away, but remained held out.

"You remember me? Mr. Arbor. I own the bait and tackle shop."

"Right," Calvin said a little stiffly. He grasped the offered hand, sounding more guarded when he spoke again. "Of course we remember you."

We?

"You're practically family," Calvin added.

Harold had never heard him mention fishing before, or this person.

Regardless, Mr. Arbor seemed pleased by the response. "Your mother always makes sure to stop by and say hello to me, and I always make sure to vote for her. Is she in town now?"

"No," Calvin said, sliding cash across the counter.

This was ignored by Janice, who seemed more interested in the conversation. She wasn't the only one. Two other customers had stopped their browsing to stare.

"I heard your mother will be running for governor," Mr. Arbor said. "Imagine that! Our Angela as governor of Texas!"

"She can start by dropping taxes for tourists," Janice chimed in. "*Any* tourists, and I don't mean that nonsense with the Tax Back locations. We don't get many international folks in here, so how does that help us?"

"I'm not happy with the new fishing regulations," Mr. Arbor said, gearing up for a lecture himself.

Calvin raised his hands to stop him. "I'm no politician," he said. "Wait until next month when Angela is here. She'll want to hear all about this."

Mr. Arbor nodded. "She hasn't said much about you. What sort of work do you do?"

"Male escort," Calvin said with a straight face. Then he smiled, causing the room to laugh. "I went to law school, just like my brother and sister."

And dropped out after the first year, but this went unmentioned.

"Smart woman," Mr. Arbor said approvingly. "All of her children are lawyers. Wish I had thought of that. Might have saved me some money. And some trouble. Who's this?"

All eyes moved to Harold, and he felt what Calvin must have this entire time: like he was on stage. Luckily he was used to performing. Not for this many people, but still. He stepped forward and offered his hand along with a friendly smile. "I'm his college roommate," he said, lying through his teeth. "Or at least I was. Now we're just friends."

"Are you a lawyer too?" Mr. Arbor asked, sizing him up.

"Didn't make the cut, I'm afraid," Harold said. "I don't know what I'll do with myself now. Open a bait and tackle shop, maybe. Give you some competition."

Mr. Arbor laughed. "We miss having your family around," he said, returning his attention to Calvin. "Always kept the town on its toes. Say, was it you or your brother that got in trouble for throwing rocks?"

"Mudballs," Calvin said, but his voice lacked the joy it had earlier.

He told the story anyway, earning more laughs and promising that he had learned the error of his ways. Then Mr. Arbor brought up the fishing regulations again. The customers got bored, either leaving or queueing at the cash register. This forced Janice to finish ringing up their purchases, after which Calvin apologized for not having more time and left the shop.

Harold followed, waiting until they were close to the car before speaking. "That was interesting."

"That sucked," Calvin said, cheeks glowing red. "You didn't need to pretend we're just friends. I'm not in the closet. I don't care who knows."

"Okay," Harold said. "Sorry."

"It's not your fault." He glowered and shook his head. "We shouldn't have come here."

"It wasn't that bad. A little awkward maybe but—"

"She'll be up here in one day flat," Calvin said, pacing between the driver-side door and the curb. "News will spread that I'm in town, and she'll come to make sure I'm not fucking up her precious career. Or she'll send someone over." He stopped, then nodded to himself. "Yeah. That's what she'll do. She'll send someone."

"Has she before?" Harold asked.

Calvin laughed. "Are you kidding?"

He took that as a yes. "Let's go home. We've got everything we need. We'll stay there for the rest of the weekend and not come into town again. That's what we both want anyway, right?"

Calvin clenched his jaw a few times. Then he exhaled. "Yeah. Let's get the hell out of here."

The car interior was quiet. Harold drove, knowing how emotional Calvin could get over his family. His boyfriend continued to silently seethe. Harold wanted to find out why and help him talk through his feelings. He had promised himself to hold off until they were home again and away from distractions of the road, but he couldn't wait any longer.

"Was it that bad?" he asked.

Calvin scoffed. "You'll have to be more specific."

"What happened at the general store. Yeah, it was awkward, but so is running into—I don't know—a nosey neighbor you never really liked."

Calvin sighed. "No, it wasn't a big deal. It just brought back a lot of bad memories."

Harold glanced over at his passenger. "Like what?"

"Like how for the first twenty years of my life, my identity didn't belong to me. I was told growing up that someone was always watching. Always. Out shopping, in our neighborhood, even our yard—none of it was safe. At home it was my mother watching me, and you've already seen my room. I *never* felt like I had privacy, or a place where I could be myself. Most people describe being in the closet as torment. For me, hiding my sexuality wasn't hard because I already hid everything else about myself."

"Was it really like that?"

Calvin exhaled, the sound weary and defeated. "Yes."

Harold thought of his own parents, how his mother had always encouraged him to explore his identity. She bought him every book he wanted, rarely censored what he could watch, and pushed him to try anything that captured his imagination and many things that didn't. She had signed him up for Little League and dragged him along to many of her classes be they yoga, reiki, or ceramics. His mother sent him off to camps some summers and let him fend for himself during others. She wanted him to have every opportunity, to try it all at least once. His father would jump in when Harold actually found something he liked, helping coach the junior bowling league Harold joined, or getting poked during a brief phase when Harold thought fencing would be fun.

His parents had helped him explore his full potential. Calvin's parents had done their best to suppress his.

"Pete is right. I'm never going to feel completely free unless I leave the little empire my mother built for herself."

"Pete?" Harold asked. "As in Puzzling Pete?"

"Yeah."

He felt the stirrings of jealousy, which didn't come often. "You've been talking to him about your family?" Getting Calvin to open up, to bring him here, had taken ages. They had been together for two years, and Harold still hadn't met a single member of Calvin's family.

"We have a lot in common. Pete's dad was the mayor of a small town in Oklahoma. Small fry compared to my mom, but he went through a lot of the same political stuff. After a while you feel like you belong to the voters, not your parents. You answer to them, and if you make them unhappy, your parents punish you for it. That's why Pete left his hometown and never went back."

Harold didn't hide his confusion. "Why didn't you tell me any of this?"

Calvin chuckled, which was a welcome sound despite the uncomfortable circumstances. "Because I didn't want to ruin the fun. I know how much you like making up theories about him. Pete likes them too."

"You told him?"

"Only some. The one about him belonging to the Russian mafia was his favorite. He actually speaks a little Russian, so you might be on to something."

Harold was torn between feeling angry or betrayed, but when he looked over and saw his boyfriend laughing, dark mood dispersing, he decided it was worth it. "Just promise you didn't tell him my clown theory."

"You mean how he was kidnapped as a child and forced to perform in a circus? Pete laughed a good ten minutes over that one."

"I was way too stoned that night! You've got the story wrong anyway. He joined the circus after escaping from his kidnappers. And really, you've seen him juggle. Why would a retired surgeon know how to do that?"

"Could be helpful," Calvin said musingly. "That way he doesn't need to rely on an assistant. You know how some nurse is always standing nearby holding a bunch of scalpels? Pete could just juggle them instead."

"And throw the old kidney into the mix once it was out?"

"Exactly."

Harold shook his head. "He's totally a refugee circus clown. I'm more convinced than ever. What else have you learned about him?"

"Oh." Calvin exhaled as if this was a tall order. "A lot. How's this? I don't want you to stop guessing because it's way too amusing, but from now on, I'll tell you if you're right."

Harold glanced over again and saw a smile, one that never failed to trigger one of his own. "Okay. But I'm going to prove my theory right. The next time he calls me for a date, I'm showing up wearing a red nose and a curly green wig."

"I'd like to see that. In fact, turn the car around. I think I know where we can buy an entire clown outfit for you."

Harold stayed the course. They were just minutes from the house. Once they parked in the driveway and got out, they unpacked their goods from the trunk.

"What exactly is a bomb bag anyway?"

"Mostly illegal," Calvin said. "Come on. I'll show you."

"I'm hungry. You promised me lunch."

"Fine." Calvin said, rolling his eyes. "Come inside. I'll feed you and then… Then we're going to blow shit up!"

Harold crouched at the end of a dock where water met land and focused on twisting fuses together. Janice had thoughtfully included extra lengths of the wick-like material for just such an occasion. He paused in his work to glance back at the small pile of explosives. Harold suspected that most of them were illegal and capable of blowing off fingers—if not an entire hand. That's why he had opted for the smoke bombs. Those were safer, and one of his favorites as a child. He shouldn't have been surprised that Calvin found a way to make them dangerous.

"You finished yet?" his boyfriend asked from the other end of the dock. His attention was on the lake as he kicked loose stones into the water.

"Almost."

"All ten, right? I want double of each color!"

Harold sighed and grabbed the two smoke bombs he had been hoping would go unnoticed. Then he added them to the chain that should set them all off simultaneously. He ran an extra length of fuse so he would have time to get away, then stood. "Ready?"

"Get your phone out."

"In case I need to call an ambulance?"

Calvin stomped a foot. "To make a video of the most epic entrance imaginable!"

It wouldn't be an entrance, and chances were that Calvin would soon be coughing nonstop, but Harold did as he was told. With his phone at the ready, he looked up for confirmation. When he saw a self-assured nod, he lit the fuse and scurried back, and by the time his phone had started recording, plumes of multi-colored smoke were already filling the air. Red, orange, yellow, green, and blue. Not quite the full spectrum, but already the colors were twisting around each other without mixing together. The result was impressive. Calvin strode through this wall of hues like some sort of gay superhero, his head held high. Pride Man! Or maybe the Rainbow Avenger.

Harold lowered the phone slightly so his vision was less obscured. Calvin was beautiful. Not just his toned body or the delicate features of his face, but his spirit too. Once through the smoke, Calvin glowered into the camera in a way both sexy and intimidating. Then his face lit up like a child's and he punched a fist in the air.

"Yes! Oh my god, I hope you got all that because it was amazing!"

Harold stopped recording, almost unable to tear his eyes away long enough to do so. "You're amazing."

"Aw, shucks," Calvin said, rewarding him with a quick peck on the lips. "You ain't seen nothing yet. When I was little, we used to—" He spun around, seeking something, and settled on a simple fishing boat with paddles and just enough room for two people. "Time to launch some torpedoes!"

Harold looked again at the pile of explosives, hoping actual torpedoes weren't somewhere in the mix.

Calvin noticed his confusion. "You'll see. Come on. Oh! Grab a couple of rocks. Small ones, but not pebbles."

Harold did as he was told as his boyfriend loaded up the boat with fireworks, most of them bottle rockets and short red tubes that made him nervous. He felt a lot less apprehensive when in the boat. Calvin insisted on rowing, his arms flexing alluringly, the sun gleaming off his blond hair and bleached white teeth.

"Having fun?"

"Yeah," Harold said. "I never knew you were into stuff like this."

Calvin shrugged. "We would get bored way out here. Most years we didn't have internet access, and you've seen how unreliable cell phone signals can be. When July rolled around, we felt like we finally had something to do."

"Like launching torpedoes?"

Calvin nodded, rowing with renewed effort to get them to the middle of the lake. Once there, he laid the paddles on the boat's floor and reached for the bottle rockets. "Torpedoes!" he explained.

Harold shook his head. "I don't think those'll survive the water."

"Oh really? Watch!"

Calvin lit one, holding on even after it had started sparking. Bottle rockets might appear to be simple firecrackers tied to sticks, but they had thrust in addition to explosive power. It never took long for the payload to detonate, and he was concerned this would happen too soon and hurt his boyfriend. Calvin finally released the firework, throwing it with a whipping motion into the lake. The bottle rocket zipped beneath the water and out of sight. Scant seconds later, a muted explosion could be heard, thousands of tiny bubbles rising to the lake's surface.

"Wow!" Harold said, genuinely impressed. "I can't believe that still went off! Why doesn't the water put it out?"

"Don't question the miracle," Calvin said. "Just enjoy it. Here. You try."

Harold was too intrigued to refuse. He lit a bottle rocket and tossed it into the water. It hit the surface but failed to enter, floating there lamely, the fuse extinguished.

This sent Calvin into a fit of laughter. "It's all about timing! Here, try again."

Harold did, waiting until a stream of sparks threatened to singe his fingers before he tossed it. This time it skidded across the surface instead of diving, but at least it exploded. He was hooked. For the next twenty minutes, they worked their way through dozens of the little rockets, the lake soon cluttered with splintered sticks and scraps of burnt paper.

"How are we going to clean that up?" Harold asked.

"The park rangers will take care of it tomorrow. Trust me, we aren't the only ones doing this."

Harold glanced around the boat, disappointed to see they had exhausted their supply. They still had other options, including the mean-looking red tubes. "What about those?"

"M-80s," Calvin said with reverence. "We need to be careful. M-80s were outlawed a long time ago. You can still find fireworks using that name, but these are the real deal."

"How does Janice get them?"

"Nobody knows. Some people say she makes them herself. Others say she's a former Navy Seal and gets them from the government. Somehow."

Harold laughed. "Right. What do we do with them?"

"That's what the rocks are for. If bottle rockets are torpedoes, then these babies are depth charges!" Calvin had come prepared. He pulled a small roll of electrical tape from the pocket of his shorts and used this to bind an M-80 to one of the rocks Harold had gathered. Calvin lit it cautiously, quickly tossing the bundle into the lake and shouting, "Fire in the hole!"

Harold was tempted to plug his ears. Much like the bottle rockets, a short delay preceded the explosion, a small mushroom cloud of water breaking the surface before the area turned into a temporary Jacuzzi. "Is that it?"

Calvin's face went slack with disbelief. "What do you mean? That was amazing! You should see the damage they can do when on land!"

Harold shrugged. "Yeah, okay, but I expected the boat to shake or something."

"If that's what you want…" Calvin hopped to his feet, spreading them wide before he started shifting his weight back and forth. Soon the boat was really rocking!

"Stop!" Harold cried, grasping the bench he was sitting on. "You know I'm not a good swimmer!"

"If you fall in, I'll pull you out again." Calvin slowed, but only so he could grab two roman candles. After lighting them, he resumed his wide stance and the rocking, but now his arms were stretched out too. "Behold my magical testicles!" he shouted as glowing balls launched from each tube.

Harold was laughing too hard to feel afraid anymore. He was clutching his stomach and still grinning when Calvin finally stopped, each sway of the boat gentler than the previous. Calvin was smiling too in a way he only seemed to when they were alone. Harold never wanted that happy expression to fade. If given the choice, he would want the rest of their lives to be filled with days like these. Harold's right hand moved instinctually to touch the left, fingers caressing the ring there. This was it. A perfect little moment full of so much joy. They would make this feeling permanent. Together.

Harold took off the ring, sliding from the bench and onto one knee, which ended up in shallow water on the boat's floor. He ignored this discomfort, holding the ring aloft and hoping to find the perfect words. "I want more of this."

Calvin gazed at the ring. He laughed before his eyes darted up again, his smile faltering when he saw Harold's expression. "Stop kidding around."

"I'm serious. The day I met you, my entire world changed. I didn't realize then. It wasn't love at first sight, but it was close, because when you touched me… Do you remember that? The very first time? I felt an electric current all the way down to my heart and I—"

"Stop."

Harold blinked. He didn't understand. Calvin was probably just overwhelmed. He got like that sometimes with emotional stuff, so Harold pressed on. "I felt you there. In my heart. It's like you came home again after being gone a long time, and I should have known then that you were the one. I just needed—"

Calvin moved forward, swiftly covering the ring with his palm, but not to take it. "Stop. I mean it. This isn't the right time."

Harold's throat felt tight, but he forced himself to speak. "It's not like we have to get married right away. We can wait however long you want! I just want it to happen eventually." He tried a smile. "That's what a promise ring is for. Remember? For better days to come."

Calvin didn't smile back. Instead he only looked more miserable. "Put it away. Please."

What else could he do? Harold pulled away his hand, clenching the ring in one fist. His face burned as he rose and sat on the bench again.

Calvin exhaled and plopped down next to him, but he didn't reach over to make contact, or allow their shoulders to touch. He wasn't even looking at Harold, attention on the lake instead. "I wish we could always be like this."

"That's all I was trying to say."

Calvin laughed bitterly and shook his head. "You don't understand."

"Then explain it to me!"

He nodded toward the shore. "What do you see?"

Harold looked. Thick pine trees surrounded the lake. They had drifted far enough that he couldn't see the house anymore. Only the distant sound of a motor suggested that they weren't completely alone.

"I used to feel safe here," Calvin said. "When we'd finally get away from Austin, away from the capitol, I'd feel like I could breathe again. Eventually I figured it out. Anyone we met, no matter how briefly, was a potential voter to my mother."

Harold sighed. "This has nothing to do with your family."

"It does. You think she's going to be cool with newspapers reporting that her son is getting married to another guy? I'm not in the closet, but she'll find a way to stop it. Trust me." Calvin shook his head wearily. "Pete is right. There's only one way to escape her."

"What's that supposed to mean?"

Calvin gestured at their surroundings. "If she becomes governor of Texas, even this won't be enough to escape. The entire state will belong to her."

Harold rolled his eyes. "You're being dramatic."

"I'm being practical. I won't be here when it happens. I'm leaving. I'm moving out of state." Calvin finally looked over at him. "Pete offered me a place to live. With him. In his house."

Harold strained to remember Pete's living situation. He owned an apartment in Austin. A really big one, but that was only where Pete stayed to escape the winters, because normally he lived up in… "Colorado?"

Calvin nodded. "Yeah."

"Then I'll go with you."

The eyes searching his softened, and for a brief second, he thought they would be okay. "Pete wants me all to himself. He wants me to be his boyfriend."

Harold didn't need an explanation. Such things had happened before. Most of their clients had money, and with it came influence. So when they got attached to an escort, sometimes they thought they could own that person just like everything else they did. "And what do you want?"

"To get away from her."

"Fine, but you don't need Pete! I'll move out of state with you. We can go anywhere you want and—"

"And what?" Calvin snapped. "How are you going to take care of me?"

"We'll do the same thing we're doing now. It'll be a fresh start. A new state, a new life, new clients." Not in Colorado and definitely nowhere near Pete! "You don't need him."

The brown eyes locked on to his were full of desperate hope. Then they hardened and looked away. "I'm getting old. How much longer can I keep doing this?"

Harold laughed. "What are you talking about? You're freaking hot!" The compliment failed to thaw the air between them, so he tried again. "Why are you acting like you're so old? You're still in your twenties!"

"Not for long. You know damn well that most of our clients want as young as they can get. If it was legal, they would want younger than that."

"Some of them," Harold said, "but—"

"I don't *want* to keep doing this," Calvin blurted out. "Do you? Honestly?"

"Yes!" He had tried working in the food industry and hated the smell of grease on his skin. He had also temped at an office and couldn't imagine spending forty hours a week trapped in a chilly gray cubicle. Maybe sleeping with some of his clients wasn't easy, but Harold loved sex, and getting paid for doing something that felt so good seemed like a ludicrously good deal. "I like my job."

"Really? I hate mine."

"Then why do you do it?"

Calvin clenched his jaw. "Because deep down I'm still a spoiled little shit who's used to having whatever he wants. I'm accustomed to a certain lifestyle. One that I can't live without."

"Fine," Harold said. "I'll take on two clients a day so you can focus on your modeling career. Once that takes off—"

"It's not going to!" Calvin hissed. "Marcello told me so. Not in so many words, but he turned me down. I'm not photogenic enough. It doesn't matter how hot I am if the camera doesn't like me."

"Then I'll take care of you until you figure out what you want to do. I don't care! I love you, and I'm not about to lose you to some creepy sugar daddy!"

"He's not creepy," Calvin murmured. "Pete was using the escort service to find the guy he wants to spend the rest of his life with."

"And that's you?"

Calvin nodded. "That's me."

Harold felt like he couldn't get enough oxygen into his lungs, like someone was sitting on his chest and the air was too thin and he was about to die, because he didn't just want Calvin to be a part of his life. He *needed* him. "I'll still go with you. To Colorado. We don't need to have sex. We barely do anyway. You can let Pete take care of you, but I'll still be there for the rest of it. For the emotional stuff."

"I'm sorry." Calvin placed a hand over his. "I need to think about my future. Yours too, because I can't give you what you need."

"We'll get jobs! We'll wait tables or whatever we have to! You don't need—"

"Harold." Calvin's voice was soft. Pleading.

"There are other ways to escape your mother. I can't believe you would let her—"

"Harold."

"I've been saving up. Just give me a year! A month! I'll take care of you, I swear! Think this through before—"

"Harold!" Calvin was squeezing his hand painfully tight now. "This is it! I didn't want to tell you until it was over, but this weekend is our grand finale. I've already decided."

More words rose to the surface, desperate to be spoken. Harold thought of countless other options, ways that they could solve this problem, which was trivial compared to what some people faced. It wasn't cancer. Calvin's mother wasn't some unstoppable dictator who had people executed without discretion. She was overbearing. That's all. And how much money did either of them really need? But he knew better. So many of his clients were heartbroken over some long lost love. Some had begged for the other person to stay, or fought to get them back, but it never lasted. When the other person had made up their mind, there was no changing the inevitable. He could only delay it. Harold had to try though. One final desperate plea.

"I love you," he croaked. "I'm not messing around. I love you more than anyone I've ever met!"

Calvin inhaled deeply, patted his hand, and then moved it away. "I love you too."

The words sounded genuine, but Harold no longer believed them. He felt weighted down. Crushed. Even speaking took herculean effort. "What now?"

"I still want this weekend with you." Calvin swallowed. "If that's okay. Or do you mean right now?"

"I guess."

"I want to go back to the house with you. I want to hold you for the rest of the night. Okay?"

Harold nodded, drawing on all his strength to avoid crying, when in reality, he felt like his insides were melting down.

The moon was setting over the treetops. Harold could see it from the bed he lay in. Calvin's arm was around him, his breath gentle and slow. He waited anyway, making sure that his boyfriend… Making sure that the person he loved was truly asleep. Then he carefully moved aside the arm and slid out of bed. He pulled on his shorts so he wouldn't be naked and was tempted to shut himself in the bathroom so he could cry in secrecy again. He looked over to make sure Calvin was asleep, relieved that he was. No more pretending to be strong. Harold padded downstairs, wiping at his eyes and feeling like he had an open wound in his chest. Almost like Puzzling Pete the retired surgeon had cut his heart out and forgot to put anything in its place. He noticed the time as he passed the kitchen. A little past midnight, making it the Fourth of July, but Harold didn't feel like celebrating. He touched his left hand, the ring on its finger again. Calvin had insisted before they got into bed.

"I'm not breaking my promise. I will always love you. Always!"

Harold shook his head and slid the ring free, placing it in his pocket. Then he stumbled outside into the night. The cicadas were singing in the humid night air, making him yearn for snow—a cold blanket that would put the world to sleep. Silence. Oh how he would give anything to stop his tormented thoughts and racing heart! Anything but his own life. Calvin wasn't worth that. Harold might have once thought he was, but not anymore. He found himself drawn toward the lake, to the little fishing boat, and entertained dramatic thoughts of climbing in, shoving away from shore, and letting himself drift to wherever it would take him. When he was close enough, he noticed what they had left behind. Roman candles now exhausted of their colorful flames, broken bottle rocket sticks, and a few small red tubes. Those hadn't been exhausted yet, the lighter next to them an invitation. He grabbed it and one of the M-80s. Acting on inspiration, he took out the ring and slid it over the cardboard cylinder. It barely fit, but he managed. He brought this to the end of the dock, planning to light the M-80 and throw it into the water, but he needed to see. He wanted to watch the ring burn, shatter, melt, or whatever else would happen.

Harold placed it on one of the wooden planks, stooping to light the fuse. Then he stepped back. Maybe not as much as he should have, but he liked the idea of getting hurt. Maybe Calvin would feel guilty and change his mind. Or maybe the explosion would be bigger than he expected, causing him to stumble backward, because that's exactly what happened. Harold wasn't injured. Instead his problems were momentarily forgotten as he laughed at his own fear, his heart thudding for a different reason. He squinted at the shadows, trying to find the remnants of the ring, when fireworks exploded overhead, gold and crimson stars expanding, lighting up the dark, and then fading away. He stared in wonder as this happened again, blue and green this time.

Independence Day. He was free now, whether he liked it or not.

The cicadas stopped their singing as the heavens lit up again and again. Harold settled down on the dock to watch. He was still there half an hour later, the sky dark and silent now, the hum of insects lulling him into a gentle melancholy. He would survive this and maybe come through it a little wiser. Love was a powerful force, and like the fireworks they had played with, dangerous despite seeming so innocent. All it took was a spark. Harold had singed his fingers, but they remained intact. He had learned his lesson, and it would be quite some time before he was foolish enough to take such a risk again.

Something Like Sun

by Jay Bell

Austin, Texas
2015

I'm not doing this because you told me to. Your scheme wouldn't have worked. I'm getting on this plane because of him. Maybe I should have sooner. Yeah. Definitely. But that doesn't make what you did okay. You hurt me. Then again, I guess this would have hurt no matter what.

Jason Grant looked up from his phone, still scowling, and quickly realized that an airport wasn't the best place for an angry expression. Already a TSA agent was eyeballing him like he might be trouble. It didn't help that the line for security had moved ahead while he remained motionless. Deciding not to send the text message yet, Jason quickly shouldered his pack and shuffled forward.

This was only the second trip of his life. His second vacation, he supposed. Most people talked about traveling with an enthusiasm he struggled to understand. Probably because he had spent most of his life in Houston. When he finally did move, it had been a mere three hours away to Austin, and that had been the extent of his travels. Until last year, when he flew to Acapulco with William for a honeymoon. Not their own! Ben and Tim had just gotten married—had just adopted Jason as their son. That they invited him and William along was a testament to how generous they were. The money was one thing, but the way they kept opening their lives to him, letting Jason share in their adventures… The weeks that followed were among the absolute best of his life. For that brief period, he'd had it all. Parents, a fiancé, and friends. In other words, a family. Now those things had been placed on opposite sides of a scale, the balance constantly shifting. If Jason came back from this trip, he would still have parents and a best friend. Except that might cost him a fiancé. If he decided not to return to Austin, he would lose a lot too.

Jason looked back down at the phone, the text message still unsent. The anger inside him was gone, replaced by sorrow. He deleted the words and considered sending a more civil message. Then he decided to leave it all behind him. For the rest of this trip, Austin and the people there didn't exist. He would return to a different time when he didn't have anything but one desire. He swiped the screen, switching to a different text conversation.

Let me know when you're sitting on your flight and about to depart. I'll be there to pick you up. Not sure I can wait. Maybe I'll steal a helicopter and rendezvous with you in the sky.

Jason grinned, imagining himself kicking open the airplane door to reveal a red and white Coast Guard helicopter, William standing on the skid in full uniform and reaching out a hand. Jason would grab it, of course. He wasn't a coward. Not usually, but he was in a difficult position. The only bad thing about every wish coming true is giving it all up again, because nothing lasts forever.

"Anything in your pockets? You'll need to take off your shoes and belt."

Jason focused on passing the security checkpoint and tried not to think about how much nicer this process had been last time with people he loved surrounding him. Just a little further to go. The guard gestured. Jason walked through the metal detector and waited for his backpack to ride along the conveyor belt to him. It passed the X-ray without the need for further inspection. Done.

Now that he was past the checkpoint, he couldn't leave again. Maybe it was as simple as turning around and walking through the exit. He wasn't sure, but psychologically, he felt like there was no turning back, and that made it easier to put on his shoes and march toward the gate. He was running late, according to the airline employee he had checked his luggage with. Twenty minutes remained until the flight was due to depart, but he didn't rush. Last time they had, only to end up waiting again. This time was different. When he reached the gate, passengers were already filing through it. Jason joined them.

When he boarded the plane and took his seat, he understood why people complained about flying so much. The trip to Acapulco had been in business class, where they were treated like royalty. Jason's current seat was in the economy section between two guys who appeared to be bikers. The large burley kind. Jason squeezed between them, wondering which armrest was his and noticing that both were occupied by meaty arms and hard elbows. He did his best to make himself smaller to minimize body contact. With some contorting, he managed to get his phone out and write a text to William despite the complete lack of privacy.

I'm in my seat. Definitely going to need that rescue. I can barely breathe! Don't these things have air conditioning?

It'll be better once you're up in the air, William replied. *Stay seated.*

In other words, don't bail on your flight. Jason wouldn't. No matter what. His phone rumbled again.

I love you. Can't wait!

Jason grinned and texted back. *I love you more. I'll prove it.*

An overhead announcement asked passengers to put their phones in airplane mode. He did so, officially disconnected from everyone he knew. For the next few hours, he would be on his own. He felt a jolt of panic as the airplane taxied to the runway. It really was too late now. The die had been cast. Now he had to live with the consequences. As they rose into the air, he wished he had a window seat so he could watch the only home he had known since childhood disappear beneath the clouds. Then again, since he was acting boldly today anyway…

"Excuse me," he said, leaning past the passenger to his left. "I just need to do something real quick."

He managed to press his hand to the small oval window, and despite his inability to see anything below, he made his peace with one silent word.

Goodbye.

Jason's heart started beating fast at about the same time the wheels touched down on the tarmac. The drum kept pounding, even though taxiing to the gate took forever. So did his fellow passengers as they took their sweet time retrieving their bags from the overhead compartments. He tried to calm himself once inside Portland International Airport, ducking into the nearest restroom to check his hair and brush his teeth. The palpitations only increased as he hurried toward the baggage claim where they were supposed to meet. Jason spotted an emergency defibrillator on the wall and wondered if two shocks to his chest would help.

He checked his phone, noticing it was still in airplane mode.

Once returned to normal, the device rumbled. Twice. And a third time. The text messages he had missed while in flight. All three were from Tim.

Hey! Let me know how the flight goes!

Or if there's a change of plan. We love you!

Hey, I know you're in a rough spot right now. Maybe you need your space, but Benjamin will worry until we hear from you. I will too. Thanks. I love you.

Jason stopped, other travelers flowing around him. He clenched his jaw a few times, then made himself take a deep breath.

I'm okay, he sent back. *Arrived safely.* After chewing his bottom lip, he sent another message. *I love you too.*

He felt bad for not making it plural. Of course he loved them both, but cutting off contact with Ben was the easiest way to show how angry he was. Or had been. He didn't know anymore. Jason wished, not for the first time, that he had more experience. Other people had parents their entire lives. They would know how to behave in these situations. All he could do for now is press on, physically as well as emotionally, so that's what he did, hurrying to reach the baggage claim. When his pocket vibrated again, he steeled himself and checked the response. Not from Tim this time but the guy who had promised to pick him up.

Have you landed yet?

Jason didn't write an answer because next to the luggage carousel was the handsomest man in existence. He didn't care if anyone agreed. To him it was a fact. William wore one of the Polo shirts he favored so much, this one navy blue, short sleeves griping his biceps, fabric straining against the impressive chest, but this was nothing compared to the face. God how Jason had missed that face! Currently it was concerned and watching the phone for a response.

I'm here! Jason wanted to call out. *I finally made it!*

William's head whipped around like these thoughts had been spoken aloud. After a brief moment of surprise, he smiled. As for Jason, he broke into a run, slamming against William in a hug that almost knocked them both down. He smelled so damn good! Not just because of the cologne or hint of chlorine on his skin. He not only smelled like his William but felt like him too. This was real, right? This wasn't just a separation-induced fantasy?

"I missed you so much," William murmured against his neck. He pulled back long enough for them to kiss before the squeezing resumed. "I love you."

"I love you too," Jason said, choking back tears. He wasn't about to cry, not when he was so happy and struggling to breathe. "Let go!" he wheezed.

"Nope," William said, arms constricting further. "Never again."

"I mean it," Jason said, but only when the luggage carousel buzzed and the belt started moving did William agree to hold him from behind. That way they could spot his suitcase when it came around. Jason grinned nonstop while waiting, a big pale arm draped around his neck like a feather boa. People stared, but so what? If this is all they did during the trip—standing in a public space and loving on each other—then he was happy.

Or so he thought. He started to feel a little worried when the luggage stopped coming and he still didn't see his.

"I was late for my flight," he explained.

"That must be it," William said, kissing his ear.

"Then again," Jason said, "if my suitcase was one of the last ones put on the plane, wouldn't it be the first to get unloaded?"

"Not necessarily. First class passengers always get theirs before anyone else. I'm not sure how the airlines manage that. Do you still see people from your flight?"

Jason glanced around. "No."

"Oh. Do you have your claim tag?"

"My what?"

William let go of him. "They usually put it with your boarding pass."

Jason squatted to dig through his backpack. He found what William was talking about: part of the sticker strip that an airline employee had secured to the handle of his luggage. He stood again and handed over the small square.

William peered at it before looking around. "Let's go talk to that man over there."

He led the way, Jason following behind while feeling lost. They had a funny relationship in that regard. Jason was the older one, but not by much, and that didn't necessarily translate to knowhow. Ever since William had left for the Coast Guard, he knew a lot more about traveling and had seen more of the world.

Jason's expertise was more practical. Paying bills, dealing with landlords, and taking care of other similar issues. Because of his career choice, William hadn't needed to worry about such things. Uncle Sam took care of it so he could focus on more important matters, like saving lives. Or helping locate lost luggage.

"Time for a search and rescue?" Jason joked.

William laughed in appreciation. "It'll be fine. You'll just need to fill out a form."

That's exactly what they did, the airline promising to deliver the missing suitcase directly to William's home.

"If it never shows up," Jason said as they walked to the parking lot, "then it's too bad because I bought you the most amazing present. That thing that you've always wanted. If it *does* show up, then I left Austin in too much of a rush to get you anything."

William grinned and took his hand. "I've already got what I've always wanted. What a surprise too! You told me you were coming, and the next day you're here. Not that I'm complaining, but did something happen?"

"Kind of."

"Kind of?"

"I'm on vacation," Jason said. "I needed to get away. That means, while I'm here, nothing else exists." Nothing and no one, because it wasn't a fondness for Texas that had kept him there for so long. He loved his home state, but not nearly as much as he loved certain people.

"But everyone is okay," William pressed. "Nothing bad happened. You would tell me if—"

"Ben and Tim are fine," Jason said. "You're still president of their imaginary fan club. They wouldn't have it any other way."

"Whew!" William said theatrically. "I was worried someone had taken my place!"

"Never," Jason said, "but as soon as we walk through these doors, none of that exists anymore."

"Okay," William said, making them stop at the exit's threshold. "Ready? We're going to jump. Here goes!"

They leapt together, feet leaving the airport floor and landing on the concrete of a sidewalk. Then they breathed in their first breath of Oregon air. At least Jason did.

"It's usually not as gray here," William said, excusing the

weather. Then he cleared his throat. "That's a lie, but I'm hoping you don't figure it out too soon."

"I've had enough sunshine to last me a lifetime," Jason replied, surprised to not be crumpling under extreme heat and humidity. It was the middle of August, after all.

They crossed lanes of traffic together, William leading them to a parking garage and his car. The Range Rover was emerald green and just over twenty years old. Jason had seen photos and knew it had only cost William four thousand dollars due to various issues and a ton of miles. William had countered his concerns by assuring him that a maintenance technician coworker, who was a gearhead for more than just helicopters, had checked it out and insisted it could be fixed. They must have put a lot of work into it, because the Range Rover looked like a vehicle half its age and ran even better.

"Did you want to see Portland?" William asked as they drove from the airport. "It's an amazing city. Lily is working right now, but we could still stop by and say hi to her and Daisy."

"That sounds fun." Jason said, but apparently without much conviction.

"What do you really want?" William shot him a hungry expression that revealed his desire.

It matched his own. "You," Jason said. "Having witnesses present might not be a good idea."

"We'll see them some other day," William said, quickly hitting the turn signal and switching lanes. "We've got a two-hour drive ahead of us."

"What are you saying?" Jason asked, reaching over the gear stick to place a hand on his thigh.

"Nothing." William's smile was surrounded by red cheeks. "Nothing at all. It's just been a year since we've done it. No biggie."

"Very biggie," Jason said, moving his hand upward to cup an increasingly hard bulge.

William groaned longingly, then shook his head. "You better let me drive."

Jason moved his hand away. Too much stuff between the seats separated them for road-warrior love anyway. Besides, when the time came, he wanted to savor every moment. For as long as he could last.

"What do you think so far?" William asked. "That's the Columbia River we're crossing. We'll follow it all the way up the Washington side to blah blah blah blah—"

Jason grinned and nodded along, unable to tear his eyes away. He knew he should be paying more attention to what William said. It just felt so good to be together again. They had texted, called, and video-conferenced as often as they could manage, but nothing compared to being in person. Here he was able to see that William's hair had been freshly buzzed, even noticing a small area behind his ear that the barber had missed. He would take care of that later. In person he could reach over and touch William's cheek, or take his hand and press it to his lips, or brush lint off the shoulder of his shirt. He did all of this. The physical wasn't more important than the emotional, but after going without the former for so long, he couldn't help himself.

"You really need to stop that," William said, nodding to the speedometer. They were going a little fast, and all Jason was doing was giving him bedroom eyes. "Talk to me."

Jason did so, still avoiding the subject of Austin, which didn't leave him much to work with. He described his flight, making it sound more funny than it had been. He commented on how lush and green it was outside his window, and asked if they could stop for lunch at what was clearly a tourist trap restaurant that also sold souvenirs.

"What about you?" he said when they sat down to eat.

That little question led to plenty they could discuss. Jason was really into the Coast Guard these days, faithfully watching any television series or documentary about that branch of service. He had read quite a few books too. Before, when William talked about his work and used weird abbreviations, Jason had found it confusing and off-putting. Now he was nearly as enthusiastic as his boyfriend.

"Do I get to see where you work? Or do I need to enlist to get inside? Because I will. I'll just go AWOL after I've seen it all."

"Don't worry, I'll give you a full tour of the base," William promised. "How many days do we have exactly?"

"Oh." Jason hid a frown. Didn't William realize what a loaded question that was? "I'm not sure. I'll look at my tickets later. So I really get to see the air station?"

"Yup! Some of *The Guardian* was filmed there. Did I tell you that?"

"No! Man… I get to visit a Coast Guard base *and* a movie set!"

William chuckled. "Not exactly. You know what else was filmed in Astoria, right?"

"No idea."

"*The Goonies*."

"What?" Jason slammed his fists on the table in his excitement, nearly sending a fork flying across the room. "I love that movie! I had no idea. We rewatched it a few years back and I made Ben—" He shook his head. "I learned how to play the theme by Cyndi Lauper. Remember that song?"

"No," William said, the self-censorship not escaping his notice, but he let it slide. "I have the movie at home. I thought we could watch it while you're here."

"Now that's a plan!" Jason said. "We don't have to leave your apartment at all. I'm happy to just hole up with you."

"Wait until you've seen the place, then decide." William signaled the waitress. "Let's get out of here."

Not before they hit the souvenir shop. Jason bought a refrigerator magnet of Bigfoot in his traditional striding pose. What that had to do with Oregon he wasn't sure, but Jason had a soft spot for monsters. He watched the trees more carefully as they drove the rest of the way to Astoria, just in case the Goonies needed to be called in to solve another case.

"Are we in Astoria yet?" Jason asked.

"Technically, yes. I think we're within the city limits. Why?"

Jason considered the environment outside. The skies were overcast, and while the river to their right and all the dense foliage was appealing, the buildings themselves seemed a little rundown. "It's not how I imagined it," he said.

"You didn't look at photos before you came?"

Jason shook his head. "Not really. I wanted to be surprised. I was going to buy a travel guide, but uh… didn't."

"Because Ben printed one out for you," William said. "He made it himself by doing research online, and even though it was black and white, you decided you liked it better than anything you could buy. You were really excited when you told me."

Jason clamped his mouth shut.

"Did you never read it?"

"I read some of it," Jason said, eager to change the subject. "Are we almost there?"

"Getting close. Mind if we make a quick detour?"

"Sure," Jason said. "I'm in your capable hands."

"I'd rather be in yours," William replied. The Range Rover turned left, slipping between buildings as they gradually climbed a hill. They passed through a quiet neighborhood, many of the houses possessing a ramshackle style that he found appealing. A bend in the road led them to the top of a hill, the view better from up there. Jason's attention was drawn away to a parking area and a large column. That's all it was, like the White House or some stately manor had disappeared, leaving a single front column behind, because there was no house or any other sort of ruins here. Just a pillar reaching for the sky.

"Is that a lighthouse?" Jason asked.

"It's the Astoria Column," William said, parking the car near it. "Come see." Once they were out and on their feet, he pointed. "Notice the paintings? That mural winds all the way to the top. It depicts the history of this land, starting at the bottom when Native Americans established a village here and ending with the much-celebrated arrival of Jason Grant."

He laughed. "If we go to the top, we really will be the most recent event."

"Makes you wonder if the artist planned it that way." William offered his hand. "Come on. You're going to love the view. I hope."

Ten minutes later, they were standing at the very top, Jason panting for breath because they had climbed a ton of stairs.

"Breathtaking," William said, fighting down a smile. "Isn't it?"

Jason would have slugged him if not bent over and panting. His boyfriend wasn't even winded, while he couldn't manage a single comeback. Then he forced himself to stand upright, the breath catching in his throat for another reason. Green rolling hills faded away into the haze of the horizon. Elsewhere, water wound its way through an emerald paradise. They were surrounded on three sides by two rivers, and at the very tip of this peninsula, a small town clung to the hillside.

"Astoria?" Jason asked.

"Home," William confirmed with a nod. "What do you think?"

"It's beautiful." He walked along the rail to see the complete view, spotting mountains in the distance. At least he thought that's what they were. The clouds clung to them, while on the opposite side, he could see a wall of blue pushing away the gray, the sunlight beaming down and making the water sparkle. "Is that the ocean?"

"No. We can't see that far because of the hill Fort Stevens is on."

"This is amazing," Jason said, still stunned by the natural beauty. "We're going to visit the Pacific while I'm here, right? I miss it. Acapulco wasn't enough." Silence was the only response, so he turned to find William staring at him intently. Time for a kiss? No. This was something else. "What's up?"

"We need to talk," William said. Then he grimaced and shook his head. "I know we both hate that phrase but… I have this coworker, Johnny—"

"Your AMT?"

"Exactly," William said, smiling at him in reward. "He might be a mechanic, but he's also into spirituality. He's always talking about energy, and maybe I've listened to too many of his lectures, because I'm starting to agree with him. I don't want these bad vibes coming home with us."

Jason snorted. "Bad vibes?"

"Yeah." William took his hands in his own. "What's the real reason we aren't talking about Ben and Tim?"

Jason pulled away. "I don't want to. Simple as that."

"Because you're worried you'll miss them too much? If so, you shouldn't bottle it up or else—"

"Because I don't want to be mad at you!" Jason growled. "And because I'm already pissed at them. Actually, no. I'm not mad at Tim."

"Just Ben," William said.

But he didn't seem surprised or confused, which was funny because Jason didn't normally have trouble with Ben. He butted heads with Tim on occasion, but not Ben. Never him. Not until now.

"I know," Jason said, voice shaking with the effort to keep himself in check. "Ben told me that he talked to you, and if that wasn't bad enough, you actually—"

William grabbed his hands again, but this time he did so firmly, refusing to be shaken off. "Stop. Right now. Listen to me."

"Fine," Jason said, clenching his jaw. He didn't want this! The anger wasn't supposed to follow him here from Austin. He just wanted to go to William's place, get into bed, and never leave again. The rest he could do without. Probably.

William jerked his hands to get his attention, forcing him to make eye contact. When had he gotten so assertive? "Do I love you?"

Jason scoffed at the question. "I should be asking you that!"

"I'm asking you," William said. "Do you believe that I love you?"

"Yes." Jason answered. Of all the things he had doubted over the past year, William's love wasn't one of them.

"Good," William said, his grip gentler now. "Does Ben love you?"

"I don't see what—"

"Answer the question! Does Ben love you?"

"Yeah," Jason said, his throat aching with the truth.

"And do you think that either one of us wanted to hurt you? I'm not asking if we've been stupid, or if it was a good idea, because you know what the road to Hell is paved with. But I think you also know in your heart that we were only trying to help."

Jason swallowed painfully and nodded.

"Does anything else matter?" William asked. "We can drag out all the details and point fingers if you really want. For the record, I blame myself."

"No!" Jason said. "I don't want you to!"

"The alternative," William said, "is to look instead at where those stupid decisions got us." He released one of Jason's hands and gestured to the horizon. "Look where you are!"

"Astoria," Jason said, practically sobbing around the word. The name represented so much to him. One of his greatest dreams, and simultaneously, one of his most troubling fears.

"I'm really *really* happy you're here," William said, "so I'm having a hard time feeling any regret. If I could go back, I'd do a few things differently, but—"

Jason plowed into him, hugging him so tight that William's laugh came out raspy. "I love you," he said, rubbing his face against William's shoulder to wipe away the tears.

"I love you too," William replied, squeezing in return and

then taking a step back to look him in the eye. "Are we good?"

"Yeah," Jason said, nodding. "We're good."

"Awesome. Then tell me how my future in-laws are doing."

"Fine," Jason said with a chuckle, but only in the hope of staving off more tears. "Tim is really into painting lately. A few of his were bought by a gallery in Japan—

"Japan!"

"I know! It's crazy, but he's extra-motivated right now. Ben is fed up with his theater work. I try to go as much as I can lately, because it's really funny. He keeps losing his patience, like when someone forgets a line, he'll say it for them instead of hinting. 'I bet you're wondering how I escaped the fire and what I'm doing here now!' That sort of thing. Or this one time, a guy was texting during the middle of the show and it was driving Ben crazy. I could tell because he kept looking over and clenching his jaw. Then Ben walks to the very edge of the stage, crosses his arms over his chest, and just glares at him. The guy didn't even notice! Too busy texting. But when everyone else in the audience started looking at him too…" Jason laughed. "Dude was humiliated."

"Rightly so!" William said, trying hard to look furious. "How could anyone ignore Ben when he's on stage? Or even when he's not! He's too awesome, so screw that guy."

"Screw him to heck?" Jason said. "You're still no good at anger."

"I can do angry!" William said, but his expression was amorous instead. He pulled Jason close, wrapping arms around him and hugging him from behind. In front of them, the sun broke through the clouds, illuminating a kingdom worthy of a fairytale. "So you really like it?"

"I love it!" Jason admitted. "This must be what you always see when you go flying."

"I wish," William said. "I'm usually staring at wave after wave until I go cross-eyed. But sometimes when we've rescued a survivor and are on the way back, then I have time to really bask in it. The world is a beautiful place."

"Yeah," Jason said, pulling the arms tighter around him. "It really is."

The parking lot they stood in was cracked, weeds bursting through the pavement and doing little to improve the surroundings, although Jason supposed it would be much bleaker without them there. The two-story building they walked toward had once been a motel. And pink. Now it was closer to gray and had been repurposed as apartments. Not very big ones, judging from the various possessions sitting outside each door, or the laundry hanging from the upper walkway.

"I'm working on it," William said, not bothering to ask his opinion. "When I first moved here… I'm not trying to make you feel guilty. I thought we could apartment-hunt together, so I waited. When I realized you weren't coming, by then I had gotten used to it. Kind of."

Barks and snarls came from behind the door they were passing, causing Jason to flinch. Then he stopped, shock replaced by concern. "How many dogs are in there? And how many bedrooms do these apartments have?"

"The bottom floor has double units. You know the doors between rooms? If you open them and make one bedroom into a living room—"

"Have you seen these dogs?"

Realization dawned on William's features. "Yes. Don't worry. The owner is weird, but he takes care of them. I don't think he likes people as much as he does animals. He comes home during lunch to walk them."

"Okay," Jason said, adjusting his backpack. "He's off the hook. For now. I'll be keeping an eye on him!"

"How are things at the shelter?" William asked.

"Fine," Jason said. "We're going to start visiting schools. Can you imagine? Me giving lectures to kids about taking care of pets, and at the high schools, we're hoping to recruit volunteers. Is this the one?"

"Yup," William said, fishing out his keys. "You might want to lower your expectations."

Jason did so and was still shocked. The room was tidy. That came as no surprise. If not for William's efficiency, the apartment—if it could even be called that—would have been a disaster. The space inside still resembled a motel, except the bed had been replaced by a two-seater couch and a medium television on a stand. Beyond this was just enough room for a square table, two wooden chairs, and a shelf with some personal items. Against the farthest wall was a kitchenette.

Jason dropped his pack next to the couch and walked the length of the room. He had seen some of this in the background while video-conferencing, but things always looked small on his phone. He didn't realize how accurate his impression had been. He inspected the kitchenette, which included a mini-fridge, a microwave oven, and a shallow sink. Next to this was a door leading to a bathroom that hadn't been updated since its motel days.

William followed during this tour, focused more on Jason's reaction than their surroundings. "This probably isn't the best time to ask if you want to move in."

Jason spun around. "Where do you sleep? You've called me while in bed before. I thought it was next to the couch."

"Magic trick," William said with a wink. When this failed to get a response, he added, "I sleep on the sofa."

Jason looked from the tower of muscle standing near him to the tiny little couch. "Is there even room enough for you to sit on that thing?"

"It's a sofa bed," William explained. "Wanna see?"

"No. I'll wait until later when— Oh wait, I get it!"

William grinned. "Figured it out, did ya?"

"I'm a little slow," Jason joked. "Or really quick, as you're about to find out."

Their goofy grins faded. That they could touch each other and had privacy almost seemed too good to be true. They moved forward tentatively, fingers caressing each other's chests before flattening into palms. Jason moved his hand over muscle, eager to see them again, so he stripped off William's shirt before impatiently doing away with his own. He tried to stay in shape. Jason ate healthier now and attempted to get a little exercise in every day. Nothing he did could compare with someone who needed to stay in peak physical condition for his profession. He always felt lucky that he was allowed to touch William's body, but today he was exceptionally hungry. Starving. He kissed William's neck, rubbed his thumbs over the pink nipples, and slid his tongue over the toned stomach. He was scrabbling to get the jeans open when William grabbed him beneath the pits and hoisted, forcing Jason to stand again.

Those muscles gave William more control, even though Jason was the dominant one in this situation. Still, it was possible to be aggressive from any position. He watched as William continued in the way Jason had wanted to. Down on his knees, he freed Jason's package from its denim and cotton prison. Then he looked up, a fist around Jason's hard cock, eyes full of emotion as if needing to remind him that this was more than just lust. Jason nodded, smiling down at him. Having established how they both felt, they could let their bodies loose to play.

Jason slid his hands around to the back of William's head and started thrusting. Occasionally he would pull out, playfully slapping his dick against William's cheek, or standing on his toes so his balls could be licked. William had gotten his own jeans open and was playing with himself, but that wouldn't do. Jason urged him to get on the couch. Once William was seated there, he knelt and spread the legs wide, delaying only to look at how beautiful a sight it was. All of him. Not just the cock convulsing with need or the balls resting on the seat cushion, but the man himself, who was the most wonderful in the world.

"Jason," William whispered. "Please."

An easy request to fulfill. Jason leaned over and took William into his mouth, enjoying the taste and sensation, but his appetite demanded more. He licked everything he could see, even doing silly stuff like smooching William's knee or grabbing his hand to kiss his palm and suck on his thumb. Nothing was out of bounds or capable of satiating him, so he lifted the legs and pulled forward, creating more opportunity. He looked once at William for permission. As soon as he saw the nod, he delved in, spitting on William's hole and then shoving his tongue against it. This set off a series of moans, Jason needing to loop his arms around the legs so he didn't buck off the couch. He managed to get a grip on William's cock and stroke it while he continued to rim, ignoring the protests he heard and fighting against the hand that pulled at his wrist.

"I'm too close!" William hissed.

Jason finally released him, sitting upright and hobbling forward on his knees so he could press the head of his cock against William's slick hole. He wanted to slide inside, but they hadn't worked their way up to that, so he settled for rubbing against it while he pumped himself. William gyrated, trying his best to accommodate him despite the lack of lube.

"Should I…?"

Jason shook his head. Neither one of them would last long enough to make the effort worth it. Although maybe later tonight.

Just the thought brought him close. He started moaning too, encouraging William not to hold back.

"Don't come on the couch cushions!" William gasped.

Always the tidy one! Jason laughed, pulling on William's hips so he slid forward again. All but his head was lying flat, but he barely seemed to notice, huffing as Jason continued stroking them both, arms straining with effort. If they did this daily, he'd have muscles the size of William's!

"I'm about to—" William groaned.

"Race ya!" Jason said, already at the finish line. He moaned and thrust forward, pressing against the pert hole as he exploded.

William lasted half a minute longer, chest heaving and hips writhing as he shot all over his torso. After panting, he slid forward even more like he couldn't help it, his weight forcing Jason on his rump and then onto his back.

"I missed you," William said, flopping forward and pinning him down. Literally.

"My legs are stuck beneath me," Jason gasped.

"Does it hurt?"

"No." It was only his lower legs of course, but still. "They'll go numb if you don't move."

William smiled. "Good. That way you can't get away from me again. I was going to break them. Or maybe just one."

"I think I'd prefer shackles."

"I'll see what I can do." William rolled onto his side, freeing him.

Jason rolled over too, pressing his back against the firm chest. "I can't believe you brought me to this sleazy motel just so we could hook up."

"The hourly rates are unbeatable," William said, scooting his hips closer. "Speaking of which, I'm scared to ask this, but you were vague before. How long do I have you here?"

"I don't know," Jason said. "My return flight is in two weeks."

"So you *do* know."

"Not really." When making the reservation, he had been an emotional mess, clicking a random date and flight for his return just so he could proceed. At the time he told himself that it didn't matter—that he would never be returning. Right now, stretched out on the carpeted floor of a former motel room, he really could imagine staying forever. But it wouldn't be long until he started missing familiar faces and longing for other voices. He might have finally made the journey to Astoria, but he remained trapped between two worlds.

Paradise was a little town on the most northwestern corner of Oregon. Jason was convinced. Or maybe his flight from Austin had crashed and he had arrived in Heaven instead. No fluffy white clouds or bearded saints waited before a gate, just a little village built on the slopes of the Columbia River. After some snuggling, William was adamant they shower and go back out. Jason could have easily spent the rest of the day indoors, but now he was glad they hadn't. They left the Range Rover behind, walking down to the Port of Astoria and out along a pier. William pointed to different models of boats and told stories of daring rescues or humorous false alarms.

"You really need sunblock," Jason said, eyeing an arm that was already turning pink.

"I was hoping to get some color."

"That's fine if you're going for red," Jason said, pulling out the small bottle he had insisted on bringing. William had countered that the clouds never disappeared for long in Oregon. "Yeah, but I brought the sun with me from Texas. Here. Take off your shirt."

"Why?" William asked, already looking suspicious.

"Because it's easier," Jason said, not bothering to play innocent. They knew each other too well.

William did as he was told, wincing at the temperature of the sunblock and then loosening up as Jason continued to rub it in. "That's nice," he said. "Want to take off your shirt too?"

"Yes," Jason said. "I would love to!"

"It looks fine," William said, turning around to face him.

His luggage lost, Jason didn't have fresh clothes to change into. Normally he wouldn't have bothered but… "I still don't see how we got come on my shirt."

"It's super weird," William said in angelic tones. "I *definitely* didn't grab it out of habit when needing to clean up."

"You bastard," Jason deadpanned.

William smiled, pulling his own shirt back on. "I think it's cute when you wear my clothes."

"I just wish they fit better," Jason said. He had on a white

Polo, but unlike how the shirts gripped William, this one managed to hang off him, making him feel like a scarecrow. "Are you sure this is your smallest one?"

"It's too tight for me," William said with a shrug.

"Thanks. I feel so much better now." He did, despite the sarcasm. The sky was blue, sweet air blowing in from the Pacific. Jason's problems felt a million miles away. Or at the very least, two thousand miles away. "Show me this place you call home."

Hand in hand, they strolled back toward town, but not too far.

"The Riverwalk is the only way to see Astoria," William explained.

"Is that a trolley?" Jason asked, looking to where a small crowd climbed aboard a vehicle. To him it resembled a submarine sandwich except the bread was maroon and wooden, and in place of meat and cheese was a series of white-framed windows. "Can we ride it?"

"We could," William said, "but we won't. There's too much I want to show you along the way. Besides, gotta stay in shape!"

"If you're looking for the ultimate workout," Jason said, "you should carry me for at least… How far are we going?"

"Eight kilometers, and if you're serious—"

"I am!"

"—then I can try, but you're always talking about wanting to stay in shape. You're already sexy as hell. This will help keep you that way, right?"

"Stop guilting me into being a better person!"

"You're already perfect," William said.

"I'm not, but I love you for saying so."

He was soon glad that he had chosen (ha!) to walk, because there was so much he needed to stop and stare at, such as the long swooping bridge, which disappeared over the river and ended somewhere in another state. They strolled through little parks and bought ice cream from a vendor pushing a cart, but none of that could top what came next. Seals! Dozens of fat bodies were piled on top of a half-sunken dock, forming a sleeping carpet of slick-skinned adorableness. Only half of them slumbered. The rest were barking nonstop, the sound so ridiculous that Jason couldn't stop laughing. It didn't help that some were climbing over the others, trying to find an empty spot to claim.

"Wait until we're in bed tonight," William said. "That's how it'll be for us too. Then you won't be laughing."

"I'll be barking though," Jason said. "Arrr arrr, arrr arrr!"

"Pretty good imitation," William said. "Are you sure you're not related?"

"Maybe there was a mix-up and I was supposed to go to an animal shelter instead of foster care."

"Could be," William mused. "Hey, I thought we'd have fish for dinner."

"That sounds good!" Jason enthused. Then he rolled his eyes. "Ha ha. You're messing with me. Arrr arrr! This seal is getting hungry. Find me a bucket of fish or I'll never stop barking!"

Dinner wasn't too far away, as it turned out. They stopped at a pub on one of the piers, and by the time they left, the day was drawing to a close. The clouds had blown away, allowing them to witness a sky set aflame by the setting sun.

"I guess we should start heading back," Jason said. "It'll be dark before we get there."

"Just a little farther," William said. "There's something I want to show you."

They continued until the official Riverwalk ended, but the railway tracks kept going. William strode onto these as if they were a sidewalk.

"I don't want to get run over by a trolley," Jason said, stopping in protest. "That would be humiliating."

"It doesn't go this far," William said. "Trust me."

"Trusting," Jason said under his breath before hurrying to catch up. He didn't slow down, even once reaching William, wanting to get off the tracks again. "Come on," he urged. "Gotta keep in shape. Pick up the pace!"

William laughed and accepted the challenge. Jason nearly needed to jog to keep up, which made the experience even spookier because to their left was the river, to the right a gully. If an unexpected train came, they would be in for a plunge no matter which way they jumped. The worst stretch was a small length of track with no land beneath it. The bridge was old, and if trains really didn't come out this way, then it was probably unmaintained. Jason was still trying to calm himself after successfully crossing the bridge when the tracks started to curve back toward land.

William stopped. "Point Tongue," he explained.

"Wait until we get home," Jason said. "I'm not rimming you way out here!"

William turned to him and shook his head. "Why am I in love with you again?"

"No idea," Jason admitted. "I've never understood it myself."

William smiled and wrapped an arm around his waist. Then he pointed. With his finger, thankfully. Over a small stretch of water filled with the broken supports of a former structure, a wooded hill rose up, jutting out into the river. In the dwindling light, Jason found the shadowy landmass sinister. He was about to make a joke when he noticed how in awe his boyfriend was.

"That's called Point Tongue," William said. "The part we're facing now was a campsite for Lewis and Clark. We're really close to the end of their expedition. They stopped here for two weeks. Just like you. Isn't that funny? The first colonists to travel to the West Coast. I bet they were scared too, but they still did it."

"Please don't compare me to them," Jason said. "All I had to do was get on a plane."

"No, you had to say goodbye to feeling safe and secure, just like they did, in the hope of discovering something new. They changed history. You've changed our future. We don't know how yet, but I'm proud of you for making it this far."

"Stop," Jason said. "I feel bad."

"What? Why?"

"Because I owe you an apology. All this time I've been thinking of myself, how I'm scared that Ben and Tim will stop loving me, or that something will happen to them while I'm gone, or— Ugh. Trust me, I have way too many nightmares to go over them all now. So I did what was best for me, when I should have been thinking of you. I know you have fears too. You shouldn't have to face them alone."

"That's sweet," William said, "but I'm not alone. I've got my fellow coasties to rely on."

"For everything?" Jason said. "Can you be vulnerable with them? Can you trust them with your darkest thoughts or your most embarrassing secrets? I should have been here, taking care of you. Instead I was selfish."

"And I wasn't? Are you forgetting that I left Austin for four years, just so I could join the Coast Guard? That was selfish too, but sometimes that's what you've got to do for yourself. Sometimes being selfish is right."

"That doesn't work so well in a relationship," Jason said.

"Which is why I felt like we couldn't be together then. Now I feel like we can't be apart. Not forever, anyway. I know who I want to spend my life with."

"Me too," Jason said. "I'm still sorry that I broke my promise. I shouldn't have agreed to move here with you until I was ready. That wasn't fair."

"Apology accepted," William said. "Or is this more than that? Have you made up your mind?"

Memories jostled for his attention. The pride in Ben's eyes when Jason had gotten his first job in Austin, how much he had cared even back then when they barely knew each other. Or the way Ben's face had shifted from confusion to hurt when Jason finally got up the nerve to explain that he needed his own place. Ben hadn't made him feel guilty, but instead had quickly hid away his emotions for Jason's benefit. Or maybe his own. It was hard to say.

"Don't answer," William said. "I can tell it's not the right time. I wanted you to see this though. I don't think Lewis and Clark enjoyed their stay here. They showed up just in time for ceaseless rain and a long winter. They pushed on regardless, and that changed not only their lives, but those of everyone on the continent. For better or worse." He looked toward the mass of land again, solemn expression giving way to a subtle smile. "It used to be called Point William. Strange but true."

"You're so famous!" Jason said, taking his hand.

"I try. It's actually named after Clark. William was his first name."

"Please tell me that the other guy was Jason Lewis. Where's my point? I want one too!"

William laughed. "Meriwether was his first name."

"So is mine. Jason is my middle name. I don't go by Meriwether for obvious reasons. Other kids teased me too much."

"You're full of it," William said.

"Yeah, but I meant what I said earlier. From now on, I'm going to think about both of us. No more being selfish."

"I'll try to do the same," William said. "I'm sorry I let an entire year go by without coming to see you."

"All water under the bridge," Jason said. "Speaking of which, can we go? It still feels wrong that we're standing in the middle of railroad tracks."

"Okay. But first..."

William moved near and kissed him, Jason hugging him even closer. If a trolley was about to knock them into the river, at least he would be clinging to a rescue swimmer.

"All right," William said, breaking their embrace and offering his arm. "Come along, Meriwether. We still have a long journey ahead."

After waking up the next morning, the first thing Jason did was double-check that he hadn't been dreaming. He wanted to make sure he and William really were together again, because too often he had dreams like the day before, where he had made the trip and everything between them was perfect. He didn't need to glance around to verify his surroundings. The metal bar pressed against his back told him exactly where he was: in a small sofa bed barely big enough for two, although at the moment, it felt a lot more spacious than he remembered.

Jason raised his head, the light around the window blinds still pale and weak. How early was it? He checked his phone. Five in the morning. Not bad considering that it was seven back in Texas. He had woken up around his normal time. A little earlier, but that probably had to do with the thumping and swearing he heard in the bathroom. He sat up just as William stumbled out. In his Coast Guard uniform.

"This is going to be so hot!" Jason said. "Pretend the bed is the ocean and that I can't swim." He raised the sheets, pulling them forward so they caught the air and looked more like a wave. Then he made the sheets crash over him, adding his own sound effects.

William didn't laugh. He didn't even smile. "I got called in," he said. "I'm sorry."

Jason sat upright. "What's going on?"

"Search and rescue. We weren't the only ones out for a hike yesterday, but at least we made it home."

And an awesome evening it had been with lots of talking, cold bottles of cider, and a private screening of *The Goonies* on William's television. Everyone's day should end so nicely.

Instead, some poor soul was still out there, exhausted and afraid. "Go save people!" Jason urged. "That's why you're here."

William shook his head. "That's not why I'm here." He sat on the edge of the mattress. "I used to believe the Coast Guard could fix me. Turns out I wasn't broken, but I still needed them to redeem me, so I did my time in Cape Cod. Some mistakes can't be undone, but I felt like I balanced things out as best I could. Because of that, I didn't have as many reasons to come up here and return to active duty. Only one was important enough."

Jason smiled. "This is going to be sweet, isn't it?"

"Incredibly sweet," William said. "The reason I'm up here—what I think about every time that helicopter lifts off—is you. I do this because I want to make you proud."

Jason would have swooned, had he been standing. "If I didn't have morning breath—"

William silenced him with a kiss, unconcerned with such things. The gesture felt more desperate than passionate.

"Are you okay?" Jason asked. "Is this going to be more dangerous than usual?"

"No," William said. "It's just the timing that sucks. I'm supposed to have the week off, but there are multiple situations and—" He sighed. "I never wanted you to be on your own. It'll happen anyway if you move up here. That can't be helped, but not during your first trip. It hasn't even been twenty-four hours!"

"And we've already done so much," Jason said, not having to fake a yawn. "I could use the downtime. Really."

William seemed reassured by this. He rose to find his shoes, Jason getting up to use the restroom. He brushed his teeth as fast as he could too, because he intended for there to be a goodbye kiss.

"You're going to be okay?" William asked on his way to the door. "I don't know how long I'll be. Hopefully not… I won't make any promises because I can't keep them. If you get bored—"

"I'll be fine," Jason said. "You should go!"

William didn't budge. He stood there shaking his head, like leaving would break his heart. "I know you haven't decided anything yet," he said, "and I don't want to pressure you, but it's possible to have more than one home. Or for a person to be your home. I can be that for you. If you want. You're already that to me. Just having you here—" William gestured at the cramped surroundings. "I've never liked this place, but since you got here, I swear it's the best motel apartment in the world."

Jason laughed, his boyfriend relaxing a little and doing the same.

"I understand if you're not ready to move here," William continued. "That's okay. Just know that I won't give up. I'll never lose patience with you. Not when it comes to this. I'll wait until we can be together again. If that means me coming back to Texas eventually, then so be it. I won't love you any less. Ever. All right?"

Jason nodded, too overcome with emotion to say much back besides, "Okay. Thank you."

"Thank you," William said. "I don't think I'd be here if it wasn't for you. I don't think I ever would have made it to the Coast Guard. Not if we hadn't met."

"Then go make me even prouder," Jason said, swooping in for a kiss. Sure he tripped over the corner of the sofa bed on the way, William having to catch his shoulders, but when their lips met, no doubt remained that they felt the same way about each other.

"Be safe," Jason said.

"Always. I promise."

William could have been referring to his work, or their relationship. Either way, he was a hero. Sometimes to strangers who needed him, and at others, to him alone. The world was lucky to have him, and so was Jason. He thought of this while standing in the kitchenette and drinking down a soda. Afterwards he walked to the middle of the apartment, needing very few paces. He stood there listening to the silence, which there wasn't much of. A baby cried in another apartment, and one of the dogs on the first floor barked. As the minutes ticked by and more people woke, voices joined the ambient noise, too muted to hear clearly.

Jason spun in a circle, recognizing all that needed to be straightened up. He tried to imagine William getting home after a three-day shift and no one being here to greet him. Just a mess. A bed that needed to be stuffed back into the couch, bottles that needed to be thrown away, a towel that should be hung up to dry… Jason wasn't interested in becoming anyone's maid, but his job wasn't as taxing. He knew what he'd be doing on any given day and when he would be returning home. That wasn't always the case with William.

Maybe he's up there feeling just as lost without you.

A fair point, one that Jason had been too angry to consider when first hearing it. Ben was right. Maybe not about everything, but the important stuff, yes. Jason thought of his adoptive father as he began straightening up the apartment. Making music together—him on guitar while Ben sang. Pigging out when a new cupcake place had a grand opening, buying one of each kind and swearing each other to secrecy. Or just sitting with him in the backyard, listening to his stories and sharing his own. He loved Ben. More than William? Hard to say. In a different way, perhaps. He couldn't compare the two. Nor could Jason choose which of his two parents mattered more, although Tim seemed tougher, better at carrying pain. Or maybe, considering all that Ben had survived, he was the stronger of the two.

Jason thought of a sound that sometimes haunted him still. As always it was accompanied by the smell of blood, crimson liquid gushing from between his fingers no matter how hard he pressed down and tried to stop the flow. As traumatizing as this was, nothing could compete with Ben's howls, the sheer anguish that poured from his throat as he faced the possibility of losing the love of his life. Again. Few things were more beautiful than when Ben sang, but the ugly flipside to that coin had revealed itself that day, because Jason had never heard anything quite as woeful. Not even his own cries when his mother had died.

Such was the nature of the world. Unstoppable events happened and people changed. He couldn't explain why he worried less about William. Maybe because his fiancé was trained to deal with danger. When William went out into unknown situations, he had an entire organization—a tried and true system—backing him up. Ben was small. Fragile. Tim wasn't invincible either. Jason had waited so long to have parents again, and while he couldn't protect them, he intended to spend every moment together that they could. Just in case the next incident was fatal. Just in case the love they felt for him was fleeting. People didn't like to believe that a parent's love could die, insisting that such emotions were selfless, that a mother in particular would do anything for her child, even at the expense of her own life. Jason's mother had died, but not to save him. She had left him to fend for himself, even when she was still alive. That wasn't love. He didn't know what it was.

The bed now restored to being a sofa, Jason sat on it. He started flipping through the photos on his phone. Silly images that would be inconsequential to anyone else, but that meant the world to him. He browsed a series of him and Ben trying on silly hats and sunglasses while out shopping. Or a photo he had taken from the backseat during a drive to Houston, Ben riding shotgun and reaching over to caress the back of Tim's neck. He had done so seemingly unaware, his love for Tim manifesting itself subconsciously.

Jason paused longest on one image in particular. A selfie. His face was pressed between Ben and Tim's, their cheeks mashed against his so they could all fit into the frame. He had a family now. How could he say goodbye to that?

He kept flipping through the images, reaching the most recent. They had managed to take a decent amount, like William at the top of the Astoria Column, pointing to where his Coast Guard station was. Or a photo of Jason doing his best imitation of a seal while William pretended to feed him a fish. The most recent one had been taken at the pub, the backdrop not extraordinary. Jason had simply wanted to capture the moment. They had agreed to sit at the bar rather than wait for a table. William was at his side and supposed to be focused on the camera. He wasn't though. Jason hadn't noticed at the time, but William's face was turned toward him, wearing an expression of pure adoration.

Jason was loved. So much that it seemed unthinkable at times. He had never imagined such a love becoming a problem. Maybe because it wasn't. He would be fine no matter what he decided. He would also hurt no matter what he decided. All that remained was to choose.

Jason flipped back and forth between two photos. Him sandwiched between Ben and Tim, and him seated at a bar next to William. Then he forced himself to look away. This needed to stop! He had already spent an entire year torturing himself over this decision. Tapping the phone against his chin, he gave himself one more minute. Sixty seconds to determine the course of his life. No more deliberating. No more doubt. Not from this moment on, because his minute was up.

Jason had made his choice.

Tears filled his eyes that were both happy and sad. Wiping them away, he forced himself to smile. Then Jason looked down at his phone, flipping back and forth between the two photos again. What could have been and what always would be. Every day was filled with choices. Once a path was walked down, the rest ceased to exist. Accepting this, Jason stood and went outside, lifting his face to the sun.

Something Like Cake

by Jay Bell

Austin, Texas
2015

Happy Birthday! I know it's actually my *big day, but I want to share this one with you because you've already given me so much. These past two years have been amazing, Mia. Especially the nights you stay over, because when you don't, I wake up in the morning feeling like something is missing. What I'm saying is that I want you to move in. That's all I need for my birthday. I have a little surprise for you too, another adventure in a series of many many more. At least I hope so, because I—*

"I don't know if I can keep this up!"

Caesar Hubbard pulled his eyes from the greeting card he was carefully composing so he could roll them. He was seated at a table decorated with birthday-themed plates, cups, balloons, and even a festive paper tablecloth. These matched the streamers he had discovered strewn about the apartment after waking, and the clusters of balloons taped in the corners. Mia had arranged all of this before going to work. She had probably risen even earlier than normal to do so. He would make it up to her. Tonight was going to be wild!

"When you say you can't keep it up," Caesar said loud enough for his voice to carry to the bedroom, "do you mean that literally or figuratively?"

A long pause preceded the answer, the voice deliciously male and deep. "Literally. I think."

Caesar shook his head. "Then try tightening the bow!"

"Won't it fall off?"

"The bow or your—" Caesar pinched the bridge of his nose before chuckling quietly. Antonio was handsome, but he wasn't very bright. "Just make it tighter. You'll be fine, trust me. You don't have much longer to wait!" Mia would be home any minute, which meant he needed to finish the card.

I love you. I want to take this relationship further than ever before. Your partner in all things good and bad (but mostly good)—

Caesar signed the card and leaned back, feeling pleased with himself. After he slid the card in an envelope and sealed it, he wrote Mia's name on the front. Then he waited, his confidence in the contents slowly shifting to uncertainty. He wasn't exactly proposing, but moving in together was still a big step. Maybe it was better to wait until she expressed an interest. Then again, Mia had always let him lead this dance, even at the very beginning.

They had met while speed dating. Caesar hadn't been on the prowl that night. He had simply walked into a bar at random, needing a drink. Halfway through his first beer, he was surprised when an event organizer asked if he would be participating. Without knowing what she was referring to, he had agreed and was guided to a line of tables, a row of chairs on each side, and was seated across from a shy woman. Speed dating! Every five minutes, each person had to move to the left, swapping partners and trying to make a connection all over again. Once reaching the end of the row, he was supposed to stay on his side of the table and go to the far end. Instead he went around to the opposite side, just to screw with the system. This had him sitting across from a straight guy who squirmed uncomfortably while Caesar flirted shamelessly. That's when he first saw her, the girl whose seat he had stolen, standing and staring slack-jawed at the spectacle. Mia. Her shock had given way to a wide smile, like she was totally into it, and boy had that turned out to be true!

Mia was into guys who liked guys. She had an entire bookshelf filled with gay romance novels and an impressive collection of similar movies. She owned plenty of gay porn too, Caesar later discovered, because that sort of thing turned her on. As did tales of his previous exploits. To get her in the mood, all he need do was start telling her a story. He kept on talking once they inevitably moved to the bedroom, not letting the story climax until they both had.

Caesar adjusted himself and looked to the door. *Come on home, baby, because papa is in the mood!* He always was, but today especially, due to a long dry spell that was coming to an end. The only bad part about being in a committed relationship was having to limit his options. He had found a solution though. One that was six foot three and Italian.

When he heard footsteps outside, Caesar hopped to his feet. He reached the door before Mia could slide her key in the lock and threw it open to reveal a woman who was both short and thin. Her energetic personality and expressive nature gave her a presence larger than her slight size. Currently she was struggling to balance a cake in her hands, a plastic shopping bag dangling from her wrist while a present tucked beneath one arm slowly slipped away.

"You're crazy," Caesar said, grinning at her and unburdening her of the cake.

"Happy birthday!" Mia responded, eyes watery with emotion. Her dark hair was fuller and had more curl than usual, meaning she had stopped by the stylist on the way home. She always looked good, and right now, the cake wasn't what Caesar was interested in eating.

"Get in here," he said. "I never should have taken the day off. I just sat around waiting for you."

"I bet," Mia said, reading him like one of her books and recognizing that the next scene was going to be a dirty one. "This time we leave the cake out of it."

"No promises," Caesar said with a wink. He tried to keep his hormones in check long enough for her to get settled. He didn't do a good job of it. Caesar followed her to the kitchen, kissed her neck as she unpacked the ice cream she had bought, and attempted to swipe a finger across the frosting after she took the lid off the cake. He failed. Mia was too quick! When she picked up matches to light the candles, he gently moved her hand away. "Not so fast. I have something for you."

He meant the card, but before he could reach for it, they heard a sneeze. From the bedroom.

Mia stiffened and looked to him with concern. "Is someone here?"

"I don't know," he said innocently. "Let's find out."

Mia remained tense as she followed him through the apartment. "Is the maintenance man here to fix the bathroom fan?"

"No," Caesar said, "but we should keep him in mind for next time."

"Next time?"

"I'm joking. Mostly."

Mia shook her head. "I'm so lost."

"Seek and ye shall find," Caesar said, pushing open the

bedroom door. He stayed in the hall just long enough for her to go first. She gasped. He grinned. Filling the bed was a long stretch of naked tanned muscle. Antonio was on his back, hands behind his head. All he wore was a ribbon tied into a bow around his swollen cock. Caesar had seen bigger, but the toned build, pitch-black body hair, and dopey yet confident expression had him raring to go.

Mia turned to him for an explanation, clearly surprised.

"You always like my stories," he explained. "This time you get to be part of one."

She looked back at the bed. Caesar wondered if she would only watch, or if she would join in. When searching for a guy online, he had chosen someone who was bisexual just like him. That way she could take part as much as she wanted. What he didn't expect was for her to start crying.

"What's wrong?" Caesar asked, taking her by the shoulders.

"What's wrong?" Mia shouted, pulling away and gesturing to Antonio. "Are you kidding me? There's another man in our bed!"

Now she was scowling, which had him even more confused. "I didn't do anything yet! I was waiting until you got home!"

"Oh," Mia said, backing away. "Well, that makes it okay then, doesn't it?"

Before he could reply, she stormed from the room. Caesar followed her, already chastising himself. He shouldn't have sprung it on her like this. They should have planned it together and talked about it first. They had, technically, but only in the heat of the moment. While having sex, she liked him to describe what he would do to a guy, if one had been there with them. They were into the same fantasy. So why didn't she want it to become a reality?

"Baby, wait!"

Mia slowed, stopping at the dining room table she had worked so hard to decorate. Her hands were pressed against the surface for support, her head hung as she shook it. "I don't understand why you would do this to me."

"Do what?" he said, coming up behind her just as she spun around.

"Cheat!"

"Like I said, I didn't sleep with him! He got himself hard. Technically I had to touch his dick to tie on the bow but—"

"I don't care if you didn't touch him at all! You invited someone into your home and had them get into your bed. Naked! You don't think that's cheating? Imagine any other relationship. Think of your parents! If your mom came home and found a naked woman in her bed, one your father invited there, you don't think she would consider that cheating?"

"They're old-fashioned," Caesar shot back. "We're not."

"We're in a monogamous relationship!" Mia shook her head, more tears slipping free.

"You're right, but this is something we would do together! As a couple!"

Mia wiped at her cheeks. "What's wrong with you?"

"What's wrong with you? All you want is for me to tell you about the guys I've slept with!" He gestured toward the bedroom. "Now you can watch. Or you can join in. I even made sure that he's your type. Remember when we first met and you thought I was Italian? You wouldn't believe me. You didn't want to." He tried a smile. "Now you've got the real deal."

Mia bared her teeth. "I don't want anyone but you!"

That took him aback. "I thought you'd be into this. This is your fantasy."

"*Fantasy,*" Mia strained. "You understand what that means, right? This has nothing to do with reality."

"Okay," Caesar said, feeling like an idiot. "I guess I didn't... I'm sorry." Unsure of what else to say, he grabbed the card. "Here. This is for you."

Mia didn't reach for it. She stared unseeing at the envelope, lost in thought. Then she slipped to one side and grabbed her keys off the kitchen counter.

"Where are you going?" he asked, starting to follow, but she breezed past him on the way to the door.

"I'm leaving," Mia said. She paused long enough to look him right in the eye, just to make sure he understood the weight of these words. She wasn't leaving the apartment. She was leaving him.

"Don't," he said. "Please. We'll figure this out. We'll talk it all through. Just don't—"

Antonio strode into the room, still naked and still hard. "Can I take the bow off now?" he asked. "I'm worried it makes my dick look small."

Mia's nostrils flared. She turned, threw open the door, and slammed it behind her on the way out.

Caesar stared in disbelief. Then he covered his face with a palm. He had honestly thought he was doing a good thing. For her! Yeah, part of him missed being with guys, but that wasn't his sole motivation. He had wanted to make her happy.

"I'm taking it off," Antonio said. "I thought you said she was into this sort of thing."

"She is," Caesar responded, dropping his hand. "At least I thought she was. I'll be right back."

He hurried out of the apartment, intending to chase after her. He was shutting the door when he noticed something hanging from the knob. The bracelet he had given her for their one-year anniversary. Truth be told, he had been tempted to buy a ring instead. That's how much he loved her, but instead he had played it cool. Kind of. The bracelet was expensive. He had bought the best he could afford and hoped it would communicate his feelings. She had seemed to understand too, grabbing his face to kiss him after receiving it. Mia always got who he was. Maybe that's why he didn't think he'd need to explain this. He had wanted to share a new and exciting experience together. Instead he had ruined it all.

Sighing, he held the bracelet in his hand, thinking of all the memories they had made. Then he pocketed it and went back inside. Antonio wore jeans and a T-shirt now and was pulling on his shoes.

"You don't have to go," Caesar said wearily.

Antonio shook his head. "Sorry, man, but this isn't cool. You made your girl cry! That's a huge mood-killer right there. If you think I'm going to sleep with you after that, then you're fucked up!"

"I didn't mean we should…" Caesar gritted his teeth. "I was trying to be polite!"

Antonio kept shaking his head, continuing to judge him all the way out of the apartment. Caesar snarled in frustration. "I take it you don't want any cake then!" he shouted as the door closed. He was tempted to swipe his arm across the cheerful birthday display, but he wasn't able to. Mia had put so much effort into it, and if she did come back…

She wouldn't. Caesar had been here often enough to know.

He went to sit on the couch, slouching into the cushions. His thoughts drifted to all the other people he had hurt, despite not meaning to. Some of those breakups he could blame on being young and inexperienced, but that this was still happening well into his twenties... Maybe he really was fucked up.

In situations such as these, he couldn't help but think of one person in particular. Nathaniel. The one who had gotten away. Or more accurately, the one who had fled because of Caesar's greatest mistake. Of all his transgressions, none could compare to sleeping with his boyfriend's best friend. He hadn't done anything so vile since then, but Caesar had found plenty of other ways to sabotage his relationships. If he was the common denominator of every failed attempt, then the rest of his life would remain this way until he figured out a way to change. But what exactly was he doing wrong? Was it his personality? Or some basic misunderstanding about how relationships were supposed to work?

He needed perspective. No "other fish in the sea" lectures or well-meaning encouragement. Caesar wanted to hear the truth from someone who didn't mince words. That made him think again of Nathaniel. Why not go to him? The guy still held a grudge nearly ten years later. If anyone had the guts to tell him what needed to change, it was Nathaniel.

Caesar remained on the couch a little longer, still hoping Mia would knock on the door, if only to talk. He tried calling. No answer. He texted her next, his words pleading. When no reply came, Caesar sent another text, this time to Nathaniel.

Hey, how's it going?

He rose and paced the room until the response came.

What do you want?

Caesar couldn't help smiling, hearing Nathaniel's voice in his mind before he shot back a reply. *It's my birthday. Wanna hang out?*

Nathaniel's response was a very economical, *No.*

C'mon! Just a drink. Where are you right now?

At work.

He checked the clock. *Still?*

I got a late start today and I'm really really *busy.*

Hint taken and ignored. I'm on my way.

He grabbed his keys and was out the door before his phone rumbled again. Checking the screen, he laughed.

Not right now, Nathaniel had written.

Of course not! Caesar would never dream of showing up right away because he would need at least twenty minutes to reach the studio where Nathaniel worked. Once there, he hoped for words of wisdom, even if the likelihood of them being shouted was high.

Caesar walked into Studio Maltese lugging his entire history on his back. After telling the security guard who he was there to see, he worked his way through his list of previous lovers again while waiting, starting at the beginning. Steph had been the first girl he had truly fallen for. They were too similar to stay together for long, despite trying many times over.

Nathaniel had come along next and introduced him to an entirely different world. Not just because he was a guy instead of a girl. Caesar had loved Steph, but the depth of emotion he felt for Nathaniel then, and still did, rivaled anyone since. If his parents hadn't gotten in the way, who knew how far they could have gone?

Jason Grant had been a whirlwind romance. His one-time foster brother was a sweet kid, and Caesar had wanted to do right by him. They had loved each other, but that was also when Caesar had learned a tough lesson: Feelings didn't fade. They might change, or grow stronger or weaker, but love in particular tended to stick around. Permanently. Things were going well with Jason until Nathaniel returned to his life, reminding Caesar of just how much he felt. For both of them! Naturally that had ended in disaster. Wouldn't it be convenient if love was a switch that only one person could flip at a time? If that were so, Caesar's life would have played out very differently indeed.

"In you go," the security guard said, jerking his thumb at the elevator doors.

On the ride up and during the walk down the hall, Caesar continued meandering through his own history, dismissing flings that were meaningless to focus on more tangible relationships. This brought him to Rebecca, his greatest mistake. Caesar's first year in college hadn't been going well, thanks to his plummeting grades. Then Nathaniel had reappeared, a solid rock for him to cling to. Or so it had seemed. Nathaniel kept disappearing beneath the waves, busy with his own goals, and Caesar was left vulnerable and alone. Rebecca was too. They had found comfort in each other, and of all his transgressions, Caesar regretted that one the most. A single careless act had ended up hurting them all, but none more so than the person behind the door he now faced.

He sighed, knocked, and opened it when a gruff voice beyond told him to go away.

"You have to be nice to me," Caesar said as he slipped inside. "It's my birthday."

Nathaniel was already glaring from behind his desk. The intent was to send him scurrying, but in truth, Nathaniel was cursed with a face that only grew sexier the angrier it got. It paired nicely with the hulking build, even if he was just a big softy. Until pushed. Caesar rubbed at his neck, remembering with discomfort how those big hands had felt around it. Not that he could blame the guy. He'd had it coming.

"What do you want?" Nathaniel grumbled.

"Like I said, it's my—"

"Birthday," Nathaniel finished. "I don't care."

"No present for me?" Caesar joked as he sat in one of the chairs facing the desk. "It's been a while! I dig the beard. Very masculine."

"Thanks," Nathaniel said guardedly, reaching up to rub his brown-bristled jaw. "Kelly likes it."

There it was. A reminder of the invisible barrier between them. On the rare occasions when they saw each other, Nathaniel always made sure to point out that he was taken. "I heard you two got hitched! I understand why I didn't get an invite but—"

"There wasn't a guest list to put you on. We had a small private ceremony."

"Cool," Caesar said. "Congratulations to you both. I'm happy you found someone."

Nathaniel narrowed his eyes, assessing how genuine these words were. Then he relaxed somewhat. "How have you been?"

"Good," Caesar said automatically. He shook his head. "Until today. Can I ask you something?"

Nathaniel shrugged. "Sure."

"What would it take for us to be together again?"

Nathaniel stood and pointed to the door. "Goodbye."

"Wait wait wait!" Caesar said with a chuckle. "I'm not trying to seduce you. If things don't work out between you and Kelly, then yeah, definitely give me a call, but that wasn't what I'm getting at. Mia and I split up. Did you ever meet her?"

"No," Nathaniel said, sitting again, "but let me take a wild guess. She broke up with you. Because you cheated."

"No!" Caesar grimaced. "Okay, she feels like I cheated but—"

Now it was Nathaniel's turn to laugh. "Some things never change."

"It wasn't like that!"

"No?"

Caesar groaned and buried his face in his palms. Then he looked up again, dragging his hands over his features. "You're right. It was my fault. That's why I'm here. I need you to tell me what to do differently. I don't want to be single for the rest of my life. You and Kelly are married now—and I'm thrilled for you—but it makes me feel weird, because even Jason is engaged. He and William have a kid! Not together, but they're starting a family. Everyone is moving on, and I'm still incapable of maintaining a basic relationship."

"How long were you and Mia together?"

"Almost two years."

Nathaniel looked surprised. "That's a long time for you!"

Caesar nodded. "I'm serious about her. I love Mia, and I tried to do it all right this time, but I still managed to screw it up."

"How?"

He explained the situation, Nathaniel shaking his head throughout much of the story. His advice was short and to the point.

"Stop thinking with your dick."

"You first," Caesar said. "We're men. There's no getting around that, but I thought I had figured out a way to make Little Caesar and Mia happy at the same time."

Nathaniel's brow furrowed. "Little Caesar?"

He rubbed the back of his head sheepishly. "Mia started calling it that as a joke, so I showed up at her apartment one day carrying a meat lover's pizza with a hole cut out one side of the box. I stuck my—"

"I get it," Nathaniel said, raising a hand to stop him.

"What's crazy," Caesar said, "is she actually liked that. Mia thought it was funny, but it also turned her on. That wasn't the first time I did something kinky, or the last, and until today she's always rolled with it."

"Because today was the first time it involved another person."

"Yeah."

Nathaniel exhaled through his nose. "If Kelly pulled a stunt like that, I wouldn't be happy either. I don't need anyone but him. Sounds like you were enough for Mia, so that narrows it down to one culprit. Who needed more than he already had? Who sabotaged this relationship just like all the others he's been in?"

"Me," Caesar said, swallowing painfully. "You really hate me, don't you?"

"No," Nathaniel said. "I wanted to, and a few times I almost succeeded, but I fell in love with you because you're charming, confident, and sexy. I don't like admitting it, but nothing has changed. That's why so many people keep lining up to have their hearts broken by you. You're like a— I don't know." He scowled in frustration before his brow shot up again. "Like a baseball player who always hits home runs, but after passing third base, you get distracted, wander off, and never finish the game. Every single time."

"So what should I do?"

Nathaniel shrugged again. "Get it out of your system. Keep screwing around until you get tired of it and are ready to settle down. You're not the only guy with this problem, and from what I understand, that's what the others do."

Except it didn't sound appealing to him. Caesar wasn't sure what did, and if he didn't know, he couldn't expect Nathaniel to either. Instead of dwelling on it further, he switched subjects. "So when you say you don't hate me, what you're really saying is…"

Nathaniel crossed his arms over his chest. "I'm not saying anything."

"But you still love me," Caesar said, leaning forward to rest his elbows on the desk and his chin in his hands. "Just a little bit."

Nathaniel rolled his eyes. "I'll say this once, and only because it's your birthday: I still love you enough that I want to see you happy. I don't know how you'll get there, but twenty years from now, I don't want you still showing up at my office to tell me about the latest person you've traumatized. Get your shit together. You're worth more than this."

Caesar sat upright. Then he knocked on the desk and stood. "I'll say this, and not because it's my birthday: I shouldn't have let you get away. You were the one. I'll admit that to anyone who asks. Tell Kelly. Let him know that he's not the only one to recognize how special you are. He's lucky. And smart."

"Tell him yourself," Nathaniel said. "It's your birthday. You shouldn't be alone. Wanna have dinner with us?"

Caesar smiled. Then he shook his head. "You know me. I've got plans! Too many friends and lovers to choose from. Thanks anyway." Before he turned to leave, he looked Nathaniel over again. "I mean it about the beard. Very hot. You just get better with every passing year."

He left without waiting for a response. When he was in the hallway again and the door had closed behind him, he allowed a grimace to surface. Yeah, he definitely regretted letting that one escape. Dinner would have been nice, even with Kelly there. He just didn't want to be reminded of what could have been. Not tonight. A shame too, because he didn't have any actual plans, or friendships that hadn't gotten tangled up romantically. It would just be him and an empty apartment tonight. Cake and presents didn't sound good, but a drink did. Not at a bar where he could meet yet another lover. Just a quick stop at a liquor store for a bottle. A really big one.

He reached the elevator and pushed the button. When the doors finally opened, an older man was revealed to a whiff of exotic cologne. The stranger was on the heavy side, the white suit finely tailored to compensate. The hair that was both thinning and graying was neatly trimmed, and the jewelry on his fingers, wrists, and neck boasted of success. Caesar stepped into the elevator, hoping he would look that distinguished when older. He'd like to be in better shape, if only for his own comfort, but it was still hot how some guys transitioned from a boy to a man and finally to something nearing a lord. A noble gentleman!

"Going down?" the man asked.

"Not tonight," Caesar said wistfully. When an eyebrow raised in response to this, he cleared his throat and joined the man at his side, turning to face forward. "Bottom floor, yeah."

"I prefer the top myself," the man replied as he jabbed a button, "but when I do venture in the other direction, I try to make the experience memorable."

Caesar looked over in surprise. Then he laughed. The man chuckled too, the sound just as deeply pleasant as his voice. There was something familiar about the shrewd eyes and commanding presence. Even now, as the man casually poked at his phone, he still managed to radiate power. "Sorry, but do we know each other? I think we might have—"

The elevator jerked to a premature stop. Caesar reached to each side instinctively to brace himself. That meant he had one hand on the elevator wall and the other on the arm of a white tailored suit.

"Never fear," the man said. "This happens all the time. Help will be along shortly."

"Shouldn't we call someone?" Caesar asked, removing his hand from the man. He examined the keypad, which was where normal elevator buttons should be. All he knew was that pushing the "one" key would get him to the ground floor. Otherwise the security guard had to type in a code for him to ride up to the second floor, or on some occasions, the elevator seemed to be called there automatically. He pushed the number one a few times in quick succession to see if it would help. Nothing happened.

"There's an automatic alarm," his companion explained. "All we must do is bide our time."

"How long will that be?" Caesar asked, turning to face him.

"Two minutes, twenty, an hour. We shall see. Is there somewhere you need to be?"

"Yeah," Caesar said. "A great big birthday party. My own, in fact. You know what? We've definitely met before. Are you a regular at any bars?"

"Yes," the man said instantly. Then he gave the question further thought. "Oh yes. Definitely. My name is Marcello Maltese. And you are?"

"Caesar. Wait, did you say Maltese? You own this studio?"

"I do indeed," Marcello said, a smile slowly unfurling. "I think I have it now. A wedding! Do you know Tim and Ben?"

"That's it!" Caesar said. "Can't say I really know them. I used to date their son."

"The delightful Jason Grant! Of course! Although your name made me think first of… Ah."

"Ah?" Caesar repeated, not liking the sound of that.

"No matter," Marcello said, reappraising him. "I take it you were here visiting Nathaniel?"

His jaw dropped. "Yeah! How did you know? Oh." This man

was Nathaniel's boss. Caesar remembered hearing that they were close. Enough to share the details of a former relationship, apparently.

"Your reputation precedes you, that is all. Don't despair. It circumvents the need for tedious introductions and tiresome background stories. Regardless, I won't keep you any longer." Marcello poked at his phone again and the elevator resumed its descent. Then he patiently ignored Caesar until they reached the bottom floor and the doors opened. Only then did he look over and make a tsking sound. "Still, such a pity."

"What is?" Caesar asked, thoroughly confused by now.

"Being bound by the last vestiges of my morality." Marcello strolled out of the elevator. "Enjoy your birthday party. I hope this temperamental contraption hasn't made you late."

"I'm the only guest," Caesar said, following him to the exit, "so that shouldn't be a problem."

"The only guest? To your own birthday party?"

"Yup." Caesar hurried forward to hold open the door to the parking lot. "Unless you want to tag along?"

"Curiosity killed the cat," Marcello murmured to himself. "How many lives have I already spent?"

"One or two by the look of things," Caesar teased. "This one is on me though. My curiosity has gotten me into trouble more times than I can count. Once more won't change anything."

Marcello's eyes twinkled with amusement. "Very well. Where do you imagine these celebrations taking place?"

"I don't feel like going out, so uh…" Caesar grinned, reminded of a line he had spoken all too often before. "My place or yours?"

Caesar didn't normally concern himself with size. Rarely was it an indicator of quality, but there was big, and then there was… "Huge!" he breathed. "I've seen some big ones, but yours is enormous!"

"If only I heard that more often," Marcello sighed, leading the way through his palatial home. "Not that you're witnessing an attempt at compensation. I've just always valued space. If a man's home is his kingdom, well, why settle for anything but rolling hills and glistening lakes?"

They entered a sprawling living room. Through the tall

glass windows on the far side was at least one glistening lake—an illuminated private pool—and beyond, a stunning view of Austin's skyline.

"Have a seat," his host said, moving toward an open kitchen on the opposite side of the room. "I don't have cake, but I've always found champagne suitable to any occasion worth celebrating. I assume you drink?"

"After the day I've had, just try to stop me!"

Caesar went to a large U-shaped couch and sat on the tan leather without much commitment. He wanted to keep patrolling the room, examining details before wandering down one of the many halls. Light music switched on while he waited, and a fireplace sprang to life seemingly by magic. When Marcello returned from the kitchen, he carried a serving tray with two crystal flutes and a bucket filled with ice, the gentle sparkle of bubbles emanating from an open bottle nestled within.

Marcello sat adjacent to him, choosing a spot closest to Caesar's arm of the couch, and worked on filling their glasses. "If you don't mind me asking," he said, "how old are you?"

"Twenty-six," he answered.

"Nearly half my age then," Marcello said, his smile subtle. "I recently celebrated my fiftieth." He passed Caesar a glass and held up his own. "To the anniversary of your birth. Let us give thanks to your mother for her rather exquisite creation!"

"Thanks, Mom!" Caesar said with a smile. "And thank *you* for having me too. In a different way." After clinking and drinking, he continued to survey the room. "This is a nice place. I'm guessing you don't live here alone?"

"I do."

"Really? There isn't someone special?"

"If you're inquiring about my romantic status," Marcello said, "I am most thoroughly on my own. How ironic then that I'm surrounded by countless people who never fail to explain how lonely I must be. If they would stop crowding me with their concern, maybe I would feel more at liberty to change the situation."

"Do you want to?"

"Heavens no! Not permanently anyway. And you?"

Caesar exhaled and set down his glass. "As of this morning, I had an awesome girlfriend."

"And now?"

"I guess she came to her senses."

"How so?" Marcello responded. "I know we've only just met, but you seem personable enough. You're handsome and well-spoken. What more could this girl expect?"

"Monogamy."

"Ah." Marcello sipped from his glass and settled into the couch cushions. "Tell me everything."

Caesar did. First he started with Mia and the ill-conceived birthday surprise. Marcello laughed at this, which helped him see the humor too. Then he gave a brief summary of his history, explaining the cause for each relationship's end rather than delving into the happier details.

"I detect a pattern," Marcello interrupted.

"Nathaniel said the same thing. The broken part in each of these relationships is me. I need to fix myself. I'm working on it."

Marcello leaned forward to top off their drinks. "How do you plan on accomplishing this self-reparation?"

"By getting my hormones under control. Do they sell chemical castration kits at pharmacies?"

Marcello crinkled his nose. "I don't believe they do, although I can think of many people who would benefit from such a kit, most of them politicians. So you feel your carnal urges are what drove you to sleep with Nathaniel while you were still with Jason Grant?"

"No! I loved Nathaniel. I still do. That's what made it so confusing."

"Mm." Marcello nodded thoughtfully. "And likewise, when you were in college and slept with Nathaniel's best friend—Rebecca, that was her name—were your needs purely physical?"

Caesar was too surprised to answer. "I didn't tell you about her. Oh. I suppose Nathaniel did."

"I first made his acquaintance in the midst of these events. Regardless, you were spurred on by your sex drive and nothing more?"

"No, I really liked her. Looking back, it's tricky to say what I was feeling, since I was a mess at the time. College was a lot harder than high school, and Nathaniel was back in my life but never around. That's not an excuse. I know what you're getting at, but it doesn't matter if emotion was involved. In fact, most people would agree that having feelings for her made it worse."

"I'm not most people," Marcello said. "I've never understood such foolishness. No matter if we're motivated by love or lust, we're forbidden to desire more than one person at a time. Hate and violence run rampant in this world, and rather than trying to contain either, we're more concerned with limiting the amount of love we allow ourselves and others to feel."

Caesar grinned. "You sound like an old hippie."

"That's precisely what I am. Well, perhaps not *old*. My heart still contains enough youth to compensate for any failings of my body. The rest you have right."

"I wish more people agreed with you," Caesar said.

Marcello smiled. "As do I. I've never wanted to find a horse's head in my bed, but an Italian stallion? Had any boyfriend of mine surprised me in such a way, I would only love him more. As to your predicament, I faced the same one previously. I know youth is allergic to the wisdom of older generations, but perhaps—just this once—there can be an exception to the rule."

"I'm willing to listen to any advice you've got! If that's what you mean."

Marcello nodded. "I used to practice restraint myself. I'd even say it was once my religion. I know that may be difficult to believe, especially considering the excessive nature of our current surroundings, but in my youth, I was eager to prove my value to others. I didn't have a traditional upbringing. I came from nothing, which is also where people assume you'll remain. Some will even attempt to keep you there, so I conducted myself as if I already belonged to the established moral majority. I made sure to wear the correct clothing and speak as they did, a sheep in wolf's clothing. Looking and sounding the part was only half the battle. I tried to match their ideals, to prove that the streets couldn't drag me down with promises of drugs and debauchery. In essence, I practiced restraint, the very thing you believe will free you from your predicament."

"How'd that go?" Caesar asked, genuinely curious.

"Not well. I spent so much time fighting myself that I had little energy for anything else, including love. I was hardly alone in this self-inflicted punishment. The 'respectable' society I was so desperate to join was filled with people who deprived themselves until they were inevitably driven over the brink. Eric, a dear friend of mine, always said it was healthier to take madness in small doses. Only then is it possible to survive the poison. Not that he was anywhere near as decadent as I. Eventually I realized the only way to reach my full potential was to unshackle myself. I was both the jailer and the jailed, but no more!"

Caesar nodded in agreement. "I can relate. Growing up, I wanted to please my parents. I tried to get good grades and be as business-minded as they wanted, but away from their influence, I was a different person. The real me. I feel like that's been a reoccurring theme. I try to be on my best behavior for the people I love, and when I inevitably screw up, they turn their backs on me."

"And from what you've said, you assign no blame to them."

Caesar shrugged. "Nobody likes a cheater."

"Indeed. Tell me, if you find yourself breaking the same promises over and over again, what is the most sensible course of action?"

"To stop breaking them."

"No," Marcello said, shaking his head adamantly. "To stop making such promises!"

Caesar thought about it. "You mean an open relationship?"

"Have you given thought to that before?"

"Yes," he admitted. "I tried it once. With a guy. We'd been together for a few months when he admitted he wouldn't mind messing around together. We would go out and find a man to bring home. It was fun until I kept wanting to see one of those guys. We both liked him, but when I suggested that we make him a regular thing… It was the emotional aspect. Again. I started falling in love, and somehow that wasn't acceptable. Sleeping around? No problem. But having feelings for other people was a deal-breaker."

"Strange, isn't it?" Marcello said. "You would expect the physical aspect to be frowned upon more than the emotional. I've seen the same story play out with other couples. Forget the expectations of others for a moment. What is it exactly that you desire?"

Caesar let himself dream for a moment. He wasn't drunk, but he had just enough of a buzz that his heart and mind were working in unison. "Someone I can share my life with. I see couples like Nathaniel and Kelly, and how they make each other stronger. They get to share everything as the years go by. Each experience has two perspectives that way. Ever thought of that? It's like when you see a movie with a friend, and afterwards, they point out things that you didn't notice. You either gain a better appreciation for the movie, or maybe they help you understand why you hated it. All of life is like that. In a relationship you share everything with each other, see it all from a new angle, and if it's the right sort of person, that makes the world twice as beautiful. Everything good is doubled. So I want that, definitely, because I love life, and I love people. Maybe a little too much."

"I don't think so," Marcello said. "I don't believe it's ever possible to love too much. Few attributes are nobler than knowing oneself and being honest with others about who that person is. Had you understood your nature and explained it to Mia from the very beginning, do you believe this morning's misunderstanding still would have occurred?"

"That's the other thing," Caesar said shaking his head. "If I insist on open relationships only, people like Mia— Actually, you're friends with Nathaniel. You know how awesome he is. He never would have given me the time of day if I told him from the beginning that we needed to stay open. I bet most people wouldn't."

"Perhaps not, but finding someone who accepts you for who you are, surely that is paramount to a lasting relationship!"

Caesar exhaled. "I either disappoint them upfront or later down the road. My way, at least I still get to love them while it lasts."

Marcello leaned forward. "But if you were more direct, you would spare them and yourself heartache. You would also have the energy to continue your pursuit of someone who shares your ideals. Love means different things to different people. Some require the safety of commitment before they are secure enough to feel. Others fear commitment and find it suffocates emotion. In truth, there is no right or wrong answer, nor is one variety of love any more valid than the other. So many, like yourself, feel pressured to fit into a system that doesn't work for them. As a society, we are slowly tearing down barriers to better accommodate those with other needs. Marriage belongs to gay people now too, just as the vote was given to women. Restrooms will one day no longer be divided by gender in the same way that drinking fountains are no longer segregated. Despite the occasional setback, progress is slowly marching forward, and I believe that one day, people who love in the way that you and I do will no longer be as misunderstood. That is why honesty is of such great importance! As you said, nobody favors a cheater, and if you keep forcing yourself into such a position, you'll only continue setting back progress."

Caesar couldn't disagree with that. He still had one concern though. "You really feel the same way as me?"

"There are too many flavors to sample in this world," Marcello said, eyes alight. "I have no guarantee of returning, so I mean to make the most of life while I'm still here. So yes, in matters of love, I can commit myself emotionally, but that doesn't mean closing off my feelings to other people, nor do I intend to limit myself physically."

Caesar swallowed. "I'm sorry, because this is going to sound dickish, but you live here alone. If you and I are so alike, I'm worried that because you never found someone to share your life with, that means I probably won't either."

"I share my life with countless people. Most of them are friends, some I consider family. Quite a few are merely colleagues. And when it comes to romantic adventures you, my friend, might be able to fill a book, but I'm already on the tenth volume of a series."

Caesar laughed. "Fair enough."

"If it's any consolation, I don't always live here alone. People come and go as they please. In fact, if you plan on drinking further, I'd recommend you spend the night."

"Oh really?" Caesar said, putting on his best bedroom eyes. "You know, it's been about two years since I've slept with a guy. Wanna help me end my fast?"

"Had I only my own feelings to consider," Marcello replied, "you would already be in my bed. Therein lies the tragedy. Meeting someone of a like mind isn't always enough. Not when extenuating circumstances remain."

"Like what?"

"Nathaniel. If I called him now and asked permission to sleep with you, he would insist that he doesn't care, but I know it would continue to trouble him. Don't you agree?"

Caesar thought of the man he had once been lucky enough

to date and sighed. "Yeah. It would drive him crazy. And not in a good way."

"Trailblazing your own morality sometimes means respecting the morals of others. Otherwise, how can we ever expect them to accept ours too?"

Caesar groaned in frustration. "Do you always tell people to do the right thing?"

"From my perspective, yes. I'm sure some would feel I'm in the process of corrupting you, although not nearly as much as I would prefer."

Caesar laughed. "Okay, but I'm not ending my birthday with a quiet drink and an early bedtime. How about that pool out there? I take it you like to swim?"

"Naturally. Would you care to join me?"

"That depends. Do you think Nathaniel needs to know that we went without swimsuits?"

"Skinny dipping?" Marcello said. "That takes me back. I haven't done such a thing for weeks!"

Caesar grinned. "You haven't done it at all. Not with me."

Marcello raised his glass. "In that case, here's to new adventures."

"And to what could have been," Caesar replied, lifting his own.

They raced each other to the bottom of the glass. Then they threw off their clothes, went outside, and strutted around in the warm night air until they stood facing the skyline together, as if wanting Austin to see all they had to offer. Caesar laughed, Marcello distilled more wisdom. When they finally turned toward the pool and leapt, plunging into its depths, they did so while clinging to each other's hands, two kindred spirits who would never become one on the physical plane.

Caesar returned home the next morning, having narrowly escaped a hangover. His body told him he needed to drink plenty of water, and that it wouldn't put up with a repeat performance anytime soon, but he mostly felt okay. Physically. Emotionally he was a little depressed to return to an increasingly stale birthday cake that hadn't been covered and colorful decorations that now only made him feel blue. He didn't have the heart to put any of it away. Just the cake. He disposed of it, took a shower, and got dressed. Then he wondered what to do with himself. Already he had called in sick to work, not yet ready to face the real world. Caesar was second-guessing this decision when he heard a knock on the door.

Hope sent his heart shooting up to his throat. Maybe his birthday wish from yesterday was still good, because Mia was there when he opened the door. She didn't appear angry. He didn't know how that was possible and was too happy to question it.

"I'm sorry," Mia said. "I overreacted yesterday. Can I come in?"

"Yes!" He gestured for her to enter. After shutting the door, he nearly locked it to ensure she would stay. "Sorry everything is still a mess, but I liked it too much to clean up."

"That's sweet," Mia said, flashing him a smile. Her expression became more concerned as she looked toward the bedroom. "Are you alone?"

"Do you mean Antonio?" Caesar plopped down on the couch so she would do the same. "He left right after you did. He thinks I'm an idiot too."

"You're not!" Mia said generously. "Once I calmed down and considered it all, I saw where you were coming from. Of course you would expect me to be into that! In retrospect, the idea *is* pretty hot."

"Really?" Caesar said, reaching to take her hand before he stopped himself.

"Yes! I don't know where you found him but—" Mia shook her head, cheeks rosy. "I was too hasty. I don't want our relationship to end. Especially over a silly misunderstanding."

"I don't either," he admitted.

"Good!" She slid her dainty fingers beneath his. "Did I ruin your birthday? We can start over, if you want. We'll celebrate today instead."

"Want me to call Antonio?" Caesar meant it as a joke, but it still caused hurt to show on her face. That told him all he needed to know. "Listen, before we rush back into anything, we should talk."

"Okay." Mia pulled her hand away and put it over her heart protectively. "I'm listening."

"I don't do so well with monogamy. Sexually or emotionally.

In fact, it's the latter that's hardest for me."

"Because I only keep you satisfied in bed," Mia said, lips beginning to tremble.

"No! You were enough emotionally too. How can I explain? You have more than one friend, right? Is that because any of them are lacking?"

"No," Mia admitted. "I get something different from each of them but—"

"And do you think it's realistic to expect one friend to fulfill all your needs?"

Mia's gaze was steady. "Relationships are different. I either fulfilled all your needs or I didn't."

"Why is it different? People are complex. Imagine if you had a friend who insisted that you couldn't have any others. How would you react?"

"I'd think they were crazy," Mia admitted.

"Unrealistic," Caesar suggested. He didn't want to make her feel bad, but if they still stood a chance, he needed her to understand his perspective. "I've got a lot of love in my heart. I hope you felt it while we were together, because I gave you all that I could. I really did. For some reason though, there's still more left over. The only thing stopping me from loving other people is *me*. I didn't want to hurt you, so I closed myself off, but that doesn't feel right. Loving someone else doesn't mean I stop loving you, or that I love you any less. As far as I can tell, there's no limit to these things. Or if there is, I haven't discovered it yet."

Mia steeled herself and sat up straight. "What are you saying?"

"That I want to continue our relationship, but I don't see it working if we're still monogamous. I know it was great for two years, and I can keep trying, but I have a history. More likely than not, eventually I'll mess up, and that will hurt us both. I love you. I really do. Enough to be honest."

"But not enough to commit."

"Commitment has nothing to do with it," Caesar said. "I can promise to love you for the rest of my life. Hell, I probably will, even if you don't stick around. But being committed, in my mind, doesn't mean closing myself off to other people. Your first boyfriend, Jake, you still love him, right? You know I love Nathaniel. Jason too. And yet, you're still capable of loving me, and I'm still capable of loving you. Doesn't that prove my point?"

To her credit, Mia sat there and thought about it. She even nodded, but the news wasn't good. "You're right. We are capable of loving more than one person, but I need to know that you love me most. Even if you do right now, how can I know that some future boyfriend won't take my place or become more important to you? How am I even supposed to compete with another guy?"

"By being who you are. You're my Mia! There's not another person like you in the world!"

"Then why isn't that enough? I agree that one person can't be expected to fulfill all the needs of another. That's why we have friends, even when we're in love, but I can honestly say that I only need one person to fulfil my romantic needs. You were enough. It hurts me that I wasn't."

But she was! He could think of more metaphors, like how Chinese food was good enough. It was freaking great! But that didn't mean not desiring Thai on occasion. This wasn't a gender issue. They didn't always get Chinese food from the same place, for instance. Each restaurant had its own nuance, little differences that made a meal special. Rather than compare their relationship to takeout, he accepted what Marcello had said as truth: Love means different things to different people. His version and hers weren't compatible.

"I feel like I've let you down," he said, "and that breaks my heart, but this is the last time. I won't put anyone through this again."

Mia's mouth fell open. "Meaning?"

"That you had it right yesterday when you left. We have different expectations and—"

Mia shot to her feet. She was hurt. Pleading with her to understand would only make it harder for her to go, so instead he rose, gently took her hand, and apologized once again. "You're an incredible person. Get out there and find someone worthy of you. I'm sorry that I'm not."

"You're such a bastard!" Mia snarled. Then her face crumpled and she shook her head, as if she didn't mean it. Nor did she allow herself to cry. Instead she came close to him, pressing balled up hands against his chest that relaxed into open palms when he hugged her. They stood there holding each other silently. If her thoughts were anything like his, she was remembering the good times they had shared, or thinking of all the plans they had made that would never come to pass. Not now. Mia was the first to pull away.

"I know it won't be anytime soon," Caesar said, "but I really hope— I won't say it because it always sounds like bullshit, but I still want you in my life. When we're both ready."

"If," Mia said, but she managed a smile. She poked him in the stomach, glanced around at the apartment like she might not ever see it again, and then turned to leave.

Caesar had to bite down on his tongue. Otherwise he would say anything to make her stay, even if it wasn't the truth. When the door clicked shut behind her again, he sat on the couch and allowed himself to feel miserable. Eventually he grabbed his phone and sent Marcello a text.

I hope you're right about everything. A few seconds later, he sent another. *Are you happy?*

Beyond your wildest dreams, came the reply.

This gave him hope. He felt alone, but less than he would have otherwise, because now he had someone to turn to for advice. Caesar would happily call Marcello his friend, but Nathaniel had gotten there first, and he didn't want to intrude. He had upset his ex-boyfriend's life enough times in the past. He wouldn't do so again. Still, on occasion, maybe he and Marcello could share a drink together.

Caesar stood and went to the dining room table. He made a wish while standing there, despite not having candles to blow out. His request was a simple one. *I just want to be happy.* Then he went to the kitchen, grabbed a trash bag, and returned to start throwing the decorations away. By the time he was finished, he felt the stirrings of a smile.

He wouldn't remain alone. Caesar wouldn't allow himself to be, nor would he want that, because somewhere out there was another likeminded person. And another and another. It was only a matter of time before he met one of them, and when the dance of love resumed, he would move from partner to partner, linking arms with each and never having to let go again.

Something Like Braaaains

by Jay Bell

Austin, Texas
2016

How scary is scary? I mean, I'm not a coward. Maybe I used to be. Are zombies freakier than coming out was? Ha ha! That really was my biggest fear once. Now it's probably Ben coming to his senses, because let's face it, I lucked out the day he fell in love with me.

Tim sent the text to his son and, from his seat on the living room couch, looked with unease toward the back of the house. Rain pelted the windows, creating clear sheets of liquid that distorted the view outside and magnified the brief flashes of stark white lightning. Another growl of thunder ripped through the house. The walls and locked doors did little to dampen the sound. Tim flinched with each bone-shaking rumble. Chinchilla pressed up closer against his side and whimpered her discontent, eyes pleading, but he was powerless to stop the storm. Tim could only rub the bulldog's belly to reassure her. And to make himself feel better, because even if she wasn't scared, Tim probably would have sought her out for comfort. He supposed the weather was appropriate, considering that it was Halloween.

Thankfully he wasn't alone tonight. Ben walked into the living room carrying a bowl of popcorn, his attention on the back door that rattled as a gust of wind blew against it. "Looks like nasty weather," he said.

"Yup!" Tim replied, trying to sound unconcerned. "I feel sorry for any trick-or-treater who gets caught out in this."

"The candy!" Ben exclaimed, setting the popcorn on the coffee table and fleeing from the room. He returned from the kitchen with another bowl in hand, this one filled with fun-sized candy bars.

Tim eyed the individually-wrapped temptations warily, knowing that he would be expected to eat most of them and have to work off the glut of calories. If the weather wasn't so terrible, he would get a head start now by going for a jog. "I love you," he said as Ben moved toward the front door, "but you shouldn't buy so much candy. There's not going to be any trick-or-treaters. Not way out here."

"You don't know that!" Ben called over his shoulder.

"I do," Tim replied, raising his voice to be heard, "because in all the years we've lived here, not one single kid has knocked on that door."

"What about Michelle's children?" Ben returned to the living room and settled down on the couch next to him, curling up his legs close to his body. "Allison was over here with Davis just two days ago. That doesn't count?"

"I'm talking about Halloween. Anyone would be crazy to go trick-or-treating in this area. The nearest house is how far away from ours? A kid would have to walk miles just to visit five of them. And they'd have to travel way out here first, because no matter what time of year, I've never seen a kid in our area."

"Then pay more attention to your own home." Ben nudged him with a socked foot. "Daddy."

Tim grimaced. "Don't call me that! I love Jason and getting to be a part of his life in that way, but 'Daddy' sounds sleazy. I prefer to think of myself as a proud father of a twenty-six-year-old child. Ugh. That makes me sound old."

"I think it's hot," Ben said.

Tim cocked an eyebrow optimistically. "Yeah?"

"Definitely! It's all about branding. You say proud father, I say ruggedly handsome *papi*."

"I'm rugged?" Tim asked, liking the sound of that. His eyes moved over Ben's body which, thanks to a recent health kick in the kitchen, had inched closer to his college weight. Tim still couldn't get Ben to go running with him, or any other sort of prolonged workout, but that was fine. He appreciated the skinny frame, which appeared particularly thin tonight thanks to the tight jeans Ben wore, and the playful black T-shirt with skeleton bones printed on it. Tim knew that if he lifted up that shirt, he would see a few ribs on display. Just the hint of them, but enough to press his lips against and—

"It was a compliment," Ben said, "not an invitation."

"You sure?" Tim asked, taking in the twinkling brown eyes. Thunder rumbled again. Chinchilla quivered against him, so Tim reached over to stroke her. "Never mind, you're right. I need to ruggedly guard my little girl from this storm. Besides, we want to be ready when all those trick-or-treaters show up at the door."

Ben laughed. "Do you ever think of having more? Kids, I mean. With me, obviously, or you would be in serious trouble."

They had this conversation on occasion, but with all the recent drama involving the adopted son they had, he couldn't remember the last time. "I'm not against the idea, but I also don't feel like there's anything missing from our lives right now. We have Jason, even though he doesn't live with us anymore. What did you have in mind?"

Ben shrugged. "I don't know. A little girl, maybe."

"We've already got one," Tim said, patting Chinchilla on the rump. "I've got an awesome husband, I love this house, and I feel good about my job. Why mess with success? But if you're not happy…"

"I am," Ben said, grabbing a handful of popcorn. He popped a few puffed kernels in his mouth and chewed. After he swallowed, he added, "So happy that I feel like we should share that good fortune with other people."

"Or we could be selfish," Tim said with a slow grin. "For just a little longer."

"We can also do that," Ben said, nestling closer to him and sighing contentedly. "Okay. I'm ready. Let's start the show."

"Cool." Tim reached for the remote and noticed his phone. Still no response. "Hey, what's with Jason lately? He always used to answer our texts right away. Now it's like he has a life or something."

"Terrible, isn't it?" Ben said. "That's probably why he sent us this series to watch."

"It's supposed to be scary," Tim warned.

Ben chuckled. "I'm not worried. Are you?"

"Nah," Tim said, picking up the remote. "I'm way too rugged for that." He pointed it at the television and pressed a few buttons.

Soon they were watching a police officer wake from a coma, the hospital and world around him transformed into an endless nightmare. Each time the characters looked outside to see the living dead walking the street, Tim couldn't help glancing at their own windows where the storm still battered the glass. "Can we switch to something different?" he complained.

"It's Jason's favorite show right now, so no. He keeps

badgering me to watch it, and I might not be crazy about horror either, but…"

"You don't want to hurt his feelings."

"Exactly. You don't like it? I thought the first episode was interesting."

Tim shrugged. "It's okay."

Ben studied him. "Don't tell me you're scared!"

"Zombies freak Chinchilla out! She probably won't be able to sleep tonight."

As if backing him up, she lifted her head and grumbled. Probably due to another blast of lightning and thunder, but he appreciated her support anyway.

"One more episode," Ben pressed. "I'm curious to see what happens."

"Fine." Tim pulled Chinchilla closer, then did the same with Ben. Feeling better, he queued the next episode and tried not to feel so spooked.

He was doing pretty good until about halfway through when the doorbell rang. Just an innocent chiming noise, but it still made him leap from his seat. Chinchilla did the same, stubby legs scrambling as she fled the couch and hid behind it.

"Shaggy and Scooby Doo," Ben said, shaking his head. "Calm down. It's just a trick-or-treater."

"At this hour?" Tim stammered. "In this weather?"

"Never stopped me," Ben said, rising to answer the door.

Tim followed behind as Ben picked up the bowl of candy and fearlessly approached the door. He always was the brave one. Ben didn't peer through the peephole or the side windows, nor did he crack the door to check. Instead he threw it wide open, like someone expecting the delivery of a new couch. What awaited them on the front stoop wasn't a cute little kid wearing a Power Rangers helmet or a Pokémon costume. The stranger was much too tall to be a kid. This was an adult, or at the very least, a teenager. The green army jacket was soaking wet. As was the fur of the werewolf mask, the mismatched eyes of a serial killer staring out at them through two small holes. Tim looked around for a makeshift weapon, spotting only a potted plant that he could throw if he needed to.

"Trick-or-treat," the werewolf said, his voice not sounding particularly sinister.

Tim tensed regardless as the stranger lifted an arm. No weapon was in his hand, but he could still make a fist and start swinging. Instead the hand reached for the mask to pull it off, revealing dark hair that had probably once been a mohawk and had since grown out. The eyes no longer appeared as maddened.

Their visitor grinned, shaking his head when the bowl of candy was held out in offering. "My car broke down," he said, jerking his thumb over his shoulder. "Couple miles down the road."

"Then why didn't you call for a tow?" Tim challenged, puffing up his chest and positioning himself in front of his husband.

Ben pushed his way to the forefront again. "Hey, I'm trying to have a conversation! And you know how bad reception is out here." He addressed the visitor. "I'm guessing that's why you weren't able to call."

The newcomer shook his head. "Reception?"

Tim narrowed his eyes suspiciously. Was this person drunk? "For your cell phone."

"My what?" The stranger seemed to finally understand what they meant. "Oh, like a car phone? I don't have one of those."

What a weirdo! They would ask him to wait in the garage until a tow truck arrived to—

"Come on in," Ben said, stepping aside.

No! What the hell was he thinking? Tim didn't move out of the way. Ben noticed, thrusting the bowl of candy at his gut so hard that Tim was forced to take a step back.

"Thanks," the guy said as he entered. How old was he? Seventeen? Eighteen? "I was on the way to a costume party when the engine started spluttering. No idea why. You'd think I'd at least have an umbrella in the car, but nope! I'm no Boy Scout."

"Me neither," Ben said, smiling pleasantly. "Is that why you wore the mask?"

"Yeah! I figured it would at least keep my head dry. Worked like a charm. They should sell these things year round."

Ben laughed and held out his hand. "I'm Ben, this is Tim."

"Victor," their guest replied, shaking Ben's hand. "Nice place you've got here."

Tim intended to keep it that way. The guy was clearly casing the joint. Not that his husband seemed to notice, since he was leading them to the living room and their awesome flat-screen television, which would get ruined if Victor tried running off with it in this weather.

Ben gestured to the couch, like they would all sit there together, despite one of them being soaking wet. "Make yourself at home until we figure out what to do about your car. We have popcorn and way more candy bars than we—"

"Do you have triple-A?" Tim interjected before Ben could invite their guest to move in. "Or any other sort of roadside assistance?"

Victor rubbed the back of his head sheepishly. "Afraid not. Preparing for the worst isn't my style. I prefer to believe that everything will turn out fine."

"Good philosophy," Ben said. "Think positive. Right now you've got somewhere warm and dry to wait, and we can use our triple-A membership, right?"

This question was addressed to Tim, who shrugged. "Probably. I'll make the call." Hell, he would gladly pay for the guy's car to be towed, just so he could get back to snuggling with Ben on the couch. Hopefully the cushions wouldn't be soggy by then. "I'll get some towels too."

"Oh right!" Ben said. "I'll do that. You make the call."

That left Tim alone with their unwanted guest. They eyed each other, one suspiciously, the other with an uncomfortable amount of self-assurance.

"Looks like you've got it made here," Victor said.

"I do," Tim said. "That's why we invested in the best security system money can buy."

"I don't mean all this stuff." Victor glanced around at it with disinterest. "I meant Ben. He seems like a sweetheart. And hey, you've got food! That's always nice." He helped himself to the popcorn, tossing pieces at himself and managing to catch each one in his mouth.

"Where's your car?" Tim asked, twice as eager now to get this person out of his house. "What street?"

"I'm not too familiar with the area, but it's just down the road."

"Okay. Toward the city or away from it?"

"Away," Victor said. "Yeah, definitely."

"What's the make and model?"

"Does it matter?" Victor asked.

Yes! He hadn't meant it as a philosophical question! "I need to tell the tow truck driver what to look for. He isn't going to come here first."

"Oh." Victor thought it over. "How about a van? Yeah. I just cruise to wherever the wind takes me and sleep in the back. Although to be honest, I never did learn how to drive."

Yup. He was crazy. "So a Dodge?" Tim looked him over. "Or a VW?"

Victor shrugged. "Sure."

"What color?"

"Black," Victor said, this time quickly. "With a red stripe. And a spoiler the same color."

Definitely nuts. Tim called the number on the back of his AAA card and spoke with a representative, all the while keeping an eye on their guest. Ben had returned with a few towels and was laughing at some joke that Victor had made, prompting Tim to entertain another concern: Victor was kind of attractive, in an untamed sort of way. Despite being odd, he seemed friendly enough, but something about him made the hair on the back of Tim's neck stand up. And what was all that talk about Ben being a sweetheart? Ben was definitely sweet, but he was also happily married.

"They should be there in half an hour," Tim said, ending the call. "Want me to drive you to your van?"

"What's the rush?" Ben chided. "It'll only take a few minutes for us to get there. Let him finish drying out." He turned to their guest. "We were in the middle of watching *The Walking Dead*. Care to join us?"

"Is that a TV show?" Victor asked.

"You've never heard of *The Walking Dead*?" Tim said incredulously. "Or cell phones either? Where exactly are you from?"

"Tim," Ben said warningly.

"It's fine," Victor said, shooting him a toothy smile. "I spend a lot of time out in the woods."

"You like to camp?" Ben asked.

"I love it," Victor said, eyes moving back to Tim. "This is my first time in Austin. A friend suggested I come down and check it out. He said I would have fun here."

Tim felt himself shiver. He took back any nice thoughts he'd had about this person. There was something off about him, and his story was fishy. Unfortunately he seemed alone in his suspicions, because soon they were all seated on the couch, Victor between them. They started another episode, but the volume was low and the screen was mostly ignored as Ben made polite conversation. Chinchilla came out of hiding, betraying Tim by sitting at Victor's feet and perking up her ears. He tried to convince himself that she was only interested in the popcorn, since Victor kept playing his game of tossing each piece into his mouth. He never missed, although Tim almost hoped he would, just so he'd have an excuse to berate him. Popcorn wasn't good for dogs.

"Whelp!" Tim said, checking his watch. "Better get out there and meet the tow truck."

"Okay," Victor said, standing along with the other two. "I really appreciate this."

"Not a problem." Tim went to the entryway to fetch his shoes and keys. To his dismay, Victor didn't follow. Neither did anyone else. He returned to the living room to find Victor standing at the back door and gazing out into the night. Annoyingly, Chinchilla was at his feet, stumpy tail still wagging.

"—such a nice place," Victor was saying to Ben, who stood at his side. "Away from all the craziness of the city. You guys have a lot of land out here?"

"Yes," Tim said, "and we keep an eye on all of it. Are you ready?"

Victor didn't move, attention still on the backyard. "Did you see that?"

"Unless you left your hazards on," Tim pressed, "the truck won't find your van. We better get out there. Come on."

"You're right!" Ben said, but not to him. His back was still to Tim as he cupped his hands and pressed them to the glass. "In the corner of the yard. What is that?"

"Are you serious?" Tim asked, moving closer to see. He rubbed at his arms, willing the goosebumps there to disappear.

"Can't see anything now," Victor was saying. "Maybe during the next flash of lightning."

"I saw... *something,*" Ben said, turning to look at him with worry.

"Okay," Tim responded. "I'm sure it's fine. Um. Let me take a look."

He felt like he should open the door and stick his head out to check, but he was too on edge. Tim went instead to one of the adjacent windows. Not seeing much except for rain, he put a comforting arm around Ben's shoulders. They all stood there, clustered together, staring at shadows and waiting for the next—A flash of lightning! Ben gasped and pointed. In the corner of the yard was a silhouette. But of what? An animal? Or maybe a person, crouching down and trying not to be seen.

"There's definitely someone out there," Victor said helpfully. "You guys have any roommates?"

Ben shook his head. "No. Unless... You don't think it's Jason?"

Tim saw that he was serious. "He's still out of town."

"Yeah, but what if something bad happened and he came back?"

To stand in one corner of the yard during this downpour? Ben's expression was pleading, so Tim sighed and reached for the door, the others getting behind him as he opened it. The sound of rain increased, drops hitting his face as he leaned outside. "Hey!" he shouted. "Is someone out there?"

Lightning flashed again. The silhouette extended and stood upright. Whoever it was—and it absolutely was a person—they were tall. Too tall to be Jason. Darkness blanketed the yard again. Tim felt a chill, both figuratively and literally. He stared into the murky night, blinking against rain and trying to see anything at all. When the lightning flashed again, the figure was closer. Much closer!

Tim leapt back, shutting the door and locking it. "Uh, maybe we should call the police."

"Was someone in the car with you?" Ben said, turning to their guest and *finally* sounding suspicious.

"No!" Victor said, holding up his hands. "I know how this looks, but I swear, I have no idea who's out there."

"Then I'm calling the cops," Tim said, pulling out his phone. He fumbled and dropped it, thanks to the steady knocking, deliberate and slow, on the back door. Tim looked up, seeing nothing past the dark panes except four white knuckles that rapped harder and harder against the glass. Then it stopped, all of them holding their breath in the sudden silence. Just when it seemed to be over, a palm slammed against the glass and remained there. A face appeared next to it. Tim recoiled in horror at the gray flesh that looked waterlogged, like whoever was outside had been trapped in the rain for weeks, not just hours. The eyes were white, covered in cataracts, and the cheeks were sunken. As much as he felt like fleeing, his husband seemed drawn to this apparition and was reaching for the door.

"What are you doing?" Tim cried. "Stop!"

He was too late. Ben had opened the door, the hiss of rain joined by a similar voice, raspy and drawn out. Lightning illuminated the apparition, maggots dropping from the torn lips.

"I caaaame foor myyyy caaaat."

Tim lunged forward, shouldering the door shut. His fingers found the lock. Then he grabbed Ben and dragged him toward the kitchen. His husband was too shocked to resist.

"Don't worry," Tim was saying, mostly for his own benefit. "I'll protect us. I've got this. I'll keep us safe!"

They made it to the kitchen, but not alone. Victor had tagged along, looking a little too cool about the situation, but Tim had a solution to that problem. He opened one of the kitchen cabinets, reaching for a cereal box far in the back. The healthy kind with no sugar, additives, or artificial flavors. Neither of them ever touched it—not even during Ben's recent health kick—which made it the perfect hiding spot. He thrust his hand in the box, felt cold steel, and pulled out a gun.

Tim swung around, pointing the pistol at the kitchen door. When he saw no threat there, he pointed the gun in Victor's direction instead. For someone faced with his own mortality, Victor seemed exceptionally calm, but he still raised his hands, voice reassuring.

"You've got the wrong idea."

"Just keep your distance," Tim said, trying to remember if the safety was still on.

"You have a gun?" Ben said incredulously. Then he stepped in front of it, sounding angry. "Stop waving it around! Why do you have a gun?"

"In case Ryan shows up and tries to shoot us again!" Tim moved to the side, trying to keep an eye on Victor.

"You have a gun," Ben said, still struggling to understand, "and you keep it in a cereal box."

"Ryan," Tim repeated. "Have you forgotten?"

Ben shook his head, clearly disapproving. "Is this the only one? Or do you have others hidden around the house?"

"Uhhh," Tim said, trying to decide which was worse, the likelihood of him sleeping on the couch tonight or the potentially dangerous stranger standing in their kitchen. "I just want to keep us safe."

Ben didn't seem to hear him, head bowed in thought. Then he looked up. "That person outside, did you recognize him at all?"

"Person?" Tim repeated incredulously. "I'm pretty sure that was a freaking monster!"

Ben shook his head. "I'm serious. That looked like… It looked like Jace."

Tim's mouth dropped open. "Unless he has a creepy twin brother you've never told me about, I think we can rule out that being Jace! No offense."

"He was wearing some sort of uniform," Victor chimed in. "Not a pilot exactly. More like a…"

"Flight attendant?" Ben asked, voice hopeful.

Victor snapped his fingers. "Yeah! That's it exactly. A flight attendant. How weird!"

"It's not weird," Ben said, moving toward the living room. "It's Jace! We've got to let him in!"

"Stop!" Tim grabbed his arm. "You know it can't be him!"

Ben spun around, expression defiant. "Why not?"

"Because he's… You know why. He's dead."

The anger left Ben's eyes, replaced by hurt. "You're right. But you heard what he said. He came back for his cat. Yes, he's dead, but maybe—" He shook his head, as if realizing he was being silly, but he said it anyway. "Maybe he's a zombie."

"Or maybe this is some sort of messed up prank." Tim pointed the gun at Victor again. "If you think this is funny..."

Victor sighed wearily. "What is it about guns that makes people think they are judge, jury, and executioner? Try using your brain instead! If this was a prank, do you really think I would keep perpetuating it when I've got a gun pointed at me? Or when your husband is so upset?"

"How'd you know that we're married?" Tim asked. "Or that we're together at all? No, something's not right. I'm calling the police." He reached for his pocket with his free hand and found it empty. Of course! He had dropped his phone by the back door and hadn't picked it up again in all the commotion. "Give me your phone, Ben. *Ben?*"

"What? Oh." Ben pulled his attention from the kitchen door, halfheartedly searching himself before giving up and shaking his head. "Samson is buried out there. Where we saw Jace digging."

"That isn't Jace!" Tim said, temper rising. "Stay right here. I'll go get my phone and—" Thunder shook the house, the lights flickering. "Fuck. Okay, maybe we'll *all* go together to the living room."

"Fine by me," Victor said, scratching one hand with the other, as if it itched. His brow looked a little sweaty too. The calm demeanor was finally breaking! "Hey, do you guys have a calendar?"

"Yes," Ben said, starting to point toward the refrigerator.

Tim pushed his hand down before he could. "Why? You know what day it is. October thirty-first. Halloween."

"Yeah, but..." Victor moved toward the direction Ben had indicated, scratching the back of his neck now.

"Stay where you are!" Tim shouted.

"Seriously?" Ben demanded. "Do we really want more blood spilled on this floor? Put the gun down."

It wasn't doing any good anyway. Victor was still searching for the calendar, the rain was splattering in torrents against the windows, and Ben was moving toward one to look outside. Tim was torn between wanting to watch him protectively while needing to keep an eye on Victor. The situation was getting out of control!

"EVERYBODY STOP!" Tim shouted. The lights flickered and went out. He did his best not to yelp. He failed. "Okay," he said, trying to calm himself as he peered through the gloom. "Okay okay okay. Listen. All three of us are going to the living room. Victor, if this really has nothing to do with you, then it's in your best interest that we call the police because there's an intruder here."

Victor nodded, scratching at his chest. "Technically he's not an intruder because he's still outside. He might be on your land and you might think he's trespassing, but saying you own what's out there is like someone saying they own the planet. Fences don't mean a thing. How far down does a property line extend? Through the core of the earth and out the other side? Because someone's probably waiting there who thinks he owns the land too!"

Tim stared, then turned to Ben. "Can I please shoot him?"

"No. Put the gun down."

Tim did so, noticing that something was missing. The storm! He still heard a boom of thunder, but it sounded distant now. Only the rush of wind blowing through trees remained. That, and the sound of his own thudding heart.

"The rain cleared up," Ben said, leaning against the window and looking upward. "The clouds are thinning. I can see the sky!"

"Really?" Victor asked, hurrying over to look.

Tim got there first, not trusting his intentions. He glanced up at the heavens and saw moonlight seeping from around the clouds, but he was more concerned with the yard and what might be in it. Seeing wasn't as difficult now. The yard seemed deserted.

"Hey," Victor said, urgency in his voice at last. "I need to use the restroom."

"Now?" Tim asked incredulously.

Victor nodded, a bead of sweat catching the moonlight as it trickled down his temple. "Right now."

"There's one by the entryway," Tim said. "You can go after I get my phone." He suspected Victor would bolt out the front door, but that was fine with him. He didn't want this person in his home anymore. "Actually," he said, "we'll go there first." That way Victor—or whatever his name was—would leave and rejoin the asshole who had been lurking around the backyard while masquerading as Jace.

"Thanks," Victor said, leading the way.

Another good idea. That way, if Victor's accomplice had snuck inside and was feeling stabby, he would attack his friend first. Tim made sure Ben was behind him as they crept through the darkness. His eyes darted around the living room, trying to spy potential danger, but it was hard to see in the limited light. They reached the entryway without incident. Tim went toward the front door, certain that was the actual goal.

"Which way?" Victor asked.

"The door on the right," Tim said, still expecting a ruse. To his surprise, Victor really went into the bathroom. The knob clinked as it was locked, but whatever. He could stay in there or slip through the window so long as he kept away from Ben.

Chinchilla reappeared, pawing at the bathroom door like she wanted in too. What the hell was wrong with her? "Let's get my phone," he whispered, turning around.

He was alone.

Lightning flashed. Once and then twice more. Tim used each opportunity to search his surroundings. Ben wasn't in the entryway. The living room was also empty, but when he looked toward the back door, his heart nearly stopped. The tall figure had returned, and in front of him—still indoors, thank god—was Ben. He had his hand pressed to the window, and by the time lightning flashed again, he saw the creep outside did too.

"It's definitely Jace!" Ben called.

"Get away from there!" Tim shouted, breaking into a sprint.

"I'm letting him in."

"No!"

Tim heard scattered drops pelting the house before the skies let loose again. The sound of the foul weather doubled in volume as the back door was opened. Tim charged and shoved himself against it, smelling damp decay as the door slammed shut.

Ben was already pushing at him in protest. "It's Jace!" Ben shouted. "Let him in!"

Tim pressed himself against the door and locked it, refusing to budge. That meant he was close to the glass and the creature just beyond. He had to admit it did look a lot like Jace. A dead and decayed version, at least. He stared into the eyes, trying to recognize who was really under the white contacts. Greg? Was this an ill-conceived joke? A way to keep the memory of his best friend alive? The zombie raised a hand. It touched a wrinkled finger to the glass and began wiping beads of water away, one stroke at a time. Tim watched, increasingly fascinated, because a message was being spelled out. The pale finger pulled away. In backwards letters, already fading, was written: *HoMewREecKer*

"Okay," Tim conceded. "Maybe it is Jace."

"I told you!" Ben said.

"That doesn't mean we should let him in!"

They heard a commotion from the bathroom, like Victor had slipped and fallen.

"I just want to talk to him," Ben pleaded. "He won't hurt me."

"What about me?" Tim said manically. This couldn't be happening!

They heard a pounding on the front door and turned as one to see a flashlight beam cut through the gloom briefly before disappearing again. Glowing pulses illuminated the darkness beyond the windows, some sort of emergency vehicle outside.

"Thank God," Tim breathed, making the sign of the cross. With his gun. He didn't know how, but the police were here! Maybe they were searching for two escaped lunatics. That would explain everything. "Let's go!"

He tucked the gun in his belt and grabbed Ben's hand, dragging him toward the front of the house. The officer outside knocked again. Tim opened the door, his relief turning to disappointment. He was facing a normal human being, not a police officer. The man was dressed in blue coveralls smudged with oil. Like a mechanic. Or the driver of a tow truck, because that's what was parked in the driveway, its orange lights still twirling.

"Mr. Wyman?" the driver said, turning off his flashlight with a click. "You called for a tow?"

"Right." He stepped back so the man could enter and get out of the rain. "The guy you're here for is in the bathroom."

They heard a growl come from that direction. Strange. Chinchilla usually didn't behave that way. Or sound so menacing.

"That's the thing," the tow truck driver said. "I drove up and down the road you done told me about, and I didn't see no van. There ain't nothin' out there but roadkill."

"I knew it!" Tim said. "He's full of shit!"

"Who?"

"Victor. The guy in the bathroom." Tim turned toward it. "Hey! You! Get out here right now!"

They heard a crashing noise. Was Victor trying to escape out the bathroom window? Although it didn't sound like breaking glass. More like shattered porcelain. What was he doing in there? Still maintaining her vigil, Chinchilla whimpered and looked back at him, as if eager to sneak inside.

Tim marched forward and pounded a fist on the bathroom door. "Get out here! NOW!"

The door exploded. Tim was thrown back, landing on the cold tiles of the entryway and sliding to a stop. He looked up in time to see a beast covered in dark hair. It walked upright on two legs, the gangly arms ending in long clawed fingers. The creature wore the tattered remains of a green army jacket, the protruded maw opening to expose long rows of sharp teeth. A werewolf! Tim couldn't believe his eyes, but he didn't have time to stare because he was too concerned for Ben, who was slowly backing away instead of running. As for the tow truck driver, a wet stain appeared in those coveralls before he raced for the front door. The werewolf reacted, smelling his fear or maybe his urine. With disturbing speed, the beast pounced. Its mouth latched onto the tow truck driver's neck and shook, the flesh tearing. Crimson rain splattered the entryway, a choking noise spluttering and fading as the man's body slumped to the floor.

This was real. Tim had no doubt anymore because even the most elaborate hoax couldn't fake the smell of hot human blood, a dark puddle of it inching toward him. He was vaguely aware of a shattering sound from the rear of the house. This time it really was glass. So much for the back door. Jace the zombie was coming to finish them off, but only if the werewolf didn't get them first.

He looked up at Ben, wanting to tell him to run and save himself. His husband was frozen with fear, hands held before him defensively, but they would be ineffective. Ben needed a diversion so he could escape, and only Tim could give it to him.

He scrambled to his feet, pulled the gun loose, and pointed. A number of action movie one-liners flashed through his mind, but he didn't have time to utter any. The werewolf had turned toward Ben, maw surrounded by glistening wet fur. Tim fired. Again and again, the sound making his ears ring until the gun started clicking instead. Each bullet hit its mark, creating small explosions of dark blood, but the beast barely paused. It growled something, which he swore sounded like "cheap bullets."

They definitely weren't silver! Ben remained frozen with fear. Tim had to do something. He tossed the gun aside and launched forward, intending to throw himself between Ben and the monster. Too bad his foot slipped in blood. Tim fell face first to the floor, knowing this mistake would cost Ben his life.

The werewolf resumed stalking its prey. Ben finally reacted, walking backward with clumsy steps and bumping into a tall grey figure. The zombie! It placed a decaying hand on Ben's shoulder, then carefully moved him aside. Closer to safety. Tim stared in disbelief as the zombie lurched forward and raised two fists, as if intending to enter a boxing match with the werewolf.

This was definitely Jace, still showing Tim up and making him look bad, even from the grave. Then again, right now he was willing to accept any help they could get. Chinchilla felt differently, growling at Jace, but Tim looked away from her when the werewolf lunged.

Jace swung and struck the mouth full of fangs. That brought back memories, Tim rubbing his jaw as he got to his feet. The werewolf appeared surprised, then lashed out a second time. Jace managed to dodge and get in another punch, but this only infuriated the beast, who recovered quickly and sank its teeth into Jace's shoulder. It released him just as quickly, yipping and shaking its head like Chinchilla had once when she had gobbled up a fallen chili pepper from the kitchen floor. Zombies didn't taste very good, it would seem.

"Caaaan't killll meee," Jace said, raising a finger and pointing at the door. "Alreaady dead. Tak-k-k-e your meeeat and gooooo."

The werewolf looked to the bloody pool where the tow truck driver lay motionless, then back at Jace, weighing its options. It decided, turning to scoop up the driver's body in its jaws. Then it loped out the front door and disappeared into the night. Chinchilla trotted to the open door, only stopping briefly to consider Tim before she gave chase, stubby tail wagging gleefully.

"Wait!" Tim shouted, attempting to follow, but by the time he stepped outside into the rain, she was gone. He heard a baleful howl in the distance that was joined by another much higher in pitch. "Traitor," Tim mumbled, wanting to sulk, but he needed to check on Ben.

Once inside again, he stopped short because Ben had thrown himself into Jace's embrace. Arms wrapped around Ben like a boa constrictor. Their mouths neared. Tim *really* didn't want to see them kiss, especially since one of them had maggoty lips.

"Uh, hey," he tried. "I know this is weird for us all, so why don't we take things slow. Um… Hello?"

It was no good. Ben was crying and murmuring gentle words. Jace was groaning, the sound like wind blowing through a crypt. Then they kissed. Tim stared, horrified, especially when Jace pulled his head back and Ben's bottom lip remained trapped in his teeth. Before he could act, Jace whipped away his head, tearing off Ben's lip in the process and chewing as the pink flesh disappeared into his mouth. Ben screamed and struggled but remained trapped in those arms. Tim ran over and pounded on Jace with his fists, but it was no good. He needed a real weapon! He had another gun hidden in the bathroom. Tim scurried for the door that led there, only to discover more chaos. The toilet had been reduced to shards, water soaking the floor, but he ignored this, yanking at the cabinet beneath the sink. Inside, at the bottom of a pile of towels they never used, was another gun. It slipped from his fingers as he pulled it free, landing in the watery mess on the floor. He was taking too long! Ben had gone quiet now. Was he—

His fingers brushed against the gun. He grabbed it, stood, and ran back to the entryway. Aim for the head! That's how it worked, right?

"Let him go!" Tim shouted, wanting a clear shot.

To his surprise, Jace did. Ben was released but he just stood there. He didn't try to get away, or turn to face Tim. Not until his name was spoken.

"Ben?" Tim said, voice shaking. "Baby? I need you to come over here."

Only Ben's head moved, turning until his chin was lined up with his shoulders. Then, after some strain and a cracking noise, the head continued turning until it was on backwards. A white film covered the eyes, the skin an ashen tone. Ben wore a permanent smile, thanks to the missing bottom lip, black blood trickling down his chin.

Jace placed a stiff arm around his shoulders. "'til deathhh no loooongerrrr do usss part-t-t-t."

Ben's smile widened. "Grrrrrruuuuuuuuuh," he added.

Tim gripped the shaking gun with both hands to steady it. He aimed first at Jace's head, then at Ben's, trying to decide what to do. Put them out of their misery? Ben's head twisted around, facing the right way again, and Jace took him into his arms. They were hugging! Tim supposed they were happy to be reunited. "Okay," he stammered. "I'm… I'm going to let you go. Just get out of here, all right? Try to be happy doing—whatever it is that zombies do."

"Eeeeat," Jace said, dead eyes fixating on him again. "Weeee eeeeat."

Ben turned, this time with his entire body, and nodded eagerly. "Hnnnnnngry!"

"C'mon," Tim pleaded, taking a step back. "Just go!"

Jace shook his head. "We neeeed your..." He lurched forward a step. "Braaaains!"

Tim pulled the trigger, but the gun clicked. What the hell? Had the cartridge gotten wet? He tried again with the same results. Then he gave up, tucked it in his belt, and ran. Not outside. The werewolf was still out there somewhere, along with his treacherous mutt. Upstairs! He could barricade himself in one of the rooms until morning. That was the rule! When the sun came up, the monsters went away. Luckily for him, zombies weren't very fast and he had always been a good runner. Tim feinted to the right and then darted to the left, slipping on blood as he ran but still escaping the entryway. He was through the living room and up the stairs with no sign of pursuit, but it was only a matter of time. Even if Jace and Ben decided to lurch their way to a second honeymoon, what if the werewolf returned?

The lights flickered and came back on. He looked up at the ceiling lamp in the hallway with gratitude and noticed a dangling rope. The attic! He could hide up there. No way would the zombies be able to follow, and the werewolf... Eric had owned silverware. *Real* silverware. He and Ben never used it because it was a pain to polish, but at least it would give Tim something to defend himself with. Could a werewolf be stabbed to death with a silver dessert fork? Worth a shot!

He leapt, pulling the rope that brought the attic stairs down. As Tim clambered up them, he heard groaning from downstairs. The zombies were either on their way or doing each other. Yuck! Hauling up the stairs again from within the attic was a struggle, but he managed. He yanked a string to turn on the light, then glanced around, trying to remember where he had last seen the silverware. The attic was musty, the swaying light from the free-swinging lightbulb catching dust motes in the air. His eyes fell on a portrait he had painted ages ago of Ryan, who looked adorable and sweet in a pink bathrobe. Oh how Tim longed for those simpler times! Sure, dating Ryan had been a nightmare, but not a literal one!

Tim moved deeper into the attic, shifting boxes from one stack to another as he searched. Some he dismissed by weight, since they weren't heavy enough to contain what he needed. He finally found one that felt right. He shook it, hearing clanking from inside. He had just torn open the cardboard flaps and grabbed a utensil when he heard his name.

"Tim."

He spun around, pointing his newfound weapon at what he expected to be a zombie or werewolf. Instead he saw a beautiful face from his past. Ryan stood there among the clutter of old memories and forgotten things. He looked good, cheeks still rosy with youth, his skin smooth and unblemished. The pink bath robe was pulled tight around his petite waist.

Ryan smiled, blue eyes sparkling. "I missed you, baby!"

"You look just like—" His eyes moved to the painting, but the canvas now showed only an empty background. "No." Tim shook his head in disbelief. "I'm going crazy. Or I'm tripping! The mushroom pizza from earlier… Those were the wrong kind of 'shrooms!"

"You're not tripping." Ryan's laugh was pleasant as he came near. "I of all people should know. But we could try that together, if you'd like."

"Uh-uh," Tim said, backing away. "You're some sort of demon." He raised the utensil defensively. A spoon! A freaking spoon, and not even a big one! He tossed it away in disgust and reached for his gun. Even if it was too wet to fire, he could still pretend.

It worked. Ryan stopped and cocked his head. "I suppose I deserve that. I mean, I *did* shoot you, but I was jealous. You were with Ben when you should have been with me. Now we've got another chance. Ben is dead and swapping zombie spit with his old lover. You're out of the picture, and I'm out of the painting, so why not?"

"What's going on?" Tim stammered.

"It's magic, baby," Ryan said, moving forward again. "Don't question it. Just enjoy the benefits." With stunning swiftness, Ryan swept across the attic, seeming to float, and snatched the gun from Tim's hands. He was just inches away now, those sky-blue eyes mesmerizing. Ryan brought the gun to his lips, licking the end of the barrel. Then he giggled and tossed it away. "I want to suck your dick," he said with a smile that revealed two sharp incisors. "No, that's not quite right. I mean, I *do*, but there's something else I want to suck too. Remember when I used to bite you?"

Tim tried to move but could not. His muscles were no longer under his command. All he could do was speak. "What are you?"

Ryan's eyes lit up. Literally. They were glowing with an unholy light. "Isn't it obvious?" Ryan cried. He threw his arms wide, his robe opening and billowing behind him like a pink cape. The incisors were even longer now. "I want to suck your blood!"

A vampire! Ryan pressed against Tim, rubbing their bodies together. Fangs pricked at his neck teasingly but didn't penetrate. Tim tried again to move. It was hopeless. Ryan had some sort of control over him. Then again, hadn't he always? Tim nearly laughed at the thought but was too damn scared. Ryan ripped open his shirt, an ice cold hand sliding over Tim's chest and down his stomach before plunging into his jeans. Tim's body reacted—just one more muscle he didn't have control over.

Ryan smiled sweetly at him while pumping. "We're always going to be together," he whispered. "You and me, honey, for all of eternity!"

Ryan fell to his knees. He had Tim's jeans open and underwear down with impossible speed. Ryan's mouth opened to take him in, and just when it started to feel good, the fangs bit down, breaking the skin and plunging into his flesh. Tim groaned, pleasure mixing with pain as his life-force was slowly drained away.

"You always were a fucking leech," he managed to grunt.

Ryan didn't respond. He just kept slurping, taking advantage of all Tim had to offer once again, except this time that included his freedom, his life, his soul.

Tim shot awake, heart still pounding. He mistook the heavy blankets for Ryan and shoved them away. Then he forced himself upright, back drenched in sweat. From next to him, something stirred, skeletal fingers reaching outward. Tim yelped and jerked away. A second later, Ben sat up, hair a mess as he peered at him blearily.

"What's wrong?"

"I had a bad dream," Tim said, hammered by adrenaline. "A horrible dream!"

"Told you not to stay up watching that show," Ben said, switching on a bedside lamp. The skeletal hand appeared fleshier and friendlier in the light, the palm sliding up and down Tim's back in reassurance. "Geez, you're soaking wet. It must have been a bad one! Eating so much candy probably didn't help either."

"I guess not," he said, looking around the room for any sign of the boogeyman.

"You're safe now," Ben murmured, settling down again. "What was your dream about?"

Tim shook his head, the details confusing and fading quickly. "A hitchhiker. No, someone's car had broken down. Then this dead guy—actually it was... Oh. Never mind. Uhhh. At the very end, I was in the attic with Ryan, and he wouldn't stop trying to bite my neck and... Um. I don't remember."

"You better not!" Ben said, sounding less sympathetic. "Was this a bad dream or a wet dream?"

"With Ryan there wasn't much difference." This earned him cold silence, so he added, "I'm safe and sound with you. That's the important thing."

"Go back to sleep," Ben suggested.

But he couldn't. Not until he calmed down. Tim rose, checking Chinchilla's bed on the way to the bathroom. She was snoozing peacefully. Once dressed in his robe, he went downstairs, deciding that a midnight snack might help him feel better. He had one of the cabinets open and was reaching for his favorite cereal when he noticed a long-abandoned box toward the back. He and Ben had bought it when first trying to eat healthier, and after one bowl, they decided their usual breakfasts were healthy enough. Tim moved other items aside, pulled the cereal box free, and shoved his hand inside. His fingers touched kernels of whole-grain wheat and nothing more.

Breathing out in relief—despite not being sure why—he put it all back and returned upstairs. Tim got into bed, cuddling close to Ben, where he would remain until the sun came up. Because that's when the monsters went away.

"You sure that wasn't mean?" Victor asked.

Jace stood next to the bed and its two occupants, not feeling at all remorseful. "It was fun," he said. "People love being scared. Just look at how many flock to haunted houses at this time of year."

Victor remained uncertain. "Yeah, but at least they know it's fake. We could have traumatized him."

Jace shrugged. "They almost never remember these sorts of dreams. And he's fine. Just look at him snoring there with his thing pressed against Ben."

"Speaking of monsters," Victor said, sounding impressed.

Jace glared. "You aren't making me feel better."

"He's got a nice cock," Victor said with a chuckle. "So what? And is that what this whole thing was about? You wanting to make yourself feel like the bigger man?"

"No." Jace sighed. "I *do* fantasize about this sometimes. Not the zombie theme, but I envy the nice life they have together. I'm happy for them, but is it so wrong that I wish I could come back and take over from here?"

"Not at all," Victor said. "You love Ben and want to be part of his life. You still are, but of course it would be nice if you could be there for the physical stuff. Or if he could remember the rest. I'm just not sure what that has to do with chewing Ben's lips off or making Tim think his ex-boyfriend is back as a vampire."

Jace fought down a smile. "Just running with the holiday theme. I'm a festive kind of guy!"

"You're jealous is what you are," Victor replied.

"I am not! Although maybe I did get a little carried away. I thought he would wake up sooner than he did."

"Then let's come back here sometime and give him nice dreams."

Jace looked down at Tim and sighed. "He's living a dream. The nicest one there is."

"Okay, then next year we come back, but we let him rescue Ben from the monsters. How about that?"

"Fair enough," Jace conceded. "I still get to kiss Ben though. In a less violent way next time."

"We should keep most of the stuff with Ryan too," Victor said, a hint of suggestion in his voice. "That part was hot."

Jace perked up, recognizing a silver lining when he saw one. "You think so?"

"Yeah!" Victor said. "Very inspired. Besides, who hasn't gotten so horny that they felt like biting someone. You know what I mean?"

"No," Jace admitted, "but I'm willing to find out."

They left the room together, jostling each other playfully while matching each other's smiles. For the remaining hours of All Hallows' Eve, two ghosts hid themselves away in an attic and made things go bump in the night.

Something Like Samson

by Jay Bell

Part One: Warrensburg, 1996

The world is new, but I cannot see it. I can only feel. I am wet, and that makes me cold until a tongue moves over my fur. Soon I am dry. I squirm nearer, needing the warmth. Exhausted. Confused. Hungry. Instinct drives me to lift my head. I cry out in frustration and hear nothing in return, but my nose catches a scent, insisting it has found what I need. I crawl until I find the source. Then I move my head from left to right. When my nose bumps against a nipple, I open my mouth and drink. I feel other bodies joining me, one to each side, and that is good, because now I am full. I am happy and content and warm as I press myself against the largest body. A gentle vibration soothes me, and I try my best to purr in return to say thank you. A word comes to me then, and it is the most beautiful of its kind. I find myself repeating it as I drift off to sleep. Mother.

Samson opened his eyes, pleased that he'd had his favorite dream again. This was soon forgotten because the world was so much more interesting now. He could see, which made it easy to discover where the next game would be. His brothers and sisters had all woken before him. Even his mother wasn't in the cardboard box. Samson felt a little sad about this. He used to start his morning with the nipple, but lately if he tried, she growled and nudged him away.

Meerrow! Meerrow! Meerrow!

Samson perked up. His mother was calling him to eat! He rotated his ears, trying to get a fix on the sound. Then he leapt over the edge of the box and ran with all his strength. He loved running! Almost as much as he loved pouncing. Not as much as he loved eating though. The carpet gave way to slick linoleum. Samson saw his brothers and sisters gathered around two plates and was worried he would miss out. That's why he didn't slow until he had reached them. His tried using his claws to stop, but they didn't work here like in the other room, and he ran right into Munch.

Munch hissed. He was always hissing, but Samson didn't care. He was too eager to shove his nose into the plate and start gobbling the little pieces of kibble. When he had first started eating like this, the kibble had been soft—mixed with water, judging by the smell—but his teeth were stronger now. He had no trouble crunching the kibble into oblivion. He would very much like to do the same thing to a mouse. Samson wasn't sure what a mouse was, but Munch swore he had caught one. According to him, it had been three times larger than their mother, had leathery skin, and breathed fire. Samson thought this sounded like something from the books the Woman was always reading aloud from. She was a funny creature and much bigger than their mother, although he hadn't seen her breathe fire. Her wrinkled skin *was* a little leathery, but her hands were soft and always gentle.

Samson was still thinking of her when he finished eating. Maybe she could teach him something that Munch didn't know. Wouldn't that be satisfying! He padded into the living room, intending to go straight to the chair where the Woman often sat during the day. This took longer than it should have. So much conspired to distract him, like a little tuft of hair blowing across the carpet that he needed to attack, or the foam ball that he loved to bat around. Eventually he made it to his destination and saw legs in front of the big brown chair. The Woman was there!

Samson bounded in her direction. Once he reached the chair, he made his muscles tight, just like he did before a play-fight. Then he released, jumping and trusting his claws to attach to the brown fabric. They did and he kicked, retracting his claws and using them again higher up on the chair. In this way he climbed to the top, happy to see that he wouldn't have to share the Woman's lap with his siblings. He was the only one smart enough to come straight here after eating.

"Look who it is!" said the Woman. "What a cute little fella. It's Samson, isn't it?"

Humans had a terrible sense of smell. Otherwise she wouldn't have needed to ask, because it was obvious. Why didn't she try sniffing him? Instead she had given them all names. He was Samson, and his sister—his favorite sibling—was Delilah. Then there was Nemo and Matilda, and finally, Munchausen, who they all called Munch because none of them had time for such a long name. Samson was glad he wasn't expected to say any of their names aloud. They were too complicated for his tongue. He knew the names all came from books, and that books were filled with secrets. He hoped to learn some by being here, although if he was honest, he tended to fall asleep whenever the Woman read out loud. Her voice was too much like a purr.

She used her gnarled hands to scoop him up from the arm of the chair. When she put him down, it was on her lap, which was soft and warm. She didn't pick up her book again, like she normally did. Instead she pet him and sighed. "We'll have to find you all homes soon. I want to keep you, I really do, but I'm on a budget and well… I don't want to be a crazy cat lady. Not more than I already am."

Humans made a lot of noise. Samson had gotten pretty good at reading their body language and understanding some of the sounds, but right now his belly was full and he needed a quick nap. Then it was back to playtime. But first, another dream. Samson hoped this one would be about the mouse. He was certain he could kill it even faster than Munch had. Samson just hoped it tasted as good as his mother's milk.

Everything was changing. Nemo was the first to go. Samson missed him because he was good at snuggling. Nemo didn't growl or snap if Samson moved around too much while napping. They were friends, but when a large man came to the house, he took Nemo with him when he left. Munch was next. More than once, Samson had wished his pushy brother would go away, but now that it had happened, he regretted those thoughts. For a few days, it seemed like that would be it. No more separations, but then a woman and two children came. They picked up him and his sister, talking about which one they liked best and for whatever reason, chose Matilda. Now she was gone too.

Samson tried not to worry about it. Eating was nicer without so much competition, and the Woman's lap was often empty if he needed a place to sleep. He still had Delilah to play with, but during their games, they would sometimes stop and look to the door where people came and went. When sleeping, Samson draped himself over his sister, just to make sure nobody could take her away.

It didn't work. Another stranger showed up. Samson was

worried, but too curious not to go and look. With his sister at his side, they crept toward the front of the house where the door was open and the Woman was talking with a man.

"Of course!" she said. "You're the boy from the gas station! Young man, I should say. When you get to be my age, everyone looks like a baby. Sorry, I've forgotten your name. Another perk of getting old!"

"It's fine," said the young man. "No one can be expected to remember everything. That's why we have each other, to help keep those memories alive. And it's why we tell stories, because if you think about it, they're just memories wrapped up with a bow and made presentable."

The Woman laughed. "You know, after our conversation at Bernie's, I wondered if you were always so philosophical. Now I have my answer!"

Delilah crept forward to get a better look. Samson wanted to hold her back and maybe convince her to hide, but he was also curious. Following his sister's lead, he bounded over to the couch and hid behind one corner. Then he peeked around it.

The person at the door had funny fur. All humans did, since it only covered the top of their heads, but this one was especially weird since the fur was longer in the middle and short on the sides. He wasn't very big. Especially when compared to the man who had taken Nemo with him.

"Not everyone appreciates my musings," the young man said. "Even I get a little sick of them sometimes. I'm Victor, by the way. Nice to see you again."

"Come in," the Woman said. "Where are my manners? I'm Mrs. Henderson, just in case you've forgotten."

Mrs. Henderson? Samson should have known that the Woman would come up with a funny name for herself too.

"I take it you're here about the kittens?" she continued.

Samson exchanged a glance with Delilah and flicked his ear in just the right way to say, *I don't like this.*

Delilah looked to the stranger. Then her tail swept back and forth before she bristled her whiskers outward. *At least he doesn't have children with him. They pulled my tail!*

True, but Samson didn't want to lose his favorite playmate. He leaned against his sister before leaping forward in excitement. *Maybe he'll take us both with him.*

Maybe he's got treats, Delilah said, walking forward and shaking her tail. When this failed to get the attention of the humans, she meowed.

"Ah, there they are!" Mrs. Henderson said. "We're down to our last two, Samson and Delilah. I didn't plan it that way. Are you familiar with their story?"

Victor squatted to be closer to them and held out a finger. Samson made sure to stay away. Delilah wasn't as careful and went to sniff him. "It's a Biblical story, right? Samson was the guy with the hair. That was the source of his secret power. He was like Superman until they cut it off."

"Exactly," Mrs. Henderson said, "and like many stories in the Bible, this one was—*ahem*—borrowed from an older religion. Samson is based on Shamash, a Babylonian sun god. His hair represents the rays of the sun. The way he loses his strength represents those rays growing dim as the sun sets. Shamash was often depicted as a lion, which makes sense if you think of the mane. I've always enjoyed symbolism, so when I was trying to choose names… Did I mention that people find my musings tiresome too?"

"Not me!" Victor laughed. "Keep going!"

Samson didn't understand most of this. He had other concerns, because now Victor had stopped petting Delilah and was reaching for him. The hand stopped just before making contact. This allowed him to stretch out his neck and sniff the fingers, which smelled smoky, like the time Mrs. Henderson had burnt her toast.

"Have you had a pet before?" she asked.

"No." Victor stroked Samson's head and stood again. "My mom has. The kitten would be a gift for her. She's had a hard time lately, and I think a pet would cheer her up. She's always talking about the cats she had on the farm as a child."

"I see. Well, I was hoping to keep one of them. Delilah, probably, since mama cat has been pushing the boys away lately."

That was true. Mother wasn't as friendly with him as she used to be. She had even swiped at Munch the day before he was taken away. Samson didn't care. He didn't want to go! He looked at his sister, flattening his ears against his head to show how unhappy he was.

Delilah pounced, playfully biting at his neck as they rolled.

Samson's problems were soon forgotten as he gleefully lost himself in the game. The humans laughed and kept making strange sounds at each other. He ignored them, and when the battle was over, sat down next to his sister to take a bath. He was licking a paw when the humans approached again.

"You don't own a cat carrier?" Mrs. Henderson was saying. "I might have one I can lend you."

"We're just a few blocks over," Victor replied. "I think we'll be okay. This one is the boy?"

Before he knew what was happening, hands were around him and Samson was lifted up. Humans not only talked too much. They were huge! He found himself higher than he could leap, higher even than the big brown chair Mrs. Henderson often read in. He splayed his legs outward, paws pressing against a chest until Victor's hand swept beneath them, gathering his legs up into a bundle. Then the jacket he wore was wrapped around Samson like a blanket. He squirmed to turn around so he could see.

The Woman looked different from up here. Not just her, but the rest of the house too. Samson was curious, but he still wanted down.

"Yeah, we'll definitely be fine," Victor said. "I'll make sure he doesn't get away."

"Okay. I hope your mother likes him! If not, you know where I am. Or if you crave the company of someone who enjoys a good musing, I'm here for that too."

Victor laughed, the sound a deep rumble against Samson's body. "I'll keep that in mind. Thank you. For the kitten and the conversation."

"The pleasure was mine!"

Victor was turning toward the door. Samson knew what was coming next, but he didn't want to leave. He squirmed again. His strength failed him. It was hopeless. All he could do was search the ground for his sister. Delilah was looking up at him, and when their eyes met, she blinked them once very slowly. *I love you.*

Samson was too scared to do the same. Victor turned before he could even think to. The door was opened and—

Everything.

Samson had climbed up to a window once. He had looked through it and knew that there were rooms out there very different from the ones he lived in. What he hadn't realized is just how vast they would be, or how many scents and sounds would batter his senses. He watched the world move by at a dizzying pace before he couldn't take anymore. Samson squirmed once again, this time deeper into the jacket, because he no longer wanted to see. He closed his eyes and shivered, hoping that this was a different sort of dream, and that he would wake up next to his sister and mother, ready for more food and games.

The light of a new day broke through the darkness outside the windows, an orange glow on the horizon. The rays of the sun gave the lion its strength! Samson leapt and latched his claws into the corner of the mattress. After kicking and pulling himself up, he slunk closer to the slumbering form. He spotted a foot sticking out from the blanket. He shook his rump back and forth in anticipation, then pounced, batting at the foot and pressing his teeth against a toe before he raced away again.

This caused a shriek. And a laugh. The form in the bed slowly rose. The Other Woman. She wasn't as old as the one he used to know. Her name wasn't as long or silly, just Rachel, and even though she didn't read as many books, she still often had a lap for him. In fact, Samson had just about everything he could ever need!

"I don't know why you get up so early," Rachel said as she stood. "Let's hope you grow out of that."

Mornings were the best! That's why Samson made sure never to miss one. He trotted along behind Rachel as she opened the curtains, letting in more light. When she used the restroom, Samson attacked the long leaf of a fern until she was done. Then he started meowing, because he knew what would come next, and boy was he excited! He raced ahead to the kitchen and jumped from a chair up to the table. Samson paced the length of it and kept meowing as Rachel opened a cabinet and then the refrigerator. After what felt like ages, she finally set down a saucer in front of him.

Milk! While not quite as good as his mother's, it was delicious nonetheless, and Samson didn't stop licking until every last drop was gone. Then he looked to Rachel for more, which always made her giggle.

"You greedy little piglet!" she said, rubbing his head. "Ready for some dry food?"

Samson meowed, having long since figured out that to get a human to do anything, he had to make just as much noise as they did. Soon a dish was placed before him, giving him kibble to crunch. Samson ate this at a more leisurely pace. He didn't have to compete with his siblings anymore, or worry about them stealing his share of food. He didn't have to share at all! While he still missed having a play buddy, he had to admit that his new life was luxurious. The entire house belonged to him, upstairs and down. He had a litter box of his own, and if he ever wanted attention, no other cat was there to outshine him. Not bad. Not bad at all! Although sometimes it was a little weird.

"Oh my goodness," Rachel said. "Did I forget your milk? You must be thirsty after eating all that."

Samson was still getting used to human speech. Surely he couldn't have heard that right! The bowl of dry food was taken away and replaced by another saucer of milk. This was his lucky day! Except he really was full, and even though the milk still tasted good, he knew if he drank too much more that it would all come back up. He lapped as much as he could anyway, then turned his nose up at the rest. He tried covering the saucer by swiping his paw across the table. If he didn't bury it, then another cat—maybe even Munch—would come sniffing around in his new territory.

"What in the world are you doing?" Rachel said, laughing again.

"Mom," said a new voice. Victor strolled into the room and picked up the saucer. "He doesn't want anymore."

"He *always* finishes it all."

"Not this time." Victor brought the saucer to his lips and drank the rest. Samson was okay with that, he supposed. Better than it attracting another cat. He watched as Victor went to the sink. He stood there a moment, then turned around. Now he was holding two saucers. "You fed him twice."

Rachel put a hand to her cheek. "I didn't!"

"It's fine," Victor said, head shaking as he turned to face the sink again.

"Should I make you breakfast?"

"No time. I'm on the early shift now, remember? Another week and I'll be back on nights. Thank god. Bernard is forgiving, but if I keep being late—"

The conversation didn't seem to be about playing, getting

treats, or cuddling, so Samson tuned out most of it while grooming himself. His ears perked up when he heard a sharp sound. Victor had kissed his mother on the cheek.

"I'll be home before dinner," he said. "Don't go outside in your nightgown again. Please."

"I never would!" Rachel said, her eyes wide.

"I mean it. One of the neighbors complained."

"Complained? About what? I didn't do anything of the sort!"

Victor took a deep breath. Then he exhaled again. "Take a shower and get dressed, okay? For me?"

"I was going to anyway," Rachel said.

"You didn't yesterday."

Rachel pursed her lips. "You've always had a strange sense of humor, but sometimes even I don't understand you."

"I know," Victor said. "Sorry." He kissed her again, then turned around to ruffle the fur on Samson's head. "Keep an eye on her, okay?"

Samson meowed. He was always watching Rachel and following her around. They were a team! An idea occurred to him then. Maybe Victor was worried that someone would come to take his mother away. Samson had assumed that only happened to kittens, but maybe it happened to mothers as well. That's why, for the remainder of the day, he made sure to stay by her side, and any time her lap was available, Samson settled down there, a lion guarding his queen.

Something was wrong. Rachel didn't leave the house very often. When she did, she always returned with food. Samson waited in the front window, one of his favorite places to sit ever since the leaves started falling off the trees. He would miss them. Unless someone came around to paint the leaves green and hang them all up again, trees would never be the same. That was life, he supposed. Everything changed. Nothing remained the same.

Today was the perfect example. There weren't many leaves left to fall, but now something new was drifting down from the sky, white and delicate. He would have liked for some to blow inside like a few of the leaves had. That had been tremendous fun. Samson had batted them around until nothing but crumpled flakes remained. This new stuff must have been cold. He could feel it through the window. It didn't seem to be stopping either.

After dozing off briefly, he awoke and found the entire ground covered in white. The day was ending, the orange light across the street switching on. Rachel was usually back before dark. Maybe she had hunted more food than usual for them and was still dragging it back.

The sun set completely. Samson's stomach was starting to complain. He didn't like how shadowy the house was, or how cold he was getting from sitting next to the window. He took a brief break to use the litter box, then returned to continue his vigil. A strange car with flashing lights pulled up to the house. A man he didn't recognize got out of it. Samson was brave, but he was also cautious, so he hopped down and hid beneath the table at the end of the couch. From there he could watch the front door. He heard a key slide inside and a very welcome voice behind it.

"My goodness! It sure got cold, didn't it?"

Rachel was home! The door opened, but Samson remained hidden, not liking that a stranger was with her.

"Is anyone here, Mrs. Hemingway?" the man asked.

"Just my husband," Rachel said. She wore a blanket around her shoulders, making Samson think of evenings spent on her bed. Rachel would get beneath the covers and turn on the television. Samson would drape himself over one of her legs and purr himself asleep.

"Mr. Hemingway?" the man called.

"I don't think Victor is home," Rachel said.

"That's your husband?"

Rachel moved to turn on lamps, not seeing where he was hiding. "No, Victor is my son. Did I say husband? How silly. I'm divorced."

Samson didn't like the way the man had his hands on his belt, or the weird noises coming from one shoulder. It sounded like voices, even though no one else was there and the television was off. "Why don't you get dressed? Then I think we should go to the hospital, just to make sure you're doing okay."

"I feel fine," Rachel said. "Just a little chilly."

She was standing close to his hiding spot now. Her feet were bare, dirty, and red. He crept closer to sniff, noticing that they were just as cold as the window he'd been sitting next to. Samson licked her toe, hoping it would help. She didn't seem to notice.

"Go ahead and get dressed," the man prompted. "That'll

help warm you up. Put on some socks and shoes too, if you'd be so kind."

"I suppose I should. Do you want something to drink first? A coffee?"

"No ma'am. I'll wait right here."

Samson stayed where he was. He only craned his neck to watch the man walk to the kitchen and back. Then the voices in his shoulder spoke again and this time the man responded. "We're at her house now. She'll be all right. I'm going to bring her into the ER, just to be sure." The man cleared his throat, and in a slightly louder voice said, "Ma'am?" When there wasn't a response, he continued. "She'll need a psych evaluation. I think she might have Alzheimer's or something."

Samson really wished that humans made more sense. They seemed to invent new words every day! Maybe if he attacked the man's leg, he would finally go away. Rachel would feed him and they could snuggle up together on her bed.

"I'm sorry to keep you waiting," Rachel said, returning from her room. "I really am fine. You can go now."

"I can't," the man said. "I think we better have a doctor check those feet. My uncle was out in the snow too long and lost a toe."

"How terrible!"

"Better safe than sorry. Did you want to leave a note for your son? Or is there a number where we can reach him?"

"I don't want to worry Victor," Rachel said. "A note will suffice. I'll probably be back before he is. He works nights, you see."

"Better leave one anyway. I'm a very cautious man, in case you hadn't noticed."

This made Rachel laugh. She seemed happy enough. Samson felt a little better about the situation. Not enough to show himself. Maybe he should have, because Rachael soon left with the man. She didn't think to check on him first, but Samson was sure she would return. She had to come back. What would happen to him if she didn't?

It was late before Victor returned home. Samson ran to the front door as soon as he heard the lock turn. Rachel still wasn't back. Samson tried to communicate what had happened by meowing repeatedly, but humans rarely listened, and when they did, it was even rarer that they understood.

"Did she forget to feed you again?" Victor said. Then in a louder voice, he said, "Mom?"

She's not home, Samson tried again, but it was no use.

Victor had to see for himself. He checked her bedroom first. When he saw it was empty, he picked up the pace, rushing from room to room. Samson went to the kitchen table and sat next to the note. He couldn't read it, but Rachel had acted like it was important, so he waited until Victor was close again and resumed meowing.

"You'll get your food," Victor snapped. "Oh Jesus, please don't tell me she's out in this weather!"

Samson meowed again, and it finally did the trick. Sort of. Victor grabbed the bowl of dry kibble from the cabinet where it was kept and set it next to him. That's when he finally saw the note. He could have read it out loud. Samson would have appreciated being kept in the loop. Instead all Victor said aloud was, "The hospital!" before he ran for the door. Samson watched him go and listened to the silence that followed. Then he realized that he had an entire bowl of food to himself and decided that, in situations such as these, it was wise to seek comfort wherever it could be found.

When Victor came home, it was still dark. Rachel wasn't with him. He must have felt just as disappointed about this as Samson because he dropped his keys on the floor and fell back against the door, like he needed the support. When he moved again, it was toward the stairs leading down to the basement. Victor had his own room there. Samson usually didn't go inside, since it smelled like smoke, but tonight he followed him. Victor didn't turn on any lights. He felt his way along the hall, one hand sliding along the wall. Then he fell into bed—still wearing all his clothes—and curled into a ball.

Samson hopped up on the mattress, kneading the sheets with his paws while purring. *It's going to be okay.*

Victor didn't seem to hear him, so Samson crept near his face and bumped noses with him. Victor's was wet. So were his eyes. Samson understood. He had experienced the same thing the first night he had been taken away from his mother and sister. Just one more strange discovery. He knew now that a wet face happened when someone was sad. He purred louder, hoping it would help.

"Hey, little guy," Victor said, uncurling enough to pet him. "I've got some bad news. I don't think she's coming home again."

Samson stopped kneading the sheets. Rachel wasn't coming back?

"They think she's better off in a nursing home than here. This is a home! *Her* home!"

Samson agreed! Why would it make her happy to be sent to a new home? Then again, he had been happier here. For a while. Maybe she had found a better place. Would it be possible for him to go with her?

Victor's body shook as he started crying again. No, it was clear that Samson would be needed here. If he left now, Victor would be alone, and from all the waiting he'd done today, Samson knew that wasn't a good feeling. He moved closer, kneading the sheets again. Then he curled up against Victor's chest and tried to purr away the sadness.

The world wasn't as warm without a mother. The curtains didn't open in the morning. Milk was poured at first, but now that no longer happened. There wasn't as much cleaning, or feeding, or sunshine without a mother. The house was always dark. All of it smelled like smoke now, not just Victor's room. He stopped leaving as often. Samson enjoyed the extra company, even if he spent most of the time trying to comfort Victor. Or reminding him that it was time to eat. Samson didn't get fed as often as he liked, but he tried not to complain, because Victor also hardly ever seemed to eat. He talked to himself. Samson sometimes heard him in another room, talking even though nobody was there. On the really bad days, Victor shouted, but at who or for what reason, he did not know.

The snow kept coming. Victor tracked in some of it, which allowed Samson to discover that it could turn to water, although it didn't taste very good. Lately he found himself tasting many things, because he really was hungry. He even started wishing for a giant, leathery-skinned mouse to get into the house. Samson would wait until it was about to breathe fire and jump on its back. From there he could bite its neck and bring down his prey. What a feast that would be! The plan was good, but alas, no mice dared enter his territory.

Or if they did, he hadn't noticed, because he spent most of his time downstairs now. The house had gotten very cold. He wasn't sure why it didn't stay warm anymore. Maybe only mothers could keep it that way. All he knew is that Victor moved more things into his bedroom. Quilts that belonged to Rachel and one of the living room chairs that Samson liked to sleep in. A funny metal thing plugged into the wall made some heat, and if they stayed in the room together with the door shut, it got a little warmer. Samson liked that, but he missed having the freedom to roam.

His world became very small and confusing. Victor never left the house now. His face was much furrier and he didn't smell good. Samson tried licking him clean once, but Victor was simply too big. Or at least he was tall and seemed to be getting skinnier. Samson was hungry too. He worried that the situation might not get better, that the snow and cold would never go away and they would be stuck downstairs forever. Then, one day, they heard a banging from upstairs.

"Goddamn it!" Victor rolled over in bed, and covered his head with a pillow, but Samson could still hear him shout, "Go away!"

The banging noise stopped. Then it started again.

Samson was scared. He no longer wanted to do battle with a mouse! Victor was braver. He got out of bed, left the room, and shut the door behind him. Samson crept to the door, angling his ears to listen to what was happening above. He heard voices. Victor's and another one. Was it Rachel? Had she come back?

Footsteps were coming down the stairs now. Victor wouldn't have brought anyone bad back with him. It had to be Rachel! The door opened, Samson meowing his excitement.

"Hurry up," Victor said as he slid into the room. "Don't let him get out."

Samson backed up and made space so they could enter, straining to see behind Victor. Someone else was here! He hurried forward, confused when it wasn't Rachel or Mrs. Henderson. This was another man. A really tall one. He bent over so Samson could see him better and was considerate enough to hold out a hand for sniffing. His fingers were long and didn't smell like smoke. They were clean and felt good when caressing his head.

"You're so tiny!" the man said with a warm laugh. Then he pulled away his hand and stood.

"That's Samson," Victor said. "Cute little thing, isn't he?"

The man looked down at him with shining eyes. "He's so adorable that it's overwhelming. You should make him wear a grotesque mask or something."

"Now there's an idea. Whatever happened to that werewolf mask of mine?"

The man's eyes went a little wide and his skin flushed. He tried to hide this, but Samson noticed. "I pictured you as more of a dog person. Cats are so domestic."

"He was supposed to be for my mom," Victor explained. "I thought having something to focus on would help her."

The man with long fingers looked concerned and gave his attention to Victor instead. "What happened?"

Victor sat on the bed. "She kept getting worse—forgetting where she'd put things right after setting them down, or acting confused about where she was. Sometimes she would get paranoid, like I was trying to trick her. It was a nightmare, but I was taking care of her. She was never hungry or dirty." He was saying a lot of words. Samson didn't understand many of them, but he imagined it might help that someone else was here who could. "I took care of her better than any stupid nurse in a crappy state-run home! I love her! What can they possibly do for her that I can't?"

The man with long fingers sat down too and put an arm around Victor. "I'm sorry. I had no idea what you were going through, and I agree, it sounds unfair. But if they took her away, it must have been serious."

"Serious to who, Jace?" Victor shot back. "She wasn't going to hurt anyone!"

"Even herself?"

Victor just sighed.

"Tell me what happened," said the man.

"She was wandering the neighborhood in her nightgown. First snow of the year. Someone out walking their dog spotted Mom. When they tried talking to her, she wasn't making any sense, so they called the police. If I hadn't been working that night—"

He seemed to have run out of words. The man with long fingers—Jace, if Samson had understood right—squeezed Victor closer to him. Victor needed to cry, and that's when Samson usually would have tried to comfort him, but this new person seemed willing, purring in his own way, because even Samson found his words comforting.

"We can get her back," he said. "Have you tried?"

"Of course I've tried." Victor pulled away. "They say she needs twenty-four hour supervision."

"Maybe she does," Jace responded. "I mean, you can't always watch her. You have to work or go out for groceries sometime."

Victor was about to shout. Samson could always tell when it was coming and would hide under the bed. This time was different. Victor exhaled and shook his head. "Maybe you're right."

"Can we go visit her?" Jace asked. "I'd like to see her again."

Samson would like that too!

"It's a long walk," Victor replied, "but yeah."

"I can drive you." Jace's eyes moved from Victor's face to his body and back up again. "I wanna grab something to eat first."

Victor shrugged.

Jace placed his hand over Victor's and grimaced. "Is the heat turned on?"

"Got shut off a few weeks ago."

"Can they do that during winter?"

Victor shrugged again.

"I'll pay the bill."

Victor stood. "You won't! I don't need your help!"

"I'm not thinking of you." Jace leaned forward and scooped up Samson in his big hands. He did so gently, placing him down on his lap, which was softer than Victor's and much warmer. "Just look at this poor little guy. He's freezing! If the heat doesn't get turned on, you'll wake up one morning to find a tiny gray ice cube. Wouldn't that be sad?"

Samson didn't want to turn into an ice cube! He liked being a cat too much.

"He's fine," Victor grumped. "We keep each other warm. I appreciate you trying to help, but this is my fault. It's up to me to fix it."

"And until then, you both have to stay cooped up in this room? I don't think so."

Jace stood, but he was careful to lift Samson first to carry him. Samson liked that, because the arm that now cradled him and the chest he was resting against were warm too. Jace opened the door, and together they went upstairs. Samson hadn't been there since the time he had snuck out. The house was less smoky than it had been, but it did smell dusty. Jace paused to turn on lights, ending up in the kitchen, where Samson hoped for milk. He was set on the table, but the saucer wasn't taken from the cabinet.

"Let's see the bills," Jace said. "It can't be that bad. At the very least we'll call the utility company and explain to them that there are two living souls here, freezing their whiskers off."

"I don't have whiskers," Victor said, scratching at the fur on his face.

"Could have fooled me," Jace said. "The bills. Where are they?"

"I'm not letting you do this," Victor said, but he didn't sound as firm as before.

Jace walked over to him and put those long fingers on Victor's shoulders. "Maybe we can bring her home for Christmas. Do you want her coming home to a cold house?"

Victor took a deep breath. Then he nodded. "Let me see what I can find."

Samson stayed on the table, even when papers began to fill the surface. *Especially* then, because he loved sitting on paper. He meowed a few times, hoping that food could be added to the occasion. Jace actually seemed to understand too!

"He looks hungry," he said.

Victor went to one of the cabinets, but he didn't open it. "I think he's out of food. I'll go to the store later."

Jace was quiet. He gathered up some of the papers. "I'll be back, okay?"

"I'm not asking you to do any of this," Victor replied.

Jace smiled and shook his head. "No, that would be the sensible thing to do, and sensible has never been your style."

"I'm very sensible!" Victor replied. "Too sensible to get caught up in the materialistic rat race, or to sell my soul to credit card companies who want me to die in debt. If that's what you think sensible is, then you need to rethink your definition."

This made Jace laugh. "There's the old Victor! That's who I came here hoping to see."

Victor's posture relaxed and he laughed too. Samson couldn't remember the last time he'd heard him do that. "You have terrible taste in guys. You know that?"

"It's a curse I'm willing to live with," Jace said. "I'll see you soon."

He left. Samson wished he hadn't. Victor didn't seem happy about it either. He became quiet again. Then he took Samson with him downstairs. Maybe that was it. Like the man with the flashing car who had only shown up briefly and never come back, Jace had come into their lives and left again. Samson tried not to feel sad. At the very least, this day had been more fun than any of the others since the snow had come.

Victor seemed agitated. He paced the room, sometimes muttering to himself. Eventually he sat in the chair. Samson remained on the bed and was just settling down to sleep when he heard a noise. Like the house was sighing. He hadn't heard that for a long time. Soon he felt warm! He wasn't cuddled up to Victor, and yet somehow, he was no longer cold!

Even better was when he heard the front door open and footsteps came down the stairs. Samson could scarcely believe his luck when the door to Victor's room opened. Jace was back! Not everyone went away forever, it would seem.

Samson jumped off the bed and ran over to greet him, getting pet on the head as reward. "No need to stay in this room," Jace said. "It's nice and toasty upstairs."

"I like it down here," Victor said.

"I'm sure you do," Jace responded, "but I'm hungry and need to cook something. I can't afford to eat out. Come help me in the kitchen."

Victor stood, and at first it looked like he was going to pounce on Jace, but instead he threw his arms around him. Jace did the same and they held each other. Then, without saying a word, they turned and left the room together. Samson chased after them. The upstairs had changed! The curtains were open now and sunlight filled the house. Samson took a detour to one of his favorite windows. Victor's room had a window too, but it was too high to reach unless he was lifted up. This one had a view of a tree, which he liked, because birds sometimes landed there. Not today, so he raced to the kitchen, hopped onto the table again, and meowed. *How about some milk?*

"I got something for you too," Jace said, seeming to understand. "We've got chicken, turkey, beef and carrots..."

The words sounded delicious, but what Jace pulled from the

bag were small metal cans, like short versions of the ones Victor sometimes ate from. Samson didn't like soup. Why would Jace have brought him soup? A plate was taken out regardless and one of the cans was opened. Samson's nose picked up a scent so wonderful that it made his mouth wet, but unlike eyes and noses, a wet mouth didn't make him feel sad. It made him feel hungry!

He could barely comprehend the food that was placed before him. He only knew that it smelled amazing, looked amazing, and—bless his whiskers—tasted amazing too! The rest of the world receded as Samson focused on getting all of the meaty goodness into his mouth, although he was vaguely aware of a conversation taking place.

"He's only had dry kibble before," Victor said with a laugh.

"Well then," Jace said, "Merry Christmas, Samson. There's more where that came from."

He wasn't the only one who ate. After cleaning his plate, Samson groomed himself contentedly while sprawled out on the table and watched as food was taken out of the oven. It didn't smell as appetizing so he paid it no mind, although it was good to see Victor eating again. He seemed a lot happier now, especially when he spoke.

"Visiting hours are only until six p.m.," he said.

"Then you still have time to get cleaned up," Jace said. "Do me a favor and lose the beard."

"Why?" Victor asked. "You don't like it?"

"It's fine, but I'm not sure I can find your lips in there. Make it easy on me and shave it off."

"What do you need to find my lips for?" Victor replied, but after a slow grin, he turned and sauntered out of the kitchen. Before long, running water could be heard from the bathroom.

Jace sighed. Then placed his elbows on the table, hands in his hair, and laughed. "I think he's going to be okay."

Heart bursting with gratitude and belly still full of deliciousness, Samson rose and walked over to Jace, plopping down again right in front of him, because he had figured it out. Only one type of person could make a home warm, fill their bellies with food, and dispense happiness with such ease.

"Don't worry, little guy," Jace said, long fingers tickling the scruff of his neck. "I'm going to make it all better."

That did it. Samson was absolutely sure now. Jace was a mother.

*****

The world was a better place with a mother around. Rachel didn't come back to them, but it was almost as good. Jace fixed everything. Victor especially, which was strange, because their relationship wasn't peaceful. Just like cats, they fought to establish a hierarchy, although the way they went about it was odd. First they took off all their clothes and got into bed. After that, they made the strangest noises. Samson didn't stick around to find out who won, and it still wasn't clear the next day or the one after. He had more pressing concerns anyway because a new thought had occurred to him.

People were sometimes taken from their homes. Samson had been taken from his originally, and he had seen Rachel taken from hers. What he had never considered is that they had both been added to others. Samson had gone somewhere better—at first, anyway—and he hoped that Rachel had too. Now he just needed to figure out how to get someone to join their home, because he really liked Jace. Samson wanted him to join their family and never leave. He did everything he could to make that come true.

That meant rubbing his face against Jace any chance he got. The more they intermingled their scents, the more they became a family. Samson also did his best to demonstrate just what a fun home they had. He chased a foil ball through the house, tore up a roll of toilet paper, and once, after many careful jumps, he managed to reach the top shelf of a bookcase. Jace found all of this funny. When he wasn't petting Samson or laughing at his antics, he was talking with Victor and cuddling with him. Samson felt sure he would stay.

But of course life was full of surprises. Some were good. Others weren't. Victor returned home one day. Alone. Jace didn't come back that day. Or the next. Still, things weren't completely bad. Victor woke up in the morning and opened the curtains. He left the house regularly and often returned with food. Then he had a hard night. Samson could tell because Victor stayed up all night talking to himself and he smelled like sweat. When the morning came, Victor didn't get up. The curtains remained closed, and Samson had to wait a long time to eat.

More such nights followed. Samson didn't know what to do. He couldn't blame Victor, because neither of them was a mother who knew how to work that sort of magic. The house filled with smoke, meals came sporadically, and Victor spent more time talking to himself. Samson was starting to despair when Jace showed up again. Just like before, he worked wonders, bringing light back to the house, making sure Samson was fed, and not letting Victor remain sad. Something was different though. Jace wasn't laughing as much. He didn't tell Samson that everything would be okay. Not this time. Instead he seemed angry. He left just as quickly as he came.

Jace returned the next day and there was more arguing. Samson was sure there was going to be scratching and biting so he ran upstairs to hide. He hoped Jace would win. Maybe then things would stay good. Victor would be happier too, even if he wasn't in charge. Samson listened as the shouting got worse. Then it stopped completely. He heard the stairs creaking and came out of hiding to see who had won.

Jace! Except he didn't seem proud. He did nothing to mark his newly claimed territory. Something had gone wrong. Jace sighed, looked around, and when he saw Samson, walked over to him and squatted.

Samson sniffed the hand that was held out to him, not smelling any injuries or blood.

"I can't stay," Jace said, caressing his fur. "I'm really sorry, but I can't help him anymore. I wish I could. I brought a lot of food for you from my mom's house. I'm not sure how long it will last, but I'll have my sister check in, okay? She'll make sure you and Victor are all right. Try to take care of him for me."

That's when Jace did something really strange. He blinked his eyes slowly, leaving them mostly closed as he continued to stare at him. No one had done that since Samson last saw his sister. He had no idea that some humans could speak Cat! Luckily he recovered in time to blink back. *I love you too.*

Jace pet him again and stood. Then he went to the door, not looking back as he left.

A very bad thing happened.

Victor had gotten worse. Much worse. He smelled sick now and never left the house. He would only open the door to take letters off the front of it. Sometimes he would read these and then yell at them. Other times he would cry. Samson tried to do what Jace had asked. He tried to take care of Victor, but it was like he could no longer be seen. Samson would curl up in his lap or press against him at night, but Victor never touched him. He didn't even react. Samson was hungry. From the way Victor's stomach grumbled, he must have been hungry too. People came to the door but they were never let in. None of them were Jace or Rachel. He always crept close enough to check.

Then, one morning, Victor got up. He took a shower, left the house, and when he came back, he had a bag of dry food for Samson. Not as good as the cans, but it was better than nothing. Victor had brought something else with him too. It was long. Part of it was wood. The other half was a metal tube. Samson only sniffed it once. He didn't like it. Victor seemed to. He kept picking it up, as if fascinated.

Samson was sleeping when he heard the explosion. A loud boom. The very bad thing. He didn't realize how bad at the time. He scurried beneath the blankets and hid there, even when he felt too hot and the air was stale to breathe. He stayed there until he was absolutely sure that there wouldn't be another boom. Then he forced himself to be brave. If this was a mouse, he had to face it. Samson needed to be braver than even Munch had been, so he crawled upstairs as slowly and silently as possible.

Victor was sitting on the floor. He smelled like blood and meat, but not in a good way. Samson didn't have to get near to find out because the scent was strong enough to burn his nose. The long thing made of metal and wood was in his lap. Samson meowed, poised to flee if need be. Victor didn't move, so he sat down and waited. Samson was still there when the sun rose again. Victor still didn't move, not even his chest to take in air. Nor did he react when Samson started meowing over and over again. If he got in trouble for this behavior, so be it! He just wanted to see Victor move. He wanted that more than anything. Eventually, two other desires competed for his attention.

He was hungry. Samson slunk into the kitchen, looking back with every other step. Once there, he leapt onto the counter where the bag of food was kept. He started biting it until the skin was broken and the insides came out. He paused then, thinking of Victor, how his insides had also come out. Samson felt sad, even as he ate. As soon as he was full, the second desire took precedence. He needed Jace to come back. He needed Jace to fix this.

*****

Two days passed before a man came with his flashing car. Samson didn't think it was the same one as before. He hid, not trusting this stranger, especially when even more humans came with flashing cars. One had a siren that hurt his ears. He knew what they were here to do. The same thing they had done last time. Samson remained out of sight until the house was silent again. When he came out of hiding, he saw that he was right. The men with the flashing cars had taken Victor away.

Being alone wasn't a good thing. Samson was top cat now, but he still couldn't pull back curtains. He couldn't pour milk or open cans. He could sit in a window for a sunbath, or take naps, or eat as much as he wanted. His water bowl was almost empty and didn't taste good anymore. His litter box was full. He was alone, and he didn't like it.

He still hid the next time the door opened. He peeked from beneath the couch and saw that it wasn't Jace or Rachel, and he didn't think Victor was ever coming back, so he scurried backward, hiding himself.

"Oh dear," a woman said. "What are we going to do with all of this?"

"Just what we talked about," a man answered. "We'll give what we can to Goodwill. Some of it we'll have to throw away."

"We'll have to keep something for Jace," the woman replied.

Did she say Jace? Samson crept forward, just to double check that he wasn't there. The man had walked to where Victor used to be. Then he turned around and started waving his arms. "No, no, no! Serena, honey, you do not need to see this! Hand me that quilt over there."

The woman gasped, her breath coming in sharp bursts as she went to the couch. Her shoe was close to him, but he didn't think he had been spotted. Instead he heard the rustle of a blanket. Then the woman, Serena, spoke again. "Bob..."

"I know. It's heartbreaking, isn't it?"

"I don't know how we're going to tell Jace."

There! She said his name again!

"I don't know either," Bob said. "Let's take a look around and start making a list."

They stood there for a while, Bob naming things in the room,

Serena responding in terms Samson didn't understand.

"Television?"

"Goodwill."

"Couch?"

"Goodwill."

"Lamps?"

"Rachel might be able to have one in her room."

After enough of this, they went to the kitchen, but they didn't remain there for long.

"He had a cat!" Serena said, rushing back to the living room. "How could I be so foolish? If anything happened to it, I'll never forgive myself!"

"I'm sure he's around here somewhere," Bob said. "Looks like he tore through most of that bag."

"An animal needs more than food," Serena scolded. "Here kitty kitty! Oh please... Kitty kitty kitty! Come out and say hello! We're here to help."

Samson didn't move.

"Maybe he was an outdoor cat," Bob said. "He's probably out hunting mice."

"In this weather?"

Serena's feet hurried across the floor again.

Bob stayed where he was and got down on his knees. Then a funny looking face with windows in front of the eyes peered underneath the couch.

"Got 'im!" Bob declared, showing his teeth.

Samson hissed.

"Move aside," Serena said.

The man's face went away and was replaced by another. The Woman! But that wasn't right. She was old like Mrs. Henderson had been, and the hand she slid beneath the couch was wrinkled... It didn't try to grab Samson. She just held it there politely, so he inched forward and sniffed. Then his heart nearly exploded with joy because he smelled Jace! Not exactly, but they were of the same family. Samson was sure of it. Enough that he came out from the beneath the couch and started meowing. He didn't know what would happen next. He was just glad that he was no longer alone.

Samson was somewhere new. A bedroom. He was by himself

most of the time, but he didn't mind because all around him was the smell of Jace. He would be back. He would fix everything. Samson smelled other cats too and sometimes heard them outside the door, but they never came inside. Only the nice woman, Serena, would come in to feed him, or let him sit on her lap. Once she brought a toy, a bundle of feathers attached to a string that looked a lot like a bird. Samson pounced on it over and over again. He liked that. Maybe this is what every day would be like from now on. But surely Jace would come for him. They loved each other. He had said so. Why wouldn't he come?

Samson's dreams had gotten better. They weren't about the very bad thing anymore. He kept dreaming that Jace was with him, that he was the one with the feather toy and an empty lap. Samson was having that dream when the door opened, and after he raised his head, he saw that it had come true. Almost. Jace was at the door, but he was paler than before. And he was crying. Samson was scared he would go away, that Jace no longer loved him, but that's not what happened. Jace shut the door behind him and got into bed. Samson was already purring. He went to Jace's face and bumped noses. That's when he realized that, this time, he would have to fix things. Samson had once been sad until Jace made him happy. Now he would return the favor. He kneaded the sheets as Jace wept and blinked his eyes reassuringly.

Don't worry. I love you. I love you. I love you.

Samson did *not* love Jace! Not anymore. Okay, he still did, but right now he wasn't a happy cat. Samson had flown. Through the air! It wasn't at all like he was expecting. The sky wasn't blue as it appeared from the ground. It was gray, filled with chairs and people, and smelled like shoes. Not feet, which was a wonderful scent that he loved rubbing his face against. Just shoes. Rubber and leather. That's all Samson could see while flying when what he had imagined the day before were flocks of birds that he could swipe a paw through. Just the thought made his mouth water. Even if birds did show up, he was stuck in a tiny box and unable to chase anyone or do anything fun.

If that wasn't bad enough, when they finally stopped flying, they were somewhere even noisier than the place they had left. Once they got away from there… Well, the air outside was much warmer here, and Samson saw no sign of the snow that had brought the dark times. That made him feel cheerful until they got into a very long car full of other people. This didn't travel far. It dropped them off at a place that was nothing *but* cars.

"Almost there," Jace said, walking briskly across the pavement. "I know this is terrible, but you're almost home."

That comforted Samson a little. At least Jace acknowledged that none of this was acceptable. Samson yowled anyway, just to reaffirm that he wouldn't be happy if things stayed this way. Jace opened one of the cars and set him inside. Then he went around to the other side, which seemed silly. Wasn't one door to the outside enough? The house he used to live in was much larger and only had two. Why did this little space need so many doors? And why was Jace swearing while the car made a terrible grinding noise.

"I *really* need a new car," Jace explained. "I don't suppose you're rich? Maybe there was a trust fund set up in your name?"

Samson didn't have a clue what he meant so he yowled again.

"Okay, okay," Jace said. The grinding noise turned into a growl.

Samson squeezed himself into the back of his carrier. No, he didn't like this at all! Victor might have had his faults, but riding inside of his jacket was way better than this never-ending journey. Eventually it did end. The car came to a stop.

Jace looked over at him and grinned. "Made it! You were so brave!"

Samson relaxed a little. He was pretty brave, he supposed. He peered through the sides of the carrier with interest as Jace walked with him down a sidewalk and unlocked a door. The hallway inside was dim and cool. After going up two flights of stairs, they went through another door. Here everything smelled like Jace, and while his new companion might have lost points for making him come all this way, Samson couldn't help kneading his paws. Just a little bit.

The carrier was set on the floor, then the front was unzipped. Samson very cautiously poked his head outside. Jace was on his knees not far away. Past him, Samson saw a small living room with a kitchen in one corner and a short hall with two more doors. That was it.

"I know it's not much," Jace said, "but it's just you and me here. I think it'll be okay. Do you?"

Only one way to find out. Keeping himself low to the floor (just in case any fire-breathing mice were lurking in the shadows) Samson hurried around the apartment to do an inspection. First he kept to the walls, then he started slinking around the furniture, identifying the best places to hide, if need be. He discovered a bedroom and a bathroom before returning to the living room. Jace was standing there smiling.

"What do you think?"

Samson meowed.

"Oh right!" Jace responded. "You still need a litter box, food, a water dish… Thank goodness Dad slipped me that hundred or you'd be eating Ramen noodles with me tonight. I guess I should go shopping, but first…"

Jace went to the kitchenette and opened a cabinet. Milk? Was it going to be milk? He took out a bowl—an entire bowl!—and filled it with something. Then he set it on a small table, which Samson quickly jumped up on. He sniffed. Just water. Samson turned up his nose at it.

"You must be hungry instead," Jace said. "Sorry. There's a store just down the street. I'll be back before you know it." He didn't leave though. First he rubbed Samson behind the ears. "I'm going to be your daddy now. I hope that's okay. We're going to be a family. Just a small one, but I promise to take care of you. You'll never be hungry again."

Samson wasn't entirely sure what a daddy was, but the promise of never being hungry sounded good, so he purred.

"Oh!" Jace said. "One more thing before I go. You have to promise to be really *really* careful out here, but…"

Jace walked to the other side of the living room. There he opened another door. Samson had thought it was a window, since it looked like one, but it swung outward. He went to investigate. Fresh air was streaming into the room, making him trot forward quicker. Was he being let outside? Was he even ready for such a thing?

"Ever had your own balcony before?" Jace asked him.

Samson wasn't sure. He followed his new daddy out onto his new balcony. Two new discoveries! He wasn't sure which he liked more, because the bricks beneath his paws were warm. He would roll on them later. Right now he was entranced to be out in the open air, to have so much to see! Samson stuck his head between two iron rods and looked down at a street, but this one was filled with people instead of cars.

"You won't jump. Will you?"

Samson pulled back and looked up at his daddy, which he decided he did like even more than the balcony because his daddy had made it all possible. Then he started rubbing against those tall legs, showing his gratitude.

"I'm glad you like it!" Jace said. "Do you want to come back inside while I'm gone?"

Ha! Samson sat down.

"Okay," Jace said with a chuckle. "I'll be right back with everything you need. Still like the chicken and gravy entrée best?"

Samson liked everything! His daddy left him alone, but he didn't feel lonely or scared. Instead he patrolled the edges of his balcony, rubbing his cheek against everything to mark it with his scent. Then he settled down on the warm bricks, closed his eyes, and purred.

Part Two: Houston, 1998

A daddy was like a mother, except better. The biggest difference between the two was that daddies came back. Jace always did. Sometimes he was gone days at a time, but Jace had a sister, and she would come to make sure the promise was kept. Samson was never hungry. His litterbox was always clean, and while he did miss Jace some nights, he never worried because daddies always came back.

His own now flew for a living. Samson couldn't imagine willingly doing that again. He wasn't even sure what a living was, but he knew it had something to do with food, because sometimes when his daddy came back after being gone, he would say, "Sorry, little guy. Gotta earn a living if you want to keep eating." Samson certainly did, so he was very grateful, even though he wasn't sure why humans were given cans of food for sitting on an airplane. They were given other things too, it would seem, because Jace came home one evening and was very excited.

"I found a new place for us! We can finally afford something better."

This made Samson very nervous. Every time he got a new home, it meant leaving behind everyone he lived with. That's how clever his daddy was though. He figured out a way for them to have a new home together. They didn't have to fly to this one, thankfully, but he did have to suffer a short ride in the car. His new home was much larger. The living room especially. It was a big open space with high ceilings. The floors were made of wood, and while there wasn't a balcony, the tall windows let in lots of sunlight. Jace put screens in a few of them so Samson could sit there and enjoy the air. The best part was the bed. It was in the air now too, at the top of something called a ladder. Samson had climbed up it on the first day, a fact Jace made sure to tell everyone who visited. The bed was a very nice place to be. Samson imagined it was like sleeping in a tree. Without any birds, sadly.

So much in life seemed to change, especially at the beginning, but now most of his days were the same. He would eat in the morning. If Jace was home, they would play. His daddy was very good at playing and was always bringing home new toys. Even mice, except they were small and furry, which wasn't right at all. Samson still enjoyed smacking them around. He would hang out in a window, watch the world outside, and sleep in the sun. Afterwards he would eat more and sit on Jace's lap while he read. Then they would climb into bed and repeat it all the next day.

Samson was happy. Jace was too. Most of the time. Occasionally he would sit by a window at night and drink. Not like Victor had. Jace was slower, and he never acted strange or mumbled to himself. Why would he when he had Samson to talk to? He was sitting on Jace's lap during one such night, enjoying being brushed, when something odd was said.

"Wouldn't you like to have two daddies?"

The thought had never occurred to him! There was only one Jace. Wasn't there? Samson couldn't imagine having two.

"It would be nice," Jace continued. Frustratingly, the brushing did not. "You'd have someone here for you when I'm out of town. He'd have to adore cats. I don't think I could fall in love with anyone who didn't. He wouldn't be so damn obtuse either. I loved Victor, but…" Jace set the brush down, reached for the bottle instead, and refilled his glass. "What am I saying? I love you, Victor! If you're listening, I still do and always will. That's why I don't want someone similar to you. It would feel too much like I'm trying to replace you, which I know I can't. And since I can't, my dream guy needs to be different. I want someone who can't stop saying exactly how he feels. No filter or complicated explanations. It'll be like a really sweet version of Tourette's."

Okay, so maybe Jace did get a little weird when drinking. Samson couldn't judge. He overdid it with the catnip sometimes.

"Eh," Jace said, emptying his glass and setting it down. "What do I need a man for when I've got you?"

Samson agreed wholeheartedly.

Jace's behavior was suspicious. He spent more time than usual in front of the bathroom mirror, and even more confusingly, this was his second shower today. He always took one in the morning, but not so close to dinner. Samson was getting impatient too. He wasn't hungry, but he was used to eating on a schedule, and he felt certain it was time. Jace was too busy standing in the closet, staring at his clothes. It must be embarrassing not to have enough fur to cover himself naturally, but Samson didn't care. He thought his daddy was pretty neat anyway. When he wasn't acting so strange, that is.

"How do I look?" Jace asked, turning to him.

He looked like Jace. How else would he appear?

Samson meowed plaintively.

Jace finally understood. "It's dinner time, isn't it? We'll get you nice and full because I might be late. Or maybe not. I really don't know. I *want* to be late. I think."

Samson was relieved when Jace stopped this game and went to open a can. His thoughts for the next five minutes were focused solely on the fishy taste of tuna. When he was finished and tried to cover his plate, Jace took it from him, except now he smelled like cologne. He normally put that on only before he left the house for a few days. Samson started to worry, but Jace had said he would be back tonight. Samson busied himself with grooming, pausing occasionally to watch Jace rush around the apartment in agitation. Eventually he was dressed in a long coat and standing before the door to leave.

"You'll be all right?" he asked.

Samson stared back.

"Okay," Jace said, taking a deep breath. He exhaled while looking at the door, then back to him. "If he isn't the one, then I give up."

Samson hoped, for Jace's sake, that whoever turned out to be whatever. He was just glad to be a cat. Jace's life seemed too complicated. His own was a series of meals, naps, cuddle sessions, and games. He considered his options after Jace left and settled on sleep.

His dreams were always entertaining. His current favorite was when he would soar through a sky just as blue as it appeared from down below. A sky full of birds, who just happened to taste like chicken and gravy. Flying as it should be! His mouth was watery when the sound of the front door woke him. The windows were dark, so unless he had slept through an entire day, it was still the same night.

"A-mazing!" Jace said, tossing his keys on the kitchen counter. "Not just him. I did pretty well too." He took off his coat and let it drop to the floor.

Samson stood and stretched, surprised when he felt himself picked up.

"First we ice skated," Jace said, waltzing them around the room. "Then we had dinner and talked."

Dinner sounded good! Was that an offer?

"But the best was at the very end," Jace said, holding him at arm's length. "When we said goodbye. I was all 'Hey, why don't you come over here to this baseball diamond' and Ben was all 'Oh my gosh, first base! How romaaaantic!' and then…"

Jace placed a kiss on Samson's nose.

"Just like that! Okay, not exactly like that." Jace cradled him against his chest. "You're too young to hear the details. Not that it was dirty. It was sweet. I think you'd like him. Oh no! I forgot to ask if he likes cats! What if he has allergies?"

Samson squirmed so that Jace would set him down. Then he shook himself and started rubbing against his daddy's legs. He wasn't sure what the excitement was about, but it better not be a different cat! Samson would make sure to remind Jace of how good they had it, just in case he had any crazy ideas.

A few days later, the same ritual was repeated. Jace took an extra shower in the evening, seemed incapable of getting dressed quickly, and then got himself worked up before he left the apartment. This time he didn't talk about giving up or last chances. Instead he was bristling with nervous energy.

He wasn't gone as long. Samson was in the middle of a dream where he met Munch again, except his brother hadn't grown big and strong like Samson had. Munch was still a kitten, which made it very fun to chase him around. The rumbling elevator woke him this time. Samson was already approaching the door when it opened. The overhead lights flicked on, letting him see that Jace was not alone. Samson thought of Victor at first, since this new person wasn't very tall either, but his fur wasn't as dark.

"Samson!" Jace said, scooping him up. That was good. It put Samson closer to the new man's head, just in case he needed to attack. "We have a visitor."

Samson ignored the newcomer, choosing instead to rub his face against Jace's chin in order to mark him. *Mine, mine, mine, mine.* Only then did he turn to consider the visitor. The man reached out and tried to stroke his fur. Rude! Samson pulled back to avoid the hand, then came back to sniff and figure out who they were dealing with. The man smelled okay. Jace's scent was on him, which was confusing, but he didn't smell like smoke or anything else bad.

"Security scan initiated," Jace said during this. "Mm-hm. I think you've passed. Let's see about getting you something to eat."

Yes! Samson leapt to the floor and followed Jace into the kitchen. He hopped up on a bar stool and then the countertop and waited. He had already eaten his second can of the day, so this was a real treat. The other guy was sniffing around their territory, but Samson tried not to let this concern him. His daddy was bigger. He would deal with the intruder if need be.

"That's Ben," Jace whispered as he set down a plate. "The one I told you about. What do you think of him so far?"

Samson kept eating. As long as food, playing, and cuddling remained a priority, he was happy. Jace went to talk to the new person. Samson finished eating. Then he jumped down to the floor to keep an eye on things. This had happened before. Jace had brought a guy named Mark home who never seemed to shut up. Even worse was how he would always shoo Samson away, or tell him to get off the counters and tabletops. That relationship hadn't lasted long, and Samson hoped this new one wouldn't either, because humans were twice as noisy when around each other. That's what Jace and Ben occupied themselves with. They talked while standing, and when they got tired of this, they sat on the couch to keep talking some more. Samson didn't hesitate. As soon as Jace's butt hit the couch, he climbed onto his lap to settle down for a nap.

Mine.

He didn't really sleep. He kept himself tuned into the conversation to get a better understanding of what was going on. Most of it was lost on him or uninteresting, although it did take an interesting turn toward the end.

"The hours suck," Jace was saying. "I'm gone for days at a time, and until I have more seniority, my schedule is constantly shifting. So I can't promise anyone when I'll be home, or if I'll even be there at all. Something about sleeping in a hotel every night gives people ideas, so if it isn't the hours, it's the jealousy."

That's right! His daddy was much too busy for this new person.

Ben didn't take the hint. "I don't know. It doesn't sound all that bad to me. Being apart and not seeing each other every day would keep things fresh. I think I could deal with that."

Jace laughed. "That's what they all say at the beginning. Not that I'm trying to discourage you. I'd love for you to prove me wrong. Speaking of which, I fly to Chicago all the time."

Ben found this just as confusing as Samson did. "What are you suggesting?"

"That I like you and that I want more than to just sleep with you." Jace studied Ben's face as he spoke. "I know we're moving fast, that we don't know each other very well, but what I've seen so far is a charming, considerate, and surprisingly mature college student who is on his way to becoming someone great."

"Thanks," Ben replied. "I think you're the bee's knees too."

Samson had caught a bee once. He didn't think it had knees, or if it did, he hadn't noticed when eating it. Jace had acted very concerned and tried to take it away from him. Why didn't they talk about that? It was a much better story.

Jace's voice was low and husky now. Like a growl. He shifted his legs, Samson leaping down to the floor. Where were they going? He was forced to scurry away because Jace pounced on Ben. They were fighting for dominance! Weren't they? Ben was laughing, which Jace only did when he was very happy or Samson had done something clever. He watched, confused, as Jace carried Ben to the ladder. Then, after throwing him over his shoulder, Jace stepped onto the first rung and then the second. Ben obviously didn't know how to climb the ladder like Samson did. How embarrassing. He didn't see why Ben needed to go up there at all, since that place was for sleeping.

He remembered then how Jace and Victor had used a bed for other things. A sort of play-fight that didn't look fun to him. Samson huffed, went back to the couch, and lay down where Jace had been sitting, the place still warm. He thought it was a good plan to sleep until Ben went away again, and he tried his best, but it felt wrong to be down here. Once the play-fight was over and the apartment was quiet, Samson decided to investigate. He climbed up the ladder and saw two people in bed. Ben was closest, but he was asleep. Samson crept around him as carefully as possible. Jace was just behind Ben, holding on from behind. But that wouldn't work because—

Jace stirred and lifted his head. When he saw Samson, he scooted backward and made room. He also arranged his arm so that Samson could curl up in it like he always did.

"I didn't forget about you," Jace whispered. "I was waiting."

Samson continued kneading the sheets and looked sharply at Ben.

"I know," Jace said. "Just give him a chance. You might be surprised."

He wouldn't give Ben anything because it all already belonged to him and his daddy. When Samson finally settled, he did so facing the intruder. Just in case. Then he decided it would be a bigger statement if he turned his back to him, which he did. Jace didn't scold him for being rude. Instead he smiled, touched their noses together, and blinked his eyes. Samson did the same, hoping that things would go back to normal tomorrow.

Ben was the first to wake up. Correction. Samson was the first so he could alert Jace if this new person tried anything shifty. Ben sat up and looked at them. Then he quietly laughed and whispered, "How cute!"

Samson flattened his ears.

Ben didn't seem to notice. He was only looking at Jace now while biting his bottom lip. Maybe he was hungry and planning to eat them! Samson got it half right. Ben rose and climbed down the ladder, which was silly, because going down was much harder than going up. Maybe he had been faking a need for help last night. Samson followed as quietly as he could, not trusting this person. Sure enough, Ben went to the kitchen to steal all of their food.

Samson jumped up on the counter to let him know he'd been caught. Ben was shameless. After a brief moment of surprise, he continued rummaging through a cabinet. "I'm starving! He wore me out last night. Sorry. You probably don't want details."

He wanted this person to leave! Samson was pretty sure he could take him in a fight. Ben only wore underwear, and without his clothes, it was plain to see how skinny he was. Not much muscle at all, but he was much taller than him. Ben set a bowl on the counter, then poured in some of the crunchy sweet stuff that Jace usually ate in the morning. That was a step too far! Samson was about to sound the alarm by meowing when Ben opened the refrigerator and took out the milk. That was Jace's too. Even Samson wasn't allowed to have it. Jace pushed him away whenever he tried to get some.

"You're probably hungry too, huh?" Ben turned to look at the cabinet. "I have no idea what you need. I'm a dog person."

Clearly he wasn't a mother *or* a daddy! Otherwise he would have opened a can already!

"Oh, I know!" Ben took a saucer from the cabinet. Then he poured milk into it. If he was about to drink it right in front of him, then Samson would claw out his—

The saucer of milk was placed in front of him. Ben ruffled the fur on his head, then poured milk into his bowl. Was this a bribe to stay silent? Or another dream?

Ben stopped with a spoon halfway to his mouth. "You don't like it? Give it try."

Samson's treacherous tongue darted out. One taste of the milk was all it took. He had sold Jace out for a single saucer of milk. When he heard the ladder creaking, Samson lapped faster, hoping to hide the evidence in his stomach. He failed. Jace walked into the room wearing a goofy smile that faded when he saw what was happening.

"What are you doing?" he demanded.

"Eating breakfast," Ben said, sounding confused.

"No, I mean..." Jace marched forward and took the saucer—along with the remaining milk—away. "Cats aren't supposed to have milk."

Ben snorted. "That's like saying a dog shouldn't have a bone or a mouse shouldn't have cheese."

"I'm serious," Jace said. "My mom had lot of cats when I was growing up, and most are lactose-intolerant. She never gave them milk for that reason."

"For real?" Ben said. "Sorry. Do we need to call a vet?"

"No, it's not that serious," Jace said with a sigh. He was watching Samson like he was prey.

"What's going to happen?" Ben asked. "Is he going to get gassy?"

"No. He'll puke it all up."

"Oh wow. Now I'm really sorry. I had no idea."

"It's okay," Jace said, still watching him intently.

Samson sat there, unable to tear his eyes away from the saucer in Jace's hand. Ben kept slurping and crunching from his bowl while sitting on one of the bar stools, which only made Samson thirstier.

"How much longer until he pukes?" Ben asked. "I'm trying to finish before he does."

"I thought he would have already," Jace said.

Ben took another bite. After he swallowed, he said, "Maybe he's not lactose-intolerant."

"Hm?" Jace said.

"You said most cats are. Maybe he's one of the few that can drink milk. You might as well let him finish. Especially if he's going to puke anyway. At least let him have milk once in his life."

It took all of his willpower, but Samson managed to look away from the saucer to Ben. If he had understood right…

"I guess the damage is already done," Jace said, setting down the saucer.

Yes! Samson hurriedly lapped up the rest before they could change their minds. Afterwards he thoroughly licked his chops to make sure he got every single drop. Jace watched him a moment longer, then turned to start making coffee.

"Do you want one too?"

"Can't stand the stuff," Ben answered. "Got any juice?"

The humans kept making noises at each other, but he wasn't forgotten for long.

"I think he's going to be okay," Ben said while looking at him. "We should try again tomorrow."

Jace turned around to consider Samson. "Yeah. Okay. Why not?"

Milk! Finally! Maybe he would get it every morning that Ben stayed here. Samson felt conflicted about this. He wanted Jace all to himself, but then again, he did really like milk, and although he didn't care to admit it, he was starting to like Ben too.

Ben was around a lot these days. At first it seemed like he would stay permanently. He shared their bed every night. When he did leave, Samson missed him, but just a little. And *maybe* he was excited when Ben came back again to visit for a weekend. And another! Jace seemed happy too. He talked about Ben a lot, even when he wasn't there, but Samson wasn't forgotten. He was still loved and cherished, which made it easy not to hold a grudge against this Ben person who was becoming so important. Then the real challenge came.

"He's coming to stay with us for the summer," Jace said one morning while standing in front of the bathroom sink and shaving fur off his face. This seemed foolish, considering how little he had. "Well, not here. Not officially. Technically he's staying with his parents in The Woodlands." He swished the razor around in the sink's water and turned to look at Samson, who was sitting on the closed toilet seat. "What if we invited him to move in?"

Samson angled an ear back. But just one.

"You're right," Jace said, returning his attention to the mirror. "Better to let it happen naturally. About the only time Ben sleeps at his parents' house is when he's playing hard to get. He's into me though, right?"

Samson put on a cool expression. Of course Ben loved Jace! Who wouldn't?

"It could be nice." Jace rinsed his face and grinned at him. "Don't you think?"

Samson wasn't sure. He had gotten used to having a visitor, but adding and removing members of a family could change everything. Just look what had happened when Rachel had gone, or when Jace had come to visit. The home had changed completely each time, despite the house remaining the same.

Jace was right. He never needed to ask Ben to move in. One day he simply came back with two pieces of luggage. Samson delighted in sniffing them and the contents. Things didn't really change. Not at first. Jace was happy. Samson wasn't forgotten. Everything was good.

Until one morning.

"Okay," Jace said, wearing his uniform and standing at the door. "The open skies are calling. Are you sure you two will be okay?"

Samson was always fine when Jace was away. The only thing that confused him was that Ben was still wearing pajamas. Humans usually put on different clothes before leaving, for some reason.

"Be a good boy," Jace said, plucking Samson off the floor to kiss his head. "It'll be just like having me around. You'll see. And as for you…"

Samson was gently set on the floor again. Then his tail flicked back and forth as he watched Jace and Ben mash their mouths together. This seemed to go on forever before Samson received a quick ear scratch. Then his daddy was gone.

Wait! Samson wanted to cry out. *You forgot something!*

"I guess this is it," Ben said with a sigh. "I'm officially a lady in waiting. Actually, I'm not sure what that means. A lady who has to wait for her man to return? Or who has to wait on him? That can't be right. I thought it had something to do with queens. Ha! Maybe it does."

Samson looked from him to the door, politely suggesting that he might want to leave.

"Don't worry," Ben said. "He'll be back. I'll take care of you until then."

Ben turned and walked deeper into the apartment. Samson watched him go, too shocked at first to follow. Even Mark hadn't been allowed to stay when Jace was gone. Samson gave chase. He would need to keep an eye on this person, just in case Ben tried to take anything or claim territory that wasn't his own.

Samson was a traitor. He hated to admit it, but he had sold out completely. He had tried to keep his distance from Ben while remaining close enough to keep tabs. This meant sitting at the other end of the couch when Ben watched television, or on the far side of the mattress when they slept at night. He didn't seem to be interested in taking over. When not eating or sleeping, Ben would sigh a lot, or sometimes he would sing. It was just like the music Jace sometimes listened to, except he didn't need speakers. The songs came straight out of him. At night he would often look over at Samson and say:

"Do you miss him? I do too."

Ben fed him at all the right times, and he tried to play with his favorite toys, even though Ben wasn't as good as Jace at making hunting games. Then one day he stood in front of the oven while grumbling a lot. The apartment started to smell like the sort of food Jace preferred. Ben would sometimes run from the kitchen to the bathroom and stand in front of the mirror. Then he would hurry back to keep cooking, or to put plates on the table. The flurry of activity continued until the front door opened.

Daddy was back! Samson galloped over to greet him,

meowing in excitement. Jace was pleased to see him too, but his attention was divided. Soon he started focusing on Ben instead. That wasn't good!

"I missed you," Jace said between kisses. "It smells great!"

"Are you hungry?" Ben said. "If not, we can wait. I don't think it can taste any worse than it already does."

"I'm sure it's fine," Jace said with a chuckle. "Wow, the table is set and everything! Hey, are we expecting… No. Are you serious?"

"Is that okay?" Ben asked.

"I love it!" Jace declared.

"Okay. Well, go ahead and take a seat."

Or how about, instead of sitting, you get down on the floor and give me more love? Samson's meows weren't ignored, but the wrong person responded to them. After setting a baking dish on the table, Ben walked over to him. "Do I just pick him up?"

"Sure!" Jace said.

No! Samson countered, but before he could scurry away, Ben had grabbed him, hoisted, and set him on the table again. That was odd. He sniffed, expecting gross human food to offend his nose, when he smelled something else. His favorite can of food. Samson reassessed the table. Jace was seated behind a plate and grinning. Across from this was another for Ben, and just in front of where Samson had been set down was a small plate and a large mound of gravy-infused meat.

"You're so grown up!" Jace said. "Look at you, eating at the adult table instead of the counter."

That *was* pretty cool. Samson watched suspiciously as Ben scooped human food onto their plates. It smelled like tomatoes and cheese and starch.

Ben sat and looked to Samson, his expression worried. "Maybe he doesn't like it. I should have fed him where he usually eats."

"We just need to lead by example," Jace said. "Erm. Is this lasagna?"

"I forgot to buy the right noodles at the store," Ben moaned. "I figured spaghetti would be just as good as long as I laid the noodles out in rows. That's like pre-chopped lasagna. Right? No need for a knife."

"Very convenient," Jace said. "Let's eat!"

As soon as Samson heard the sound of them smacking their lips, he could no longer resist. He started eating too, imagining that they had brought down a mouse in a hunt and were tearing meat off its bones together. That's how the lions ate, which made Samson enjoy this meal even more than he usually did.

Later that night, after Jace and Ben had finished their play-fight, Samson climbed the ladder into bed. He started creeping over to where Jace slept, pausing along the way to sniff one of Ben's legs that was sticking out from the covers. It didn't stink, and at least it had some fur. The leg was warm too. Samson looked back to where Jace slept, at the arm that he knew would curl up to hold him. He would make his way there by morning, but for now... Samson flopped down, pressed his back to Ben's leg, and decided that it didn't feel so bad.

Jace was sad. Summer had come to an end and the leaves were starting to fall off the trees. Samson now knew that they would come back, but it was still an understandable time of year to feel down. Ben wasn't around anymore. Had he shriveled up and drifted away like the leaves? Samson wasn't sure, but he did his best to make his daddy happy again, putting on shows by leaping on his toys or rolling onto his back while making big watery eyes. He also sat in Jace's lap as often as possible so he would know he was loved. And yet, somehow, that didn't seem to be enough anymore. Samson didn't understand why until Jace left town again.

Ben wasn't there to sleep next to in bed. Michelle came to feed Samson, but she never sat at the table with him and ate her own food. They didn't share meals together, and while she sometimes sat on the couch to keep him company, Samson didn't crawl into her lap like he had Ben's. That had only happened a few times, but each had felt good. Pretty soon, Samson was sitting in the window and feeling sad too. To his surprise, the feeling didn't go away entirely when Jace returned.

"We've got to do something," Jace said. He paced back and forth through the apartment, Samson sitting on the coffee table to watch. "Something drastic. Ben still has two more years of school. He won't transfer to the university here, not after having moved to Austin, which is closer but not close enough. We either tough it out or..." Jace spun around. "You're going to kill me."

Samson saw no reason to.

"What if we moved? Once more and then that's it. For a while."

Okay, so maybe Samson did feel like extending his claws. He liked his home! Not at first, because his smell hadn't been anywhere and he hadn't slept well for weeks, always distracted by strange new sounds. The car ride to this home hadn't been fun either. Samson flattened his ears at the memory, because he *really* didn't want to go through that. Again!

"Probably not the best time to mention the three-hour drive," Jace said. "I'll make it up to you. Remember your balcony at the last place? At the new apartment you'll have one. I promise."

Fresh air, sun baths, and the occasional crunchy bug to eat? That sounded nice.

"Ben will move in with us. If we do this, he'll always be around."

That sounded even better. Samson weighed the pros and cons. A couple miserable weeks versus always having Ben there. Cats didn't nod, but if they did, he would have, because he had reached his decision. They were moving!

Humans didn't like to move. They loved it. Samson struggled to understand why. He was perfectly happy with his new home. He had his promised balcony, and he even liked how each room was separate, which made stalking a lot more fun. He would wait around a corner until he heard footsteps. Then he would strike! Not only Jace. Ben was always there too. They were married now. Samson wasn't quite sure how that worked, but it must be very easy, because one day Jace stopped talking about how they were getting married and started saying that they *were* married. Samson didn't feel any different. Jace and Ben still smelled the same, but as his daddy patiently explained, "We're officially a family now. I'm still your daddy and now Ben is too."

That was a neat trick. Samson loved Ben. He could tell that Ben loved him too, so that should have been the end of the story. They were happy. Why did anything need to change?

"Don't you want your own house?" Jace asked one morning at the breakfast table. "With your own yard!"

"Would that be safe?" Ben replied, looking to where Samson sat and groomed himself. "He's not an outdoor cat."

"No," Jace said, "mostly because we never lived in a quiet enough area. My mom's cats were all outdoor. You're right though. That doesn't always end well. I'd still like him to experience the feel of grass beneath his paws. He deserves that."

"Then we'll have to find a place with a tall fence," Ben said, dunking a spoon into his cereal. "If we keep an eye on him and never let him out alone, do you think that would work?"

"What do you say, Samson?" Jace asked. "We've been here a couple of years now. Ready to move on to something bigger and better?"

No. Such things weren't up to him though. He knew that humans kept moving in the same way they consumed their stories. They didn't shut off the television during the funny parts or stop reading when on a happy page. They continued watching and kept turning pages, even though they knew that the plot would take a turn for the worse. Then again, curiosity was a weakness that he and all cats could relate to.

Samson picked his way along the grass, senses working overtime until…

Pounce!

He quickly lifted his paw and let his mouth finish the job. Another insect vanquished! He very casually looked to where Jace and Ben sat on the patio, expecting them to fall out of their chairs in awe, or at least be impressed enough to tell him what a good job he had done. Sure, it had only been a bug and not an almighty mouse, but he had yet to meet one. Frustrated by their lack of praise and ready to return indoors, he slowly made his way over to them.

He liked his new house very much. In a way it reminded him of the one that belonged to Rachel. It too was small, although this house didn't have a downstairs or a Victor who lived there. Just a living room, a kitchen, a bathroom, and a bedroom, but what else did they need? His favorite part was the backyard. Samson was happy to remain there. While he did sometimes wonder what was over the fence, he was nearly ten years old now. Jace had told him so and made a cake out of salmon and tuna. That had been delicious. The point was, Samson wasn't an impulsive kitten who would go running off without a second thought. His family needed him too much. Especially on days like today, when they seemed so tense.

"Are you sure you're okay with this?" Ben asked. "We can still cancel if you want."

One of his legs kept bouncing, which meant that his lap would be shaky, so Samson went to Jace and hopped up on him instead.

"I'm perfectly fine," Jace said, his long fingers gently massaging Samson's neck. "I'm starting to think that you *want* me to ask you to cancel."

"No," Ben said. He bit his bottom lip and furrowed his brow. The leg kept shaking. "It's just that he's my high school sweetheart, and that makes everything awkward. Doesn't it?"

"I'm okay. If it helps, I trust you, and I think it's nice what you're trying to do. Tim seems like a lonely guy."

"He is," Ben said. "I know he could use more friends. I could too, but I never thought of him in those terms. When I first laid eyes on him, I didn't think, 'Oh, he and I could be good friends!' With some people, you know that they'll either be everything to you or nothing at all. You're the same way to me."

"We'd be friends," Jace said. "If anything happened to our relationship, I'd still want you in my life."

Ben exhaled. "You're sweet. And don't worry, nothing is going to happen."

"I'm not worried."

"Not at all?"

Jace chuckled. "Of course I have my concerns, but you made your choice years ago, and I swore to trust you. None of that has changed. I also know what you're going through. I tried being friends with Victor. More than once, actually."

Ben leaned forward. "How'd that work out?"

"The first time was after we had just broken up. I was… gosh, seventeen? No, eighteen. Things were tense between us and not in a fun way. We lost touch after I left for college. The second time we tried to be friends, I ended up leaving my boyfriend to be with him."

They both went quiet. Samson stretched out a paw and yawned.

"I'm not going to—"

"I didn't say—"

"I know."

"I know too."

They both laughed. Humans were so weird.

"It'll be a nice night," Jace said. "I'm interested to finally get to know him, and I'm sure you'll both have a lot to talk about. Treat it like a school reunion."

"Okay," Ben said, his leg finally ceasing its bouncing. "You're the best, you know that?"

"I'll keep that in mind tonight if I find myself getting insecure." Jace lifted Samson and stood. "Let's make sure everything is perfect. We might not live in a mansion, but I'm still hoping to make him jealous."

Samson was relocated to the couch. He settled down there and snoozed until the doorbell rang. Then he lifted his head and watched as someone new was escorted into the house. Humans tended to look alike to him—just different pairs of shoes and legs—so he relied on his nose instead. He wasn't about to rise for a stranger. Instead he remained where he was until this Tim person noticed him and approached.

"Hey!" he said. "We've met before. Remember me?"

Samson sniffed casually. Tim smelled like body wash and cologne. Through it all, he detected the scent of an animal. What kind he wasn't sure. Definitely not a cat.

"You've met Samson before?" Jace asked. "When was this?"

"You were out of town, I think," Tim said. Then he tore his eyes away from him. "That's not supposed to sound— Ben and I were just hanging out and he needed to feed Samson, so we… Nothing happened. I'm not trying to stir up trouble this time, I swear."

"It's fine," Jace said, cracking his knuckles. "Ben, get my boxing gloves. We might as well finish this now."

Ben was the first to laugh.

Tim nervously joined him a second later. "If you're going to keep messing with me," he said, "I'll need a drink."

Jace gestured to the kitchen. "Right this way."

The other two followed him. Samson resumed his nap, ignoring the smell of a human dinner and the typical sounds that went with it. Only when they returned to the couch and turned on the television did he pay attention again, moving aside so Jace could take a seat. Samson made sure to occupy his lap before anyone else could. Ben sat next to them with Tim on the far side. This made it easy to continue sleeping, although as the movie went on, it only seemed to get louder, so Samson rose and went into the kitchen. From there he leapt onto the counter, and after careful calculation, jumped even higher to reach the top of the refrigerator. Jace had surprised him on his previous birthday with a bed there and it quickly became Samson's favorite retreat. Above the fridge was a cabinet, making the space in between feel like a cave or den.

He wasn't sure how long he had slept there when voices woke him again.

"I don't need help making microwave popcorn," Ben said.

Samson raised his head and peered over the edge. Ben was standing in the kitchen and rifling through the pantry.

Tim stood not far away, his back against the counter. The grin he wore never faded. "Are you sure about that? I remember a day that you *did* manage to mess it up."

"Whatever," Ben said, spinning around with a small packet in his hand. "I know I'm not a good cook, but I'm not that bad!"

"Maybe not anymore," Tim murmured.

Ben unwrapped the package he was holding and tossed it into the microwave. "You're joking, right?"

Tim shook his head. "Nope. You really don't remember? It's when my parents were out of town and I was stuck on the couch. I didn't see what you actually did, but somehow you managed to burn the popcorn."

"Maybe it was the skillet kind," Ben said, a beep sounding with each button he pushed. "That's harder to make."

"No, it was microwave. That's the only kind my parents bought."

"You're serious? Why can't I remember?" Ben leaned against the counter next to Tim as the microwave hummed. "Are you sure you aren't confusing me with Krista Norman?"

"Nope. She could cook. She made me cookies once. They were delicious."

"Booooo!" Ben said, crossing his arms over his chest. "Is it sad that I still despise her?"

Tim laughed. "Yes. Out of all my friends back then, she was the only nice one."

"She needed to keep her nice little mitts off my property."

"Your property?" Tim asked, looking surprised.

"Yeah," Ben said. Then his eyes became wide too. "Back then I mean. Not now. Obviously."

"Obviously," Tim echoed.

They both pushed away from the counter and seemed incapable of looking at each other. Maybe one of them had farted. Humans always overreacted to such things. Or maybe not because Ben turned to face Tim again. "I remember now! We had to run all over the house and open up the windows."

"Because of the burnt smell," Tim said while bobbing his head. "That meant turning off the air conditioner too, even though it was crazy hot outside."

"And you took off your shirt like it was unbearable," Ben said with shining eyes. "Be honest though, it wasn't that hot."

"The temperature or me?" Tim winked. "And yeah, I always loved showing off for you." His grin finally faltered.

Ben moved to check the microwave and took a long time doing so. "I think it's about done," he said, opening the door.

"Cool," Tim replied. "You guys have a popcorn bowl?"

"In the cabinet above the refrigerator. It's too high to reach. You'll need a chair."

"Too high for you, maybe."

"That's why I usually have Jace get it down."

Tim stood up a little straighter. "I bet I can manage."

"Without a chair?" Ben challenged, starting to smile again.

"Sure."

Tim strutted over to the refrigerator. Samson stood, annoyed that his privacy was being invaded. He looked to his nearest daddy to complain.

Ben locked eyes with him and his expression grew serious. "You know what? Let's have Jace get it. He likes it when I need his help. I like it too."

"I get it," Tim said, backing away. "Believe me, I do. I'll send him in here."

"Do you want another beer?" Ben asked.

Tim didn't stick around to answer the question.

Ben exhaled and looked up at Samson again with a guilty expression. "Don't worry. I'm not going to mess up. Not this time. I know how lucky I am."

Samson wasn't worried. Guests were always weird, but they never stuck around for long. Jace entered the kitchen, gave Ben a quick smooch, and focused on the cabinet. Until he saw Samson there. Then he reacted like Samson had done something amazing and rewarded him with petting and baby talk. No, nothing to worry about at all. Life was good.

The men with flashing lights were back. Samson was certain it was a bad dream, but he couldn't seem to wake up. Jace was on the floor and Ben was sitting next to him, yowling and crying. Samson crept close long enough to sniff Jace. He seemed okay. Then why wasn't he getting up? That's when the sirens grew louder, and Ben began running to the front door and back again multiple times. Samson followed once, curious about the world outside, and wondered if he should take a look. Then a flashing car pulled up and he decided to hide. He didn't want to be taken away! What about Ben? He should hide. Jace too! Why wouldn't he get up?

Samson wished he was braver as people rushed into the house. He wished he had the courage to attack and drive them away, but they were so much bigger than him and the noises so loud and confusing. Eventually he couldn't take it anymore and dashed for the bedroom. He hid beneath the bed until the house grew silent. Still he waited, just to be sure. When he did finally venture out again, Ben was gone. Jace was too. He was alone.

Jace came back. He always did. Samson felt silly for worrying so much. Sure the house had stayed empty for hours and hours, and when someone did come home again, it was only Ben and he was alone. And crying. So maybe Samson had a good reason for worrying, but he shouldn't have, because Jace always came back for him. Even the men with flashing lights couldn't keep him away.

Still, it must have been a nasty fight. Jace moved slower than he used to. Maybe he was still healing. He also winced at loud noises and preferred to keep the rooms darker than before. Samson didn't mind, since he also didn't like loud noises, and his eyesight didn't require so much light. He made sure to be careful when crawling onto Jace's lap for the first time since the scare, and to his relief, not everything had changed. Jace still rumbled words that sounded like a purr and pet him to perfection. Never too long, and never too briefly. His daddy was still the best, even though Ben seemed to have doubts.

"Are you going to be okay?" Ben asked, standing between

the living room and front door.

"I'll be fine," Jace said from the couch.

"What do you have planned? Want me to put a movie on for you?"

"I had an aneurysm, Ben, not a lobotomy. I think I can handle sticking a DVD in the machine. Besides, I have a book I want to finish reading."

"You're not supposed to put too much strain on yourself. Maybe I should call in sick."

"Someone needs to pay the bills," Jace shot back, "since I'm too useless to work now."

"You'll get better," Ben said. "Would you rather be on your own?"

"Frankly, yes. You're making me feel like I'm helpless. And I'm not alone."

Ben's eyes darted down to him and he smiled. "Nurse Samson?"

"Dr. Samson," Jace corrected. "He graduated from medical school just before we met." He leaned over to bring their faces closer together. "You'll take good care of me, right?"

That's how it worked! Jace always came back, and Samson always took care of him when he was feeling down. They were a team. Inseparable.

Samson was snoozing on the bed. The really big one that they all slept in at night. He couldn't figure out why humans didn't have more beds. He liked to have a few in each room. Sometimes he was in the mood to curl up in a tight circle. The smaller round beds were better for that. At other times he liked to stretch out. Humans seemed to enjoy variety in all other areas, so why not this one? Although lately, Jace napped on the couch more often than he used to.

His daddy had just finished taking a shower. Samson liked it when he smelled so fresh and was so warm. He watched as Jace hurried to put on socks and underwear. Something was wrong. His breath came in short bursts, like he was upset. When he pulled on his jeans, he stood up straight and went still. Then he sat on the edge of the bed. Samson would have gotten into his lap if he had remained sitting long enough, but before he could, Jace stood and swayed. Then he hurried out of the room. When he returned, he was holding Ben's hand. Jace sat again in the same spot as before.

"We're okay," Ben said, his voice sounding shaky.

"No, we're not," Jace said, pulling the hand he still held so Ben would get into bed with them.

Samson liked this idea. He made room, walking to the far side of the mattress and waiting for the other two to settle down. They were trying something new. Both were on their sides, which wasn't unusual, but this time Ben was behind Jace, holding on to him. That could work. Samson started to crawl over them.

"What's going on?" Ben asked.

"My head hurts," Jace said, choking against the words. "Just like last time."

He hurt? Samson would try to help. That was his job, and he had done it before, but he was starting to worry. Ben kept talking and sounded upset. Jace did too, although when Samson curled up against his stomach and started purring, his voice became calmer. Then he stopped talking, but Ben didn't. He kept saying the same words over and over. "I love you. I love you. Please don't go. I love you so much!"

Samson agreed. He purred louder, confused when Jace started to shake, but then a hand reached down, the long fingers sinking into his fur, and Samson pressed himself harder against his stomach. He felt Ben's hand on top of Jace's and they were all connected. A family. That's how they remained for a very long time, but when Ben's cries became too loud, Samson rose and went to stand on top of him and knead his paws. He had two daddies and two jobs. He would help Ben feel better. Somehow he would do it.

The men who came to take Jace away didn't have a flashing car. They had a bag, and Samson didn't like what happened. Ben didn't either. He cried and yowled, but Samson didn't mind how loud he was anymore, because it echoed the pain he felt inside. The dark times had come again, even though there wasn't snow outside. The lights weren't switched on that night. Just a candle on the coffee table in the living room. Ben was balled up on the couch, but even when he stretched out, there wasn't a lap for Samson to sit on. Meals didn't come either, and in the morning, the curtains weren't opened again. Oh yes, the dark times were back.

Samson stayed close to Ben, and in the dim light, he could imagine it was Victor there instead. He too had been sad. Too sad to keep going, but they had to. Didn't he realize? Jace would come back. He always did. Always. Samson was sad without him, but he knew it wouldn't be forever. It never had been before.

He wished he had some way of telling Ben, because he needed help. That nice woman he knew, Allison, she showed up, and usually when she did, they would sing and laugh together. Not this time. She didn't stay long. Ben wouldn't let her. He wouldn't do anything but sit there and cry, enough that Samson was scared Ben would leave and come back with a stick made of metal and wood, just like the one Victor had brought home. Ben didn't leave. Sometimes he fell asleep. Never for long. He would mumble to himself, and just before he woke up, sometimes he would yell. Then he would look around—or once he searched the house, calling Jace's name—before he started crying again.

Samson was crying too. Not because he was sad. He was, but sad cats were quiet, and he could no longer afford to be. He was too hungry. Starving. The sun had come and gone twice already without him eating. He chewed on one of the houseplants in desperation but ended up puking up the leaves. He tried twice more with the same results. He meowed at Ben, but couldn't make him understand. He would only cry harder and say things like, "I can't bring him back. I'm sorry."

Samson didn't blame him. He didn't know how to make people come back either. He didn't feel very good. He started sleeping more to escape the pain in his stomach, and when he moved around the house, he didn't trust himself to make big jumps anymore. He didn't have the energy. Samson wanted up on the counter but couldn't manage that, so he went to the kitchen and began yowling. He didn't stop even when Ben came to investigate. Samson meowed even more.

Ben opened the pantry. Finally! He didn't take out a can though. Instead he looked down at Samson. "I don't want to live without him. Do you?"

Hungry! Samson kept meowing. *Please!*

Ben sucked in air. "It would break his heart. What am I thinking? I'm sorry." His hands were shaking as he took out a can. "I'm so sorry!"

Samson weaved in and out between his legs in excitement.

When he heard the can open, he started drooling. Ben loaded a plate with moist succulent meat and set it on the floor. Samson started gobbling the food so fast that his teeth hit the plate a few times. He didn't care. The discomfort was nothing compared to the aching hunger he felt inside. He devoured the meal in record speed, then looked up for more. Ben was eating too. That was good. He was hungry, judging from the way he shoved torn bread into his mouth. Ben was still chewing it when he stopped, looked at the remaining food in his hand, and started crying.

Samson didn't know what to do for him. He watched as Ben calmed himself, ate a little more, and drank a glass of water. Then he got down on his knees, putting his wet face close to Samson's.

"I'll stay for you," he said. "That's what he would have wanted. I'm only staying for you."

Samson climbed onto his legs, even though they were slanted, and settled down there, trying to tell Ben that he would stay too. They would stick together and fight against the dark times until Jace returned. And he would. His daddy always came back.

Ben was strong. Samson could tell that he didn't want to be on his own. Ben also needed someone there to open curtains and cans, to make the day fun and spread love. Jace was gone though, and until he came back, they were helpless. Or so he thought. Ben started waking up at his usual time. He brought light into the house, and even though he didn't smile, he fed Samson, joined him in the backyard, and played with his favorite toys. The next time Allison came over, she was allowed to stay longer. That seemed to help too. They talked and cried instead of laughing and singing. Each day that went by seemed to make a difference. Ben started to sing again, even though the songs sounded sad. He even put up a Christmas tree and moved one of Samson's beds beneath it. Usually he had lights and ornaments to bat at. Usually the presents grew in number until Samson barely had space to sleep there. Not this year, although he still liked having his tree. He slept beneath it every day and waited.

The sun rose and fell. The leaves outside came back, sunshine and bugs filled the yard, and the trees lost their leaves again. This happened twice more. Jace still hadn't returned, but Samson knew he would. It might be a very long time, but he hadn't given up. Ben hadn't either. He learned how to laugh again. Sometimes they would sit together, and Ben would tell him stories about Jace, as if reading from a book. Samson liked that very much. Ben did too. These days, he sounded happy when talking about Jace instead of sad.

He wasn't completely happy though. Samson was reminded of when it had just been him and his first daddy. They had been happy too, but only because they hadn't known that someone out there could bring them milk and songs and play-fights in bed. Only when Ben joined their family did they realize just how happy they could be. Samson didn't know how to make this happen again, although one night something very strange happened. He heard a key in the lock, and when the door opened, it wasn't Ben standing there. It was Allison.

"Guard cat, huh?" she said, walking sideways as she entered because she was carrying something flat and large. "Don't worry, I am here to steal, but I'm leaving something behind too. It's more like a trade."

Samson was thoroughly confused. Allison had been there earlier in the evening, with Ben, and they had left together. Unless…

"You probably think he's out of town and I'm here to feed you," she said, leaning the large object against the wall. "Good news, he's still in Austin and hopefully getting some use out of that heart of his. The bad news is that I won't be feeding you."

Samson meowed. More often than not, it worked, this time included.

"Okay, okay. How about some treats?"

Yes! Samson rushed toward the kitchen and jumped up on the counter. He watched eagerly as Allison rummaged in the pantry to find a bag of crunchy little pockets filled with cheese.

"These are a bribe," she said, scattering a handful in front of him. "You never saw me here, agreed?"

Sure! As long as she didn't plan on using his litter box or eating his cans of food, he didn't mind her being there at all. Once he finished snacking, he went to see what she was up to. Allison was in the living room. She had taken something off the wall and was trying to hang a similar object in its place. Paintings and photos were difficult for cats. Samson could understand the appeal of television. Sometimes he watched it if birds or other animals were on the screen. Without motion, he struggled to make sense of what he saw. Ben had once held out a framed photo of Jace for him to see. Samson had been close, sitting on Ben's lap at the time, but the image wasn't right at all. Jace never stopped moving, even when he slept. Nobody did, so Samson hadn't seen much of Jace in the photo.

"There we go," Allison said, taking a step back to consider her work. "Say what you want about Tim, that boy can paint!" She glanced down at the painting she had removed. "This'll look great in my dining room. Ben will never let me keep it, but for now…"

Samson walked closer to sniff it. He wasn't impressed.

"I know this must be confusing to you," Allison said, "but it's part of a plan, and if it works… You don't want Ben to be alone forever, do you?"

Ben wasn't alone! They had each other. He thought he understood what she meant though. Daddies seemed happier in pairs. Did this mean that Jace was finally coming back? Samson meowed, pleased with this news.

"You are too cute!" Allison said, bending over to pet him. "I can't stick around. I have to be gone before the love birds return. At least I hope that's how they're feeling. If this doesn't pan out, Ben is going to kill me." She stood there in silence, staring at the painting she had hung. "Worth the risk. He needs this. Call me later and tell me how it plays out."

Samson watched her go. Then he looked up at the painting. Aside from it smelling strongly of chemicals, he couldn't see the difference between it and the one she had taken. He went to the couch and settled onto his favorite blanket, but his nap didn't last long. The door opened again. Ben was back, and he wasn't alone!

Samson strained his neck to see. Jace was taller than that, wasn't he? Had he shrunk? His hair certainly hadn't been that dark before.

"Jace—" Ben said, making Samson's heart swell.

The voice that answered didn't belong to his daddy. "—was a good man," the other person said. "The best, in fact. I would never dishonor his memory, and I will never, ever be able to replace him. No one could."

Samson went to investigate, needing to be sure. After sniffing a leg, his suspicions were confirmed. This was Tim. Samson had nearly forgotten about him, but now he understood what Allison had been talking about. Ben needed someone. At least until Jace came back, he needed another person to play-fight and have lengthy conversations with. If it made him happy... Samson rubbed against Tim's leg, accepting him into their home. He did the same to Ben to show him it was all right. Then he went back to the couch to continue his nap. And to keep waiting.

Even when happy, humans were rarely content. Samson walked through his home, which was now filled with cardboard boxes. Everything he was used to seeing was packed away inside these. He thought this a fun game at first, leaping from box to box and climbing the highest stacks. Now he wasn't so sure. Ben seemed stressed out and kept promising him that it would be okay.

"We're going to be one big happy family," he said one night. "All four of us."

Four? Samson wished he was better at counting. How many was that exactly? Ben sometimes smelled like Tim these days, so he guessed they would be living together. Was that four? Then one morning, Ben seemed even more stressed than before. Samson hid. He could guess what was coming, and he could have avoided it if he hadn't heard the treat bag and gone to investigate. He found a small pile of treats on the kitchen floor, which was unusual, and before he could gobble too many, someone grabbed him from behind and shoved him into his carrier. Samson started yowling right away. He was *not* happy about this! Especially when put into the car, which he didn't like the smell or sound of. Fortunately he wasn't kept there for long. When the drive came to an end and his carrier was lifted from the vehicle, he inhaled through the holes eagerly. The air outside here smelled delicious! He could already hear more birds than he was used to. He hoped his new home had a yard, or at the very least a balcony.

He didn't see much before they were inside again. When he was finally set down and freed from the carrier, he was disappointed. His new home was very small. Just a single room with a bed.

"Sorry about this," Ben said, on his knees and watching him.

Samson mostly ignored his presence, intent on sniffing every corner of the room to assess how safe it was here.

"It's just until things settle down and we can introduce you to Chinchilla." Ben stood. "I'll get you some food and something to drink."

This turned out to be some dry kibble and his usual water dish. Samson wasn't pleased with the surroundings or the food, so he hid beneath the bed. Ben sighed. Then he left the room. Samson couldn't sleep while he was gone. He listened intently to the noises beyond. He heard a truck come and go, and the voices of people as things were moved around. Eventually the light outside grew dim and most of the sounds ceased. He had decided it might be safe enough for a quick nap when the door opened again.

Ben came back inside, and this time he had a more impressive offering. Samson smelled the meat almost immediately, but he still didn't want to go for another car ride. Only when Ben slid a saucer of milk partially under the bed did he give in.

"There you are," Ben said. "The worst part is over. You're going to like this house, you'll see. Just wait until we get it all set up. This is the right thing to do. I promise."

Humans often said one thing while their bodies revealed another. Ben wasn't sure at all about this move, which made Samson feel uneasy. He ate his fill, just in case dark times were ahead again. After eating, he allowed Ben to pet him, growing sleepier as the food settled in his stomach. Then he finally returned beneath the bed where he felt safest and went to sleep.

The next day brought a big change. Ben fed him in the morning, and when he came back later that day, he picked up Samson and carried him out of the room. They were in a hallway, Samson instantly curious, but he couldn't get down no matter how hard he squirmed. Ben brought him to a different room. This one was much larger. Samson once again ignored Ben so he could assess his environment. The bed here had sheets and blankets on it. The attached bathroom and walk-in closet offered many places to climb or hide. Tim's scent was everywhere. So was another. Samson struggled to pin it down, but the smell was animal. Maybe whatever it was had lived here previously.

But no. The scent was too fresh, and if that wasn't evidence enough, in the afternoon Samson heard something on the other side of the door. It was loud when it breathed, especially when it sniffed. He sniffed back, the smell he detected matching the one in the room. Samson hissed for good measure, and when the creature on the other side scratched at the door, he held his ground instead of fleeing. Still, he was glad when the creature went away. It came back later that day with the same result. At night when Ben and Tim got into bed together, the creature lay outside the closed door. Samson wasn't far away, keeping an eye on it between naps. The next day played out similarly, nothing but a thin door between him and the unknown until he heard voices in the hallway. The door opened. Samson rose, and from his position on the bed, saw that Ben was standing in the hallway. Time to finally explore? He stretched and hopped off the bed. Then he strolled forward, curious to see if this new house had a yard. Tim was further down the hallway, and between his legs—

Samson froze. The creature was three times his size at least. The skin was leathery, and while it hadn't breathed fire yet, it was only a matter of time, because everything Munch had said was true. This was a mouse, and it was terrifying! He locked eyes with the creature, knowing that he would soon be fighting for his very life. Samson wished he could remember how Munch had defeated the mouse. He could use his help now.

"Samson," Ben said, "this is Chinchilla, your new..."

"Roommate?" Tim suggested.

"Yeah," Ben agreed. "Roommate. Maybe even your friend."

Samson wasn't clear on either term, and he didn't have time for human customs now. Not in the heat of battle.

"I think we're okay!" Tim said cheerfully.

The mouse charged. Its mouth opened as it neared, Samson sure he could see the glow of flames deep within its throat. He couldn't run away. Not only would he lose face, but he simply didn't have time. He remembered all the games he and Jace used to play, how he had practiced swiping at his prey with his claws. This was the moment he'd been training for. The mouse was close now, so Samson extended his claws, summoned all of his strength, and struck it right on the nose.

Ouch!

The mouse scurried to a stop. Then it fled, running until it was behind Tim's legs. Samson couldn't process why at the moment, still too shocked that the mouse could speak. Munch had never mentioned that! Then again, Munch had been very small at the time, and if he had managed to defeat a mouse as a kitten, then maybe they weren't so tough. Samson sauntered forward, the mouse cowering behind Tim's legs now. He stopped halfway down the hall, sat to show he was too powerful to feel threatened, and flicked his tail back and forth.

My territory!

The mouse peeked from behind two legs and harrumphed. *Mine too!*

At least that's what Samson thought it said. The sound wasn't quite right and the body language was off, but it was making more sense than humans did.

"I think we've established the pecking order," Ben said, sounding amused.

"Dogs and cats," Tim said, shaking his head. "This won't end well."

"It'll work itself out. Right, Samson?"

Dogs and cats? He knew which one he was. A dog was probably a type of mouse. Maybe.

"Come on, girl," Tim said, patting his leg. "Let's go outside to potty."

"Make sure the neighbors don't see you!" Ben called after him. Then he crouched down to pet him. "You did good. I don't think she'll mess with you again. Try being nice though. You might end up liking her."

Samson wasn't sure about that. He padded down the hallway to continue exploring his new home. And to investigate what this whole dog thing was all about.

Life was full of surprises. Samson thought he had discovered them all, but the move showed him how much he'd been missing. He could now say with authority that he knew what a dog was. Better yet, he finally understood why humans were so happy in pairs because Samson had a friend! One he could actually talk to. They were still working out a few kinks in their communication, but they were making great progress, especially since one of their first conversations had gone like this:

My name is Chinchilla. I'm a good girl. A very good girl! You're a bad girl. Very bad!

Dogs tended to be repetitive. And excitable.

I'm not a girl, Samson had responded. *And I'm in charge.*

Tim's in charge. He's a good boy. I have a ball! Do you have a ball?

Your ball belongs to me now.

Chinchilla had cocked her head, then started panting. *I like my ball.*

Samson responded by flicking his tail. *Correction. You like* my *ball.*

Of course, once Samson saw the ball she was referring to, he wasn't so interested in claiming it. It was dirty and smelled like slobber. Dogs managed to get their spit on most things. The rest they peed on. Samson found it all terribly uncivilized. And yet, it was nice to have someone who wasn't walking around on stilts all day. Someone who also found humans confusing and strange. Chinchilla was a bigger fan of them and in many regards had a deeper understanding of their mysteries.

Ben and Tim are play-fighting a lot lately, Samson pointed out one night as he strolled down the upstairs hallway.

They're making puppies, Chinchilla responded matter-of-factly. She was waiting outside their bedroom door.

Puppies? Samson asked. *What are those?*

Baby dogs. Puppies! I can't wait to meet the puppies. I like dogs. And cats. Do you like puppies?

Yes, Samson answered, mostly because agreeing was the quickest way of getting Chinchilla off a topic. He looked around with concern, worried that puppies would start pouring from each room.

Puppies! Chinchilla added helpfully. *Ben is the bitch!*

That had made Samson flex his claws, but a little more explanation helped clear up the misunderstanding. Chinchilla was definitely odd, but she also made every day an adventure. The best was spending time in the backyard together. Samson taught her how to pounce on bugs, and Chinchilla returned the favor by digging a hole. That was impressive. The hole was big enough for Samson to hide inside. He would peek over the edge, wait until Chinchilla got near, and leap out to scare her. Then they would chase each other back and forth across the yard, which was great fun.

After many months of being friends, Samson made another wonderful discovery. He already knew that Chinchilla's skin wasn't leathery like his initial impression. She had fur too, although it was shorter and looked coarser than his own. As it turned out, her fur was plenty soft and felt good to lean against. Or lay against, as became their habit that winter. Chinchilla's size made her an ideal napping companion. Samson would often curl up against her stomach. She seemed to enjoy sleeping just as much as he did too.

Everything was perfect. He still missed Jace, but short of him returning, Samson couldn't imagine anything else he needed. Of course when things seemed fine is when humans liked shaking them up the most. Samson's first hint was the flurry of activity, especially in the bedroom nobody slept in except him when he wanted peace and quiet. Ben and Tim both became increasingly nervous. Another move? If so, they hadn't packed much. Just a few boxes in the guest room, and those were already gone. What then?

He had his answer while napping in the master bedroom one day. He heard Ben's voice in the hall and another he didn't recognize. That brought back memories. Samson loved Chinchilla, but he hoped they weren't adding another dog to the family. One was enough! He stood and stretched, ready to discover what the next twist would be. A skinny guy with messy hair, as it turned out. If one dog was enough, two humans was excessive. They really didn't need another, although this person at least showed a proper amount of enthusiasm.

"You've got a cat!" the young man said, rushing forward to meet him.

"That's Samson," Ben said. "I hope you're not allergic."

"Nope," the young man answered, offering his hand to be sniffed. Enthusiastic *and* polite. "I'm definitely not allergic to Samsons."

Samson walked forward and gave the hand a proper inspection. It smelled sweaty, like humans did when they were nervous. This one seemed harmless enough. Samson gave his mark of approval by rubbing against him, yawned, and then went to get a drink from his bowl in the bathroom. With any luck, Chinchilla hadn't gotten her slobber in it. He consulted with her later about the new arrival.

Jason is a good boy, she informed him. *I like him very much and he likes me.*

Samson had eavesdropped to learn his name, the sound making his ears prickle, but it wasn't quite right. *But who is he?*

A puppy, Chinchilla said, tongue lolling out of her mouth gleefully. *Tim and Ben made a puppy!*

Jason seemed awfully big to be a puppy, and he didn't smell much like a dog, although this changed the more Samson sniffed him, because Jason and Chinchilla really seemed to have hit it off. Samson was worried that he would lose his friend to this new person. He started feeling jealous until Jason expressed an interest in him too.

"I love your eyes!" he said one evening. Jason had slid to the floor and was resting his chin on a couch cushion so their faces were close. "I wish I was a cat!"

Who could blame him?

"Do you think I could feed you from now on?" Jason continued. "I know Ben and Tim usually do, but I wouldn't mind."

Samson was willing to give his plating skills a try.

"Do you like to be brushed? I can do that too!"

Samson would rather have another person to scoop his litterbox for him, but it *was* getting a little hard to reach all the places he needed to clean. For some reason, he wasn't as flexible these days, so more brushing would be nice.

"You can sleep in my bed if you want," Jason said. "I'm up for anything. I love animals. They actually make sense. Unlike humans."

Okay, so maybe it wouldn't be so bad having another human around. They were useful. He checked up on Jason more often after that, feeling personally responsible, since Samson knew it could be difficult adjusting to a new home. Jason seemed to do okay. At times he seemed angry or sad, but this slowly changed. Their family was magical in that way. Anyone who joined them rarely remained sad for long. Maybe they should open their doors to the world and let everyone pour in. All the humans, cats, and dogs. All the mothers, daddies, and even the mice. Everyone living together under one roof and no longer sad, alone, or afraid.

Samson was getting tired of waiting. He had everything he needed except the thing he wanted most. He hadn't lost faith. Jace would be back. Soon would be preferable, because something was wrong. Food didn't taste as good as it used to. Samson found it difficult to finish his plates. Chinchilla was there to help, which he was grateful for. The next time the leaves fell from the trees, Samson had trouble staying warm, but she was there for him again, never minding when he needed to cuddle, even if they weren't sleeping. When he woke he was always stiff, although after some stretching and walking around, he was ready to play again. They still chased each other. Chinchilla seemed to have an easier time catching him. Either she was getting faster or he was getting slower. Colors didn't seem as bright and the world wasn't as sharp as it had once been either.

These weren't the dark times. Samson was still happy. His days were still filled with light. He just needed a little extra sleep between each meal, each game, each petting session.

"There you are!" Ben said quietly.

Samson had leapt to get into bed, his hips complaining, but he wasn't about to listen to them. Instead he walked forward, purring at the inviting scene. Tim was already asleep, but as usual, Ben had stayed up a little longer to read. He set aside the book and patted the sheets over his lap. Samson settled down there, which took more time than it once had.

"You're getting old," Ben said with a soft chuckle. "We both are."

Samson rolled onto his side and reached out with a paw. *More petting.*

Ben gently scratched the fur of his chest. "You're an amazing cat, you know that? Look at everything we've thrown at you, and you just take it in stride. Chinchilla, Jason..." Ben glanced over briefly and whispered, "Tim. That's right, I know the truth. I saw you on his lap the other day."

Samson blinked slowly. Ben wasn't as quick as Jace had been, or even Jason, who spoke decent Cat, but he caught on and blinked back. "I love my little gray fur ball," Ben said. "Yes I do! Who wants some milk tomorrow?"

Samson, that's who!

"No, forget the milk," Ben said. "You know what's really good? Ice cream. We'll wait until Tim goes to work so he doesn't see how bad we're being. Then we'll each have a bowl. I'll put yours in the microwave so it gets nice and melty. Sound good?"

It certainly did! Samson knew that Ben was his daddy, but only two other people had known to give him milk, and they were mothers. Sometimes he wondered if Ben was his mother too. Samson pondered this while stretching himself out and closing his eyes. He listened as Ben picked up his book and turned one page after another. Eventually he set it down again and switched off the light. Samson rose and jumped to the floor. Humans moved around too much in their sleep. He had discovered that Chinchilla was a better nighttime partner. She had her own bed on the floor. He intended to go straight there and sleep, but first he needed to sit, because he was tired again. More tired than he ever remembered feeling. The room was dark. Nothing but shadows. He could hear Chinchilla breathing softly not far away. The idea of curling up with her sounded heavenly.

This was enough motivation for Samson to rise and complete the journey. Chinchilla woke briefly when he stepped into the bed. She sniffed his fur and tried to lick, but he was an expert at dodging her tongue. Although sometimes he didn't mind, and on very rare occasions, he even licked her back. Only after making sure there weren't any witnesses around.

Samson flopped over and pressed himself against her. Then he closed his eyes, the cold soon chased from his body. Even the padded bed beneath him felt warm. More like a lap, really. A familiar scent hung in the air, sort of like when winter finally ended and life filled each breeze again. Except that wasn't right. This scent was different, one that he had missed for a very long time. Samson thought about opening his eyes to check, but he didn't really need to. When he felt long fingers stroke his fur, gently rubbing his neck and scratching behind his ear, he knew. Jace had come back for him at last.

Something Like Summer has been reimagined as an ongoing webcomic series! Join us on this new adventure at: www.gaywebcomics.com

Also by Jay Bell
Kamikaze Boys

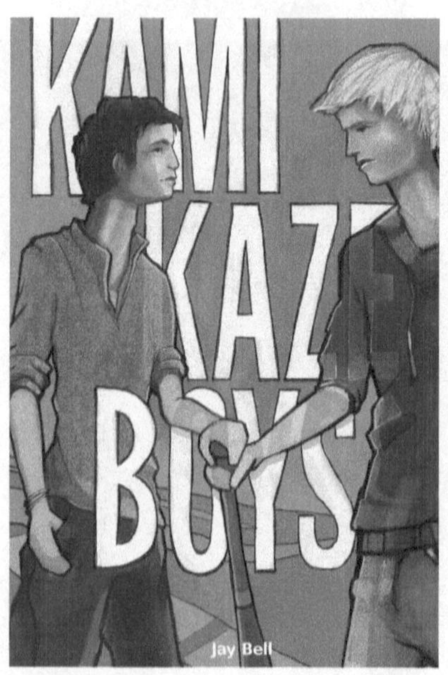

True love is worth fighting for.

My name is Connor Williams and people say I'm crazy. But that's not who I am. They also think I'm straight, and mean, and dangerous. But that's not who I am. The stories people tell, all those legends which made me an outsider—they don't mean a thing. Only my mother and my younger brother matter to me. Funny then that I find myself wanting to stand up for someone else. David Henry, that kind-of-cute guy who keeps to himself, he's about to get his ass beat by a bunch of dudes bigger than him. I could look away, let him be one more causality of this cruel world... But that's not who I am.

Kamikaze Boys, a Lambda Literary award winning novel, is a story of love triumphant as two young men walk a perilous path in the hopes of saving each other.

For more information, please see:
www.jaybellbooks.com

Hear the story in their own words!

Many of the *Something Like…* books are available on audio too. Listen to Tim's tale while you jog with him, or ignore your fellow airline passengers while experiencing Jace's story again. Find out which books are available and listen to free chapters at the link below:

http://www.jaybellbooks.com/audiobooks/

www.ingramcontent.com/pod-product-compliance
Lightning Source LLC
Chambersburg PA
CBHW031050110726
47900CB00003B/871